THE WILD OPERATIVES COLLECTION

Vivienne Savage

Thank you for joining us!

V. Savage

Payne & Taylor Publishing

ISBN-10: 0-9903817-6-5
ISBN-13: 978-0-9903817-6-1
www.viviennesavage.com
Editor: Hot Tree Editing
Graphic Artist: Mirella Santana

Table of Contents

BOOK 1: THE RIGHT TO BEAR ARMS

Chapter One

~DANIELA~

The black bear appeared in my yard for the first time one late Friday night.

I had just awakened from a nightmare around half past three. The recurring bad dream of my home on fire left me too unsettled to remain in bed for long, so I slid from beneath the blanket and pulled a light robe over my nude body. I preferred sleeping au naturel, with nothing between me and the silk sheets.

After stepping downstairs to fetch a glass of cool water, I peered through the sliding glass doors for a look into the moonlit rear yard. My landlord, as of six months ago, owned enough acreage for a forest preserve. With my house situated at the very edge of the woodland growth, I was often treated to an array of beautiful creatures. It made me feel like a Latina Snow White.

It was a completely different atmosphere than my last home in the suburbs. I thought I'd hate the hour long commute to work each day, but it gave me time to unwind behind the wheel, sip coffee, and sing to the morning radio. On the way home, I chatted with my mom, usually trying to convince her I was all right on my own. She didn't trust that Michael would leave me alone.

Officially, I was ending my first month as a single woman after eleven years of an unhappy, emotionally and physically abusive marriage. Michael judged every aspect of my existence, from the style of my hair to the weight I gained during our marriage. Nothing made him happy, and in the end, when he lost his job and came home drunk, he fell asleep with a lit cigarette in his hand and cost us our home.

My parents saw the signs, and when we turned to them for a place to live, they forbid Michael to come into their home. He raged and swore at them, cursed at me, and finally pushed me over the edge until I accepted their ultimatum. A month later, I filed for divorce.

I was alone since then with my share of the insurance claim, starting fresh with the life I deserved in a little rural town in Texas named Quickdraw. I sighed and sipped my water. That was when I noticed the dark shape in my brand new hammock.

"What the hell?" I flipped on the porch light, casting a yellow glow over the formerly dark yard. A bear lay in the hammock, sprawled on its back, so deeply asleep that the light didn't even disturb it.

The sight was so ridiculous that I spent the first minute giggling crazily after I turned out the light. Russ, my neighbor down the lane, had warned me when I moved in that all kinds of predatory creatures came out of the woods and to be careful if I had any pets. I didn't. Not anymore. Mimi, my Sphynx kitten, had died in the fire.

I slept easier after seeing the bear and imagined that if my ex came tiptoeing through my yard, he'd have Yogi to deal with for his transgressions. Following a night of more peaceful dreams, I showered and squeezed into a pair of yoga pants with a sports bra and oversized t-shirt. My hair, curly and black, fell in damp ringlets down my back. I shook them out with one hand and stepped outside onto my porch with my unopened mail, a book, and a steaming mug of coffee.

The kiss of a morning breeze touched my cheeks and rustled my dark hair, waking me before I even had the first sip of my drink. I dropped into a patio chair and grunted when I saw the bill collection notices for Michael Rodriguez. I set those aside, making the snail mail trash pile. Taking comfort in the chirping birds, my eyes swept over the yard and noticed… the bear hadn't moved. In my head, I decided the laziness made him a boy. He lay there, so still in the hammock that I thought he was dead. Squinting, I could see the steady rise and fall of his chest. Was he ill? Should I call animal control? What if they shot him?

I gulped down a few hot mouthfuls of coffee as if it were liquid courage before rushing inside to fetch steak leftovers from the fridge. I warmed them up in the microwave just enough to knock off the cold then tossed them in a pan before returning outside. My furry friend hadn't left yet. He groggily raised his head to look at me with his big brown eyes. Friendly eyes. Docile eyes. In and out with each steady breath, I steeled my nerves and slowly proceeded forward with my offering. He watched me as closely as I watched him, maybe feeling the same amount of fear. I approached in two step increments, judged his reaction to the human encroaching on his space, then continued closer. Once I was about twenty yards from the bear, I placed the pan on the grass. My heart had never beat so fast, not even when Michael terrorized me in my own home. My ex-husband had been a monster, but this wild animal could take me as a threat and kill me within seconds.

"Would you like a nice, delicious breakfast?" I asked him in my calmest voice, as if I were speaking to a puppy. I saw him drop from the hammock, and as he moved closer, I distanced until I was inside. I watched him from the other side of the glass doors until he finished his meal and walked away.

Early Monday morning, I found him in the hammock again but awake, seeming to wait for me to emerge from the house to see him. Scared out of my wits again, I brought leftover taco casserole this time.

Something about his chocolate brown stare assured me I was safe. He didn't rush me or make an aggressive move, never coming closer than the place where I set his food. This time, I settled tentatively in the patio chair and watched him eat out of the pan. Michael had never appreciated my cooking so much as this wild animal.

I grinned and enjoyed his distant company until at last he ambled off into the woods and disappeared from my sight.

My newfound friend made visiting my lawn a habit. Each night, I cooked more than necessary and set aside a portion. Each morning, he waited for me in the hammock where he watched me approach with eerily intelligent eyes. Our daily ritual became something I needed, until I no longer remembered when the animal transitioned from being a bear to simply 'my bear.'

"Daniela, it's a wild animal. Hasn't anyone told you that you shouldn't be feeding them?"

"Why the hell not?" I demanded. "It's been two weeks, Papa. If he was going to hurt me, he would have by now."

My father sighed into the phone line. "You're wasting food. Let the untamed, dangerous animal forage for his own meals, sweetheart, before he becomes too used to people. Do you know what happens when wild animals become used to eating from people?"

I didn't answer him. "I'll be careful, Papa, promise. Look, I have to go; I'm pulling in for gas." He was right, but I didn't care. This was something that was completely mine, and I enjoyed the company. It had become the one selfish thing I wanted.

The gas station was an older one without a debit card reader by the pumps. Forced to go inside to pay with cash first, I meandered to the ancient fridge and grabbed a cream soda before checking out at the cashier.

"Afternoon, Mrs. Rodriguez," a friendly voice spoke up behind me. I glanced over my shoulder to see a broad chest beneath a striped button down shirt. Unconsciously, my eyes scanned down over Wranglers and dusty brown cowboy boots. They fit the body they adorned quite well, alluding to the muscular physique beneath. Once I swung my eyes back up over his muscular chest, I tilted my head to look up into a pair of warm brown eyes. Russell, the homeowner from down the road, lived alone with a massive German shepherd he'd brought back with him from the war in Afghanistan. The sexy Army vet was one flex away from bursting his shirt sleeves every time I saw him. His jeans didn't fit him like a second skin, but he wore them right, fitted appropriately to his tall frame without sagging.

"Actually, it's Reyes again now," I told Russell with a tired smile. "But really, Daniela is fine."

"My mistake, ma'am."

"Daniela," I corrected him again, laughing. He was such a sweet man. When the UPS guy dropped off a package for him at my house once, I drove my car down to the end of the lane to bring it to him. He'd answered the door in boxers and given me the thrill of my life. Thirty seconds of conversation on his porch while his face lit up red as a tomato, made the couple minutes of my time worth it. I grinned the entire drive back home that day, daydreaming about his tight pecs and healthy summer browned skin. He didn't have a tan line on him.

"Habit." Russell grinned back this time. If he wanted to be more of a country stereotype, he only needed the Stetson on his head and a Marlboro between his lips.

The gas clerk cleared her throat to lure my attention back to the fact that I was at the front of the line. I passed her a twenty with a quick request to put the change for my soda on pump three.

"Anyway, it's been nice running into you, Russell."

"All my friends call me Russ," he corrected me this time. "Drive safe, Daniela. I hope you're on the way in. There's supposed to be one helluva storm tonight."

"I'll be home in a few minutes," I assured him.

The Texas weather wasn't so friendly lately, and I hoped my bear would be okay, that he had shelter wherever he lived in the woods.

Dismal clouds swept in from the east as I hurried outside to pump the gas.

A few scattered raindrops pelted my windshield along the way home. The one thing I loathed was that my ex got our truck in the divorce settlement. I walked away with the older sedan. It made driving down the unpaved country roads a chore during the rainy weather, when the ground became a sea of orange clay and muck.

I made it home as the heavier rain began, just in time to see a lanky figure leaving the truck parked in my driveway.

Shit. Michael was here.

"What are you doing here, Mike?" I demanded hotly while springing from my car to confront him. He wasn't my husband anymore, and I had nothing to fear from him. He couldn't hurt me now, I told myself again and again.

My ex-husband had three years of age on me. We met at college a few weeks after I moved into the dorms when I was too young and doe-eyed to see through his charismatic act. Mike had dazzled me with his good looks, popularity, and position on our school's sports team. Eventually, I fell for his game off the field, and we got married less than a year later. I believed every promise, and we tried to build a family after my graduation.

The first time he hit me was after I miscarried our son. The hospital bills made money run tight for the two of us, so I had made a dozen excuses for his short temper by shouldering the blame. I'd told myself I was so lucky to have a handsome, hard-working husband who would let me stay at home to recover, and that his stress was my fault. Years later, I finally saw past his good looks and realized he wasn't the man I married. I didn't deserve his abuse and he didn't deserve *me.*

I'd probably still be with him if our house hadn't burned down.

"*Hola*, Daniela." He always spoke Spanish when he wanted something or was trying to butter me up. Back in the beginning of our relationship, I had loved his rich baritone and the sweet nothings he whispered in our families' native language. Mike's friends once joked that he could sweet talk the panties off a nun. "*Vine a hablar—*"

"No," I cut him off. "I have nothing to say to you, and you can talk to my damned front door if you think I'm listening to anything you say."

He flashed me a grin that reminded me of how I swooned in college. He'd made me feel so special then. "Don't pretend you don't miss me, Daniela. It's raining. Let's go inside and talk about—" The weather was ruining his perfectly gelled hair. Deep down, I knew his tidy appearance was probably for his new girlfriend and not for me.

"I said *no*."

~RUSS~

Rough weather was blowing in from the Gulf, yet another one of those storms that tended to knock down all the trees and leave branches scattered over my yard. I didn't look forward to the work, but Trigger and I were bound to have some busy days ahead of us.

If not for the forecast predicting a 90 percent chance of rain, I would have left my dog to roam outside in the fresh air. Trigger would be waiting for me by the door by the time I got home to my cabin at the edge of the woods.

With the radio turned to my favorite country station, I cruised down the uneven dirt road. Some guy I didn't recognize stood in the driveway beside Ms. Reyes, gesturing with his hands and angling his body aggressively toward her.

I couldn't pass by her house in good faith without knowing she'd be all right, so I pulled over beside the ditch and rolled down the passenger side window. Spanish shouts filtered through to me, spoken too fast for my failing memory to translate. I hadn't taken Spanish in years and never acquired more than a passing knowledge of the language and the phrase "*¿Donde está el baño?*" Keeping up with it took a backseat to learning Russian and Arabic during my twenty years in the Army. Admittedly, I spoke the former better than the latter.

"Everything okay, Ms. Reyes?" I hollered out to her. Issues like this were why I kept a Mossberg in the locked cabinet built into my truck's rear cab seats. During these dangerous times, a man had to protect his life and property, and I sure didn't plan to rely on the local police department. I lived about fifteen minutes outside of town down a long and narrow dirt road a half mile past Ms. Reyes' rented house. I knew her landlord. Ian was a close friend of mine and the squad leader of our elite group. When he told me the new neighbor showed signs of being an abused woman, I promised to keep an eye on her — watch out for her if I could.

"No, I'm—"

"She's fine," the man yelled back in English. As he shot a dirty look toward my truck, I noticed his stereotypical pencil mustache, which made him resemble a Disney villain. My bad feeling was worsened by Daniela's red cheeks and stiff posture. I hated bullies.

I gave him a dubious look. "Yeah?" I thought of all the times good Samaritans rushed to the rescue and ended up getting shot or worse. Stepping from the truck, I rounded the front end with my Mossberg held down at my side. The guy backed up with his hands held up.

"Whoa, man. You can't just go around aiming shit like that at people. I didn't do anything here."

"I didn't aim anything at you *yet*," I replied. "Is he giving you problems, Daniela?"

"Who the hell are you, man?"

"Just a member of the friendly neighborhood watch," I told him with an easy smile. "We don't take kindly to troublemakers in these parts." I drawled it out, hoping he got the picture: *I'm a country boy and I will light you up if you hurt this woman.*

Thunder rumbled overhead. The rain didn't bother me much, but I could tell Daniela was cold. Her black hair was plastered to her head and her lips trembled. The thin, pale blue cashmere sweater she had on may as well have been transparent since she was soaked through. It did nothing to disguise the dark bra worn beneath or the fact that her nipples were tightly stiffened from the cold, and… And I needed to keep my mind on track.

"Go home, Mike," Daniela muttered, drawing away toward her house with both arms wrapped around herself. "We have nothing more to discuss. It's over."

Mike ignored her. "You think you're big because you've got that shotgun, don't you? Bet you wouldn't be shit without it. You're a coward, man."

I glanced at the troublemaker beside his big, overpriced truck, and deduced he was probably the ex-husband she moved here to escape. "Daniela?"

"I don't want any trouble," she whispered. Ian was right. She was a domestic violence survivor, and I'd put my life savings down on this asshole being her former abuser.

"Go on up on the porch, Daniela, before you catch a cold." I maneuvered in close until I was beside her, my body between hers and Mike.

"This has nothing to do with you, asshole, so get back in your damn truck and get the hell out of here. Daniela, you keep your fat ass where it is until I say you can go."

I passed the shotgun into her hands and advanced on her ex.

"You want to do this? I'm right here."

I let him score the first hit. His fists were light and fast without any power behind them, barely more than a swat to my face and a second to the ribs. I knew guys like him from sparring in the military during training sessions. They were the small ones, lithe in build and stream-lined, the sort who favored a lot of fancy footwork. His speed didn't help him; I only had to hit him once. My fist crashed into pretty boy's jaw and knocked him backward onto the wet pavement, barely bruising my knuckles in the process. The satisfying crack of impact made me grin.

"Good enough to bully a woman, but you can't beat on me, can you? Come on. I'm waitin'."

He glared up at me from the ground, his face wet with rain and tears no doubt. I hit like a freight train when I wanted to, and for him, I'd held nothing back.

"You want to fuck her that bad? You can have her. She only has two tricks, and once you get tired of her laying there, you'll be ready to give her back and go back to fucking your cousin in the woods."

When I stepped toward him to finish what I started, he sprang up from the ground and darted around his truck. He hopped into the driver's seat and peeled out of the drive. Once he rumbled out of sight, I turned my attention back to Daniela.

She was mortified, and I couldn't blame her one bit. Avoiding any chance of meeting my eyes, her trembling hands passed the shotgun back to me while her face turned away.

"Daniela? You okay, darlin'?"

"I'm fine," she lied through her teeth.

"Why don't you go on inside and get dry? He won't be back tonight." He'd be going to the ER to get an x-ray if he knew what was good for him.

"Yeah, I should… He didn't hurt you, right? I'm so sorry you got dragged into this."

"Ain't nothin' to apologize for, ma'am. Give a holler if he bothers you again."

I waited for the lock to click into place before I headed back to my truck, wiping water from my face. Once I reached home, I parked under the carport and headed inside to receive a greeting from my best friend. Trigger met me at the door with his tail wagging.

"Hey there, boy. Missed you," I rubbed his ears a few times then kicked off my boots while he ran out and handled his business. I shed my soaking wet clothes and tossed them into the bathroom hamper, delaying my usual afternoon routine for a shower.

I was starved by the time I finished, changed, and poured a couple generous scoops of food into Trigger's bowl. I settled for a cold sandwich, too hopeless in the kitchen to make much more than stew and chili. Sometimes a little old lady from down the road brought me a casserole and a pie, but I survived the rest of the time on crockpot soup and barbecue from the grill.

"Met a real jerk today, boy. You'd have had fun with him." Trigger's soulful brown eyes gazed into mine with understanding. "But I think I did the right thing."

I hoped I did. Back while I was away on my sixth deployment, one of our neighbors gave my wife, Katie, a load of trouble about her songbirds shitting on his car. She'd argued with him, headstrong and stubborn to the very last word, and then one day, she'd gone outside to find little feathered bodies in different corners of the yard.

Ian had been our other neighbor and home to enjoy his R&R, and after she despaired, he'd taken it upon himself to set up a hidden camera angled into our yard. When the cops wouldn't take action without proof, Ian did the work and gave the evidence to them. Our bullying neighbor paid some hefty fines, and eventually, more songbirds returned to our feeders.

I didn't know my wife was sick then. She kept it hidden, and her birds were a way for her to deal with her physical pain. She hadn't wanted to worry me while I was away in Afghanistan. At the end, I barely made it home in time to say goodbye to her, and by then, I'd lost precious time I could have held her in my arms.

Daniela wasn't my wife, but she was someone's daughter, someone's sister maybe, and I wanted to look after her the way Ian had once helped my Katie when she needed a hand. The next time her ex showed up uninvited, I'd break him in half. Better yet, I'd teach the woman to do it herself.

Chapter Two

~DANIELA~

"I've never been so embarrassed in all of my life," I blurted into the phone.

My younger sister chuckled. I could picture her reclined in bed, twisting a strand of her dark red hair around one finger. "Your neighbor sounds like a nice guy. Married?" Marta asked.

"No. Word in the neighborhood is he moved here after his wife died."

"Then maybe you need to—"

I cut her off quickly. "I do not need to bone him, Marta. Back off that train."

I loved my sister, but she thought everything could be fixed by hopping on the D. Sometimes that was the truth, but in most cases, fucking the problem away wasn't a realistic solution. I'd tried that with Michael for a decade to no avail.

"Well, damn. Sorry for trying to make a suggestion."

The rain storm continued to rage outside, blowing through the trees so hard their green tops bowed. I probably wouldn't see my bear in the morning, and that disappointed me more than it should.

"Ugh. I'm sorry. I took a hot shower, but I'm still kind of cold from being out in the rain. I guess it's making me irritable."

"Get under the blankets with a drink, sis. I'll talk to you soon. Take it easy this weekend and don't let Michael spoil it."

"I won't," I promised. "Love you. Night."

After we ended our phone call, I traipsed downstairs to make a hot mug of cocoa with the chocolate my dad brought back from a business trip to Mexico. A sudden flash of lightning revealed my empty yard, accompanied by crashing thunder that nearly made me spill the milk. I poured a liberal amount of Bailey's into the finished cup, returned upstairs, and tucked myself into bed with the lights dimmed.

I dreamed of bears that night — of running barefoot through the overgrown woods bordering my home with the scent of the wet trees and moist earth all around me. He was leading me somewhere, but I wasn't fast enough to keep pace. The chase continued until my tiring leg muscles gave out and I collapsed to the mossy bottom of the forest floor.

Convinced my bear had abandoned me, I lay motionless, waiting for the cramps in my legs to fade. Gentle hands caressed me, and when my eyes opened, I gazed up into warm brown eyes and tousled dark hair. Russell had the perfect chest, touched by a scattering of black hair over chiseled pecs. His abs were rock-hard and flawless, the kind I could bounce a quarter off. He wore only jeans, but the hard bulge beneath his zipper responded to my touch, twitching when my fingers stroked over the denim.

His mouth crashed into mine, the perfect kiss, breath-stealing, hungry, and impatient for more. Our tongues tangled to the rhythm of our rising passion while his eager hands traced my shape. I soon realized I was completely naked. Bared. Heat rose to my cheeks as a masculine palm scooped my large breast.

The scent of the open forest surrounded us, carrying juniper and damp earth. The cool soil beneath my back became the perfect cushion as my lover's head dipped. He was dragging his mouth over me, kiss by kiss, inch by inch, tasting me until he reached my quivering breasts, closing his lips around my left nipple. Moist heat surrounded the aching tip; then his teeth skimmed over the edge of the tightly puckered flesh.

His fingertips had the calloused texture of a man who worked with his hands. Slender but strong digits crawled over my hips — the ones I used to loathe for their width — introducing me to the scratch of his roughened skin.

I startled awake when his fingers dove into my pussy, sprawled on my back with the sheets tangled around my legs. I couldn't remember the last time I'd woken from a dream so stirred up, but the aching need I felt was undeniable. Sliding my fingers down my body, I traced the path my dream lover had taken, skimming over my full breasts, then down to my hips. The dream had ended there, but I wanted more.

I sighed. Masturbating wasn't going to scratch the itch I had for a man.

"I'm losing my mind. Dreaming about bears and sexy widowed Army men," I groaned into one hand. As far as I was concerned, I hoped to never run into my gorgeous neighbor again after that humiliating debacle in my front yard.

I left the bed with Sergeant Sexy on my mind. Wearing only a thin robe over my curves, I invaded the kitchen and fried up a heavy breakfast of potatoes, chorizo, and eggs.

Michael would have bitched, claiming the meal would add a few more inches to my thighs. The more he stressed me about my weight, the more I seemed to gain. I couldn't even fit a calf into my old jeans, but I was happy now and free of the constant dieting to try to please him. I'd never be content with the jiggling of my thighs, but I didn't miss food diaries and slaving over a treadmill.

The rain had ended sometime during the night, leaving a layer of moisture on the patio and the world beyond it. I sighed and watched from the glass door instead of going outside to enjoy the birds flitting to my bird feeder. It was doomed to be one hell of a muggy, uncomfortable Texas day. Leaning against the glass door with my plate in hand, I shoveled food in my mouth and muttered about the unfortunate weather.

Then I saw him. The bear shuffled past at a lumbering pace. He glanced at the hammock in passing, like it had become habit for him now, too.

Impulse made me throw open the door. "Wait, don't go!"

The bear halted immediately and turned his face toward me.

"I have eggs!" I called out to him, feeling silly the very moment the words left my mouth.

Without considering how absurd it was to expect him to understand me and wait, I hurried back to the stove and shoveled most of my plate into the cooling skillet. The bear had not left when I came back outside, standing still behind the leafy ferns. I ventured forward a few feet and set the heavy cast iron on the grass, then backed away slowly. The breeze caught my loosely sashed robe and blew it open, but with no one present but the bear to see it I didn't care.

I humanized him when I imagined appreciation in his deep brown eyes. Brown eyes that struck me as familiar when I watched him from afar. The animal ate his meal and continued out of the yard, but he left me with the lasting impression that he would continue to return.

If I could feed a bear, I could feed the lonely man down the road. It was the least I could do after he defended me. As my furry friend continued on his passage through my yard, I fetched the empty pan and rushed back inside to place it in the sink.

"I'll bake him a… what should I bake him?"

I considered the American flag flying in his yard, the time served in the military, and the southern drawl that attracted me to him.

Apple pie. There was nothing more American than apple pie, unless I stenciled a bald eagle on the crust maybe. One glance at my half-empty fruit bowl foiled that. I'd given the last of my apples to my bear a couple of days ago.

"Pecan, it is," I announced. Grinning, I fetched my recipe box and began to gather ingredients. Two hours later, I had a cooling pecan pie and a stupid plan that all depended on the man actually being home on a Saturday afternoon.

It cost another half an hour to ransack my closet for something that screamed confidence without telling him I was easy. After trying on a dozen tops with varying amounts of cleavage, I laughed at myself and tugged on a sports bra, teal racerback tank, and black yoga pants with a blue-green roll over top. The stretchy Lycra hugged my curves and drew positive attention to my ass, but the tank's scoop neck front highlighted my boobs.

His dog announced my arrival by barking at me from the yard. The eager animal, beautiful with a lush brown and black coat and big shining eyes, loped back and forth by the handmade fence.

The fence was a work in progress, constructed entirely from thin tree trunks and thick branches. The unfinished side wall had a huge gap the dog charged through to reach me.

"Shit," I muttered aloud, just as the shepherd came bounding toward me.

"Trigger!" My attention jerked from the animal as Russell's authoritative voice rang out. He rounded the corner clothed in only jeans, which rode so low they exposed the carved muscle at his hipbones. My drooling had nothing to do with the pie in my hands, and everything to do with the hunk heading toward me. "How's it goin', Daniela?"

"Oh, just fine… Nice dog," I murmured, feeling foolish.

The man was all muscle, with the physique of a fitness trainer at the gym. Or a boxer. What was I doing here? He probably had a girlfriend I didn't know about who would flounce out in the shirt he wasn't wearing. She'd show off her sex-tousled hair and bikini body while looking down her nose at the frumpy divorcee bringing pecan pie to her boyfriend. Rumor said he was widowed, but he lived such a private life at the end of the lane that it was all I knew of him. All anyone really knew about him, besides his fondness for charity and giving back to the community as a volunteer firefighter.

"He wouldn't have hurt you. I swear, now that we're both retired, he's forgotten his manners along with his training. He just wanted to love you a little."

Trigger dropped his haunches to the ground and sat beside Russ. He whined until I reached out to rub behind his ears. After that, he galloped merrily away.

"I brought a pecan pie. You know, to say thanks for last night. I realized I must have seemed really ungrateful for what you did."

"Aw, it wasn't anything big."

He didn't have a bruise on his face from when Michael hit him. Not even a minor red mark. When my ex hit me, he'd always left muscle-deep stains of color that lasted days.

"No, it was. You… you didn't have to stop, but you did, and I really appreciate it. No one would have looked twice back home." Too many neighbors had known and ignored it. The depressing thought threatened to deflate my mood, so I quickly shook it off and offered out the pie. "Anyway, I don't mean to keep you—"

"You're not keeping me," he blurted out. "Was just finishing up some work out back, is all, but you're welcome to come in. I planned to put some burgers on the grill…"

"I don't want to intrude."

His grin gave his face a youthfulness that brightened his chocolate brown eyes. "Nah, we'd enjoy the company, wouldn't we, Trigger?"

The dog barked from across the yard, voicing his agreement.

"Thanks."

Russ led me around to the back of the cabin where a respectable vegetable garden bordered the rear edge of a spacious lot. I caught sight of a few flowering fruit trees and recognized peach blossoms.

"Was the garden here too along with the fruit trees?" I asked.

"Nah. I did that. Ian planted an orchard out here back when he lived on this land. I just sort of took it over when I sold my old house and bought this off him," Russ explained. He set the pie on the table beneath the shade. "Have a seat."

I sank into a chair on the covered deck and watched him stack the firewood. His muscles flexed and bulged beneath the sheen of sweat. A tiny trickle ran down his sculpted back. I ached to wipe it away with a washcloth… beneath a steaming hot shower.

Despite my reservations about hitting on a widower, my mind had other plans, which involved mentally sketching out his body sans jeans. I moistened my dry lips with my tongue and watched him move around his yard until eventually, a green blur snatched my attention away.

"Just gimme a chance to shower, and I'll be right back. You're welcome inside if you—"

"I'm fine here," I spoke up, offering him a big smile. "You have hummingbirds."

"I do. I like to keep the feeders filled when their migration comes through this way."

With the hummingbirds and occasional songbird as company, I relaxed on the deck while Russ showered inside. Trigger appeared at my side to nudge his furry head beneath my left hand, so I spent the rest of the time petting him until Russ emerged with a covered tray. He had more meat than one man could reasonably eat.

And he'd put on a shirt. *Dammit.*

"Is there anything I can help you out with?"

"Hm?" He glanced over a shoulder at me. The man had a smile that could thaw ice and melt the coldest hearts. "Not really. I've got the grill covered."

"But are you planning to make anything to go with this really impressive assortment of meat?"

"Uh, no."

"Would you like something to go with it?"

Uncertainty flickered across his face. "Like what?"

"Rice, potato salad, pasta… something," I offered.

"You're offering to cook for me?"

"Sure. I baked for you, didn't I?"

Something about my suggestion brought a perplexed raise to his brows. They knit in consternation before he gave a nod. "Whatever you want to make is just fine with me, Daniela."

"Great. I'll just rummage around until I find everything I need, if you don't mind."

He didn't, so I entered his kitchen, washed my hands, and gathered all of the ingredients needed to make a potato salad and a few other sides. I'd just removed the macaroni and placed the cheesy garlic bread into the oven when Russ stepped up beside me. I began to worry that I made too much and had overdone it.

"God, that smells amazing. Been about forever since…"

He didn't finish his thoughts, but his expression made sense to me. No one had probably cooked for him like this since his wife. No one but me. It created an instant link between us like the connection between my bear and me. I wanted to be the woman who made his meals.

"Anytime you want to come over and have dinner with me is fine, Russ. I'm still not used to cooking for just one." I smiled. "I'm home by five or six every day."

"I noticed that." Russ cleared his throat and moved away to refill his dog's bowl. Trigger had been giving him a sorrowful look. "If you don't mind me asking, what is it you do for work?"

"Me?" I laughed and poured two glasses of sweet tea. "Nothing exciting, I assure you. I'm a loan officer at Prime Advantage Bank of Texas. What about you? You're retired Army, right?"

"Yeah. Twenty-three years. Brought Trigger back with me when they retired him. Now I teach classes down at the gym and help out the fire department. Gives me something to do."

Twenty-three years of service. I whistled and tried to estimate his age at a glance. He didn't look over forty, his body honed and fit, as if his athleticism had stopped the clock and turned back time a few years. I didn't see a trace of gray in his wavy hair.

"What kind of classes?"

"Self-defense. I throw in a few military combat techniques and give instruction on how to disable a man. Nobody will be an overnight brawler, but they'll be able to take a guy down and run away for help." He glanced at me, warmth filling his brown eyes. "Sometimes I give private lessons to young women with ex-assholes who don't know when to let go."

"I really wish you didn't see that."

"I'm really glad I did. You can tell me to shut up if it's none of my business, but I'm making an honest offer, Daniela."

"To teach me?"

He nodded his head. "Yeah. Do you have a gun in the house?"

"No. My dad tried to offer me one, but I don't know the first thing about what to do with it. And… my ex had one, but he didn't want me to learn how to shoot it." He was probably afraid I'd take it and pop him with it. There were times I was tempted. Sometimes, I wondered if all those years I spent under his thumb made me as pitiful as I felt back then.

"You about done here in the kitchen?" he asked suddenly.

"I just need to take the garlic bread out."

Russ disappeared and returned as I removed the last component of our meal from the oven. "That looks great, Daniela."

He leaned a shotgun against the cabinet beside me. I stared at it.

"What's that for?"

"It's for you," he replied.

"I can't cook with a gun."

"It ain't for you to cook with, darlin'."

While the burgers and hotdogs cooled, Russ took me out to the edge of the property where he introduced me to an enormous mound of soil as high as a person was tall.

"This is how you load it. I'm going to remove the shells and watch you do it now."

"I don't know what the hell you just did, Russ."

So he repeated it again, slower this time, guiding me through each step down to removing the safety. Once I had four shells in the unwieldy firearm, he helped me into position with his strong hands. The same hands I felt in my dream, powerful working-man's hands with rough finger pads toughened by a busy lifestyle.

"Don't lean back, darlin'. It'll knock you on your ass. You want the stock right here in this pocket in your shoulder." Russ was a good teacher, or maybe I just liked the way his hands felt on me. "It's going to kick back at you, just keep that in mind and fire it when you're ready." He cupped his hands over my ears.

This was crazy, but his low and encouraging voice gave me confidence. As instructed, I took a deep breath, let it out, and then squeezed the trigger. The butt of the shotgun struck me hard, an abrupt punch to my shoulder. I staggered back against him after underestimating the recoil. If not for Russ' presence behind me, I would have landed on my butt in the dirt.

He caught me easily, and the secure embrace of his arms around my middle turned my knees into jelly. The excitement was a head rush that weakened my legs, born from the turn-on of having a smoking-hot man behind me and firing a gun for the first time. I liked it. I liked both feelings.

"Never saw firing a gun make a lady swoon before."

"Maybe it's not the gun," I said. I told myself it wasn't my imagination, and that his arms really did tighten briefly around me. With his hard chest against my back, I would have happily leaned against him all evening. I tilted my head back against his shoulder and breathed in the subtle scent of his aftershave.

"Wanna try it again?"

"Yes!"

I wasted another three shells into the dirt mound then Russ talked me through reloading. We went through the motions two more times before our growling bellies insisted we return to the porch.

He seemed as reluctant to part as I felt, but he pushed the gun back into my hands when I tried to offer it to him.

"What are you doing?"

"It's yours now."

"Russ, I can't take—"

"The first rule of having any firearm is that you don't point it at someone unless you mean to shoot it, Daniela. Remember that. Please take it. I'll feel better knowing you have a way to protect yourself."

With his shotgun beside my chair, we settled at the patio table and enjoyed his entree of cheese-stuffed grilled burgers. The heat of spicy pepper jack accompanied every bite, creating a symphony of flavors. My sweet tea was the perfect compliment.

"You told me you couldn't cook."

"I don't consider grilling to be the same as cooking, darlin'. Not really." He gestured toward the leftover potato salad on his plate. "Now that's cooking. I try, hence having all the groceries for it, but it's a hot mess when I'm done. You can't buy food like this from the store. "

"Yes, you can. It's called the deli at Wal-Mart."

Russ shot me a look, but his good-natured amusement showed through his faux grimace. "That's not what I meant. I mean, sure you can buy a tub of it from the store, but it'll never taste the same as a meal made with love in your own kitchen."

"I'll agree with you there." Russ and I chatted into the evening until the threat of mosquitoes chased us inside. There, he opened a bottle of peach brandy and we talked longer about our families — or rather, my huge family and his lack of one. Trigger wriggled in beside me and laid his head in my lap the whole time we talked.

"I'm sorry, Russ… I knew you were a widower, but I didn't know it was so recent."

A hint of a sad smile touched his lips. "Two years ain't that recent. Not really. I sold the house after that, put in for my retirement, and moved out this way for the privacy. The big home and picket fence was always what Katie wanted anyway."

And now he lived alone with his dog. My heart ached for the man who had served his country for two decades, only to lose the woman who mattered most to him. Life wasn't fair, and Russ' circumstances were a prime example of the universe's cruelty.

Our talk turned to happier topics after that, and he told me stories about my landlord. Apparently, he and Ian were fishing buddies who met first as neighbors while living in military housing. Later, they served together in a unique cross-branch squad that wasn't known to the public by name.

"So you were sort of like… what? Delta Force? Seal Team 6?" He sounded sexier and sexier by the second. I imagined him in complete combat armor, a military grade shotgun in his hands, moving in formation with a group of similarly equipped soldiers. My breath caught in my throat.

"You could call it that. I can't say a whole lot about it, but I can say we did a lot of good here at home and in the Middle East. I retired as a Master Sergeant, but I'm kinda still on contract. When I retired, I agreed to let them recall me as needed."

I didn't even realize how late it had gotten until my phone buzzed. I silenced the call from my sister and gaped at the time.

"Wow, it's eight already. I should probably get going, just let me help you get everything cleaned up."

"You cooked it; I'll handle the dishes." His lazy grin made my heart speed into a gallop. Looking as good as he did in a t-shirt and jeans, lounging in an armchair, should be illegal.

"Sorry, bud, you're gonna have to let me up now." Trigger whined and didn't budge, content to remain where he was. I laughed and scratched his head. "I'll rub your ears again next time."

Because I really hoped there would be a next time.

Trigger padded off and Russ walked me out. He held the door for me like a gentleman.

"I had fun today, Russ, thank you."

"I'm real glad you dropped by."

Maybe we had the same thing on our minds when I stood on the front porch, wringing my hands together, fretting, and doubting myself. When his lips touched mine, a jolt of electricity shot through me and a warm feeling zipped right to my core, reminding me of how long it had been since the last time I'd gotten laid. A year almost?

No, I told myself firmly. You are not going to try to fuck this man on the first date. I set some limits in my head as we separated. In reality, the kiss hadn't been as long as it seemed in my mind and nothing more than the corners of our mouths had touched. In fact, I was positive he'd been aiming for my cheek, but I had turned my head like an idiot.

Once I finished mentally cursing myself, I put a sunny smile on my face and let the memory of his lips bolster my confidence. Just as I planned to invite him to dinner, Russ beat me to the punch.

"I'd… like to do this again soon, Daniela. If you'd like."

"I would."

Relief flooded his features, as if he'd been afraid I'd turn him down. That idea never passed through my mind. It wasn't just that he was sexy as all get out — he was a great guy, too. I had honestly enjoyed chatting with him all afternoon.

Chapter Three

~Russ~

The conversation and dinner with Daniela seemed to cure my wanderlust for the entire evening. By the time she left, the desire to strip out of my clothes and enjoy an evening stroll was long gone. The bear in me was equally satisfied by her company. Something about her appealed to my inner beast and soothed the animal at the core of my spirit. Had my bear recognized her as a potential mate?

It was that attraction that had drawn me to use her rear yard as my path each night. When I saw her brand new hammock stretched between the trees, impulse drove me to climb aboard and make myself comfortable for a while. I didn't count on passing out until past dawn, and I didn't count on her seeing me. I certainly didn't count on her feeding me.

I'd taken a shine to Daniela from the very first time she offered me food while unaware of my true identity. It took a special sort of person to accept a wild animal in their backyard without any intentions of shooting it. Reappearing afterward required a battle of ethics — was it immoral to return morning after morning, knowing she'd provide me a meal, or was my animal form facilitating something we both seemed to crave?

I was born this way. Most shifters inherited the trait from a parent, with exception to a few of our magical brethren like the loup-garou. A werewolf could infect a mortal human on the full moon, transferring a spark of the magic that allowed them to shapeshift. Most purists didn't believe in creating new blood from lowly humans though. I'd run into a couple inbred packs in my day that would give Harry Potter's Death Eaters a run for their money.

While we were all uniquely different, we had a couple of similarities between our species. All shifters got the wanderlust from time to time, an irresistible urge to go back to our animal roots and roam through our native habitats. I could sate mine by taking a walk in my own backyard, but others, like my pal Taylor, weren't so lucky.

He had to drive into the country to shed his human flesh and prowl the hills in his natural mountain lion state. Ian was probably the safest among us. It took a bold bastard to shoot at our national bird. As for the rest of our old squad, their animal talents ranged from conspicuous to damned near invisible.

I spent half of my enlistment period as a Special Forces operative in an elite group exclusive to shapeshifters. Ian was the second generation leader of the squad, following in his father's footsteps. Together, we were unstoppable and we accomplished the impossible, handling critical government jobs from infiltration to surveillance.

Since I was officially out of the Army, I remained on as a contracted employee. Lucky for me, they hadn't needed me back for anything big since my retirement. It'd be a lie to say I wasn't relieved for the break from war and battle, but I received damned good paychecks as a consultant. Between that and my Army pension, I was financially secure to enjoy life without any monetary concerns.

After Daniela was gone, I laid in my bed imagining the pressure of her lips beneath mine. The feeling of lust for a woman had been gone for so long that its return almost struck me as foreign.

There'd been no one since Katie, and wanting Daniela almost felt like a betrayal to my wife of sixteen years. The rational part of me also knew she wouldn't want me to sulk at home in eternal mourning of her memory.

To make use of my surplus meat from the grill out, I invited Daniela over again the next night. During a dinner of reheated burgers and sweet tea, we shared stories about our recent achievements. She planned to go back to school for her master's degree, something her ex had strictly forbidden while they were married. In retrospect, I wish I'd punched him a couple more times before the coward ran away.

"So, what do you think about coming with me to the gym this Saturday for a couple lessons with my other students?"

"I don't know…"

"It'll be fun."

Daniela dragged in a breath and settled back in her chair. "Me and the gym sort of have issues."

"What if I promise not to make you sweat much, and to buy you ice cream afterward?"

"Frozen yogurt?"

"Deal," I agreed, laughing.

Two nights later, she invited me over for chicken enchiladas and sopapillas. We lit a couple of mosquito torches and sat out back while the hummingbirds visited her deck. I wondered if her feeders and apparent love of the birds were initially what lured me to linger on her property.

By Saturday, Daniela had improved her speed at loading and unloading the shotgun, and she was ready to begin her combat tactics lessons. My small class met two weekends a month and had several regulars who all had found their way to me for varying reasons. Some of them wanted to get fit, a few did it for shits and giggles, and then there were women like Daniela, learning to defend their lives against true danger.

Since there were a couple of new faces, I made everyone introduce themselves at the start of the class. After they warmed up with stretches and light calisthenics — during which Daniela shot me dirty looks — I moved to the front of the class to begin the real lesson.

"Today, we're going to begin with palm heel strikes and shin rakes. They're easy to do in close quarters, and it doesn't take a lot of power to hurt someone. First, I need a volunteer."

To no one's surprise, a busty blonde girl raised her hand from the front of the class. Juliette always offered, and her motivation was transparent. I sighed. Her fair hair and porcelain skin didn't do a thing for me. I liked them dark-haired and exotic, with big brown eyes and even larger bottoms. If there wasn't enough meat on a woman for me to squeeze with my hands, they held no interest for me.

"Daniela? Would you come up front and give me a hand?"

"Oh, I don't know—"

I grinned at her and patted the training dummy beside me. "C'mon, I promise Bob here won't bite."

The gym had provided two body opponent bags when I started my class over a year ago. I donated a third to help out when my classes became popular. The stern-faced, plastisol torso gave the students a realistic visual representation of where to strike an attacker.

"If someone gets in your space and won't back down, a strike to their nose or throat with the heel of your palm is gonna make them rethink things quick."

Using Daniela as my model, I walked her and the class through the motions then paired them up into small groups.

"Lock your elbow when you do it, Daniela. Like that. Put some power into it. The more you practice it now, the easier it'll be if you actually have to do it."

As much as I'd have liked to, I didn't stay with Daniela the entire lesson. I paired her with Blake, a high schooler who'd been bullied since coming out of the closet last year. He didn't really need the lessons anymore, but he enjoyed helping during classes and seemed to look up to me. Even said he planned to join the ROTC when he went to college. He made a good practice partner for my gal while I moved around the room and helped everyone with their technique. Wait, when did I begin to think of her as mine?

"Good everyone. Real good. Bring your gloves next time, y'all. I want to pair you off for sparring matches."

"Can I fight you again, Russ?" Blake asked.

"Sure can. You're faster than I am, so maybe you'll kick my ass this time."

After giving them reminders to stay hydrated, I dismissed the class and started to store equipment away. Daniela helped me out until I shooed her aside to drink and rest. She'd done well in her first class. During the ride home, she quizzed me about my Army training and why I'd decided to teach self-defense.

"Part of it was for something to do, I guess. After twenty years of being busy, having completely idle hands made me twitchy. Besides, I like helping people."

"You're good at it. I went to the gym once. Well, Mike made me go. He paid some trainer to work with me, but the lady was a real hard-core bitch who screamed a lot." Daniela turned her gaze to the moving scenery outside. "I got discouraged and didn't want to go back and…" She went quiet and I filled in the blanks. Her asshole of an ex probably didn't take well to the money lost.

I flicked the turn signal, slowed, and drifted off the interstate toward a building marked with a colorful pink and orange sign. According to the sign, Flora's Fro-Yo had about a dozen special flavors.

"Wait, what are you doing?" I stole a glance to the passenger seat to see Daniela's quizzical expression and wide brown eyes staring back at me.

"I promised you frozen yogurt, remember?"

"You just whipped like a thousand calories off me," she said pointedly.

"Now I'm putting it back on you," I replied while pulling into the parking lot.

"You don't think…" She paused again, huffed a breath, and simply laughed before shaking her head. "All right then. It's your treat though."

"I wouldn't dream of letting you pay."

I filled my paper cup to the top and encouraged Daniela to do the same. While I wasn't looking, she tried to serve herself a tiny dieter's portion, like I'd judge her for wanting more than a spoonful.

"How am I gonna steal some of your flavor if there's only one bite to take?" My friendly tease seemed to do the trick, convincing her to take a more generous helping. After filling up her bowl, we picked out toppings for each other.

We devoured our frosty treats beneath a covered table outside, enjoying a pleasant Texas breeze. It was the perfect way to cool off after a tough workout session. I didn't think the day could get any better, but Daniela proved me wrong with an innocent kiss to my cheek. Her cool lips left a tingling warmth on my skin long after she pulled away.

"I had fun today."

"You're welcome to join again anytime. Just let me know and you can bum a ride with me."

I dropped her off an hour later, after a relaxing stroll through the town square where we walked hand in hand and I bought her flowers from a local vendor. The close knit community was one of my reasons for moving to Quickdraw's little municipality, aside from the badass name. Around this time of the year, the farmers' markets were in full swing.

"You didn't have to buy me this, you know." She sniffed the fragrant white blooms on the potted gardenia topiary I bought for her. It would be a perfect addition to her home and, I hoped, something that would make her think of me whenever she looked at it.

"That's the funny thing about gifts. Don't need a reason to give 'em."

With my truck parked beside her little sedan, neither of us moved.

"Go have a hot soak, darlin'. You'll be feeling that workout later."

Daniela lingered in the passenger seat and glanced back at me with one hand on the door handle. I couldn't let her leave like this, with things hanging in the air between us. So I trusted my gut and pulled her back to me, then leaned in and claimed her lips.

One arm hooked behind my left shoulder, her fingers tangling in my hair. She dragged me in closer, equally eager and filled with as much yearning. One hand grasped the front of my t-shirt initially, and then she placed my hand against her breast. I squeezed and kneaded the plump swell beneath my fingers, pinching the stiffening nipple through her thin t-shirt and bra. She had the perfect pair. They were more than a handful for even my large palms, and the tips were hard bullet points I wanted to suck into my mouth.

Her fingers danced over my zipper, a playful tease that I couldn't bear. My cock swelled even more under her touch and became so hard it hurt to remain in my jeans.

Not like this. As much as I wanted her, I didn't want our first time together to be in a cramped truck cab like we were a couple of randy teenagers. I became conflicted between having her in the truck or dragging her outside. Fantasies danced through my mind of bending her over in the grass and sweet-smelling clover, of raising that luscious ass of hers to the air, spreading her thighs, and thrusting into her tight hole.

The effort to pull away from Dani's sweet little mouth exhausted my willpower. I groaned then finally twisted my face away. "Baby… baby, wait."

"Wait?" She panted against my cheek, each breathless exhale making me wonder how sexy she'd sound in the throes of orgasm.

I kissed her again, raw with my hunger and need for her. The bear in me demanded satisfaction, but the man warred against bestial instincts and implored me to be patient. When I made love to Daniela, I wanted us to enjoy every second, unrushed, unhurried, and not sore from putting her through the ringer at the gym.

The sexy minx nibbled my lower lip and playfully tugged it when the kiss ended. Her dark eyes smoldered. "What are we waiting for?"

"Not now, darlin'."

"Not now?" Her brows drew together in confusion.

Regret filled me as I dragged in a deep breath and got myself under control. "Not now," I repeated. "You're tired and…" I had trouble separating my hand from her tits. I squeezed one again and watched her arch into my palm. "When I do make love to you, it won't be in a parked truck." I couldn't wait to dive inside of her, but also couldn't justify putting sexual need in front of manners.

"Come inside." Her invitation preceded a hot blush.

"I wanna do this right, Daniela." I eased forward and kissed her again, keeping it light and tender. Her breathy sigh nearly did me in, but I managed to pull back. "Next weekend, I want to take you out. A real date, one that doesn't involve guns or punches."

"What's a real date?"

I couldn't tell if lust made her sarcastic, or if she honestly didn't know. I didn't put it past her douche of an ex to have never treated her to an honest-to-goodness night on the town. "Dinner and dancing," I replied, maintaining a straight face. I didn't want to laugh if she was that clueless.

"Dinner and dancing?" Daniela gave me a dubious look, skipping her brown eyes over me and letting them linger on my crotch. My cock jumped beneath my jeans, throbbing with renewed need. "What kind of dancing are we talking about?" Leaning forward to reach me, her lips drifted over my jaw and traveled lower until she found the pulse point in my throat. She sucked gently and nipped, filling my head with images of her gorgeous lips around my length, sliding up and down with frenzied abandon.

"There's a country western bar called Spurs, near Houston. It'll be a nice ride." I groaned and tried to focus on something neutral. Baseball. The unforgiving Middle Eastern sun. MREs. When that worked, I patted her thigh and nudged her back from me.

Daniela fixed me with a skeptical look. "What am I supposed to wear to a country western bar? I'm not a cowgirl."

"Every woman in Texas has a pair of boots, darlin'," I exaggerated.

"I don't," she insisted.

"Aw, hell, it doesn't really matter what you decide to wear. We're going there for fun. It's not a fashion show."

"Okay." She pursed her lips in thought, glanced away, and then peeked back at me again through her curly hair. "Friday sound good to you?"

"It sounds perfect."

"Are you sure you don't want to come in for… a cup of coffee?" She fixed me a coy look.

"Positive," I replied, grinning the whole while. It wasn't forced anymore. The longer we waited, the sweeter it would be, and I planned to make certain every second delayed was worth it.

Chapter Four

~Russ~

My prediction wasn't far from the mark. Daniela phoned Sunday morning to inform me she couldn't touch her toes without straining her hamstrings to the limit.

"Take another hot soak and work on your stretching," I advised. "Do you need anything?"

My question received silence in return, a long pause finally answered by, "No."

"Are you okay?" I ventured.

"Yeah… just worried about something. Hey, Russ? You're outside a lot, right?"

"Most of the time when I'm home, I'm outside. What's up?"

"Have you seen any unusual wild animals around this area?"

Shit. I inhaled a deep breath and decided to play it dumb. Spending time with Daniela in person had come at a cost; I couldn't visit her backyard in my wild shape. I preferred talking to her as a human and sitting with her at the dinner table. Stealing kisses as a bear wasn't feasible.

"Define unusual."

She laughed suddenly. "Never mind. I'm being silly. I'm gonna go take that bath and relax. I'll talk to you later."

Despite her aches and pains, Daniela attended my Tuesday evening class. When we were outside of the gym, I took her back to the rear of my property to resume our lessons with the guns. She was a natural at it.

Friday night, I parked my pickup in her driveway and stepped from the vehicle to retrieve her for our first official date. She must have been waiting for me by the window.

My date stepped onto the porch and locked the door behind her, bearing little resemblance to the uncertain woman I had become accustomed to seeing during the week. Her frumpy sweats and yoga pants had been replaced by tiny denim shorts with pockets that protruded below the frayed hem. I watched her strut toward my truck fully aware of how goddamned sexy she looked. She had to be, and in my mind, it was an intentional show just for me. I was so entranced I almost forgot to step up to greet her.

"You look amazing," I complimented her once I moved in place to intercept her arrival. I opened the passenger door and gestured to the seat.

"Did you expect anything else?" she teased. For my benefit, she did a little twirl on the driveway before turning to climb into the cab. Her movement exposed her plump bottom to me and how the shorts clung to her full hips. I wanted to squeeze her ass, daring to imagine how amazing it would feel bare beneath my hands.

I'd met women at the gym Daniela's size who shied away from sexy clothes, fearing they were too large to dress provocatively. God, she proved them wrong. The little length accentuated her thick thighs. They were full, but slightly firm at the same time, with small dimples that trailed beneath the cut off hem. I wanted to kiss each and every one and learn the taste of her skin.

"Thought you didn't have boots," I spoke up after sliding into my seat. We buckled up and I reversed from the drive to embark on our date.

"I may or may not have made a shopping trip to the boot shop a couple days ago." She crossed her legs. I had trouble tearing my gaze away from her thighs to check out the knee-high suede boots she wore. The brown and teal was a fetching combination against her skin.

Teal must be her favorite color. I saw it on her often.

"I hope you broke them in because I'm not going easy on you tonight." The thought of her making a special shopping trip for our date made me smile.

"Yeah, the sales lady had some tips." She grinned back at me.

We spent the hour-long drive with pleasant chatter that continued into dinner at my favorite steak house. From there it was a quick jaunt over to the dancehall where I planned to spin her around the floor and see her enjoying herself. I let her choose our drinks for the night, only to receive a surprise when she chose double shots of cherry vodka sours. Between the booze and all of our dancing, Daniela curled up in her seat and dozed off ten minutes into the drive home. We didn't leave until two; neither of us had wanted the night to end.

Unfortunately, a flash downpour delayed our arrival home, and when I returned to our neighborhood, I didn't pass a single house with power. I passed two dimmed trailers and one black house along the way to Daniela's place. Her automatic porch light was off, too. One glance at her peaceful face was all it took to make the decision to bring her back to my place. Only an asshole could drop a woman off at a pitch-dark home to ride out the downpour alone.

I parked beneath the carport and left Daniela behind briefly to unlock my front door. I didn't have a garage yet, but there were plans in the making to build one with my own hands. After I turned on one of the battery-powered lanterns by the entrance, I returned for my girl and lifted her into my arms. I bumped the door shut behind me and carried her into the house when the rain dwindled to a drizzle. With the lantern guiding me, I set Daniela on the couch, removed her boots, and peeled off her socks. I didn't dare to undress her any further, but my conscience couldn't leave her there on the sofa either.

"Russ?" she murmured drowsily just as I was about to lay her in my bed.

"Hm?"

"Where are we?"

"The power's out in the neighborhood. I brought you back to my place. Sorry… I can get you home now if you want. Even got some candles to spare if you need them."

"No, thank you." Her lips fluttered against my cheek at first, then another attempt found my lips. A hint of cherry flavored her mouth and made each darting press of her tongue as sweet as the next. "Where's your bathroom? I feel sort of scummy. Someone spilled a drink on me when I stepped away to the restroom."

"One second. Lemme get you some light."

I set her down and located a second battery lamp. We placed that on the bathroom counter, then I gave her one of my clean shirts to change into since hers reeked of beer. A few minutes later, the shower squeaked on, prompting my thoughts to wander. Once, when she'd rushed outside to bring me breakfast, the wind had kicked open her robe and exposed her amazing body. One memory was enough to stiffen my cock, filling me with so much lust I retreated to the couch before I could make a fool of myself while delirious with exhaustion.

Trigger joined me after I settled in and closed my eyes. He set his furry face against my lap, and together we both dozed off for a short while.

"Why are you out here?" Daniela's voice pierced through the dream fog. I snapped awake and jerked my head toward her in alarm before registering the familiarity in her voice… and digesting her half-dressed appearance.

I'd given her the shirt, thinking she'd replace her beer-stained blouse and settle down to rest. She surprised me by stepping from my bedroom in only the thin white cotton. Without a bra or her panties beneath it, it may as well have been invisible. Her big breasts quivered with each seductive step, each nipple a pebble-hard tip.

"Just thinking and having a sit with Trigger. Ain't that right, boy?" My fingers smoothed over his dark fur.

"You know, there's room for you in that big bed, too."

"I didn't want to assume…"

Daniela moved into view and stood in front of me. Her fingers curled into my leather belt and pulled until I rose up to my feet to join her. Without a word, she unbuckled it and pulled it free of the loops. Kissing me, she pushed up against my body, wriggling just right to apply pressure against the hard bulge beneath my jeans. I breathed a sigh of relief when she popped the button and lowered my zipper.

"Daniela… are you sure about this?" I couldn't lay down in bed with a drunk woman. No matter how much I wanted her, no matter how much I wanted to discover the heat of her body, I couldn't claim her as mine if our night out had inebriated her beyond making a good decision.

It didn't matter that she'd tried to invite me inside once. This was now, a wholly different time, a completely different situation.

"I think I slept off most of the alcohol, Russ, if that's what you mean. I'm sober. Completely sober to know what I want."

That was all I needed to hear.

~Daniela~

With my fingers in Russ' belt loops, I guided him back with me into the bedroom. My heart pounded the entire time, my belly doing somersaults and nervous flips. All those years of marriage meant I'd only ever slept with one man. No one but my ex-husband and my doctor knew what I looked like naked.

"Do you have any idea how sexy you looked tonight on the dance floor?" Russ asked me, his voice husky and thick with desire.

"If this is any indication, then yes," I replied boldly. I cupped my palm against the bulged mound behind the opening in his boxer briefs.

He was already half hard, as impressive in a semi-aroused state as my ex had been with a full erection.

"Get undressed, Dani… Let me see you."

Hesitating, I glanced up to his brown eyes and saw the raw need in his expression. A shirt with no undergarments was as bold as it came for me. I shied away from removing my borrowed tee in favor of unbuttoning his shirt first. To control my nerves, I kept my eyes on his handsome face the whole time until I shoved it back from his shoulders. The LED in his battery-powered lantern emitted a soft, aqua-colored glow that highlighted each muscular plane and chiseled dip.

His jeans and boxers came last. I shoved my fingers into the elastic band and lowered to a crouch, tugging denim and cotton with me. Without looking at the hard-on I had bared, I took in a few nervous breaths as he kicked both aside. After a few seconds, I risked glancing up.

Russ had the largest dick I'd ever seen in all of my life. Not just long, but thick too, the perfect amount of girth, which I couldn't close my fingers completely around. It rose from a patch of neat black curls that felt almost silky beneath my fingers. I stroked him and slid my fingers over his cock in a teasing pump. My pussy throbbed in anticipation of having him inside me, and when I tentatively raised my eyes to his face, I saw the same urgent hunger mirrored in his features.

"You're wearin' too much now, Daniela."

He pulled me back up to join him, and then my shirt was gone too, tossed aside as Russ took charge and backed me against the mattress. His lips descended to mine, a desperate crash of our mouths that ended when his knee parted my thighs, and his questing finger delved between them. One of his strong arms curled around my back and held me close, while the other remained between my legs. Through it all, I tried to focus on gliding my fist up and down his length. Our mutual touching continued until his middle and index fingers became slick with my need.

"You're so wet, baby… I want you so bad right now." He dipped his head to wrap his lips around my left nipple. He then tongued the stiff budded tip until all I could imagine was that same dexterous movement against my clit. "Tell me you're mine. Say it," he growled.

"Yours," I answered on another hitched breath. His thumb flicked my clit, igniting a series of sparks that started at my aching pussy and radiated out to every limb. I was ready to explode, and he hadn't even entered me yet. Thank God, I'd gone in for a wax the previous day.

"Please, Russell, I can't wait. I *need* you inside me."

The thick comforter cushioned my fall onto the bed and Russ' weight settled over me, my softer curves molding against his firm muscle. Then he still denied me the penetration I wanted by raising onto his forearms and gazing down at my body, bathed in the pale glow of an emergency light. I wondered what he saw when he looked down at my fluffy curves, my round belly, and large tits. Every part of me quivered each time I took a breath.

He answered my silent ruminations without words. His lips lowered to my stomach to place a kiss beside my navel. After he pushed back onto his knees, his mouth brushed my inner thigh next, assuming a worshipful pose that clenched my insides with desire.

"Every inch of you is beautiful, Daniela. Every damn inch."

By the time Russ lowered atop my body again, I was beyond ready. He pressed into me, stretching and filling my slick channel with his large girth. I moaned and tilted my head back against the pillow when our bodies bumped close and the base of his dick nudged my clit.

Russ guided my leg over his hip and kneaded his fingers against my thigh, wedging our pelvises even closer together. The deep penetration was amazing. Filled completely, I had no idea where I began and he ended, as if we made one complete whole.

"You feel so good." He groaned softly against my ear. His first gentle movements left me breathless, but tender churning strokes and slow lovemaking wasn't what I craved, not tonight. Something wanton and desperate had developed inside of me, created from the long and chaste months during my divorce process.

"I'm not delicate. I won't break. Russ, please, please," I begged, gripping at his upper arms. At my request, he surged forward anew, claiming me deep and hard. I shuddered beneath him and hooked my other leg around his hip, clinging with both hands to his shoulders.

The next thrust shook the headboard against the wall. He didn't give me the chance to recover, every stroke fast on the heels of another. Over and over he rolled his hips, slamming into me, fucking me until I writhed beneath him. Each staccato bang accompanied my breathy cries for more. I moved beneath him, raising my hips, grinding against him, and burying my fingernails into his shoulder until I was sure to leave crescent shaped divots behind.

No part of my body remained neglected for long while Russ made love to me. His hand slid beneath my thigh, squeezed, and delivered a playful slap against my ass. He kneaded the flesh within his hand and lowered reverent kisses to my breasts. By the time he found my lips again, I was ready to melt.

"You're so perfect," he confided in me. "I've wanted to kiss you like this for weeks."

"You're so big... so big," I breathed out, desperate for something, anything to say to him in return. The building pressure was too much, unbearable tension stretching inside me. His huge cock filled me so tight that the slightest bump of his body made contact with my clit. His low, sexy growl set my soul on fire. I was right on the edge and nothing but the greedy, fast-paced strokes of his dick could quench the need I had for him.

"Come for me, darlin'," he breathed against my ear. Passion thickened his voice until I could tell he was pushed to the limits of his restraint and close to coming, too, holding back until I had my climax. Each piston of his dick made stars explode in my vision, introducing me to an ecstasy I'd never experienced with Michael. My ex-husband *thought* he was God's gift to women — but Russ was a true gift given to *me*.

"Russell… Oh God, oh God!" My back lifted from the sheets and every muscle tensed.

His hot and frenzied rhythm faltered, telling me he was close. Each groan from his lips was heaven to my ears, the most beautiful music, the sound of a man soon to join me in mutual satisfaction. The grunt of my name accompanied the most mind-blowing climax I ever experienced. The tension snapped with one burst of pleasure and I lost myself to pure sensation. Russ' fingers tightened on my hips and he pounded against me with increasing urgency until I felt him swell in release. I never came with a man before in a mutual orgasm. All I could do was cling tight to him and ride it out.

At the end, my arms became limp and heavy at my sides. I tried to raise one hand to stroke down his chest, only to sigh in contentment when Russ pulled me near.

"I don't think I have any words that wouldn't be an understatement," I murmured against his shoulder. "Amazing." My entire body seemed to float as my eyes drifted shut. Tremulous aftershocks rippled along his cock, squeezing him to a timed rhythm. He lingered until the last pulse ended, then groaned and shifted inside me, as reluctant to part from my body as I was to fall asleep. I wanted more of him.

"There'll be more where that came from in the morning." He must have read my mind. The warm chuckle he gave afterward made me tingle all the way to my toes.

"Thank you, Russ… tonight was perfect."

With the blankets pulled above us, I buried my face against his throat and let my dreams carry me away.

Chapter Five

~Daniela~

The insides of my thighs and my hips were bruised. After awakening, I had crawled from the empty bed and examined myself in the bathroom mirror. Then I showered again, donned my borrowed t-shirt, and sought out my new lover.

I found Russ sitting on the deck with a mug of black coffee in his hand. I had learned he drank it dark, strong, and with only a couple spoons of sugar.

"Morning," he greeted me with a faint smile. I raked my eyes over his half-naked body. A pair of boxers and nothing else clothed him, which meant my eyes immediately zeroed in on the little slit opening in the front, hoping to catch a sight of his cock. "You sleep well?"

"Mm. Must have. I feel great." I ran my fingers through my drying hair and tried to tame the damp curls.

Russ didn't seem to care that I looked like crap. He set his coffee down and tugged me into his arms. I breathed him in. He smelled good, his scent striking me as something familiar even though I couldn't place it in my memory.

"Why are you out here alone?"

"Trigger needed to go out, and I didn't want to wake you if I could help it. The power must have come on again sometime during the night." He glanced through the kitchen's window pane at the flashing digital numbers above his stove.

"I like to spend my mornings on my back patio, too. I, uh, have a regular bear visitor. You ever seen him wandering around out here?"

Russ glanced over the yard. "A bear, huh?" He stroked his stubbled chin thoughtfully.

"I Googled a little. I think he's an American black bear. I saw him every day for a couple weeks and then… one day he stopped visiting. I know it's silly, but I'm worried about him."

"Sweetheart, he's a wild animal. I'm sure he's off somewhere climbing a tree or doing whatever bears do," Russ assured me.

"But what if someone shot him?"

"I don't think bears stay in one place for so long, Daniela. That's probably why you haven't seen him."

His words didn't convince me. My frown deepened a little more as I stepped into his kitchen and threw together brunch. I ruined the first batch of eggs when Russ eased into place behind me and flipped his t-shirt above my waist. His hands skimmed over my ass, and with one foot, he nudged my stance apart.

"Russ… I'm cooking," I attempted to warn him. His lips descended to the back of my neck and one hand moved between my legs. He played with my pussy, using dexterous, strong fingers to glide over my clit.

"Russ… what are you…" Butter popped in the skillet as the smell of burning eggs reached my nose. I barely had the focus to turn off the stove before his middle finger delved into my body. "Russss," I hissed out between my teeth. I didn't just want his dick, I craved it, desperate to connect our bodies in intimacy again. Using protection had never occurred to me — I'd gotten an IUD over a year ago, terrified of carrying Michael's baby in the final months of our marriage.

Something told me Russ wasn't so worried about that. And while we hadn't discussed it between us, I was sure he was clean, too. Maybe I was placing too much faith in him, but I believed it when he told me there had been no woman since his wife.

"How are you so good with your hands?" I groaned out, tilting my head back and rocking my hips to the motion of his fingers.

He didn't answer. His thick cock brushed against my folds, and then his hips snapped forward. He buried himself within me in a single thrust, filling my body and making me whole again.

Russ moved me away from the stove and faced me toward the wide island instead. I gripped the counter edge and bent over it. With this new position and his big cock, he penetrated deeper than I was accustomed to receiving. The unfamiliar sensation stirred something indescribable inside me, bouncing against the end of my tight channel without mercy. He introduced me to pleasure and pain, quick and bright sparks of discomfort that faded into bliss on every stroke.

"I could spend the entire day like this with you, discovering every way I can make you scream."

"I love it when you talk that way." My sweet boyfriend, the southern gentleman, said the sexiest things. Thank God we made it official to continue dating. I guided his free hand beneath my shirt to my breast. He circled his finger around the tip until it stiffened to a hard point. I wanted it in his mouth, and at the same time, I craved the way he took charge and claimed me from behind. With Russ, it wasn't a demeaning position used to exert dominance over me. It was pure and primal lovemaking, his heavy balls slapping against my clit with each thrust.

"You're wearin' too much to be in this house," he muttered against my ear. His voice sent shivers through me, and before I could protest, he had grabbed the bottom of the t-shirt and tugged it up until I raised my arms to facilitate its loss.

In the sunlight streaming through his kitchen windows, there was no hiding my imperfections. My curls tumbled over my bare shoulders and down my back. Through his glass patio doors, I could see only a faint hint of our reflection. His larger frame hovered above me from behind, a huge bear of a man and every bit the example of physical fitness. He made me appear tiny by comparison despite my thick curves.

"You're so beautiful, Daniela. Fuck." He grabbed a handful of my ass and slapped it until it jiggled. "I love this."

I was already about to come, and he'd barely even started. My trembling thighs and tensed body were the first indication he received, and then on his next stroke, I orgasmed hard. My pussy clenched around his steel-hard length, milking him and urging him to join me. I felt him stiffen behind me, burying his face against my skin while stubbornly resisting the lure.

"Russ, oh God, baby, please…"

"Not yet, sweetheart." He nibbled my shoulder and continued his slow strokes through my release. "I want you to do that again. I want you to come so hard for me that you'll never want to wear another scrap of clothing in this house."

"Again?" My voice squeaked up an octave and earned his affectionate chuckle. An honest orgasm had come so rarely with Mike that I had become accustomed to faking it. Two climaxes in one session seemed like a fairy tale, despite my lover's apparent experience. The promise of another orgasm made my body clench around him again in anticipation. He churned through it, teasing me with shallow dips and the occasional forward snap that planted him fully inside me. When those happened, my eyes rolled in my head and I almost fainted against the kitchen island.

He pinched and teased my nipples, treating them to the textured tips of his fingers. The rough scrape of his callouses made me whimper out loud. "Russ… Russ..." I groaned low, rocking with and without him.

Russell wasn't satisfied until I was sobbing out his name and tightening around him anew. His long and deep strokes stimulated me in a wholly different way, angling against my cervix. The building pressure made me writhe and groan for more.

I reached back to seize a handful of his hair, unable to do anything more than hold him in place, scream his name, and frantically throw my hips back and forth to ride the crest of his movements.

"Don't stop, don't stop!"

Russ nipped my ear. The husky growl from him was as animalistic as his tireless pacing. He filled me again and again, spearing my body at depths I never experienced before. Then he pinched my nipple, stretching it, introducing me to a hint of pain. The sudden sting struck as the ideal contrast to my pleasure and the two sensations merged together.

The moment was too intense, and I felt as if I were shattering into a million pieces that would never be whole again. My walls spasmed around his dick in a series of shockwave contractions, clinging to him the entire time I came. The sensation was different and alien, pulsing through my core until my trembling knees almost gave in. Russ' arms kept me standing. "Russsss," I keened his name aloud while tugging his scalp. My other fingers buried into his wrist, my nails biting into his skin, but my sexy Army sergeant never uttered a cross word. Instead, he sank deep and met his own release, pulsing inside me. My only regret was that I couldn't see his face to enjoy the way he clenched his jaw and squeezed his eyes tight as he came.

I sagged against the counter with my cheek on the cool marble. Panting hard and fast, I couldn't compose a thought, much less utter a word to praise my lover.

Neither of us moved. Russ seemed as content as I was to lay against me, trapping my body against his kitchen counter with his heavier and larger bulk. I closed my eyes, sighed, and enjoyed the close moment between us.

"I'd make love to you every day like this if I could, Daniela."

I wanted to cry. I wanted to call him a liar, but most of all, I wanted to trust him and accept every word. I wanted to believe a man could truly find me attractive again after a decade of the worst degradation and abuse. I wanted to believe in Russ.

When he finally slipped out of me, my legs had regained their strength. I dipped down without making eye contact to grab my shirt and begin pulling it on, but Russell stopped me with a hand on my wrist.

"Don't. Please."

"Don't?"

"I meant it, Daniela. Don't hide from me, baby."

"I'm not hiding," I lied. "Just getting dressed."

His body stepped in snugly behind me, his cheek against my hair and his arm wrapped around my middle in a tender embrace that left me feeling cherished. "No one here but you and me, darlin'."

"Do you really think I look all right?"

"No, I don't just think you look all right. I think you're stunning from head to toe. Not just on the outside, but here too." Russ placed his hand over my heart. "Come on. I'll run a bath for us to have a soak before you get into this kitchen again."

Trusting Russ, I let him take me by the hand and lead me. Our first bath together was the icing on top of everything else we'd shared since our date, and we held each other until the cooling water pruned our bodies. Afterward, while toweling each other off, we exchanged slow, drugging kisses that made me lightheaded.

He surprised me with a sudden question. "Why is it so hard for you to believe I like you the way you are?"

"I've never met a guy who looks like you who cares to be with someone like me… When I married my ex, I was a lot skinnier than I am now. He hated that I gained weight." Back then, my good-looking ex-husband had the physique of a slim running back. His lean build and tight muscular tone gave him a sleek appearance in a football uniform and in my bed.

"You think because I look like this, that it means I want my woman to be small and dainty?" His laughter made me twist around to look up at him in confusion.

"Don't you think girls like Juliette are hot?"

"She's obviously not the woman I want, now, is she?" His hand glided over my damp skin and cupped my breast, a gesture that seemed more for comfort than any attempt to arouse himself or me. "My wife was… she wasn't much smaller than you when I married her. Taller, maybe, and that made her seem skinnier, but I always appreciated how she had some meat on her. She was thin after the sickness, but the woman I keep in my heart and memories was almost as thick as you. And you know what, baby? I wouldn't change either of you for anything."

He hadn't shared much about his wife beyond the assurance of her passing and that he was truly a single man. I hadn't noticed a photo of her yet in the house, but of course, I also hadn't seen his bedroom with more than the weak light of a lantern.

"You really loved her."

"Completely."

I didn't make it back to my house until late afternoon, and if not for Russ' keen sight, I probably wouldn't have noticed something was wrong until the next day when I came down for work.

"Baby, was your car always scratched up like that on the driver's side?"

"Scratched up?" I leapt out of his truck and ran toward my car for a better look. A long horizontal scar ran from the front tire down the side until it reached the rear light. A sick feeling churned in my stomach and my body went cold. I couldn't feel my toes or my fingers anymore.

"Shit," Russ muttered from the other side of my car. I glanced over at his red face, tensed frame, and clenched fists. I dreaded crossing over for a look, but I did it anyway. Someone had scratched the word 'BITCH' into my passenger door in capital letters.

Closer inspection revealed the dash had already been defaced with a particular 'C' word I didn't want in my vocabulary. My driver and passenger side windows were also on the seats along with pooled rain. Someone had bashed those out.

"Who would do this?" Tears burned my eyes and my throat tightened. I knew exactly who. Mike. My driveway swam in my vision, blurred by tears and dizziness. Passing around the front of my car revealed the last of the damage. I stepped on fragments of glass from the shattered headlights.

I couldn't drive to work like this. A sob tore from my throat as I slammed one fist into the hood of my car. If insurance didn't cover all of the damages to the electrical system, I'd be forced to buy a new car.

"Breathe, darlin'." Strong arms surrounded me while I struggled to get enough air in my lungs. "Slow it down and breathe, Daniela."

While I struggled to get it under control, Russ made a call to the local police department. Someone came out and took a statement. After I told them about my ex-husband and how he must have come last night while I was away on a date, the cop said he'd follow up on that and keep me updated on any news.

Russell offered to stay with me, but respected my wish to be alone. I called in sick to work when Monday came and spent it beneath the blankets in bed. I didn't want to see anyone, and I didn't want anyone to see me.

***

I didn't venture out of the house until the second day after my car was vandalized. With a book in one hand and a cup of tea in the other, I retreated to the backyard where I hoped the sunshine would pull me out of my funk. Before settling in the hammock, I placed my cell phone and drink on the wrought iron table beside it.

The shade trees helped set the perfect atmosphere for a lazy afternoon. Between my spiced chai, the chirping birds, and my raunchy romance about a sexy FBI agent, my mood lifted enough for me to be able to shyly send a text message to Russ.

In hindsight, I felt awful about sending him away so fast and rushing into my house to have a pity party. It wasn't his fault my psychotic ex-husband keyed my car, but I hadn't wanted him to see me fall apart.

Hi, Russ, I sent to him. I waited a few minutes, listening to the chirping birds. When he didn't respond an hour later, my worsening anxiety forced me to send another message. *I'm sorry for chasing you away and ignoring you. I miss you.*

"He's probably at work in a fitness class or something," I muttered. I tossed the phone back onto the table and returned to my book. Things steamed up, forcing the agent to choose between the professionalism of the job and mutual attraction with the woman in his charge. He tried to keep her at a distance, only to fail as she pressed and pursued him by bringing attention to his arousal.

By the time they finally kissed, I was so engrossed in the book that the world around me ceased to matter.

"Always reading that romanticized feminist bullshit. Don't you know real men don't act like that?" Mike's voice came from behind me and sent my heart into a wild rhythm. I hadn't heard him approach.

My thoughts turned immediately to the shotgun Russell had been training me to use, and the fact that it was in my bedroom closet. I got up and put the hammock between us.

"Aren't you glad to see me? I came way out here to this shithole for you."

"Get out of here, Mike, or I'll call the cops. I know what you did to my car."

"Did what to your car? Oh, you mean that pile of shit in your driveway right now? I don't know what you're talking about." He made a feint to the left, spun, and caught me on the other side as I made a run for my deck. "Why are you trying to run from me, Daniela? Don't you miss me?" He nudged me up against the tree and trapped me with his body. I smelled the alcohol on his breath.

"I hate you."

"You miss me. You know, when the divorce papers came, I couldn't believe you had the balls to file on me… but I knew you'd never make it on your own. Admit it, chica. You're not happy here. You want to come home to a real man."

"I'm happier here than I've ever been with you," I spat at him.

"Who were you fucking Friday night?"

Mike wouldn't ever own up to damaging my car, but I knew it was him, and I knew he did it because I wasn't home. I shivered and glanced to the side, wondering if my voice would carry to Russ' house. Would he hear me if I screamed? Unlikely. Was he even home? The unanswered text messages told me no.

"It's none of your business where I was."

"Was it that big fucker with the shotgun? Were you fucking him? I told you, this pussy is mine and—"

Mike reached below my waist as if he meant to cup me between the legs. I didn't give him a chance to make contact with me. My hand flew out into his nose, a perfect palm-heel strike that caught him off guard. I had Russ to thank for his lessons. After my ex stumbled back, holding his face, I took off across the yard. I ran without looking back over my shoulder, pushing myself to get distance between us. I would have never looked back if not for the roar.

"Ah, fuck, fuck!" Mike screamed.

I whirled around and lost my footing. Without a chance of regaining my balance, I stumbled back and sat hard on the ground. My bear had returned, except this time he wasn't the placid creature I'd come to admire. He was a growling beast that charged forward through the underbrush, all teeth and ferocious claws.

"Daniela! Do something before it kills me!"

Even if I'd wanted to help, what could I do? I was frozen, too petrified to move. The experts claimed the safest way to end an encounter with a wild bear was to play dead. I hoped they were right.

I heard something ripping, more screams, and the pounding of feet on the ground. Michael must have escaped and left me there to die. I laid there quiet and still, tears streaming down my face. My dad had been right all along. With no hope of making it off the ground and into my house, I laid on the grass with my eyes tightly shut and prayed.

Something warm and dry touched my face, then the heated, warm bulk of a heavily furred body dropped onto the grass beside me. I opened my eyes to find myself face to face with my bear. My heart skipped a beat, and for a moment, I didn't know whether to scream, cry, or pass out. I ended up holding my breath and waiting for a death by mauling.

"Please don't kill me."

The bear responded with a huff of warm air across my cheek, still and nonthreatening. Going as slow as I could, I sat up, hoping and praying the wild animal beside me remained passive. His deep brown eyes never left me as he twisted around and dropped his large head in my lap.

"Hi," I whispered softly. Unable to believe my luck, I stroked my palm down his dark fur. His unbelievably warm coat was coarser than expected. "Were you trying to help me?"

I didn't expect an answer from him, but his intelligent eyes reminded me of rich, warm cocoa. It jarred a memory in my mind.

"If I go inside to get you a snack, will you stay here?"

I had a friend in college who later went on to veterinary school. She told me animals could feel love and tenderness more than they could understand the spoken word. My attempt to convey my affection for him appeared to work; the bear removed his head from my thigh and wandered to my hammock. When I returned with my offerings of pecans and cold salmon from the fridge, I discovered my visitor had made himself at home.

"Thank you for running him away. I bet he won't come back again after that scare." If not for my four-legged defender, I would have called the police and reported Michael, but I was afraid he'd weave some story about a dangerous animal to them, too. People in these parts tended to shoot first and ask questions later when an animal was involved in a dispute.

I didn't know the first thing about bears beyond what Google told me regarding their diet. Cautiously, I extended the glass bowl of pecans toward him with one hand and a plate of fish with the other. He leaned over and ate directly out of the bowl.

"They're all yours. Go ahead," I coaxed him when he stopped to peer up at me. "I worried about you. I worried so much when you didn't come back." Why did it feel like he could understand me?

In my mind, I drew a half a dozen outlandish conclusions, but out of them all, only one made sense. Maybe he was a pet someone had raised from a cub and released again. If that was the case, his behavior would make sense and explain why he sought human interaction. Because I'd fed him, he took Michael's aggression as a threat and protected me.

That had to be it.

My bear didn't leave until after dinner. I cooked in the kitchen while he lounged outside, then I split the helpings and offered half in a mixing bowl. Thirty minutes after he trundled away out of sight, my cell phone rang with a call from Russ.

"Daniela? Are you okay? What's wrong?"

"What made you think something was wrong?"

"I… well, I laid down to read on the sofa when I came back from the gym and fell asleep all afternoon, you know. Funny thing. Woke up to a couple of messages you sent hours ago and just had this bad feeling."

I nudged the phone between my ear and shoulder to hold it in place while I filled the dishwasher. "Nope. Everything's fine now." Fine because of my bear. A sudden rush of emotion brought stinging tears to my eyes. I held back the sniffle and smiled. "Missed you."

"If you'd like me to… If you're feeling up to company this evening, just say the word."

"Word," I whispered into the phone.

"I'll see you soon."

The phone rang again after I hung up. My sister's name popped up in the caller ID window along with a selfie I took last year during a visit to Austin to see her. I made the three-hour drive as often as I could.

"Hey, sis. Feeling better today?" I didn't answer her calls yesterday and only replied to a text with a vague inference that I was ill.

"No," I replied before launching into a summary of the recent events, beginning with my return home Saturday and ending with my rescue by bear.

"Are you kidding me? You're not going to call the cops on that asshole because you're afraid they're going to shoot some rabid bear? Daniela, it could have eaten you!"

Normally I was the one to talk sense into my younger sister, but the role reversal was sobering. "But he didn't. I swear, it was like… like he understood me."

"Sweetie, forget about the damn bear. You need to report Mike to the police so they can arrest his stalker ass."

I knew she was right, but I couldn't do it. Michael would spin his lies, and by the time he finished talking, the cops would think he'd rescued me from a deadly mauling and saved *me*. I didn't want to leave it up to chance; I couldn't risk my fuzzy friend's life.

"Daniela? You still there?"

A set of powerful headlights shone through the living room window. I parted the curtains for a look into the driveway to confirm it was Russ before I sprang to the door and opened it. He waved to me as he approached. "Russ is here. I better go."

"When do I get to meet Mr. Tall, Dark, and Sexy Marine Guy?"

"Army not Marines, and when you actually bring your ass down here."

"When you move out of the place called Quickdraw I'll come visit you. Until then, you're on your own. What the hell is it with this state and the dumb town names?"

"As if a town called Atropos is any better," I teased. Texas seemed to have something with stealing names from mythology and other countries. Paris, Texas. Athens. Sparta. Corpus Christi.

"Yeah, yeah, yeah. Okay, love ya, sis. Come visit soon."

"Love you, too. Maybe this weekend."

I disconnected the call and smiled up at my man. "Hey, you."

"Hey." His gaze flickered toward the cellphone in my hand. "I'm not interrupting anything, am I?"

"No. I was just chatting with my sister and stuff. Come on in."

Russ offered out a long, paper-wrapped box tied with blue ribbon and leaned in for a kiss. His lips against mine washed away the final vestiges of my horrendous day. I didn't need a gift, only him.

"You certainly know how to greet a girl."

"Only my favorite girl, darlin'." His grin made me melt, sending a jolt of heat straight to my gut. "Gonna look inside?"

Ripping into the paper like a kid at Christmas revealed a box full of chocolates from a local candy shop. My favorite sweets were nestled in pretty gold and silver foil wrappers.

"I can't believe you brought me two dozen of these. Eat a few with me."

"I bought 'em for you."

I plucked one of the chocolate, pecan, and caramel clusters from the box and touched the delicious morsels to his lower lip until he took the bait. "I want to apologize to you for how I behaved the other day… it's not your fault."

"You had every right to feel down, Daniela. That no-good bastard defaced your property and… well, those aren't the kind of things you call a lady. He better hope I don't catch him sniffing around here again."

"Again?" I paused in nibbling a chocolate to stare at him.

Russ grunted and went to the fridge to pour himself a glass of sweet tea. "I punched him in your driveway," he reminded me gently. "And I'll kick his ass again the next time I see him."

"Russ… He came by *again*. Today." Although I was certain I'd regret telling Russ, I told him about my encounter with Michael. His expression changed, undergoing rapid transitions between angry and neutral.

"Really though, baby, be honest with me. Are you all right? Why didn't you call me?"

"I'm fine. I was terrified for a little bit, and not just of Mike…" A bite of gooey chocolate and caramel gave me an excuse to be silent.

"You should have called the cops, sweetheart."

"I didn't want a hunt put out on the bear."

Russ shook his head. "I'm sure the bear can take care of himself. Call the police," he coaxed me, reminding me of my sister's plea. If she phoned my parents and relayed the story of what I told her, I was toast.

"You sound like Marta," I grumbled.

"She's your sister, right? You haven't said much about her. What's she like?"

"Well, she looks just like me but a little taller, skinnier, and prettier—"

"Prettier because she's skinnier?" he asked, raising his brows.

"Well, yeah."

"How many damn times do I have to say you're gorgeous, Daniela. Don't you dare think otherwise for a second just 'cause you got… a little more of you to love."

I stared across the counter at him, unable to take my disbelieving eyes off his straight face. It wasn't the sincerity in his words that threw me off balance — it was the corny line. "There's going to be a lot more to love after finishing these chocolates," I quipped.

His big grin spread a little wider. "Nothing wrong with that." He fed me another chocolate.

"You have no idea how great it feels to have a guy who loves to eat as much as I do." I grinned and nibbled his fingers playfully. "Come on. Let's go start up a movie." I finally bought a sofa when I passed by a yard sale in town.

With our candies in hand, I dragged Russ into the newly decorated living room. He wasn't impressed by my tiny loveseat, and his furrowed brow made me burst into a fit of giggles.

"All this space and you have this teensy couch."

"Hey! It was almost free!" Looking around my living room, I couldn't argue with his observation. "To be honest with you, all my rooms are like this. Ian's charging me a pittance for how much square footage I have in here. I use the third bedroom for storing my appliance boxes and stuff in case I have to move again."

There were two bedrooms upstairs across the hall from one another. I had one fixed up like a guest room in case my sister decided to swing into town, and the one downstairs held all of the boxes leftover from my new appliances.

"Sweetheart, why don't you splurge a little and get yourself some nice things. I know somebody who works on the sales floor at Ashley's. She'll cut you an amazing deal—"

"We are *not* using your amazing connections."

"And why the hell not?" he demanded.

Indeed. Why the hell not? My brow creased as we settled into place. "Fuck it. Give her a call. I should have insurance claims money left over after I pay the deductible for my car repairs."

"Great, I'll let Roxella know that we'll be—"

My phone rang with an incoming call from my mother and father. I didn't get a chance to say a word in greeting.

"Why are you not calling the police, Daniela? The man is crazy. He could return and do anything. Call the police right this moment."

"Mama, please." I sighed into the phone. "I know Marta made it sound worse than it is, but I'm fine. I have a shotgun and I will fill him full of holes if he comes back again."

"You have a gun now, *querida*? Where did you get a gun? Daniela, I don't know if you should be alone in that house right now."

"But I'm not alone, Mama. Russ is here. Besides, my vehicle is trashed and I can't go anywhere right now without a car."

My dad didn't waste a second. In the span of a heartbeat, he barked his own questions into the phone. "Who the hell is Russ and why should I trust him to keep you safe? Who is he?"

I was going to wring Marta's neck.

"I should have killed that bastard Michael when he first laid his hands on you," my father raged into the phone. He was beyond the edge of reason now. "Who is this Russ?"

"Papa, relax. Russ is my neighbor and he's an Army vet, okay? He's been teaching me to shoot and…" I peeked over at Russ' amused expression. "We're dating."

That shut both my parents up quickly. I could hear them in the background though, speaking rapid-fire Spanish to one another. It sounded muffled, so I guessed one of them — likely my mother — had a hand over the receiver.

"When were you planning to tell us you were dating someone, *mija*?"

"Soon, Mom. I was planning on telling you soon, but I'm not sixteen years old anymore." I rolled my eyes and swatted Russell's arm when he chuckled at my expense. As loud as my folks were talking, he could probably overhear their end of the conversation.

My father returned to the line. "We planned to come visit for your birthday anyway this weekend, but we'll meet this Russ person, too."

"Can't wait," I chirped back. If I sounded anything less than thrilled, they'd both take off work and come to see me by the ass crack of dawn instead. "See you then. Love you both." After ending the call, I shook my head and turned to face Russ. He promptly burst out laughing.

My parents would love him. Of that, I had no doubt whatsoever. I knew they would because… I was beginning to love him, too.

Chapter Six

~DANIELA~

To ease some of my stress, Russ had a friend down at the fire department come to tow my car into Houston while he drove me to work the next day. He promised me he'd found a body shop with reasonable prices, owned by an old friend of his from the Army. Apparently, the guy retired and opened a business at the start of the year. It was booming, but he promised to squeeze me in.

My boss peeked in on me during my scheduled lunch hour and helped herself to a visitor seat while sipping her Starbucks.

"I'm glad you came back today, Daniela."

"Me, too. I feel silly for laying around so long over something so stupid. A car can be fixed, you know?" I'd already told her the full truth, unable to lie to Laura for long. She was a good woman, and had been an even greater friend over the past couple of years since I first came to work for her.

"Are you going to need a ride home?" Laura asked. "I'm going up to Huntsville to visit my daughter and grandkids this evening. She needs me to babysit. I don't mind swinging by your area."

"Oh no, my boyfriend is coming back by to get me."

The older woman raised one steel gray brow. "A boyfriend, huh? What happened to 'I never want another man again?'" she asked, much to my embarrassment.

"Yeah well… he sort of snuck his way in there."

"Those are usually the best sort, dear." Laura had recognized the signs of an abused woman before my family even realized what was wrong. She'd tried two years earlier to convince me to move out, even offering me a place to stay. I didn't know who celebrated my divorce the most, her or my family. "So tell me about him."

"He's great," I offered without the satisfying details she wanted.

Laura plucked a peppermint from my candy dish and hurled it at me. "That tells me *nothing*."

"Army vet, owns his own home, has a sweet dog he brought back from Afghanistan."

The divulgence of a few details satisfied her. "You can't go wrong with a man who loves animals," Laura replied, nodding.

Michael had hated pets. That should have been my first sign not to trust him.

"Russell took me dancing for our first night out on the town. He taught me a few line dances."

"Would he be that handsome fella looking around the lobby?"

A peek outside my office door revealed my handsome boyfriend stood just a few yards beyond the lobby doors. Jeans, tees, and western boots were a staple of his wardrobe that I'd come to expect from him. A black cap announcing he was a veteran of the U.S. Army covered his wavy black hair. Russell drew admiring glances from the tellers and a few waiting customers in the queue. Not that he seemed to notice, or if he did, he didn't acknowledge them. His muscles bulged as he crossed his arms against his chest and spoke with one of my coworkers. Beth pointed toward my office. When Russ turned to peer through the glass, a big grin split his face.

"Yeah, that's him. Crap, he's super early. I told him five."

"Well go on then, don't keep him waiting. I'll see you tomorrow."

"But it's only noon!"

"And we will manage without you as we did over the weekend. Go on. Shoo."

"Thanks for understanding, Laura. I didn't mean to put you guys out while I was gone."

Her warm smile assured me that my worries were unfounded. "You never call in. Don't think anything of it."

I hugged her, grabbed my purse, and dashed out to meet up with Russ just as someone was thanking him for his service. In the most unprofessional act I've ever committed since landing my job, I threw myself into his arms and hugged him in front of everyone. I had to lay my claim, like an animal marking her territory. *Mine.* All mine, I conveyed in one fierce embrace.

"Well hello to you too, darlin'." Russell caught me up easily against him and snuck a chaste kiss in against my brow. His scruffy face tickled my skin, making me giggle.

"I didn't expect to see you this early."

"I was in the area to check up with my friend about your vehicle. Thought I'd come by and see if you had an hour free for lunch."

"Well, I do, but I ate… and my boss just assumed you were

coming to take me home. So I'm afraid you're stuck with me for more than an hour."

"In that case, would you like to come meet Taylor?"

"Sure."

I found Trigger waiting outside of the bank on the cement walkway, harnessed but without a leash. Passing bank customers complimented us on our dog's exceptional behavior like I'd had some kind of hand in his training.

"Oh, he's not my dog," I blurted out while Russ grinned alongside me.

"He loves her more than me," Russ drawled.

Trigger placed his head beneath my hand and bumped my fingers for a pet. I stroked him and realized how much I had to look like a liar.

"He certainly seems to love you," the grinning stranger said.

I hopped into the passenger seat while Russ buckled Trigger into the rear cab. The extra step taken to guarantee his fur baby's safety endeared me to him more.

It took us fifteen minutes to reach Wild Side Auto Body & Lube. A sleek, feline silhouette, too muscular to be a house kitty, made up the logo.

Russ' friend was a baby-faced man, but probably in his early-to-middle thirties. When I first met Russ, I estimated the same thing about him. He claimed to be forty-three, but I didn't see the age on him either. Taylor wore his hair and goatee closely trimmed, his appearance fastidiously groomed. Like Russ, he didn't have an ounce of body fat on him. He was all lean muscle in a more compact, slimmer build.

When Taylor took his shades off, my breath caught in my chest. His eyes were glacier blue, a vivid contrast against his brown sugar-hued skin. His rich voice sounded the way velvet should feel, smooth and sensual.

Knowing what my landlord looked like, I tried to imagine Russ, Ian, and Taylor side by side until I feared my ovaries were going to explode.

"Uh… I'm..." What was my name? The guys glanced at me and patiently waited while I fumbled through an introduction. Taylor probably thought his friend was dating an idiot. "I'm… Daniela," I tried again.

He shook my hand politely and grinned. "Taylor. Glad to finally meet you. How long has this guy been keeping you a closely guarded secret?"

"Oh, uh…" The amusement on Russell's face when I glanced over at him was enough to snap me out of my temporary stupidity. "A few weeks now, maybe. Thanks for taking my car on short notice."

"No problem. What happened to you was a damn shame. We're working on getting your ride back to you good as new."

Good as new… My ancient 2003 Chevy Malibu would never be good as new. I chuckled a little and nodded. "I'd be glad to just have the scratches off and a couple new headlamps."

"And tires. The asshole kinda popped those too," Taylor added. As my expression fell — a byproduct of my concern for the rising costs — he held out both hands toward me and quickly said, "Your insurance should be enough to cover most of it, trust me."

I relaxed and nodded again. "Still, I appreciate this. When I saw the water damage, I was sure I'd have to suck it up and get a new vehicle."

"No, ma'am. I got a guy on staff who's a good electrician. As long as the insurance checks out and they're cool with our plan, we ought to have it back to you within a week."

"That fast?"

"If I can, it'll be done."

I liked Taylor as much I liked Ian. His open, friendly attitude eased my anxiety and brought a smile to my face.

We hung around the auto body shop with him for a while. They told me stories of their time together as a squad, in which they were both sergeants, one a weapons specialist, the other an engineer.

"Oh yeah. This guy was real serious about his weapons training. And God help the idiot who touched his guns. You so much as got a fingerprint on his babies and he'd throw the biggest hissy-fit you ever saw."

"I wasn't that bad," Russ protested.

One look at Russ' red-cheeked face made me think otherwise. I knew how much he loved his guns, and he'd had me breaking them down and learning to clean them with him days after our lessons began.

We hung around with Taylor for an hour longer before I thanked him again and Russ drove me home. We had dinner together and snuggled up to a movie, growing closer with each passing day.

In the morning, I woke first and tiptoed to the kitchen door to search for my bear. While the bacon fried in the pan, I snuck outside to walk through the yard, only to return to the kitchen when my furry friend didn't greet me at the tree line.

It set the beginning of a new pattern for the remainder of the week. Russell and Trigger slept over each night, but my bear stayed away no matter how much bacon I left outside for him.

I had one, but I missed the other.

Chapter Seven

~ Daniela ~

A late Friday night with Russ meant I overslept Saturday morning. Long after he went home to handle his household chores and business, I lounged in bed and dreamed of the bright days ahead of me, contrasted by the hardships left behind. I also dreamed of all the things Russ had done to me over the course of the night. My thighs still ached, but I wouldn't take any of it back or utter a single complaint. The man was insatiable and he'd awakened a similar hunger in me. I couldn't get enough of him.

I would have slept deep into the afternoon if a determined caller didn't ring me over and over. I nearly swatted the cell phone off my nightstand to peer at the caller ID. Ian MacArthur, my landlord, would be about the only person who didn't catch the hint.

"Hello?" I answered.

"Good afternoon, Ms. Reyes. I'm on my way out to see about some security upgrades to the property. Is this a poor time?"

What made him think that? Was it the two missed calls or my exhausted voice? "Huh? Oh, no!" Then his words sank in and cleared my befuddled brain. "No, it's not a bad time. What security upgrades?"

"Glad to hear it. I'll be round in about, oh, fifteen minutes or so to explain it all to you. I'm going to grab Russ on my way and utilize him for my manual labor." I could picture his wide grin and playful wink with his words.

"See you then."

After hanging up the phone, I flew into the shower then brushed my teeth in an effort to look less like a zombie. My hair was a total loss, so I twisted it into a quick bun and bounced to the front door just as Ian's SUV pulled into the drive.

My landlord was a fox. When I first answered the ad on Craigslist advertising this place, I expected some ancient old man in his seventies with too much space to care for the land anymore. I didn't count on a smoking hot guy with a chiseled body and bright hazel eyes.

Stand him next to my hunky boyfriend and it was enough to make a girl spontaneously orgasm. The only way things could be hotter would be if Taylor were here too, and I seriously didn't know if I could handle that much sexy all at once.

"Morning, boys. Or afternoon I guess."

Russell greeted me with a kiss, which was better than any caffeine jolt I'd get from the coffee brewing inside. I forgot all about Ian until the man cleared his throat.

"Sorry. Hi, Mr. MacArthur." Ian was of ambiguous age and race, his dark brown hair worn too closely trimmed to identify the texture, and his features too youthful to be beyond his forties. His eyes were his best feature, the pale golden color of champagne, and absolutely gorgeous within his bronze tanned face.

Ian gave us both a skeptical look. "I think since you're boning each other, we can all be on a first name basis now, right?"

"Christ, Ian," Russ muttered. Seconds later when the grin seeped into his expression, I could tell this sort of joking was normal for them. The friendly banter helped to offset my embarrassment.

"Well, I know I'm not wrong," Ian teased.

"Since he's in the mood to be an ass, you can always call him Colonel," Russ suggested in a playful tone, nudging my arm. "He loves that."

"I'll stick with Ian out of those options, thanks," I replied.

"We're going to install a home burglary system here. I know Russ gave you a boomstick," he began, referring to my shotgun, "but it doesn't hurt to have another measure of defense, right?"

I flushed. Between Russ and all of the firepower in my bedroom right now, my house should have been the safest on the block. "I prefer the house alarm to be honest. I don't know if I could shoot someone." Even if that man was my abusive ex.

"Let's hope you're never in the position where you have to," Ian said.

While they worked around my house, I baked a peach cobbler to accompany the plate of roast beef sandwiches and sweet tea for their lunch. They placed alarm sensors in each ground floor window and doorway entrance, which would alert me and the police of shattering glass. The last of the work involved two hidden cameras. Ian angled one onto my patio and directed the other to my driveway. Motion sensing lights would warn about anything larger than a squirrel wandering through my yard, and since I had no immediate neighbors on either side of me, the bulbs were as bright as the sun.

"Thanks for the lunch, Daniela. It seems like we're all good here, so I'll get out of your hair and check in with you next month. Let me know if you need anything."

"Hold on a second. Let me write you a check for next month's rent while you're here."

Ian waved it off and headed for the door. "Nah. Don't worry about the rent. I feel bad about what happened here. I didn't take security into account when I rented this house out to you—"

"You had no way to know my ex was an asshole," I argued with him.

"Be that as it may, I won't take a dime from you next month."

Russell's vanilla ice cream and peach cobbler distracted him. I'd thrown together a good meal for the two hardworking men, and, of course, his belly seemed to take precedence. "Russ," I hissed at him. "Make him take my rent."

"Are you kidding? He's rich. He won't even miss whatever you're paying him," Russ assured me. "Go on and get, Ian."

"Much obliged," he called before he dipped out the door. I stared in frustration at the empty doorway then shot a dirty look at Russ. He was no help.

"Look, when the colonel makes up his mind about something, there's no changing it. He was the same way in the field, and I expect he'll be the same way till we bury his stubborn ass."

"Fine." I didn't like it, but I didn't see a way around it.

"C'mere." Russell tugged me close and gave me something else to think about.

Chapter Eight

~Russ~

Once Ian was gone, I distracted Daniela with a foot massage in front of a romantic comedy marathon. I let her choose the flicks and pretended to care about the couples on the television. Their scripted angst and relationship troubles didn't hold a candle to the dilemma I was facing.

How could I possibly tell the woman I had grown to care about that I wasn't technically human? How could I tell her the bear she missed so badly hadn't left her, and I'd been here all along watching out for her? Sooner or later, something would have to give before the guilt consumed me.

"Will Trigger be okay? Do you need to go let him out?"

Her words pulled me out of my inner musings. "Oh, he's fine. I ran over to let him out when Ian was finishing up the wiring on the last camera. He's better with that sort of stuff."

"Mm… you think so? Good."

"Good that Trigger's not gonna make a mess or good that Ian's better at wiring?" I teased.

"Both." She tapped the power button on the remote while half of the movie remained.

"Huh?"

"There's something else I want to show you," Daniela explained. With one hand in mine, she coaxed me from the couch and guided me upstairs toward her bedroom.

"Ready for bed already, darlin'?"

"No. I actually had something else in mind."

"Yeah?" I drew her in close and bent down to claim a kiss. "What's that?"

"You'll see."

Sleeping over a couple times that week made me familiar with the ultra-feminine space. Purple lace curtains over blackout shades matched a satin comforter over the queen-size bed. She left me in the center of the bedroom and struck a match to light the candles at the bedside. The aroma of ginger and citrus permeated the room, exotic and bold like my spicy Latina.

Her fingers slid beneath my t-shirt hem and over my abs. Creeping the cotton higher, she dipped her head to kiss each inch of skin she revealed. Something had gotten her into the mood, and hell if I knew what it was. Her fingers glided over me, tracing my muscles at first before a breathy order issued from her lips. God, she sounded like a sex kitten when she brought out the sensual whispers and her heavier accent.

"Lay down."

"You in the mood to be a cowgirl today?" I pictured her on top of me, bouncing up and down on my length with all of her energy. My stiffening cock reacted to the visual with a twitch.

"I said lay down."

I underestimated Daniela's strength. With one shove, she knocked me back onto her bed and advanced on me to unfasten my belt. She didn't waste movements with flirtation or teasing. She jerked my pants down again for the second time in our relationship to reveal the bulge in my dark green boxer briefs.

Taking the lead this way was a new side to her, and it was the sexiest thing any woman had ever done for me; foreign but far from unwanted. As she drew my stiffening cock from my boxers and tugged them down, a single stroke of her hands brought me to complete arousal. My dick jutted up, hard and pulsing with need, seeming too big for her small hands. When she curled her fingers around me, I realized my perception was right. It *was* too large, the base so wide when completely aroused that her fingers and thumb didn't touch.

While she stepped back from me to undress, I maintained a one-fisted grip of my cock and jerked off while she stripped. She'd been shy around me once. Too wounded by years of verbal abuse to trust me with her body. I drank her in without shame and visually devoured the sight of her bare breasts.

"You're so beautiful, Daniela. I could watch you all day." The short time since our last lovemaking seemed like years. My balls were heavy and full beneath her fingertips as she replaced my hand with hers on my dick. I groaned and tilted my head back against the pillows, exposed and completely naked for her enjoyment. I loved it when she rode me, moving above my body like a goddess, her full breasts offered to my hands and mouth. The newfound confidence she displayed aroused the hell out of me, and I couldn't wait for her to climb on.

"Oh, yeah?" she asked, a hint of flirtatious humor in her voice. "What's your favorite part of me?" She dipped her head to flit her tongue against my sensitive crown. I moaned and tried to cling to my intelligence.

"Your… your… fuck," I breathed out as her mouth descended next. Daniela had never tried sucking me off before, and as much as I enjoyed a good blow job, I had never pushed her to try. She took in a quarter of my length and withdrew until only the tip remained. I wanted to thrust my hips upward to claim every inch of her throat.

"My fuck? I'm not sure I know what part that is," she teased.

Before I could say anything more, she ducked her head down and took my cock back between her lips. I couldn't form another coherent sentence and succumbed to the skill of her mouth.

Skill was an understatement. As she dragged backward and left a slick sheen on my dick, I shuddered and anxiously awaited her return. The playful light had returned to her eyes, the glow that I missed since her ex damaged her car. She consumed me again in a single stroke and began to draw me in to completion. One inch at a time, my shaft disappeared past her plump lips, a welcome sight that I watched to the last second.

I wasn't a small man in the least. Back in my dating days, before I met my wife, nothing less than a large condom would comfortably fit around my thick girth. And since Dani had told me she was protected, I didn't have to bother with one now. I trusted her.

"Dan… Dani, wait… I'm too much for you," I barely breathed out. She peeked up at me with a mischievous sparkle in her eyes, swallowed to loosen her throat, and thrust the final inches of my length past her lips. Despite my size, she deep throated me so proficiently that I gripped the sheets and gasped in surprise. She cradled me from tip to base, completely and wholly plunged into her throat until her nose pressed against the dark curls at my pelvis.

She kneaded my balls and gently squeezed the weight in her hands as she pulled back. Her tongue teased my sensitive cockhead and prodded the hole, lapping away a clear droplet beading from the tip. I became helplessly captive in her competent hands as she came alive with enthusiasm and drew me in deep again.

"Dani, sweet Lord, baby. I can't keep…" I wouldn't last long if she continued at this rate.

Daniela made cock sucking seem like an art. She slid her mouth to the tip and engulfed me anew with zeal. Something in her had changed, and I lacked the concentration or willpower to investigate it. I became her willing captive, a slave to her talents each time my dick disappeared between her lips and down her throat.

I didn't warn her of my impending orgasm, nor did I need to. Our on-and-off intimacy over the past couple of weeks had given her time to learn me well. She drew back, her mouth leaving me entirely before she swiped a bottle of clear oil from the bedside table. Within seconds, she'd squirted it until my dick glistened with more than her spittle. Before I could even voice a moan of complaint, she leaned forward and took me between her breasts. Using her forearms to press them in tight together, she slid her body up and down, trapping me within her oiled cleavage.

"Holy shit!" My shocked brain couldn't dredge up any finer compliments. Utterly entranced, my eyes followed her up and down motion over my cock, and my hips surged upward.

"Come for me, Russ," she urged.

My fingers tightened in the sheets, my abs tensed, and an explosion of come jetted over her generous tits. I watched the entire display from start to finish, treated to the hottest thing I ever witnessed in all of my life. She made it a spectacle, sort of a show for me to enjoy.

"Wow." My voice sounded raw. I laid there atop her girlish comforters, boneless as a fish. "You did… wow," I repeated again on the next breath.

"You don't mind that I didn't, you know… swallow?" Her fingers had replaced her breasts, and she ran them down my softening dick with tender, slow strokes.

I wanted to ask what idiot put that foolish notion in her head, but I already knew. "No. No, pretty sure I don't mind," I replied. A blow job was a blow job, and the one given to me was stellar. I groaned and forced myself to sit up and gaze down at her. Daniela had knelt at the edge of the bed, a naked but beautiful mess covered in my cum. The sight made me groan anew, but my dying erection remained lifeless. Not now, but soon, I'd have to have her again and feel her body trembling around me.

Sudsing her up in the steamy shower was more than enough to invigorate me. We eventually moved into the shower to clean up, but my good intentions didn't last. I lifted Dani up, planted her ass against the wet wall, and drove into her hot and fast. By the time the water went tepid, we were both ready to collapse into the sheets for a long night of sleep.

My bear had bonded with her, driving me head over heels in love. I wanted to tell her the truth, and all I needed to do was figure out how.

Chapter Nine

~DANIELA~

Mama and Papa showed up bright and early Sunday morning for brunch. They brought Marta along with them to prove that my new town of residence wasn't filled with gun-toting Texans ready to pump us full of lead.

"Happy birthday, *mi hermana!*" Marta threw her arms around me and practically knocked me off my feet before I could invite them inside. Laughing, I squeezed her back and accepted hugs from both of my parents, too.

"Your place is so big. Whoa." Marta twisted all around and then peered at my brand new leather sectional. Russ and I had picked it up during the week and I really loved it. I didn't regret the decision to let him talk me into buying nice things.

"This is a very beautiful neighborhood, Daniela." My mother stared around the foyer as they removed their shoes.

"This house is so large," my father commented, echoing my sister's sentiments. "Are you sure this is in your budget?"

Leave it to my dad to worry about my future funds.

"My landlord is an Air Force veteran. You know, the kind of guy who goes off and does contract missions for the government now. Honestly, Papa? I think I'm mostly house-sitting for him."

"What happens when he wants to move back in?" Marta plopped down on the couch and kicked the footrest up.

"I don't think that's going to happen anytime soon. He's always flying somewhere to do mercenary work. And well…" Was living with Russ out of the question once a few months passed and we became close enough to invade each other's space on a daily basis? I liked the thought of making him breakfast every morning.

"Come on, lemme show you outside. He has this amazing deck out there."

We chilled on the patio, chatted, and played catch-up on the big events in my life. By the time I finished telling the three of them all about Russ, my mom had begun to clap her hands with joy.

"Where is he? Does he not want to meet us?" Mama asked.

"It's not that. He really does want to meet you, but he teaches self-defense classes sometimes on Sunday afternoons. It was already scheduled. I promise, I'll fetch Russ once he's home and we'll all meet up in Huntsville for dinner around seven."

My father didn't appear convinced. It took a little more to win him over sometimes. "We'll go check in to our hotel rooms then."

"Are you sure you don't want to stay here?" I asked, probably for the tenth time.

"No, no, we don't want to put you out. Besides, you know your father, he goes to bed early and likes to have the TV on loud." My mom grimaced but had no true malice in her tone. After thirty years of marriage, she liked to have a movie blasting, too. She just wouldn't admit it.

"Which is why I have a room of my own," Marta added with a cheeky grin. "Rafael is going to meet us for dinner as well, okay?"

Marta's boyfriend was, like his namesake, an artist, and he attended one of the nearby schools. I didn't think their long distance relationship would hold while she attended a college three hours away. But it did endure, and had held for the past year since she'd transferred away for a better program at a larger university in San Antonio. My mother and I were positive he'd be popping the question soon. We'd then have a beautiful wedding to plan for once she graduated.

About an hour later, Russ' pickup rumbled by. I waited until he phoned me with an enthusiastic happy birthday before I embarked on the five minute walk to his place. He met me on the porch with a sweet kiss then invited me to his backyard.

"Got you something today on my way home."

"You didn't have to get me anything, Russ, really." Having him was more than enough for me. Plus, agreeing to brave my family this early in our relationship felt like a gift all its own.

"What did I say about gifts, hmm?"

I kept the gardenia he bought for me in my bedroom window. The rich scent of the flowers made my room smell divine, an ever present memory of the man who gave them to me. While I had discovered my generous boyfriend made more money in one year than I'd earned in a decade, I still felt off sometimes about accepting gifts from him that cost more than ten dollars. He outdid himself this time.

The gift-wrapped box opened to reveal a glossy snub-nosed

revolver with an ivory grip. It gleamed like silver, and may very well have been plated with it for all I knew. "Russ, I can't accept this."

The boyish grin on his handsome face melted my heart. It made his chocolate brown eyes light up. "Yes, you can. Happy birthday. Now load it up and get your sweet ass over here to test it out."

According to Russ, I was amazing with a shotgun. We'd practiced on and off at his home and even visited a range to shoot one of his handguns. Apparently, he wanted to reward my progress with a brand new Smith & Wesson revolver for my birthday.

Michael had given me an apron and brand new skillet once for a birthday, then demanded to know why I didn't get into the kitchen to make him some bacon. He didn't appreciate the lip I gave him afterward, and once I got off the floor, I made him a great breakfast with my new gifts.

This was different. This was a gift from the heart and one meant purely for me. Russ led me over to his firing mound where he'd already posted up a new silhouette. I'd blasted a fist-sized hole into the last one from repeated shots and developing precision. The area was all set up for me, my goggles and earmuffs waiting on the small table with a box of bullets. While he watched me, I loaded six rounds, flicked the safety, and took aim. He didn't lurk behind me anymore these days, nor did he coach and remind me with gentle cues. Patient as ever, he leaned against a tree and pulled out his phone to text.

Slow is smooth, I reminded myself. And smooth is fast. I used to jam my finger down on the trigger and become discouraged when the gun jumped in my hands. My bullets would fly wildly into the silhouette's gut or shoulder, never striking the mark. This time, the bark preceded a hole in the silhouette's face where the nose belonged. Satisfied, I fired again until the gun clicked empty then I set it down on the table and walked up to examine my work.

"You don't have to keep it if you don't want to."

"Russ—"

He eased up behind me and curled one arm around my waist. "I did get you a backup gift just in case. I just wanted to give this one to you first—"

"I love it, and I'll be happy to take it home." I twisted within his embrace and threw my arms around his neck. "It's awesome. I love it, and I—" Love you. A strange feeling rolled through my belly and tensed my muscles. I couldn't speak it aloud, but the realization snuck into my thoughts and stole my breath. I did. If I didn't love him, then it was a feeling damned close to love. "I think you're amazing."

"I hope you think I'm amazing still after this confession. Your car is ready. Taylor actually finished it last night, but I told him to hold on to it until today since it's your birthday."

I shoved him in the chest. "Get out."

"Sorry! I didn't think one day would impact things."

"It doesn't, but you could have at least told me. You can tell him he's an asshole too for not calling me."

"Well, you can tell him yourself. He just pulled into my driveway about five minutes ago."

"I want to shoot you with my new gun."

"You won't after you see your car."

I ran ahead of Russ for the front lawn. Taylor's tow truck was parked on the road but my car was in the drive. He emerged from my Chevy Malibu and shut the door just as I passed the corner. I didn't even recognize it. My modest midnight blue sedan had been transformed, replaced by a sleek twin in vibrant teal green and purple. My favorite colors. Russ had told him my favorite colors, and better than that, was the fact that he'd noticed them at all. Screaming, I leapt up and down in place then hugged Russ tightly before rushing over for a better look.

Tears streamed down my face as I circled around my Malibu. An aqua-hued galaxy faded into a deep plum with silver and white stars, then back to teal again at the trunk end of the car. Taylor had taken my plain vehicle and transformed it into a universe on wheels. Tinted windows all around concealed any changes inside, but there were enough on the outside to hold my attention.

"I have hubcaps now! Fancy hubcaps!" I blubbered. The metallic teal practically glowed in the sunshine.

"You haven't had a look inside yet," Taylor said.

I flew to the driver's door and opened it. My dull gray interior had been trashed from the day I bought the used car, and worsened by Michael smoking inside of it. I slipped into the seat and inhaled the new car smell of synthetic charcoal grey leather. The steering wheel cover featured my favorite cartoon fairy and felt smooth as satin under my hands.

"Start it up," Taylor encouraged.

He'd left the keys in, so I fired up the ignition, noticing the dash instruments were all changed. Digital readouts glowed back at me. I screamed.

"I think she likes it, man," Taylor said with a laugh. He and Russell high-fived each other.

"How much do I owe you?"

"Nothing, sweetie. Your insurance covered most of the necessities. I mean, that jackass did some damage, and thanks to the storm, your insurance covered an overhaul on your electrical system. I had fun and threw in a few things sitting around the shop. Shit someone ordered and changed their mind about that we never sent back. Believe me, it was a relief getting rid of all that junk lying around."

"There's no way you threw in all of this."

"Naw, I didn't. The paint job upgrade is gratis, so are the new wheels and tint job on your windows. As for the rest... well… we'll consider the deductible and other extras covered by a charitable donor." He glanced at Russ.

"Russ, you didn't."

"I'm not claiming or denying it," Russ replied.

After I jumped out of the car, I flung myself against Russ for the second or third time. Who could keep count? I embraced him fiercely and peppered his face with kisses while his friend laughed. "Was this my other present?" I asked.

"Yeah… Happy birthday, Dani. You deserve this. C'mon, Taylor. Tell her what all's in the car."

"Sure thing, bro. All right. First off, me and the guys placed a brand new alarm on this girl. It has an invisible sensing field that'll alert you of any interference. If the car windows are shattered again, it'll send a message to the police. And… you can control it through your smartphone once you download the app. I know how y'all chicks are about your phones."

I threw myself into Russ' arms and hugged him until his rich laughter filled my ears.

"What the hell? I'm the one who did the work. Where's my hug?" Taylor demanded.

"Get your own woman," Russ muttered to him.

I couldn't help myself. I peeled myself off Russ and hugged his friend tight. "It looks amazing!"

"Damn straight it does." Taylor lifted me off my feet for a brief spin then passed me back over into Russ' arms. "Well, I do believe my work here is done."

"You hold on a sec. Need to talk to you about something," I heard Russ saying to his friend as I wandered around my vehicle again, touching and stroking the flawless paint job. "Dani, I made reservations for us. You wanna go change?" he asked me.

"Should I drive the car home?"

"Hell yeah. Take it home and change. I'll be over in a sec." He passed my new revolver to me with the safety on. I would have forgotten and left it with him if he didn't.

We'd already talked and discussed the possibility of enrolling myself into a concealed handgun class. With my new S&W, I felt more confident about carrying for my protection. I drove my new-to-me car home, squealing joyously the entire way like a child on Christmas. I even triggered the alarm the moment I shut the car door.

Once inside, I set my shiny revolver on the kitchen counter and darted upstairs to my bedroom to change. A quick rummage in the closet provided a cream, off-the-shoulder dress with a billowy bodice. The perfect amount of cleavage.

I let my hair down and misted it with lavender water to refresh my curls. Russ appreciated my casual looks, adored me without makeup, and simply liked me for being me. With him, I could be myself.

Had I ever felt so in love with Michael? A giddy feeling overtook me until I giggled crazily in the bathroom. I applied some sweet, peach-flavored gloss to my lips and admired my hair again. My dress emphasized my cleavage and tits.

"Maybe just a little make-up." I peered down into the makeup kit and selected a brush for my eyeshadow palette. When I glanced up again, a frowning face peered back at me through the mirror. There was a man standing behind me in the open bathroom door to my bedroom. I shrieked and whirled around to face my ex-husband in the most unlikely place I ever expected to find him. My home. Mike was in my home, violating the private sanctity of my new residence.

"You look like a slut." Mike's gaze lingered on my breasts. He was at least ten pounds thinner. His gaunt face had hollowed a bit, and his bloodshot eyes told a tale I knew well. He'd been up all night drinking and the binge had extended to the day. The smell of tequila wafted off him and assaulted my nose. Shit. Why hadn't I set the house alarm, too?

"I look great. That's why you're here, isn't it? No one else wants to put up with your shit, right?"

The shotgun was in my closet, behind Mike, and far out of my reach. All I had at hand was a jar of cream eyeshadow and an Avon make-up brush with a tapered black handle.

I could make a stand here and now. I weighed more than he did and I knew how to deliver a punch now. Those thoughts of dispensing physical justice died as quickly as they were formed though once I saw the gun tucked into his waist. Fists and a makeup brush weren't any match for a firearm.

A terrifying realization occurred, bringing with it a flash of cold understanding that struck me like ice water. A man only arrived at his ex-wife's house with a gun for one reason, and one reason only. He'd kill me whether I fought or not.

Two years ago, I would have cowered. I rushed him instead and shoved all of my weight behind my hand. The blunt end of the makeup brush sank into his shoulder. He punched me and screamed in pain, but my sudden attack gave me the upper hand. With my weight, I knocked him over and darted into the hall.

"You bitch!"

Get downstairs, get downstairs. The alarm Ian had installed included a panic button. I could activate it from the box beside the door or my phone — which I had left in my car with my purse. In my excitement over everything, I'd left the keys behind, figuring I wouldn't need them.

Unlike my old home in the suburbs on the postage-stamp-sized yard, I didn't have neighbors for nearly a mile down the road. Screaming from inside my house wouldn't do a thing but strain my vocal cords.

Mike thundered down the stairs behind me. Something whizzed past my head and the front window shattered. It took my mind a second to register that Mike had actually fired a bullet. At me. It wasn't about wanting to slap me around or intimidate me anymore. He'd come to finish me off for good.

Abandoning my idea to reach the front door and the security system box, I immediately turned the corner to duck out of his line of sight. I ran toward the kitchen with tears streaming down my cheeks. My revolver was on the counter and I grabbed it without pausing.

"No one gets to have you but me!" Another bullet zinged past and struck the cabinets.

"You're crazy!" I yelled back. Sunshine blinded me as I slammed the patio door open and darted outside. Distance was what I needed. Distance and Russell.

"Help me!" I screamed at the top of my lungs. "Somebody help!"

Another shot rang out, but this time I had no idea where it struck. Mike's aim was lousy, much to my favor, but I didn't dare to count on that fortune continuing.

"Get back here, you fat whore. Gonna leave me and just spread your legs for the next man to come along?"

I didn't know how many bullets a Glock could hold, but the rounds in Mike's handgun seemed never-ending.

"Ungrateful bitch, you don't get to leave me. Not after everything I gave you."

I spun on my heels and took off for the front lawn where my new car waited for me. With the revolver in my hands, I felt like a coward. Who ran from a man with a gun when they had a weapon of their own?

"Get your fat ass back here!"

Another shot rang out, and then wind rushed past me. An enormous jet black blur hurtled by my left side. My mind didn't move quickly enough to register the things happening at that moment. Mike's startled scream, the roar, and another gunshot made me stop cold in my tracks.

I turned to see my bear upon Mike, shoving him into the grass and mauling him with unforgiving claws. Then my ex-husband fired point-blank into my bear's belly. The sudden explosion of pain must have startled the animal who released his prey and reared back, allowing Michael to scurry to his feet. Blood streamed down my ex-husband's chest as he raised the gun and shot my bear again.

A few days before, I told Ian I didn't think I could shoot a man. Given the choice between my bear and my ex, there was no competition. My mind had never been clearer. I raised the revolver, peered down its sight, prayed, and slowly pulled the trigger. Michael jerked back as the round struck his shoulder then I fired again. I fired until the last report echoed and the revolver was empty.

I didn't know how many times I hit him, and I didn't care. I tossed the gun aside and rushed to my bear's side. Blood pooled on the grass around his lush black fur.

"No!" I shrieked. I threw myself to my knees beside him, feeling more helpless than ever. Michael's glassy eyes stared up at the sky, but all of my concern was with my bear. My protector. "Don't die. Please don't die."

I could call for a veterinarian, couldn't I? If a vet could operate on a horse or a cow in some pasture, couldn't they save my bear? With his blood on my hands, I rushed into the house and dialed 911 from the kitchen. I had no idea what gibberish I screamed into the line, too distraught to make sense beyond yelling that 'he' was dying and to send someone please.

As I stepped onto the patio deck again, I saw my bear shambling to his feet and lumbering toward the tree line. Everything I knew about wild animals told me to keep my distance, but my love for him drove me forward across the grass.

"No, don't move. You can't go like this. You're hurt!"

He proved me wrong and put on a burst of speed that took him through the brush and into the forest. For an injured animal, he moved quickly and disappeared beyond the tree line. Instinct made me give chase.

Branches whipped at my face and slapped my skin, scraping my exposed skin with every step. I ran barefoot after him despite the difference in our speed. With his blood on the forest floor, it wasn't too hard to track him. He left a trail that I followed with ease.

It was like my dream, only this time, I ignored the burning in my calves and thighs to tear through wilderness. My chest heaved and my lungs burned for air. I wasn't in shape and my body hated me for every step, but I knew in my soul that if I let him run this time, I'd never see him again.

The bear rustled through the bushes ahead of me and escaped the overgrown woods into a manicured rear lawn. I knew this yard. This half-finished wooden fence. I knew those carrot tops and green tomatoes, as well as the bountiful number of white peaches dangling from the branches of an enormous tree.

"Russ!" I called. "Russ! Help!" I screamed again for him. I found the bear sprawled in the middle of the garden, still bleeding from both injuries. The gunshot left a ragged exit hole and a smaller entry, both congealed with blood. With no other option, I fell to my knees beside him and slid my fingers over his dark coat. "I'm here. I'm here. Shh…"

If he did die, I wanted him to go feeling loved. I'd known somehow since the first day he dined with me, that my words were understood. Gazing down at him now I saw the keen understanding in his pain-filled eyes.

"Russ!" I called out again. Comforting the animal as he died became my top priority. If I could do nothing else but remain at his side, I'd do that at the very least. With tears streaking down my cheeks, I turned my face toward the log cabin and waited for my boyfriend to emerge. Where was he?

The bear moved beneath my hand. The coarse sensation of thick bear fur receded away until bare skin and smooth muscle was in its place, confusing my perceptions of what I last saw with what I felt. I blinked down toward the animal and gaped.

The creature under my hand was no longer a bear. A human male lay on his side, his body contorted with agony and pain. "Russ?" I jerked my hand back from my boyfriend's brawny arm. He didn't wear a scrap of clothing, but the most undeniable proof was the identical holes in his midsection. Two entries and one exit. I stared.

"Dan… Daniela. I need you to… I need you to get my first aid kit. It's on the..." He groaned and controlled his breathing. "Bottom kitchen drawer, below the microwave."

"You were a bear. You were a bear a moment ago. Russ, what's happening? Why were you my bear?"

"I'll tell you everything. Fuck, this hurts." Russ groaned and tried to sit up until I pressed a hand to his shoulder.

"Don't move!"

I dashed into the cabin and retrieved the kit as directed. Once beside him again and on my knees, I used the only medical know-how I had to apply pressure to his bleeding wound. "You need a doctor. You're losing so much blood, Russ."

"No." He shook his head and grunted. "No hospitals. You need to go back to your place, Dani. Tell the police what happened and say the bear ran away. It'll all be on camera."

"I'm not leaving you like this!"

"You have to. I'll be fine here. I promise you, baby. Just do as I'm asking you to do, please."

"But—"

"Darlin', please. I know you don't have much love for your ex, but… but you need to meet the police there. Tell them what happened."

I knew he was right. I'd shot Mike and there was no way to cover that up or deny it. If I fled the scene, I'd be looked on with suspicion.

Terror had numbed me. The chase through my home, Mike's attempt to kill me, and the shoot out on the lawn had made his transition from bear to man seem almost simple by comparison. Choking on my tears, I nodded and rose to my feet.

When I returned to my yard, Mike's motionless shape remained in the same place where I left him, or rather, where I shot him. I shuddered and couldn't force myself to go see if he was still breathing. I'd leave that to the professionals.

Less than a minute later, the small-town cops swarmed into my yard. I stayed where I was with my hands out in the open and my gun lying on the ground.

"Ma'am? Ma'am, are you hurt?"

I shook my head and pressed my lips together in a failing effort to remain calm. My boyfriend was a bear, my ex almost murdered me in my own home, and I'd shot a man for the first time. The reality of gun ownership didn't empower me; I felt terrified and waited for them to haul me away next.

"I think she's in shock. Ma'am, we need you to tell us what happened here."

"He… my ex-husband broke into my house and tried to kill me. I shot him." I didn't realize I was hyperventilating until the world dimmed and I was suddenly sitting on the damp grass. One of the EMS workers had lowered me to the ground. Another handed me a bag while speaking gentle instructions to breathe into it.

"Hey, I remember this house. There's an open vandalism case on her car," one of the officers said.

"Can you tell us what happened to your ex-husband?"

"He's shown up uninvited a few times, but this time he came into my house," I told the two policemen. "He shot at me with his gun."

They introduced themselves as Officer Hunt and Officer Perry. I nodded a lot and answered their questions with short answers before directing one of them to the security console inside of the house. Surveillance ran 24 hours a day whether or not I armed the actual system itself. Hunt, the lanky and taller officer with a thick southern accent, headed over to review the tape while Perry remained near me with the paramedics. Drained and exhausted, I didn't argue when the female EMT guided me to their van and onto the stretcher to rest.

Hunt returned to the van. "Yup. Everything's like she said. The bear came from the front of the home to intercept her husband and from there, she shot him after he fired into the animal. You say you were feeding him, ma'am?"

"Ex-husband," I stressed, "and, yes. I fed him almost every day. He was a good bear." I shivered beneath the blanket the paramedic had draped over my body. It wasn't enough to warm me.

"Gotta say I agree. He may have saved your life," Perry said.

An hour later, Mike's body had been removed from my lawn by the local examiner. The police had my report, but I promised to drive up to the department the following day to make an official statement.

After they were gone, I paced the floor then washed my face in the kitchen sink. My glass window had been trashed and fixing it wasn't my first priority. With no other alternative, I armed the security system and stepped outside into the cooling night air.

Dreading the worst, that I would return to find him bled out in the grass, I made the long walk to Russ' cabin only to step into the yard and find it empty. Russ wasn't there. Trigger barked to announce my entrance into the otherwise quiet cabin, meeting me at the door and licking my fingers eagerly.

"Where's your daddy, boy?" He whined and turned tail to scramble out of the room. He led me to Russ, who sat in his recliner with a few square bandages on his abdomen. I had to presume more were on his back.

"Oh, thank God!"

"Daniella… You should be with the paramedics, darlin'. Are you okay?" He stood up from the chair to greet me, despite his pale features.

"Forget *me*, Russ. What about you? He shot you so many times! You need a doctor… you need… you need help." Watching Mike shoot him had been traumatizing enough. Now I fretted over the very real possibility that he could bleed out before my very eyes.

"Shhh. Only twice, and it's okay. I'm not gonna die over a couple bullets, I swear. An old Navy friend is on the way to help me out. I think there's one lodged in me, so I'm not gonna have a happy evening here."

Tears brimmed over my eyes at the sight of him. So bold, courageous, and dumb! My ex fills him with holes and he has the nerve to worry about me? Assured that he wouldn't die on the spot in front of me, my mind latched on to the next conflict.

"Fine. Then you have to tell me what's going on. I need to know what's happening." I needed to know why the animal I had loved, nurtured, and worried for turned out to be the man I adored. My hands trembled, and it was debatable whether the shake came from fear or rage.

"All right," Russ agreed without argument. "But I need you to understand this first, Daniela. I planned to tell you everything tonight. All of it."

"Tell me now."

He sighed. "I'm a werebear. Thousands more like me exist around the world."

I tried to moisten my lips with my tongue. "Like a werewolf?"

A faint smile ghosted its way across his lips. "Sorta like that, except we're born this way. None of that biting nonsense."

"I don't… understand why you kept this from me so long. *You're* my bear? You slept in my hammock. You ate the food I made for you. You did all of these things, but you couldn't tell me you were a human being and able to understand every word I told you."

"Dani—"

I held up a hand and cut him off. "I feel like the world's biggest fool. I came back here afraid to find you a fucking cold corpse, but you're moving better by the second. Were you even hurt at all? Are you faking that too?"

"No!" he shouted.

"How many lies have you told me?"

"I've never lied to you," Russ insisted as he took a step toward me. He reached with one hand and I quickly back peddled away. Fresh tears sprang to my eyes. The trauma of the day should have dried them completely, but with my rising anger, I found myself wiping my face with my wrists all over again. "Dani… Baby, please."

"Don't *baby* me, Russ. How many lies have you told me?"

"None." He glanced at his abdomen and peeled off the corner of the bandage. The wound appeared raw and tender, but at least a few days old. I stared at him. "Shapeshifters heal faster than humans, Dani." I gazed into his brown eyes and saw my furry guardian protector who watched over me. He was still the Russ I'd come to love so much.

Together, we sat down on the sofa, close enough for our thighs to touch. This time when I shivered, the weight of his arm lowered around me instead of an impersonal blanket. Allowing Russ to pull me closer, I placed my cheek against his shoulder and closed my eyes.

"My mother is a bear shifter like me. I inherited this from her when I was born. Ian inherited his gift from his father and grandfather." I jerked my head up to stare at him. "Yeah. Ian and Taylor both."

"They're bears like you?"

"No, not bears," Russ answered. "They'll probably be a bit ruffled when they learn I told you this, but I don't want any more secrets between us. Ian's a bald eagle and Taylor's a cougar. All the members of my old squad are shifters of some kind, including the doc coming to patch me up."

The words falling from his lips sounded preposterous but, at the same time, they were weighted with the absolute truth. His earnest and open expression told me he wasn't making it all up. He wasn't crazy and neither was I for the memory I had of him transforming.

"You didn't think you should tell me this before?"

"I wanted to. Dani, please. Just imagine if every time one of us dated a girl, we told her about all this. That's not how you keep a secret."

The uneasy feeling in my gut diminished, leaving a cold ache in its place. He hadn't trusted me, but we were still so new in our relationship that I couldn't hold it against him completely. "What about the visits to my yard? You knew I was worried about my bear — about you." The animal I had come to love was also the man I cared for, creating an overlap my heart couldn't reconcile.

"I, uh…" Russell blushed and hung his head. "I'm sorry, Daniela. That first night I never really meant to fall asleep. Then you came outside with food, so brave and kind, not even a little afraid that there was a bear in your yard."

"But why did you keep coming back?" Had he been watching me like some peeping Tom? I dismissed the absurd thought the moment it popped into my head. Russell wasn't like that. "I just… I feel so stupid."

"There's no other way to tell you how sorry I am for deceiving you, Dani. I guess… I knew right then from the start that you were the woman for me. I couldn't get you off my mind. When one of my kind meets our mate, it forms a connection nothing can shake. I never thought I'd have another like that after Katie died… then I met you. You, Dani. You're the most important thing in my world. It just took me a while to realize it was happening again. I understand until tonight that my bear recognized you."

I wanted to stay pissed, but his near brush with death smoothed the edge off my anger. Before I knew it, I was wrapping my arms around him tightly without regard to his healing injuries. I kissed his face and ran my fingers over his mussed waves.

"You could have died, you dumb, dumb man." I dragged in a deep breath, which shuddered out of my lungs. My mind's eye replaced the events in my head, showing me a bleeding bear, and then minutes later, a bleeding man amidst the carrot tops, riddled with bullet wounds in his powerful torso.

"And I could have lost you. I'd do it again without hesitation."

"But you saved me, Russ. You came to my rescue and you saved me."

"No, baby. You saved yourself. I just helped you to do it."

Chapter Ten

2 MONTHS LATER

~DANIELA~

Trigger bounded back and forth between the porch and the open gate where the men brought up my leather sectional. Watching the three of them sweat under the noonday sun came as a reward for deferring to Russ' old-fashioned terms. Women weren't supposed to lift heavy things *if* a man could do it for them. I sipped lemonade and grinned as taut muscles shifted under suntanned flesh. They were a sexy gradient of skin tones, beginning with Russ' country tan and ending with Taylor's caramel brown. Ian was somewhere in between, the product of a mixed marriage with Native American blood. I'd finally dug that information out of him and made him promise to tell me stories about the Ojibwe Nation.

"Man, can we take a break yet? She's been working us all day," Taylor complained during the next trip to Russ' truck, setting one of my boxes down too heavily. Glassware clinked from inside it.

"Hey, buddy. You break my expensive dishes and you can forget eating dinner. I'll open you a can of tuna," I called out in a teasing threat.

"Yes, ma'am!" Taylor quickly replied.

Russ was too much of a gentleman to allow me to participate in moving my belongings. When moving day came, he recruited his two pals to help instead.

"How the hell did you get so much stuff in eight months?" Ian asked. "Where did all of this come from?"

I nodded toward Russ, my enabler who either encouraged me to spend on a whim, or later returned to buy the things he saw me eyeballing too closely in the store. Protesting his frequent but generous purchases had been a waste of time. Russ insisted that he had earned the money, and if it couldn't bring us happiness, what good was it to have it at all? Between all the new acquisitions and what I'd received after the divorce from friends and family helping me out with my new start in life, I had a truckload of boxes.

"Figures," my former landlord grumbled.

At first, Ian wasn't so happy about Russ deciding to spill the beans about their military group. He understood the reason, and knew it was inevitable, but it didn't make him happy that a civilian knew about their world. I assuaged them of their worries by promising I'd never tell a soul, as long as they let me see them in their natural states, of course. They were as handsome as a bear, eagle, and mountain lion as they had been as men, only their fur and feathers permitted me to stroke them without shame.

"How soon do you need me to finish the clean-up on the house, Ian?" I asked him.

"Take your time. I'm not planning to rent it out again. Hell, I might move in myself and enjoy small-town life for a while. I haven't lived here in years."

"It's a nice town," I agreed.

While they worked, I whipped together a pan of chicken enchiladas and later baked sugar cookies to give the hard working fellas a carb rush. After they were gone, Russ and I returned to our porch where we opened a bottle of wine and watched the sunset. The moment was bittersweet, the beginning of a new life with a man I loved and a farewell to the single existence I created in the wake of my divorce.

Even my family loved him once they finally had the chance to meet him the night I killed Michael. He'd earned my father's respect once we told him the gun Russ gave me was responsible for my dirtbag ex meeting his end. Then my mother hugged me tightly and Russ even tighter, because if not for his insistence on learning to use a weapon, I would have been dead. I had no idea how he kept a straight face through the pain.

Russ became quiet after his buddies were gone. He was throwing a ball across the yard for Trigger to chase and occasionally return to us; he was so silent I had to fret.

"You're not regretting it, are you?" I asked suddenly to break the silence between us.

Russ laughed and patted my thigh. "Too late to change your mind now. I don't think you could bribe Taylor to come back and move things again," he teased.

"I know… I just… I'm glad for the chance to start over. What's on your mind?"

Sensing the heavy emotion in my heart, or perhaps seeing it on my face, Russ turned to me and cupped one hand to my cheek. I turned my head and brushed my lips against his palm.

"You are. I was thinking about how much… I love you, Daniela, and I want you to be happy. Here with me and Trigger."

A field of tears shimmered over my sight, distorting Russ from my vision. His thumb swept over my left cheek to clear it away once they began to fall. "

"I *am* happy." Happier than I'd ever been. "Russ, I love you. I wouldn't be here otherwise."

And I knew Russell would never become unworthy of that love. In the few months since our first date, my bear had more than proven he deserved every ounce of my affection.

BOOK 2: LET US PREY

Chapter One

~IAN~

Normally, I was a morning person, but the drone of a church sermon had me bleary-eyed and half asleep with my head dipping down little by little as the hour wore on. My grandmother had sweet-talked me into escorting her to Sunday worship for nefarious reasons.

She claimed the visit was to socialize, but I knew the truth. She wanted to introduce me to the divorced daughters of her friends. Once the preacher had his say, I was doomed to a fate of awkward conversation with middle-aged singles who would pretend to hang on every word I said while feigning interest in something besides my looks and income.

I sat beside Gram with my phone on vibrate in my pocket, expecting an important call from the Secretary of Defense to come at any moment. Or at least hoping for one. The government didn't stop for Sunday prayer sessions, and neither did war. As a retired Air Force Colonel and acting leader of a special squad of operatives, I retained certain privileges.

I was also a shapeshifter, an ability I inherited from my late grandfather. My fondest memories were of him sharing old tales about how our kind came to be. At my age, I should have had a son of my own, or even a daughter with whom I could share the story of Brother Eagle's gift to the people of the Ojibwe Nation.

"Please open your hymn books," a man announced to us from the pulpit.

My groan earned me a sharp elbow in the ribs from Gram, prompting me to hush and focus my attention elsewhere. *Ring, phone, ring,* I pleaded internally.

Once the singing began, led by the small choir up front, I scanned the church pews. I saw George Banks making eyes at his mistress, his wife unaware the entire time. A few teens texted with their phones in their laps while their disapproving parents stared at them. Chuckling, I nearly gave in and did the same… then I saw her.

A young woman sat alone in the rear of the church, isolated from the rest of the worshippers. She wore a plain white blouse and a dull, dove-grey skirt in a modest length. Its style wouldn't have flattered most women's curves, but her assets were so generous Houdini couldn't have hidden them. The perfect amount of hip and thick thighs. I knew without a doubt she'd have a bottom to match.

"Who's she?" I asked in a low murmur while the rest of the congregation sang the words to some hymn I didn't know.

Gram swatted me. "Ian," she hissed under her breath.

"Well?" I insisted.

"Her name is Leigh," she whispered.

"You're telling me nothing, Gram."

"She's a young woman who made poor choices, from what I hear."

From a woman who loved her share of gossip, I was disappointed by the ambiguity.

I spent the rest of the services stealing glances at Leigh, lost in her melancholy beauty and serene features. Church couldn't end fast enough, and when it did, I was the first from my seat. Following morning worship, the congregation gathered in the reception hall where they all enjoyed a spread of baked goods and casserole dishes. Gram had me carry in a peach cobbler as our donation prior to the service.

"Ian, where are you going?" I heard my grandmother calling.

"I'll be right back, Gram."

Two middle-aged women approached Leigh. One of them was Pastor Stevens' wife, a woman known for causing trouble. I tuned in to eavesdrop and pick up what I could as I narrowed the distance.

"Leigh, where's your contribution to our lunch? Don't you plan to stick around for once?" Lettie asked.

The other woman, Myrtle, made a disgusted sound like she was coughing up something in her throat. "I don't even know why you make the effort with her. She's only gonna dive out again, as usual."

Leigh blushed from the scooped neck of her blouse to the top of her ears. With her porcelain complexion and fair hair, there was no hiding the embarrassment. Whatever she said in reply was too low for my keen ears to pick up, but it was apparent she was excusing herself.

Our eyes met from across the foyer, and I caught my breath as if I'd been sucker-punched. Her grey irises were as pale as the rest of her, clear as a pre-dawn sky. She broke eye contact first and looked away.

The sorrow in Leigh's features called to the eagle inside me, and before I knew it, I was sprinting to the door. When I descended the steps, I saw her scurrying down the sidewalk at a brisk power walk. Two teen boys, one blond and one dark-haired, were hooting and making catcalls at her, being general pricks.

"Don't see why you're leaving so quickly. You need all the Jesus you can get!" the blond called to her.

I frowned and brushed past them.

"Oh shit," the dark-haired boy muttered.

"Why didn't you say MacArthur was nearby?" the other asked.

"Didn't see him," the blond whispered.

"Hold on a second!" I called to Leigh.

Leigh slowed ahead of me and peeked back over her shoulder, uncertainty on her face. "Me?"

"You shouldn't let them run you off, ma'am."

"Leigh," she corrected. "Leigh Denton."

"Ian MacArthur."

Her eyes went as round as two buttons. "You're a lot younger than I thought you were."

"Thanks? Uh, you seem to know about me, but I don't know the first thing about you."

"You're like a legend around here, Mr. MacArthur. They named the new food pantry after you, and the town library's named after your father."

A grin slipped onto my face. "Ian," I corrected her this time. "And they named it after my grandfather."

Leigh studied me then gazed at our surroundings with distrust, her big gray eyes darting to each side. "Did I do something wrong? Is that why they sent you after me?"

"Not at all. Actually, I was going to ask why you weren't sticking around."

Leigh fidgeted and avoided meeting my eyes. "They don't really like me, but I like to go hear the singing." She resumed her walk again, clutching a tattered grey, synthetic leather purse against her side. It probably cost her five dollars at the general store.

"And the luncheon?" I prodded, keeping pace with her.

"It's rude to take when you don't contribute. I'm not a mooch," she snapped back, revealing more with her defensiveness.

"Can't cook?" I asked. Maybe I was a legend in these parts, but she didn't seem impressed or willing to slow for me.

"I cook fine, I guess."

When I attempted to strike up conversation again, she picked up speed to leave me behind. She was a tall girl with a long stride, easily 5'10 or taller and just a couple inches below my own height. While her skirt was modest, it didn't conceal the strength of her calves and legs.

Taking the hint, I suppressed the urge to give chase. My eagle fought against my willpower, suddenly a screaming and raging beast. In all of my years, it had never reacted with as much intensity over a woman. Many shifters spent our entire lives looking for the right person — our soulmate so to speak — and in Leigh, I'd found mine. She crossed the next street and disappeared into a dilapidated home barely larger than my garden tool shack. Most houses in the poorer side of Quickdraw were uninhabitable tinder boxes ready to collapse.

Leigh remained on my mind during the walk back to the church. Someone had hurt that girl, making her cold and unreceptive to even innocent friendship. I found Gram waiting for me on the steps with a frown on her face.

"Ian, where were you?"

"I walked home the young woman Lettie and Myrtle were harassing. Saw some boys bothering her outside, too."

"Don't be getting yourself mixed up in other folks' problems, sweetheart. I had a word with Marjorie, and she says Leigh is all kinds of trouble. The criminal sort."

"Marjorie is also known to bouts of wild exaggeration," I pointed out.

"True enough, true enough," she admitted. "But most all here say the same. I just want you to be careful. You get into enough trouble with that team of yours."

"Gram, I love you, but I can make my own decisions. Are you ready to go home, or do you plan to hang around with the ladies?"

With frail and bony fingers, she pulled her shawl around her shoulders and gazed toward the car. "I'd like to go home, I think. It's too cold to socialize outdoors."

The girl with the pale eyes remained on my mind during the drive to my grandmother's home and throughout the distraction Gram made to redirect me. The cooking and cleaning got done, but I performed every task with my mind in another place. My thoughts returned to Leigh's curvy body. I'd always loved when girls were on the plump side.

"You're still thinking about Leigh, aren't you, Ian?"

I blinked away from my half-assed job at rinsing the plates for the dishwasher. "Sorry, Gram."

"Well?" With the assistance of her cane, she moved closer and lowered to one of the chairs in the kitchen's breakfast nook. Due to advanced arthritis, she couldn't wash dishes in the sink or lift them from the machine's basket without a struggle. When I returned to town, I made it a habit to pop in to do the small things for her until we could find a replacement aid. She fired the last one for stealing from the house, or rather, I did after Gram tipped me off to missing belongings and I logged into the nannycam for a look.

"Ian, I'm waiting." Old age hadn't made her patient.

"I think she's the one," I confessed.

"Ah." No arguments. No denials. Gram knew better than to fight against shifter instincts or to question the recognition of fated mates. Seventy years ago, she'd been one, too. "Well then, what do you plan to do? She's young and she's got many problems, Ian. Perhaps too many even for you."

I shook my head. "Everybody has problems, Gram, including you. I'm going to get to know her and find a way to help, and I don't care what anybody here says or how they gossip about it."

Gram gave me a reassuring smile. "Good. That's the boy I raised."

Leigh would be mine, and I'd do anything to convince her I was worthy of becoming hers.

***

I didn't have to ask around much to dig up the truth on Leigh. Two years ago, drama went down with the young woman renting my house when her stalker ex-husband keyed her car. After the cops got involved, I befriended the guys on the small, six-person police force and enlisted their help to watch out for her.

"What's the deal with Leigh Denton?" I asked.

Sergeant Jacob Hunt sighed. "Did she steal from you?"

"No! Christ. Jumping to conclusions a little, aren't you? No, she didn't steal from me. I'm asking because I witnessed some odd behavior the other day during church service, and I want to know why it happened."

"Leigh Denton is a mess of trouble, man. I know she's pretty, but you don't want to get caught up in her issues. Why don't you tap a contact or two and look at her police record—"

I cut him off before he began the usual spiel. "You *are* my contact and you *are* the police. I want to hear what you have to say instead of pulling up her entire criminal background check, all right?"

"Point made. All right. You didn't hear all of the gritty details from me, but she lost custody of her infant about three months ago."

"Why?" I asked.

"The baby was born with neonatal withdrawal syndrome related to opiate use. Codeine is Leigh's drug of choice. Her boyfriend has a twenty-five year stretch at Ferguson Unit for dealing a whole plethora of narcotics."

Hunt's news hit me like a bucket of cold water. Lapsing into silence, I let the news wash over me and took a few moments to digest it all. When I saw Leigh, I didn't see a woman out for her next fix — I saw *and felt* a wounded soul crying for help. "What else?"

"She's got a juvie record for shoplifting, too. Stole a couple televisions from Wal-Mart. Got busted with a flat screen."

"How the hell do you steal a television from Wal-Mart?"

"Back when the Quickdraw Wal-Mart was new a couple years back, they didn't run as tight a ship as they do now. She went into the store, bought a television, and took it out to her friends in the parking lot. Then she returned to the store, fetched the second television, and cruised through the other exit doors with her receipt. She would have probably gotten away with it if she didn't try to hit the store up again after the shift change. Someone had reported strange behavior to loss prevention, and they were watching for any more suspicious acts."

Even as I took in all of the damning evidence against Leigh's character, something told me there was more to the story. I stroked my chin and gazed out the police department window. "What about her family?"

"Only child of deceased parents. Her mother, Louise Denton, was killed in a car wreck when she was five. Gregory Denton died a couple years back of laryngeal cancer. She lives in his old place on the North side."

"Tell me about the boyfriend." I used my phone to take notes.

"He was this good-for-nothing punk named Dennis James. When we busted him, he had enough prescription narcotics to stock his own pharmacy, Ian."

"Dealing for someone big or working his own business?"

"Who knows? One minute he was telling us all this shit about how he'd be out in a day; a few hours later, he's got his mouth shut tighter than a Baptist preacher's asshole."

I chuckled at the imagery. "What did the investigation turn up?"

"Turns out him and his boys were robbing elderly people while they were asleep or out of the home and selling them on the market. He even stole from his own parents, and they're good, respectable people."

I thought back to the girl I caught pinching my grandmother's lorazepam one pill at a time. "Was Ms. Denton involved in the theft or distribution?"

"No, nothing we found or could prove. She seemed genuinely shocked when she heard the charges against him," Jacob said.

His words cleared the rest of my reservations. "Okay. So she wasn't shooting meth, she wasn't dealing, and as far as you know, she hasn't stolen anything since she was a kid."

"Why are you asking about this anyway?"

I had to think fast, searching for any excuse that would suffice and save me from admitting we were soul mates and sounding like I was out of my mind. "Gram needs a new home health aide and I thought about hiring Leigh. That's all."

Jacob gave me an uncertain look. "I'd keep a daily count of Mrs. MacArthur's medication then."

"I plan to after the last one we told you about, but I'm also a firm believer in giving people a chance."

"Let's hope your generosity doesn't bite you in the ass this time."

"Yeah, yeah, yeah. How's your boy doing anyway?" I swapped the subject to Hunt's seventeen-year-old son and his plans to enlist.

"Good, good. Danny took those practice placement tests, and they said he'd be a good fit for some of those technical jobs they have in the armed forces. Of course, he wants to take the language test and try his hand at linguistics."

"I was certain he was going to go with the Air Force. They take linguists, too, you know."

"Heh. Well, you know how boys are. Once his buddies going into the Army all called it the Chairforce, there wasn't much hope of getting him to go. I thought he'd at least enroll in college first," Jacob said.

I scowled at him. "There's less sitting involved than they'd have him believe. Either way, he'll get some good experience out of it and money for college. Maybe he'll come back to Quickdraw one day and work alongside you."

Jacob and I hung around his desk for a while longer before a call pulled him from the station to settle a fender bender dispute at the gas station. I went home to my personal office where I sat behind the computer and phoned a friend.

"Argus? Hope I caught you at a good time."

"Always have time for you, Ian. What can I do for you today?" he asked in his easygoing voice.

"I need you to draft up some legal paperwork for me about a job."

Chapter Two

~LEIGH~

Just before Daddy died, he signed his old Ford F-150 over into my name. Letting go of it for a few grand was one of the hardest decisions I ever had to make, but the money helped to make ends meet until I found a job.

With less than seven hundred dollars of it left to my name and few worldly possessions, I threw myself into finding gainful employment before I lost everything. Time at the library consumed most of the week, allowing me to fill out online applications at every business within fifty miles.

Days without Sophia passed into weeks and became months. The ache in my heart was a hollow, barren field where my baby belonged. Two days a week wasn't enough time, but I needed firm footing beneath me before the court returned her to my care. I failed her and *myself* when I didn't seek professional help during pregnancy.

Back then, I thought they'd judge me and take my baby away if I asked for help. In the end, they did it anyway by citing child endangerment. After CPS took her away, I spent the first weeks cursing the medical staff who reported me and laying blame everywhere but the place it belonged. Myself.

The driver of the carpool to Ferguson Unit honked from the side of the road. I ran out and joined two other women in the backseat after passing ten dollars to the driver. An hour later, an intimidating prison loomed ahead of us, a massive brick facility with two layers of perimeter fencing and harsh razor wire. Impassive guards armed with AR-15s watched us from towers in passing.

I shivered and scurried along with the rest of the flock, feeling like a sheep herded to pasture. The other ladies wore makeup, but my face was bland and intentionally unappealing. They wore dresses and tight-fitting tops. I wore jeans and a light cardigan over a V-neck, which I fastened before entering the facility.

The humiliating shakedown procedures were just part of the sacrifice I made to see Dennis. I turned my pockets inside out, set my shoes in the bin for the x-ray machine, and walked through the metal detector with my hands raised. A female officer ran her fingers down my body, sliding her palms down my spine then the backs of her hands down my ass. Her smaller build placed her at an inconvenience and forced her to stand on tiptoe and lean uncomfortably close to reach around my thicker frame. Once she was satisfied I didn't have drugs and cigarettes stuffed into my meager bra, she shooed me to get out of her line.

I was shuffled into a visitation room for an impersonal meeting behind glass walls. I sat nervously on my chair with my hands folded over my lap. I'd never gone into a prison before in all of my life, but the dismal, gray-painted cinder blocks and dirty floor depressed me.

I tensed the moment Dennis entered the room and sat opposite me with a thick pane of glass between us.

He looked as good as I remembered, with full lips, chiseled features, and a strong jaw. I'd always loved his cocoa brown skin and the contrast between our complexions. At a glance, I could tell he'd picked up some weight and broadened his shoulders with muscle. Figures in the penitentiary he'd have nothing better to do than work out, but the plain white uniform didn't do his athletic body the justice it deserved.

"What took you so long to finally come here and visit me? You don't write and you didn't register to accept calls from me."

"I don't have a vehicle anymore, Dennis. I had to sell Daddy's truck a couple months ago to make ends meet."

The honest truth didn't seem to satisfy him. "Yeah, all right. That don't explain why you didn't register. I could have been calling you by now, baby."

The last affection I had for Dennis died on the day he'd gotten himself locked away for a quarter of a century on an unnecessary crime. I hated knowing Sophia would grow up without a father for the mistakes he made. We should have been raising her together.

"I've been too busy trying to find a job to sit at home on the phone, Dennis. Besides, I don't know how to register," I lied.

"Damn. Fair enough." His brown eyes drifted to the inmate beside him. The guy's family had purchased him a pile of chips and four icy Cokes from the overpriced vending machine.

"I came to talk to you about Sophia," I spoke up to direct the conversation.

"Buy me a Coke first, Leigh."

I shook my head. "Don't have it on me."

"What? You can't even buy me a soda while you're here?"

"I don't have the money," I repeated, voice low. "No one told me I could bring quarters for the machines."

"It's a fucking buck, Leigh. You mean to tell me you don't have a goddamn dollar to spare for me?"

"I wouldn't even be here if I didn't carpool with a group. I gave them ten dollars to get here." I had an electric bill to pay and groceries to buy. While he received three hot meals and a cot courtesy of Texas, I was left to fend for myself.

"Then what the hell are you doing here, girl? It's not like you even tried to pretty yourself up," he fussed at me. I swear he said those things just to be an asshole and hurt me.

"Pretty myself up for a prison visit? Like I said, I came to talk about Sophia and getting her back. Or at least seeing her more often." Had he even been listening to me? "Can't you talk to them? They're your parents, Dennis."

"You know how Ma and Dad are. I can't tell them nothin' from in here."

"Tell them to let me see her more."

"Hell, Leigh, you see her more than I do. You think they bring her up here for me to see her?"

"Yeah, well whose damn fault is that?" I snapped back.

A couple of prison guards in stiff gray suits glanced our way. When the male officer moved as if he intended to come over, I dropped my voice again.

"Listen, Dennis. Sophia is my baby. Ours. She doesn't belong with her grandparents. She needs a mom, and them keeping her from me when I've been clean isn't for her benefit. They're doing it because they're pissed at us."

"Bitch, are you even clean for real this time? How many days did you tell me you were done and not to get you any more pills, but the moment I offered a bottle, you were ready to take them?" he mocked me.

"I *am* clean," I hissed. Counting backward from ten in my head helped me calm down. "I haven't touched so much as an aspirin since they discharged me from the hospital." I must have looked hostile, because the officer was on his way back again. I stood up from my seat and beat him to the punch. "Our visit is over. I'm leaving. Don't expect to see me back again."

I spent the rest of the two hours outside on the curb, the occasional passing car the only witness to my silent tears. Eventually, the shudders ended and I was able to embrace a future without Dennis in my life. In our lives, if I could pull it together and meet the requirements set by the court.

I had to have a job, and I needed it yesterday.

***

"Thanks again for the ride," I said to Kelly. The blonde woman in the driver's seat smiled at me.

"No problem, sweetheart. You email me next time you need a ride up there."

Positive I'd never go back, I smiled and nodded. "Sure." I waved and let myself inside, kicked off my shoes, and locked the door behind me.

My dad's home had seen better days, and with him gone, I couldn't replace the leaking roof. But it was a house, and it was better than some people had. Once I secured a job, I'd be able to change things and do him proud. I'd get the windows replaced and a new roof over my head. I'd have a new bedroom door to replace the one the cops knocked down when they arrested Dennis. I'd need the floors covered in something eventually, so Sophia wouldn't have to crawl on hard cement.

A quick shower let me wash the stink of the prison from my skin and hair. I could still smell it, the stench of a few thousand men and sweaty guards in a cement box without any air circulation. I shivered, remembering the way some of the inmates had stared at me with lust in their eyes despite my perceived plain appearance.

Someone beat on the door just as I toweled off in the tiny closet of a bathroom. I squeezed into panties, shorts, and an off- the-shoulder t-shirt then stepped barefoot into the narrow hall. I twisted my hair into a bun on the way to answer it. My tee revealed my lack of a bra, but without much on top to warrant wearing one all of the time, I thought I was safe from any lookie-loos wanting to steal a peek. My pear-shaped body meant I carried all of my junk in the trunk.

Caution made me pause before opening the door, and a quick glance through the parted window shades revealed an unfamiliar black SUV parked alongside the road. I frowned and angled my body for a peek at the stoop.

Ian MacArthur stood on the porch, his hands folded behind his back. The sexy military vet wore a black leather jacket and dark shades over his unusual, strangely colored eyes. The t-shirt on his body stretched taut over every muscular ridge, a second skin in navy blue.

"What the hell is he doing here?" I whispered. The next sharp rap on the door made me jerk back; then a surge of courage prompted me to crack it open and peek out at him. "Hello?"

"Good evening, Leigh. This a good time for a talk?"

"I just got out the shower."

"I can wait for you to get dressed," he said pleasantly.

"I am dressed." I paused and looked down at my chunky thighs. My current state of dress was inappropriate for meeting with the grandson of our town's founder. "What do you want, Mr. MacArthur?"

"To offer you a job."

I opened the door to stare at him. "Bullshit."

"Give me a second and hear me out. I'm told you're in need of a job. As luck would have it, I need an employee."

It was too good to be true, the perfect solution to my problem at the ideal time. I gazed at the handsome man on my doorstep and felt a cold stab of shame streak through me when I realized he could see the room behind me. The rough concrete floors needed another sweep, but it was the least of my troubles when I had a spreading water stain on the ceiling.

"May I come in to talk?"

"We can talk out here." I scurried outside and shut the door behind me.

"I want to offer you a job. You see, I work out of town and my grandmother's getting up in her years. The home health agency only gives her so many hours on the weekends, and she won't hire a housekeeper through the week or allow me to do it for her."

A flash of rage shot through me. "Housekeeping? Is this a joke? Is that it? Did you come to have a laugh at me too because no one wants to hire me for a real job in this shithole?"

"Leigh—"

"Fuck you, Mr. MacArthur. You can go to hell along with everyone else."

I slammed the door in his face before the tears began, and within moments, I was reduced to uncontrollable sobs. Damn him. Damn him and everyone else laughing behind my back. In the privacy of my own home, I wiped at the hot flood trickling down my cheeks and succumbed to my anguish. I needed a legitimate, tax-paying job, and under the table work cleaning bathtubs wouldn't cut it.

Maybe I brought it on myself, but why couldn't they just allow me to wallow in my own well-deserved punishment without rubbing in the salt?

"Leigh?" Ian's soft voice penetrated my flimsy door. A glance through the peephole showed the man hadn't moved. "I only want to talk to you for a moment. I'm not here to make fun or judge you. If you'd just let me come in for a moment to talk..."

"Is it a real job?"

"A real job," he confirmed.

I opened the door for him again after I wiped my face. "Okay."

When Ian entered and removed his glasses, he barely gave my sparsely decorated home a glance. His eyes lingered on me, resting on my face instead of my thick thighs and single bare shoulder. His features held no judgment and lacked the mockery I expected.

"Thank you. I brought the paperwork with me, and you can keep it to review overnight if you'd like, or sign it now and I'll take it with me. Choice is yours."

He offered me a manila folder filled with official looking papers and not like something he'd typed up at home. The fancy letterhead and watermark featured a wolf's head logo from the law offices of Argus Prescott.

"I'm sorry for losing my temper and slamming the door," I apologized. "Can I get you anything? I have…" *Nothing. I have nothing to offer him except tap water*. Soda wasn't in my budget lately. Food stamps could only get a single person so far.

"Water's great."

I set the papers on the coffee table — a handmade, beautiful piece my dad had carved and assembled himself about ten years ago — then gestured for him to have a seat on the paisley green sofa. I returned with his glass of ice water and joined him.

"Thank you, Leigh. Why don't you take a moment to review those while I'm here in case you have any questions."

My hands shook as I lifted the thin folder and flipped it open for a look. Responsibilities of the job and daily duties, a schedule, protocols for calling in sick, and a close set of rules to follow. He'd outlined everything professionally, complete with information about healthcare and vacation days.

"Vacation days?" I asked.

"Twenty-one days a year with two weeks advance notice so I can be there for her in your stead. I expect you to be at Gram's place five days a week. You've got two paid sick days a month, but they'll add up and won't expire so make them count. But keep in mind, I'd prefer if my grandmother wasn't made ill because you forced yourself on the job with the flu, got it?"

"Okay. What's my pay?"

"Fifteen dollars an hour to start, paid every Friday. If you like it a month from now, I'll raise you to twenty."

Tears stung my eyes. "I… you want to pay me twenty dollars an hour to clean your grandmother's house?" Sniffling and wiping my cheeks, I tried to maintain a calm expression. I couldn't. Emotion burned my throat and tears spilled over my face too quickly to be dried for long. "This isn't a joke?" I repeated again.

"It isn't a joke."

"Why help me? Why?"

"Well, I hope you're not too mad at me, but I asked about you, and the way I see it, there's a little girl depending on her mama finding a stable job. And I have a legally blind grandmother with rheumatoid arthritis. We need each other, right?" Ian asked.

I wanted to throw my arms around him and smother his neatly groomed face in kisses. "Thank you. Thank you so much, Mr. MacArthur—"

"Ian," he said again with a pleasant smile on his handsome face. "Just call me Ian."

"Ian," I agreed. Shock made it impossible to convey my gratitude without floundering for words. I repeated the simplest ones. "Thank you."

"If you don't mind, I'd like to ask you a couple of questions for my own curiosity."

My belly sank a little, like a lead weight hit the bottom of my gut. "Okay."

"I know you've had some drug problems, Leigh. I want to believe it won't be a problem again. I'm not one to mince words, so I'm sorry if I offend you but… what happened? Did your boyfriend get you hooked?"

"It *won't* be a problem again," I quickly blurted out, too defensive. "This is a bit of a long story, and it's no excuse, but it started in college. I played volleyball until I blew out my knee at the start of my junior year. Surgery was out of the question because my dad was fighting cancer."

"Right. You probably couldn't afford two sets of medical bills," Ian deduced.

"Yes. So my doc prescribed me some codeine while I did physical therapy. I got into therapeutic horseback riding at this ranch at the edge of town, volunteering to help the kids in exchange for riding lessons and time with the therapist. Loved it. At the start of my senior year, Dad's cancer got worse. I dropped out to care for him and the ranch closed down due to lack of funds. They weren't getting enough money to care for the horses even though the therapist and trainer volunteered their time. Because I'd dropped out of school, I lost my student insurance plan."

Ian shook his head. "I wish I'd known about the ranch's troubles. I knew they shut down, but never heard about why. I must have been away at the time."

"Yeah. It was really sad. I couldn't afford my doctor or a new therapist, so Dennis supplied me with codeine. I was too stupid to ask where it came from. Or I didn't care. I was hurting and always needed one more to get through a day with Dad. The laryngectomy didn't help him, you know? The surgeon missed some of the cancer, and it metastasized to his lymph nodes. He came home here to die instead of hospice in a facility."

I swallowed and focused on my lap, fearing if I looked up at Ian, I'd see the judgment in his handsome face. Stealing a quick glance revealed compassion instead.

"I wanted to get help, Ian. I did. By the time I realized I had a problem, I was pregnant. I tried to kick it a dozen times on my own, but I was so afraid they'd take her from me. If I had it to do over again, I'd have never started taking them." Time had given my knee the chance to heal, but I'd probably benefit from resuming therapy.

Ian's fingers brushed the top of my hand in a reassuring stroke and left goose bumps in their wake. "It's behind you now, Leigh. What about your boyfriend?"

"We're done. I don't even know what I saw in him anymore. His parents used to love me, you know?" These days, I couldn't get them to talk to me unless it was my scheduled visit to see Sophia.

"What about the theft? Do I have to worry about you stealing?"

I shook my head. "I stole a television a couple years back when my dad lost his job and we fell on hard times. Welfare office was going to take forever to process our case, and your food pantry didn't exist back then."

"So you stole a TV to sell for money to buy food?"

My cheeks flared with heat. "It only made things worse for us and was a dumb thing to do. I can't take it back and undo it, but I'll always regret the way he looked at me when we had to go to court. I shamed him and myself trying to take the easy way out."

Ian and I talked a while longer while I reviewed the rest of the papers. At the conclusion of our meeting, he wished me a good evening and made his way outside onto the pebbled road. He was gone and out of sight a few minutes later, leaving me to marvel over my change in luck.

I finally had the chance I needed to earn Sophia back. My prayers had been answered.

Chapter Three

~Leigh~

My change in luck was too good to be true, leading me to believe I'd make the two-mile walk to Mrs. MacArthur's house to meet an old lady who loathed me on sight. I was wrong. She drew me into a motherly embrace and kissed my cheek before inviting me inside.

Two hours later, I finished cleaning the kitchen from top to bottom. I reached all the nooks and crannies Ian neglected whenever he visited to help. Afterward, I tried to move on to the master bedroom of the small six room ranch style home, but Mrs. MacArthur dragged me into the living room and made me sit with her.

We watched soap operas until noon then I made her lunch, which she insisted on sharing.

"Sweetheart, if you're going to make lunch for me, you have to make something for yourself. It's just not right to watch someone else eat."

"Mrs. MacArthur, I don't think your grandson wants me eating your food while I'm here."

"Baby, my grandson didn't hire you to be my maid. He wants you to give me company, and *I* say I don't like to eat alone."

I made another sandwich for myself and took out fish to thaw for dinner. By the time Ian arrived from a day of work in Houston, doing whatever it was rich and sexy guys like him did, I'd whipped together a delicious meal for the three of us to enjoy.

After we ate, I scrubbed the dishes and cleaned my mess. I kissed Mrs. MacArthur, who firmly insisted on me calling her Betty, on the cheek and hugged her tight.

"Will I see you at the same time tomorrow?" she asked.

"Of course."

I left her house with a big smile on my face and a feeling of self-worth I never knew was possible. Before my feet touched the sidewalk, the door opened again to frame Ian's tall body.

"If you wait just a sec, I can give you a ride home, Leigh."

His black Escalade chirped when he released the door locks by remote. A second later, the lights flashed and the engine powered on with a roar. I stared at him.

"Mr. Mac— Ian, you don't have to drive me home. I like the walk."

"I'd like to talk to you," he countered.

I was positive he intended to fire me for some unknown transgression. My mind jumped to every worst possible conclusion until he stepped from his grandmother's house precisely a minute later and flashed me a great big grin.

It wasn't fair for one man to be so damned good looking. Ian's high cheekbones made him resemble his late grandfather the most. There were old black and white photos of our town founder in the house. He was a handsome Native American man with flowing black hair past his shoulders and equally pale eyes. It must have been a family trait.

"So, tell me how you like it." Ian fastened his seatbelt and waited for me to do the same. I clicked in quickly.

"Betty and I had an awesome time. I think she sees better than she lets you believe though. You wouldn't believe how she moves around the kitchen."

"Nah, she's just good at fooling you. You'll catch on," he assured me.

Tucked into his car, I was keenly aware of everything about him. His cologne was subtle, a scent I associated with cool wind snaking between sweet autumn trees. Resisting the temptation to lean over and breathe him in became an exercise in willpower.

"You said you wanted to talk," I prompted.

"When's your next appearance in court?"

"I'm supposed to report having a job by next week, then we reconvene next month. The judge only gave me so much time to prove I can make a stable environment for Sophia." I nervously bit my lower lip and stole another glance at my new boss. "I guess I have the job part done."

"Then I'd better give you an advance on your paycheck so you can get a head start on providing the stable environment part."

"An advance?"

He pulled out his wallet and a giant roll of cash bigger than anything I ever saw outside of a bank. I stared at him in amazement as he handed over ten crisp hundred dollar bills.

"What about the taxes?" I asked lamely. Math wasn't my preferred subject of study in school, but I was positive 40 hours at 15 dollars wouldn't add up to a grand.

Ian chuckled. "Well, we'll just pretend between you and me that I paid you in exact change. Don't count on it next time though. I'll pay by check and you can open a bank account to cash it."

"Okay," I agreed while focusing on my lap. It was a better alternative to staring at my boss and melting over the way his grin crinkled his pale eyes at the corners. Or how he had just the perfect amount of scruff on his tanned face.

"I have big expectations out of you, Leigh. I trust you won't relapse, but if you ever need to talk, I want you to call me, all right?" He passed me a business card with a U.S. Air Force eagle emblem above a blue banner announcing him as a veteran.

COLONEL IAN MACARTHUR, RETIRED

MACARTHUR SECURITY, CO.

(936) 555-5555

"There's my cell phone number. You're welcome to contact me at any time and any hour. I'll always answer if I can."

"Why are you being so good to me?"

Ian pulled out from the drive without answering right away. The houses passed by outside and the sky dimmed.

"My ancestors believed in strengthening the community and the people who lived in it. I look at you and I see a woman striving to make positive changes in her life. That's something I respect, Leigh."

The differences between the north and south sides of Quickdraw were vast; our main toad bisected the town into two distinct areas. Betty MacArthur lived on the south side and only a brisk walk from the town police department, which shared a building with the fire department and city hall. On my side, there weren't as many pretty gardens and the homes were smaller.

"Do you want a ride in the morning?" The streetlamp outside my house flickered as he pulled up. Further down the road, a group of teens collected near another street corner with their hands in their pockets. They watched us like hawks.

"No, I like the walk. Really," I assured him. "It wakes me up and helps get me going."

"All right. It'll make me feel better if you wait for me in the evening though. The news is probably spreading through town right this moment, but there was a shooting only a couple blocks over sometime last night. Heard about it on my way out to work this morning."

"A shooting in my neighborhood?" The chilling news didn't surprise me.

"Yep. Looked like a drug deal gone bad or something. No one died, but the cops took both of them into custody."

"Thanks, Ian. Anyway, Betty is amazing, and I'm glad you trust me with her care. I loved hearing her stories."

"Good. I'll see you tomorrow on my way in from work. Take care." He paused, the moment stretching for eternity between us. "I'm proud of you, Leigh. You're doing great."

"Thanks," I whispered. "Bye, Ian." Stunned, I stepped from the car and barely shut the door with shaky fingers. Proud of me? He barely knew me.

He lingered until I was safely inside and the door was shut. After locking up, I ran my fingers over the green bills in my hand and wept myself to exhaustion. My life was finally turning around, and I had my own personal guardian angel to thank for it.

~Ian~

Leigh haunted my memories long after I returned home, a persistent force invading my thoughts until I stripped out of my clothes and walked onto the rear patio. I hit the pause button on the security camera first — I didn't need a digital record of what I planned to do.

I let the eagle overtake me, inflicting a sharp crack of pain to both of my arms, snapping my bones and reshaping me into a compact, feathered body. Whenever I left the ground behind and took to the air, the world around me gained a new level of clarity.

Flying past Russ and Dani's house gave me a glimpse of her with their new horse, Daisy. Russ was building a barn while his girlfriend of two years hosed the mare down after a ride. I envied him when we realized Dani was his fated mate, their binding obscured by the lingering traces of his grief for the one he'd already lost.

Dani peered up and shielded her eyes against the setting sun. She waved to me and I called back to her in return. I left them behind and soared toward the town.

Quickdraw wasn't the same place of my childhood. Sickness had infested its soul. The wind carried me over to the south side where Gram lived. I wish she'd stay with me, but she wanted to have neighbors in walking distance. She wanted to see children playing ball in their yards and walking dogs down the street.

I wanted Leigh's baby to become the great-grandchild Gram deserved. As my flight path brought me toward the north side, I scanned the ground below me and took in the sight. Wealth and comfort bled away to barren, sandy yards and unpaved streets. Circling around gave me the chance to scout the area near Leigh's home and descend to a light post at the street corner.

Criminal activity bustled at her neighbor's home. A car pulled up and stalled in front of it, waiting until a little boy ran down with a baggie of weed. The kid, no more than seven or eight, took the money back up to his father.

A scrawny, malnourished dog trotted down the road with swinging teats close to dragging the dusty road. Leigh's door opened to frame her in shorts and an oversized tee. She held a small bowl in her hand piled with rice. When she approached the road, the dog paused and met her halfway. The animal snapped up the offering.

"I wish I had more for you," she said.

"Hey, Leigh! Why do you bother feedin' that ugly thing? Why don't you let me shoot it and put it out of its misery?" one of the men called from her neighbor's porch.

Leigh shook her head. "Actually, I'm thinking of keeping her. She comes this way every couple of days, and I don't think anyone owns her."

"Bitch, you don't even got a job. How you gonna take care of a dog?"

"I do now," she called back. She ran her fingers over the dog's floppy ears and straightened from her crouch. Her eyes raised to me then became large as saucers. "Holy shit, it's a bald eagle!"

"I'll be damned. It is," one of the neighbors said.

I came down closer to her and glided to the low chain-link fence around her house. Leigh gasped and didn't move while I preened my flight feathers. A handful of yards distanced us, but my eagle craved contact. I wanted to feel her fingers over my wings and to touch my beak against her soft cheek.

"I wish I had a camera… it's beautiful," Leigh murmured.

"Better get your mutt inside before the bird takes a bite out of it," one of the guys called.

"Eagles don't eat dogs," Leigh argued.

"Bet if the fucker was a rat dog, it would've taken off with it by now." The guys howled with laughter while Leigh backed away with the canine.

The reservation in her eyes told me she didn't want to go inside. She wanted to watch me as much as I wanted to watch her.

"I'm telling you. There ain't no reason a big bird like that's sitting around except to find its next meal, Leigh."

Gray eyes watched me the entire time she led the hungry dog up her porch steps. After the mongrel was safely indoors, Leigh returned with a disposable camera.

"I can't believe he's still here. Two shots left…"

The neighbors moved on to another conversation. A woman brought them fresh beer and another drug-seeking customer arrived. Leigh glanced at them with morose eyes and sighed.

Desperate to take her sadness away, I glided to the dusty walking stone in front of her porch. She shrieked and stumbled back against the door, banging her hip in the process.

"Leigh, you okay?" the concerned neighbor woman called.

"Shit. I thought the thing was attacking her," one of the guys commented.

"Maybe I should shoot it," one of the guys threatened.

"No!" Leigh screamed at them. "It's not doing anything."

A couple men chuckled. "You ain't no Disney princess, lil mama. Let us chase it off before it hurts you."

"Fuck you," she seethed at him, revealing a stubborn streak. The young woman approached despite their warnings. With my beak closed and tilted down, I watched her hesitate until I closed the gap and touched my feathered head against her bare knee.

"Oh, my God. Oh, my God," she whispered under her breath.

"Maybe it's sick," one of them speculated. When I didn't fly into a vicious rage or attack, they lost interest in watching. Our moment became truly ours, and then her fingers were against the nape of my feathered neck.

"You're so big," she breathed out loud. My mind traveled to other places, wondering if she'd say the same thing in bed once I was above her and our naked limbs were twined. The dangerous line of thought tempted my beast, so I pulled away before I lost all control. Leigh startled back as I snapped out my wings. A powerful flap lifted me into the air, where I circled twice before riding an air current away from her home.

My survey of north Quickdraw yielded similar results of criminal behavior and sketchy individuals. Why weren't the police doing anything?

I returned to my house before absolute darkness fell and showered once I was inside. The memory of her touch didn't fade.

Leigh. She was mine, and soon, I'd be hers too.

Chapter Four

One Month Later

~Leigh~

Betty and I passed out candy alone for Halloween until Ian arrived in a Captain America costume. Petunia lay on the porch beside us, large and near the end of her pregnancy. We'd have puppies soon.

I eyeballed Ian from top to bottom as he kissed his grandmother's cheek. The fitted costume suited his physique, sexy as all get out and too authentic to be cheap.

"I think I'll be going inside now," Betty said. "This cold is too much for my arthritis, you know."

"It's barely a breeze," I protested.

She ignored me and continued inside. "I'll see you Tuesday, Leigh. Good luck. Goodnight, Ian."

Without thinking anything else of it, I turned back to Ian. His costume deserved my attention. "I wish I knew you were going to dress up. I would have done the same," I teased, nudging his ribs with my elbow. "Why *are* you dressed up?"

"I visit Texas Children's Hospital each year on Halloween," he explained. "It's sort of a tradition between me and some of the other guys in my squad. We go on down to Houston and tell stories to the kids."

"How long have you been doing this sort of thing?"

"This is the fourth year for me," he admitted. Petunia lumbered over and set her face on his knee until he scratched behind her ears. My dog loved him.

"Isn't Cap another branch and rank?" I asked innocently. I unwrapped a Hershey's kiss and held it in my mouth until it melted.

"Well, yeah, technically…"

Ian had a fresh shave for his Halloween role, and if he wore his hair long, he would have been a dead ringer for his grandfather. My gentle ribbing brought out a blush, its warm hue complementary to the exotic complexion he'd inherited from his grandmother and grandfather. I had discovered Betty was biracial, too; the daughter of a white man and black woman, but so fair-skinned it wasn't easily apparent. I eagerly listened to her stories of love existing during a time when society was against them.

"The part in the movie was definitely miscast," I said. After unwrapping a second chocolate and offering it to him from my fingers, I held my breath when he took it without hesitation, his lips closing around my fingertips. Ian and I had a kind of easygoing flirtation between us.

"You think so, huh?"

"I know so."

We hung out together for an hour longer as roving bands of children came for treats. My biggest regret was that I couldn't take Sophia to the yearly Trick or Treat social at the church in an adorable costume.

Ian jingled the keys to his SUV. "Guess you're off the clock now officially. Thanks for hanging around past your usual hours."

"Are you kidding? We had a blast. I love decorating for the holidays. Any holiday, really." We piled into the car and buckled our seatbelts. When we reached my neighborhood, we passed the usual gang of teenagers standing beneath a dimmed street lamp. We both knew what they were doing, but the local police didn't care about the small fry dealers.

"How do you feel about Monday?" Ian asked to break the silence.

"I always have trouble sleeping the night before a visit with her. Every other weekend isn't enough. I want to see her every day and let her know I haven't forgotten her and haven't abandoned her."

"It's because you love her, Leigh."

"Sometimes I worry I need her more than she needs me." Until her big gray eyes gazed up at me with something resembling recognition during my last visit. "I miss her so bad, Ian. I just wish they'd let me bring her home for a few hours. Even a night. Why do they think I'd go through all of these hoops just to hurt her? I mean, on Monday the judge is just going to review my case and see I fulfilled all his requirements, right?"

"It takes time to regain trust, sweetheart. But you're doing the right thing now playing it by their rules. Look at how far it's gotten you." He parked in front of my house.

I nodded, feeling foolish for the tears stinging my eyes. Only a few more days, and my nightmare would be over. Sniffling, I wiped my face with the back of my hand, then was taken by surprise when Ian pulled me into his arms. I became hyperaware of too many things at once: the earthy, familiar scent of juniper and woodsy pine I associated with him, his strength, how perfect we fit together when I set my cheek against his shoulder, and how much I wished he saw me as more than a charity case to save.

"Do you have a ride over?" he asked.

Once my emotions were under complete control, I leaned back from Ian and separated. "It's a ten minute walk. Their house is just up on Amarillo Drive." Uphill into a nicer area of town.

"What about to the courthouse?"

"Uh…" Shit. I drove Daddy's truck last time, and without it, I didn't have a way to reach the courthouse twenty miles away.

"As luck would have it, my schedule is clear Monday."

Ian probably had some sexy girlfriend waiting for him at home. Most of the town, including me, didn't know much about his personal life. And any attempts to wheedle information out of Betty resulted in absolute failure. He struck me as a private individual with a big heart, and ever since our evening ritual began, he'd never once hit on me in the car. Never made a pass at me.

Of course not, I thought, suddenly irritated with myself. Ian was a real gentleman, the kind of guy idealized in time period romances depicting the south. Once I reminded myself his interest in me was purely charitable, I suppressed the urge to do anything more than lean across the truck's center console for a hug. I threw both arms around Ian, catching him off guard with the ferocity of my embrace.

"Thank you, Ian. *Thank you.*"

"It was my pleasure, Leigh. I…" He squeezed me a little tighter, imparting a sense of safety I'd missed. Why was the second hug better than the first? "Maybe it's wrong to ask now, but I wondered if you'd like to join me for dinner Monday somewhere. Alone and without Gram."

My heart stuttered and missed a beat. "Dinner?"

"Yeah, an evening out."

I swallowed nervously, fearing I misread a friendly celebration offer. "Like a date?" I whispered.

"Like a date. We could catch a movie after your hearing, unless they let you take Sophia home with you right off. We'll just swing dinner somewhere kid-friendly then."

As if to compensate for seeming to stop, my heart slammed wildly in my chest, pulsing so hard I could barely hear him above the rushing sound filling my ears. "A date?"

"I do believe that's what the cool kids call it these days."

"Yes. Yes. I want to." I really wanted to, so much I was afraid I'd ruin the moment by speaking something foolish out loud. To spare myself any embarrassment, I turned my face toward his cheek and brushed my lips against his skin. "My hearing is at nine forty-five." I leaned back to look at him.

"I'll be here by eight o'clock."

I stepped out of the SUV then gently lifted Petunia from the rear seat. Ian waited for us to get inside the house and close the door before he drove away.

Between his advance bonus and my first couple paychecks, Daddy's old house looked like a home again. Ian had helped me paint and seal the ugly cement floors a week ago. The marbleized appearance gleamed with a smooth finish beneath a few tidy floor rugs. I couldn't show him enough gratitude for taking me to the store.

My roof no longer leaked. He and his friend Russ spent one sunny autumn afternoon on the ladders and did the repairs without charging me until I forced them to accept the cost of supplies.

"I can't wait to bring Sophia home." I had outlet covers, a secondhand crib, and everything needed to welcome her. Betty was eager to meet my child and swore up and down Sophia was welcome to attend my work duties with me every day. As Ian didn't have children, she looked forward to having a baby in her company.

My life was really taking a turn for the better, and I owed it all to one stubborn man named Ian MacArthur. Grinning, I kicked off my shoes and locked the door behind me. I was on cloud nine.

As part of my recovery, I'd become a creature of habit and took comfort in following the same routine each night. Following my shower, I fetched a yogurt cup from the fridge and settled cross-legged on the couch to watch the local news. As I toweled my hair dry, the weather forecast was interrupted by a Breaking News report.

"Ferguson Unit is under a prison lockdown following a riot that took place this evening. Correctional officers were forced to deploy chemical agents to regain control of the recreation facilities and report no officers were harmed during the events. Numerous injuries and three fatalities are reported at this time among the inmate population.

TDCJ has not released any names, pending notification of the families."

My brow creased as the news carried on without any further elaboration.

Although I had no true reason to worry about him, I laid down in bed hoping Dennis hadn't been one of those inmates on the recreation yard. By morning, I was in better spirits and able to enjoy the brisk stroll to the James residence. The couple who could have once been my in-laws lived in a quaint, cottage-style home on the south side of the main road.

They'd given Dennis everything, so I couldn't imagine what led him to dealing drugs. His father answered the door as usual, looking worn and unkempt. I'd seen him this way before after a night of beers with his friends.

"Good morning, Mr. Ja—"

He cut me off before I finished my greeting. "We're not up for supervising your visit today, Leigh. Go home."

"What do you mean I can't see her? It's my day. I get four hours today," I argued.

"Not today, Leigh."

"Why not?" I demanded hotly. His hangover had nothing to do with my child and me.

"Dennis is dead, and we'd like to mourn him in peace, without you here to remind us why he was in prison in the first place."

The fire and anger dimmed in an instant. "What? But no one called. No one told me."

"Our son was killed in a riot last night, or don't you care?"

"I…" He'd torn the rug out from under me. My eyes filled with unshed tears and I stared at him, wordlessly opening and closing my mouth. Dennis was dead. Killed and gone in the blink of an eye. My child was without a father.

"Go on now, Leigh. You're not welcome here."

Sour acid burned up my throat, but I swallowed back the urge to throw up. I didn't recall much of the walk home. Sharp pain radiated through my chest and consumed my very soul. All I could think about was Sophia, and what this meant for her. Dennis had been condemned to twenty-five years, but he would have managed a mediocre presence. Now she had no father. Not even a deadbeat to flit through her childhood like a passing shadow in the night.

"Hey, do you remember when this asshole promised we'd all go on an escort to Iran without even asking if we were interested?" Russ asked.

"Who doesn't?" Sasha replied.

"You got paid for it," I grumbled. "I couldn't help it was an all or nothin' deal."

"He's still at it. Guess who got roped into an afternoon of roof repairs a couple weeks back?" Russ pointed a thumb at himself. "Ian's turned into a true angel of benevolence since retiring. I expect he'll open his own soup kitchen for the homeless by Christmas."

Russ quieted down once he found himself on the receiving end of a dirty look.

Since my retirement, the group of us met at least once a month to unwind and play catch-up on each other's lives. My house was preferred for the pool I'd had built last year, unless we hung out at Sasha's penthouse in Houston. The youngest member of our team, a marine named Nadir, remained in active duty and was missing from our get-together.

Taylor's feline instincts let him hone in on my discomfort. Like a true jackass, he picked up where Russ left off. "So, what's happening with the hot girl?"

Playing dumb, I shrugged and raised my beer to my lips for another swig. "What hot girl?" They'd never let me live it down if they knew my eagle had responded to a girl less than half my age.

"The blonde with the booty," Taylor replied, gesturing with his hands for emphasis. "The one taking care of your grandmother."

"Ooh, spill it, Ian." Sasha flicked a bottle cap into the trash. Her lazy sprawl on the lawn chair was reminiscent of her lioness form, relaxed but deceptively alert. She twisted a lock of golden hair around her finger and grinned.

"Looks like the cat's out of the bag now, man. You may as well spill it," Taylor said with an unapologetic shrug. Russ must have told him everything, because I sure hadn't.

"Thanks, Russ. Really."

"You're welcome."

"It's us, Ian," Juni chimed in. The tiniest and quietest member of our squad gazed at me with a reassuring smile on her face. The wind kicked a few strands of dark hair into her almond shaped eyes.

"Her name's Leigh," I began after a sigh. I laid out the entire story, beginning with our chance meeting at church and ending with my decision to help her regain complete custody of her child. By the end, I'd prepared myself for laughter and merciless teasing for my gullible actions. Who gave so much money and time to a stranger they barely knew?

No one laughed.

"Well?"

Sasha shook her head. "You're a great guy, Ian. She's lucky."

"That makes you and Russ now. Funny, I always imagined ladies-man Taylor would get snagged up first." Juni passed fresh beers around the circle while Russ checked the smoked meat on the grill.

Sasha grunted and went inside. I guess she was still sore from letting go of her relationship with Taylor. We all knew why it had to happen, but it didn't ease the tender feelings on either side.

She was a lion, he was a cougar — interbreeding between our shifter species never worked out, and once the call of nature ran its course, our children were the ones to suffer most. If they survived. None of us could resist mating once we had a treasured spouse. I was already beginning to feel the tug toward Leigh, a desperate and raw urgency I denied each time we were in close proximity.

"Just you watch," Taylor said, trying to move past the awkward silence. "You'll be next, Junebug."

"Doubtful. Male rabbits are kind of pussies." Her lighthearted statement was meant to amuse us, but I heard the undercurrent of disappointment.

My phone's ringtone sang out to alert me to an incoming call then Leigh's name popped up in the caller ID window. "Hang on a sec, guys. I'll be right back."

Leaving them to laugh and make fun of male bunny shifters, I stepped aside out of shifter hearing range and answered the call. "Hi, Leigh."

"Dennis is dead. Someone stabbed him to death last night at the prison in a riot."

If anything, I'd expected to hear a heartwarming story about holding her baby again, or good news about mending the damaged relationship between her and the grandparents. She stunned me. "A prison riot? Shit. I'm sorry, hon."

"I don't even know why it's bothering me. It's not like… like we were together anymore."

"Sweetheart, it's natural to mourn him. He was a part of your life for a long while. You had a child with him."

"And now they won't let me see her," she sniffled over the line. "I mean… I sorta get why, but it's still hard, ya know? Anyway, I didn't mean to ruin your Saturday."

"You didn't ruin anything. Would you be happier if I came over?"

"No, it's all right. I'm sorry, Ian. I'm sorry."

"Stop apologizing. I did say if you ever need to talk, I'm here for you."

Leigh sniffled. "Yeah. Anyway, enjoy your Saturday, Ian. I'll see you tomorrow morning at church."

I told her goodbye and ended the call, but I returned to the deck to find four sets of eyes watching me.

"That sounded serious," Juni spoke up tentatively. She bit her lower lip and dropped her shoulders a little. She hadn't meant to eavesdrop, but her sharp hearing picked up everything. "Are things okay?"

"Remember the ex I told you about in prison? Yeah well, somebody shanked him last night. Dead. His folks denied Leigh her scheduled visitation with her kid."

"Sounds like she needs a friend then," Russ commented. "Why are you still here?"

"She said she didn't need me to come over and would see me at church."

"Don't be daft, Ian." Sasha rolled her eyes and shook her head. "When we women tell you to stay away, we actually want you to come."

"What the fuck kind of mind game is that?" Taylor asked. "Why can't you just tell us you want us around?"

"Because then you whine about us being needy," Sasha fired back.

"Okay, okay. Before this devolves into the usual, I guess I'll head out and check on her. Sorry, guys."

"We'll be here when you get back. Not like we're driving anywhere," Taylor said. He shrugged.

"We'll hold down the fort. Here." Juni jumped up and plucked the first two steaks off the grill. We had one extra T-bone because Russ had forgotten she didn't eat meat. Within minutes, she prepared a tidy to-go package, including some of the cobbler Dani sent over with Russ.

With our meals and a bottle of merlot in my possession, I drove over to Leigh's house and knocked on the door. The neighbors watched me from their porch, filled with curiosity.

"Sup, MacArthur. Sure see you around here often. Y'all datin' now or something?" the guy asked.

Given the chance to stake my claim, I ran with it and nodded. "Yup. She's all mine now." I knocked again. "Steak delivery for Leigh Denton," I called, hoping to lure her from inside.

"Heard 'bout what happened to Dennis. Can't say it surprised me much."

"Yeah? I thought the prison system was safe these days."

"About as safe as a prison can be if you keep your mouth shut."

I didn't get a chance to inquire further. The door slowly creaked open to reveal Leigh. Her puffy face and red eyes confirmed my suspicions, proving no matter how much she claimed to be okay on the phone, she really wasn't fine at all.

"Ian? I told you not to come."

"I brought you dinner, sweetheart. You can kick me out after you take it."

After she stepped aside to let me in, I set Juni's care package on the kitchen counter and turned around just in time to receive an armful of woman. I ran my fingers through her fair hair and eventually coaxed her to sit with me on the couch. I held her until the worst of her sobs subsided and she removed her cheek from my soaked shoulder.

"I'm s—"

"Apologize one more time and I'm gonna go and take my steaks with me."

Leigh's sniffles dwindled to weak giggles.

"When I say I'm here for you, Leigh, I mean it. You can talk as much as you want or just be quiet. It won't bother me a bit." I settled back into the couch arm and watched her. Uncertain, cloud-grey eyes studied me in return.

"I hate him so much for what he did to us," she whispered once the initial silence ended. "I used to blame him for my relapses, making up excuses all the time."

"And now you don't," I encouraged her.

Leigh nodded. "Not anymore. I spent the first month after they took Sophia thinking, 'If he didn't supply me, I could have kicked it. It's his fault.' Then I realized I was looking at it all wrong. He didn't put the pills in my mouth. I did."

In another time and place, I might have judged her too for her shitty decisions. Poor choices may have hurt her child, but the law was putting her through a mother's nightmare to get her back.

"Everything just went to hell when my dad got sick. I just feel so lost right now."

"Well, I'm pretty sure a full belly and a good movie will help a little."

With a little effort, I managed to get Leigh to eat a filling meal. The solemn mood gradually tapered off over the course of a made for TV movie. We dug into peach cobbler and took turns swigging from the merlot bottle once I assured her no one would barge in to point fingers for her decision to have a sip. A pain killer addiction didn't make her an alcoholic.

"I feel weird drinking straight out of the bottle," she murmured. "Wish I had glasses."

"It's okay, hon. There's nobody here to see us drinking like a pair of classless lushes," I reminded her. "It's only us, and I'm not telling. Unless the judge is hiding in the bushes outside your window, we're good."

Afterward, when we were both stuffed and she was clearly tipsy, she leaned against me and kissed my cheek. Her palm slipped over my chest, idly trailing up and down my torso. "Hey, Ian?"

"Hm?" God, she smelled sweet. As much as I wanted to kiss her and submit to the needs of my feral half, the man in me said to wait. Now wasn't the time to put the moves on her. Not when she was mourning and not when there was a gorgeous wine flush on her cheeks. My stiffening cock provoked a slew of lustful thoughts, imagining Leigh beneath me with her head thrown back. I wanted to feel her nails against my shoulders and tight body milking my release.

I couldn't deny my eagle much longer.

"Thanks for coming."

"It's nothin', sweetheart. Hey, instead of meeting at church tomorrow would you like to come meet some friends of mine who are in town right now?"

"You mean skip?"

"Exactly. I'm pretty sure the big man upstairs will understand, as upset as you are. You can come join us all for a big brunch since they're staying at my house tonight."

Leigh leaned back to look at me with guilt in her large, gray eyes. "Oh, Ian, you had friends over and you abandoned them to come see me? I couldn't intrude—"

"Psshaw. They'll love you. Besides, Dani will be glad to have some non-military company there. She tends to bug out and just send over treats if it's only us." I guided her back over to me with one arm around her. She came over willingly and nestled close.

"Dani?"

"Russel's girlfriend. You met him, you know, the guy who helped me out with your roof repairs."

"The big guy who looks like a bear wearing a Stetson?"

My grin widened a little. "Yeah, that one."

"Mm, he was nice. You were both so nice," she mumbled against my shoulder.

I thought I'd imagined her checking us both out when we were cooling off beneath her peach tree with our shirts off and the case of beer I fetched from the corner store. Then Russ confirmed it on the way home, and we both had a good chuckle.

Another glance down confirmed she had fallen asleep, her face closer to my neck. Without waking Leigh, I slipped my arms beneath her body and raised her up from the sofa. Her cramped bedroom was neat and tidy, with little more than a full-sized bed and a banged up dresser. Photos of her decorated the mirror in a collage style, fastened by tiny squares of tape. I tucked her in and took a moment to look at them on my way out the door.

The young woman in the high school graduation photos was at least forty pounds lighter, slim at the waist and hip. Without the cap and gown, her modest black dress revealed long legs and toned, athletic arms. Sliding my eyes back and forth between the photo and the real woman in the bed, I drew comparisons between Leigh's thicker waist, rounder face, and the picture's smaller proportions. The only thing I preferred about her younger visage was the careless smile on her face. It touched her eyes and overflowed with happiness. The Leigh I knew never smiled as freely.

After tidying up her living room, I borrowed her second bed pillow and sprawled on her new sofa. The smell of the manufacturer and showroom floor was gone, replaced by her scent. I let the memory of her touch carry me off to sleep.

Chapter Five

~LEIGH~

I awakened without any regrets about my evening of wine sipping with Ian and spent my first conscious minute remembering the way his abs flexed beneath my stroking fingertips. The man had a stomach I wanted to kiss.

My old clock told me it was half past ten, long past the hour I usually got up to prepare for church in the morning. I groggily slipped out of bed and ran my fingers through my disheveled hair.

Just as I was preparing to set out clothes, a strange sound from my living room startled me out of the daily routine. With my dad's Louisville slugger in my hands, I tiptoed to the hall where a peek revealed Ian stretched facedown across my couch. Snoring.

I sighed.

After I spread a blanket over the chilly man, I shuffled into the bathroom and got in the shower. I made sure my legs were damned silky, wrapped a towel around myself, and stepped into the hall just in time to come face to face with Ian as he emerged from the kitchen with a glass of OJ. The kitchen doorway placed him barely two yards from me.

"Uh..." I clutched the towel a little tighter. It was tiny scrap of rectangular terry cloth insufficient for my tall frame, coming to a stop higher than mid-thigh. It barely covered my ass in the back and left an inch wide strip of my side visible. Ian's eyes followed the narrow path of ivory.

"Morning, Leigh. Hope it was okay to raid your fridge."

"Morning," I whispered back. The two yards between us became mere inches as he bridged the gap before I could shuffle into the bedroom to die of embarrassment. Beads of water glistened upon my cheeks and arms, droplets occasionally splattering against the floor from my dripping hair.

Ian moved a slick strand from my face and tucked it behind my ear. The casual gesture made me tremble with rising anticipation of the next touch. Thankfully, the plush fabric of my newer bath towel concealed how stiff my nipples hardened beneath it.

"Leigh?"

"Hm?"

"Do you have a bathing suit?"

"A b-bathing suit?" I stammered.

"It's a pool party, sweetheart."

"A pool party in November?"

"We're only a couple days into November, and it's Texas, darlin'. Sixty-five degrees out there today." His cocky, uneven grin warmed my heart. "Plus it's a heated pool."

"Oh! Just gimme a second to figure out if I have one I can still fit in."

Ian's lips brushed against my temple. "Take your time."

My favorite pre-pregnancy two-piece was a no. I didn't feel confident enough to strut my stuff in front of strangers bound to resemble the cast from Magic Mike. I settled on a blue, halter style tankini with a white polka dot print and modest boy shorts instead.

While he waited outside, I rummaged for the perfect ensemble to accentuate my curves. The sea-green pleated skirt I found suited my above average height and swished around my legs, and when paired with a wide belt to emphasize my waist, confidence surged through me as I looked in the mirror.

I emerged from my bedroom to whistles and enthused catcalls. "You look *amazing*."

"I do?" I came up short of grabbing my purse from the coffee table and stared at him.

"Pffft. As if you ever had any doubt about it."

I did, but he didn't need to know that.

***

Ian's home was a spacious, two story nestled outside Quickdraw city limits. The massive backyard deserved its own zip code and housed an in-ground, rectangle pool with its own dive board. Sasha and Juni had stretched a volleyball net between both sides.

"C'mon, Leigh. We need one more for a game of volleyball. Ian claims you've got a badass spike," Taylor called.

"And Russ will cry if their side is short a person," Sasha added.

"I will not," Russ protested.

"He will," Dani confirmed from a lawn chair on the deck. "I'd play, but I'm feeling sort of tired from pulling those extra hours at work all week. Just gonna sit here and read a bit."

"I don't know, guys. I haven't played in a couple years." I tried to imagine myself leaping around in the water and jiggling while Sasha pranced in her white mesh bikini. The hot little number evoked instantaneous feelings of inferiority.

Then I realized they didn't care. No one gave me a cross look for my swimsuit choice.

"C'mon over to the dark side," Russ encouraged.

"Bet I can spike one past you," Ian taunted.

Fuck it. The only person who cares about my rolls is me. Overcoming my biggest fear, I joined them in the pool and had the time of my life. The best part of all was discovering the passing of years barely dulled my skills. By the third game, it was all coming back to me in a rush. My adrenaline pumped when Ian and Russ began arguing over sharing me.

"Guys, guys. I'll swap with Sasha next game."

"But we don't want her!" Taylor cried.

The intensity of Sasha's dirty look made Taylor recoil. "Sorry. Uh, I mean… We'd love to have you, baby doll! You can have Leigh back, Ian."

We played three more games before the tough soldiers threw in the towel. Ian picked me up and swung me around in a circle, laughing because I'd won him 500 bucks off Taylor.

"Told you she had a better spike game than you," Ian taunted him.

"You brought in a ringer, man. Not cool," Taylor grumbled while the girls dragged me away to chat.

"Do you kickbox?" Juni asked.

"No, I've never tried it. Not sure it'd be so good for my knee."

"Oh." Juni flushed. "You can tell me to mind my own business if you want. I was just thinking you have great legs for it. The guy I train with has worked with people with knee injuries before, you know."

"Really?"

"Yeah." The slimmer girl beside me had a set of muscular thighs I envied, so I couldn't imagine her believing mine were great for anything. Her modest, navy blue one-piece covered more than Sasha's bathing suit, but Juni lacked my insecurity and wore it with pride.

If I can look at her and see she looks great, why couldn't I feel the same way about myself?

"I've never really considered kickboxing before, but it could be fun once I've saved up some. I know I won't have a job with Betty forever."

Ian's glance made me regret my words. I bit my lip and ducked my head down, wishing I'd phrased it better.

"Why don't you apply to return to school?" Sasha's question pierced the tension like a knife slicing butter. I aimed an appreciative smile to her.

"I don't know. Maybe it'll be possible once Sophia is in school. I have a year of courses to finish and daycare is too pricey."

"Check and find out if any of the courses you need are available online," Dani chimed in. "I'm going to get a start on my master's and have a couple I can do from home."

By the time Russ announced the barbecue was ready, Dani had fetched a pecan pie from indoors. I ate without shame or fear of judgment, stuffing myself with delicious ribs and sweets until I slumped uselessly against Ian's chair. He slipped an arm around my shoulders, inviting me to snuggle close.

"Your friends throw good parties," I mumbled.

"The best." I may have been surrounded by hot military men, but his was the only body I wanted to cuddle.

At the end of the evening when Ian dropped me off at home, I kissed his cheek before leaving the vehicle.

"Thanks for today."

"Looks like they all loved you, sweetheart."

"I loved meeting them too."

It was a struggle to unwind for bed after a day with Ian's amazing, nonjudgmental friends. With only hours to go before between me and the biggest day of my entire life, I sipped chamomile tea to soothe my nerves. Sophia and Ian's faces blessed my dreams once I finally fell into slumber.

***

My custody hearing should have been an open and shut case. It started with Judge Ritts asking for my proof of employment, which I provided when I passed over my pay stubs.

"How do you plan to continue working once Sophia is in your care, Ms. Denton?"

"I have an agreement with my boss and client. Sophia will come to work with me each day."

"That isn't very professional. A child in a working environment?"

"They've both encouraged it. I brought a written statement from her and my employer." I slid those to him. Ritts set both aside when he finished reading then he sighed.

"I received a report from child protective services about the state of your home. I couldn't in good faith allow her to return to you until I've received proof it's hazard free."

Thanks to Ian's advice, I came prepared with a few Polaroids. I set those in front of the judge, too, and watched him exchange a dubious glance with Sophia's grandparents.

Everything seemed to lean in my favor, pending another drug screening and a home assessment by CPS. Then Mr. and Mrs. James had their lawyer drop a bombshell on me.

They wanted to retain custody of my little girl and claimed they would give her the life I never could. When the judge asked me if I would voluntarily surrender my parental rights, it took every ounce of my control to decline without profanity. I glanced behind me to see Ian staring daggers at the judge, his jaw clenched. He was angry, but I couldn't breathe. All of the air was leached from my lungs, my emotional pain manifesting as physical agony I'd never felt before.

Judge Ritts demanded more proof I could provide a stable home. Apparently my employment, growing bank account, and sobriety didn't count. We would reconvene in a month to decide the fate of my parental privileges. I left the courtroom feeling numb from head to toe, barely aware of my surroundings or that Ian was guiding me to his Escalade by one arm. My foggy head made it difficult to focus, and I stumbled going down the steps. Ian steadied me.

"Hey, I've got you. Slow down, Leigh."

"I've done everything. Everything they asked," I whispered. My body was numb, useless as he guided me.

"The Good Ol' Boy System at work," Ian muttered. He shook his head and opened my car door.

Despite Dennis' crimes, his mother and father were still highly respected in the community. As far as our fellow residents believed, his wrongdoing wasn't because they'd spared the rod and spoiled the child — it was me, the junkie and corruptor who led him down his wayward path. I had the drug history and criminal background he didn't have prior to his arrest. Dennis got caught up in my bullshit, and now he was dead at the young age of twenty-five, his light extinguished too soon.

"What do I do now, Ian?"

"We'll fight it. My friend, Argus, specializes in finances, but I'll ask him if he can recommend an associate in family law. I should have gotten you a lawyer to begin with."

"I can't afford a lawyer."

"*I* will pay for it."

"And I can't ask for you to do it!"

"You're not asking me, but I'm telling you this will happen, and you'll owe me nothing for it. Because it's the right thing to do, and I wouldn't be able to sleep at night if I don't."

"There has to be a way to do this without costing you a lot of money."

Ian rubbed his chin thoughtfully and gazed into the distance. "I'll have a word with them. We can try conversation first. I'll talk it out with Mr. James, and we can do this like men."

"It's not going to be easy, Ian. You can't just strut into someone's house and lay down the law like you're back in the Arm—"

"Air Force," he corrected me.

"Air Force," I gritted out through my teeth. "They don't have any reason to believe a single word you say to them. They don't have a reason to trust *me*. What? Do you think I haven't tried to get through to them?"

"I understand, Leigh."

The thing I hated about Ian was no matter how much I ranted and raged, he kept a cool head and waited it out as I transitioned from despair to fury.

"The hell you do!" My sharp scream startled me, but it failed to coax a reaction out of him. "What do you know except that your current charity case is about to lose her daughter for good? Why do you even care? You don't have anything to gain from this. Why are you here at all?"

"Are you done?" he asked gently.

Sniffling, I wiped my eyes with his handkerchief and nodded. Crying was exhausting business.

"Good. You want to know why I care so much, so I'll tell you, Leigh. I care because after my dad died, *my* mom gave me up. She didn't want me. When Gramps passed away, it was just Grams and me and a lot of people didn't think she could raise a little boy alone. Maybe she didn't make your mistakes, but she did right by me. I believe you mean it when you swear you're off the drugs."

The story of Ian's family history jarred me out of my self-pity session. I stared at him through the haze of my tears. "She gave you up?"

"Yeah. I was about to celebrate my sixth birthday. She walked out of my life and didn't try to contact me until she heard I had a big military commission. Tried to write her son the Colonel, and she made sure to ask me for money, too."

I couldn't imagine walking away from a child without a damned good reason for doing it.

"Did she ever tell you why?"

"Yeah, she did." Ian's pained smile told me everything I needed to know. I didn't pry. "Anyway, why don't we go and have lunch to give them a chance to return home."

"They won't listen to you, Ian."

"They will. Trust me. When I finish with what I have to say, they'll be glad to give Sophia back to you."

Chapter Six

~IAN~

I knocked on the door to the James household without a single plan in my head. I knew they loved the kid, but what they had decided to do went above and beyond the call of justice. They were trying to replace their child with someone else's daughter.

Leigh made her mistakes, but she'd received her punishments and fulfilled every stipulation set by the law. So why hadn't the judge restored custody at the hearing? I had my guesses.

Someone peeked at me through the peephole then I heard the rustling of a security chain. As the door cracked open, I assumed my most unintimidating stance, with my hands folded together behind my back and my spine straight.

The portly older man in the doorway smiled at me, no doubt aware of the reason for my visit. "Mr. MacArthur, what can we do for you?"

"I'd like to talk to you about Leigh and Sophia. May I come in?"

Mr. James stiffened and clenched his jaw. "I think we've spoken enough about Leigh and Sophia."

The whole town knew I served in the military. I had a reputation here, and I certainly didn't plan to fuck it up by scaring an old man in his own home. I wanted to chat with him on the level, but he was making it hard to remain patient when I couldn't even get a foot in the door.

"You haven't talked with me personally on the matter," I said quietly. "You can let me in now, or you can wait until I contact a lawyer. Which will it be?"

"Lawyer" was the magic word. The old man let me in this time, and we took seats in the living room, him in his chair and me on the sofa.

"I'm sorry about your son, but I'm going to cut straight to the point, Mr. James. None of you have any reason at all to suspect Leigh hasn't turned over a new leaf. She's clean. She's passed every piss test the state has thrown at her. She's working—"

"At a job you created for her," the man cut in.

"A job is a job," I replied mildly. "This recent request is a slap to the face. Don't you think it's been long enough? A child deserves to have a mother. Leigh loves Sophia. She'd do anything for her — has done everything for her. She's been clean almost four months."

"And when she relapses, then what? Sophia's gonna be the one to suffer."

"She won't."

"You don't know that," he insisted while rocking in his chair.

"You can't punish her for something she hasn't done yet, either."

"She is my grandbaby. I'm not going to let her mom ruin her life, not when we can give her better."

The way they gave Dennis better? I bit back the retort and kept the irritation from my expression and my voice. "Sophia will have a great home. With her mom."

"In that ramshackle drug den of hers? No, Mr. MacArthur, I don't think so."

"No. In *my* home. I plan to marry Leigh. We're on our way to the city hall now for the marriage license," I spit out. My temper got the best of me and took charge, sweeping me down a road I couldn't reverse. "I'm going to marry her and adopt Sophia. So you can listen to me now and back off, or wait to see the both of us in court. I promise you, it's going to be costly, and you won't like the outcome if we take the legal route."

I knew he had Judge Ritts in his pocket, and their fishing buddy friendship was the reason Leigh couldn't get a fair shot. What Mr. James and Judge Ritts didn't know was one fucking phone call from me would have him removed by morning. I was willing to take a chance and call in a favor.

***

"What do you mean we're getting married?"

"I kind of lost my temper and said I plan to marry you. Then I said we'll see them in court."

For my safety, I decided to lay the news on Leigh after we were on the road and driving toward the next town.

"Where are we going?" Leigh demanded.

"To buy a marriage license."

"Fuck no. I'm not marrying you."

"Well, you might want to listen to the rest of what I have to say before you make up your mind."

Leigh settled back in her seat and fixed me with a scowl so dark it could curdle milk. I winced and turned my attention back to the road. "I'm waiting."

"If I'm married to you, I have the legal right to stand beside you in court. And just between you and me, I have a military history, no criminal record, and enough money to buy half this town. Alternatively, I can also pull a lot of strings to get Judge Ritts disbarred. What he did today was a severe miscarriage of our justice system, and I'll be damned if I allow him to get away with it. You met their requirements."

"I don't know, Ian. He's been a judge for forty years. He's not a bad man. It'll ruin him and drag his name through the mud."

"But he's discriminating against you," I pointed out.

"I know but—"

"Do you want Sophia back?"

Leigh silenced. With her eyes on the window, a thoughtful expression came over her pretty face. She'd made mistakes, but the James' decisions would follow her for a lifetime. "I want my baby, Ian."

"Marry me, Leigh. I have a big house you and Sophia are welcomed to share with me."

"What about…" She cleared her throat and gestured between us. "I mean, we haven't even had a first date. Not really. Marriage is..."

"It's convenient for both of us. In a year or so, after you finish school, we can have it annulled or divorce to go our separate ways. I'll make sure you're comfortable." Like hell we would. My deepest hope was she'd come to feel for me what I felt for her.

"So that's it? A fake marriage and I get to live in a big house?"

"Did you expect more?" I took a shot in the dark and stole a look at her from the corner of my eye. "Some kind of perverted sex stipulation?"

Hot color spread over her face. Bingo.

"Sex is a very personal, intimate thing for me, Leigh. It goes against my principles to expect you to lay down with me just because I'm giving you a hand."

Maybe it had something to do with my shifter half. Eagles mated for life, and the few times I'd have had sex with a woman simply to satisfy a craving, the lack of attachment made me feel empty inside. Incomplete. It was an impression I couldn't shake, too intense to risk repeating unnecessarily.

"It's personal for me, too," Leigh confided.

"I meant what I said about taking you out and getting to know you better, Leigh. Look, my house is big enough for you to have your own bedroom. We'll take it slow and see how things develop."

"What if I don't want to marry you?"

"Then I'll find you the best lawyer I can retain on short notice and we'll take this to court."

"What if I marry you and it gets awkward?"

"Then in a year, they'll see you haven't relapsed and we can split." The idea had its charm and gave me a year to show her I could be the man she wanted for the rest of her life.

"Okay."

"Okay what?"

"I'll marry you."

"Church or courthouse?" I glanced over at her and grinned. Leigh wiped the tears from her face with one hand and grinned back at me.

"Courthouse. Think I've had enough of church for a while."

***

"Wait, wait, what?" Russ choked on his beer until his girlfriend slapped him on the back.

"I said I need a best man. A witness. Whatever it is."

"You're joking, right?"

Dani swatted Russ. "I don't see him laughing, hon. Of course we'll come, Ian."

"Thanks, Daniela, it means a lot to me."

"Hold on a minute now. Don't you think you're rushing into this? Have you talked to her or told her *why* you feel so strongly about her already?" Russ asked.

Daniela rolled her eyes. "Don't listen to the bear stalker over here. If there's one thing I've learned about you strange shifters, it's that your hearts lead you to the right place."

Abashed, Russ exhaled a low sigh. "Sorry. I guess she's right, but are you sure this is what you want to do?"

"I had all night to think about it, Russ. We were supposed to have our first official date yesterday, but after we bought a marriage license at the county courthouse, I spent the evening letting her cry on my shoulder instead," I said.

"What I don't get is why it's taken so long for Ian to find his fated mate," Dani mused.

"There could be any number of reasons, darlin'. Could be he wasn't truly ready to settle down," Russ explained.

I nodded in confirmation. "Have you ever heard the saying 'there's someone for everyone'? It really should be 'there's a few people for everyone' because as our life circumstances change…"

"So do the people we're destined to find," Russ said. "Katie was always the woman for me, but her death made room for you, Dani. You were my other soul mate, the one I never knew I had. Because I'd bonded once in my life, it took a while for me to realize you and I bonded."

"You guys make it sound so romantic. It would make a beautiful movie plot line, I bet. A tale of a man searching his whole life for his other half, only to find her where he least expects her."

"Yeah, in a church of all places," I grunted.

"My dad used to say church was the best place to find 'em," Russ commented.

"I guess that's why Dani found your lazy ass in her yard like some hairy sleeping beauty instead of down the road at the Methodist church around the corner."

Russ grunted this time. "Anyway, back to your problem. We'll be there. Just let us know if you need anything else, like help moving her things."

Where would I be without the support of my friends? "Nah. We're going to start tomorrow."

We waited two days instead, taking Wednesday as a cooling off time away from each other to decide what was best. While waiting, I contacted Argus and placed my thumb on a couple contacts who owed me favors. I prepared for the worst possible outcome, which was Leigh deciding she wanted me to go after Judge Ritts.

Alternatively, if she wanted to fight, a fancy lawyer from San Antonio was waiting to come to the rescue. The man was so good my pal Argus claimed by the time he finished our defense, Sophia would be back in Leigh's care and her grandparents would be paying child support.

Leigh didn't want that either.

By Thursday, I drove up in my Escalade to find her wrapping photo frames and small keepsakes. Russ planned to visit later in the evening to fetch her couch with his pickup. It was too new to leave behind like the bed.

I waited until the next day, after she was long gone and clear of reprisal before calling the police department about her dealing neighbors. While Leigh unpacked some of her clothes into her new bedroom, I snuck away into my office and got on the line to the Quickdraw Police Department.

"We're aware of some problems from that house, Mr. MacArthur," the young woman said. She didn't sound like an officer and had to be one of the girls in the office since I knew we had an all-male force.

"Excuse me?" I asked. "If your officers are aware of it, why aren't they doing anything?"

"I can't answer those questions over the—"

"I'd like to speak to the chief." She put me through a ten minute wait before Montgomery answered the line.

"What can I do for you, Mr. MacArthur?"

"There are people openly dealing drugs down on Denning Street and you aren't doing anything about it?"

"We've gotten calls, Mr. MacArthur, nothing else. There's no proof of wrongdoing there."

"That's bullshit, Montgomery, and you know it. I sat outside Leigh's house fifteen minutes the other day and saw everything I needed to know. They've even got the little kid rushing down the steps to peddle their dope because they're too lazy to get off their asses." Leigh had a card from her CPS caseworker, and while I hated to get any parent into trouble with the law, my conscience wouldn't allow it to rest. I had to call.

"Now hold on a minute, Ian."

"Oh, now we're on a first name basis, are we? My fiancée is out of that house now, but I want to know what you plan to do about it. I can drive through north side at any hour of the day and catch a handful of drug deals going down by the Dixie Quarters. Why is this happening?"

"There are things happening behind the scenes that I can't discuss," Montgomery said. His snide tone made me wish I could strangle him over the line. "Sometimes, it's to our benefit to allow some small fish to go free until we catch the keepers, if you get my drift."

"*Some* small fish to go free? It's become very apparent that Quickdraw has a 100% catch and release program in effect," I said dryly.

Montgomery silenced. I pictured him fuming in his office and grinned. "I won't discuss police matters over the line, MacArthur. I can only tell you to take comfort in knowing we've got it under control."

"Thanks for your time." I ended the call and glanced up to see Leigh in the doorway, frowning.

"Is everything okay, Ian?"

"Oh, everything's great. Nothing I can't handle," I said. She didn't need to be bothered any more on the matter. "Did you get Petunia settled in yet?"

"Oh yeah. She loves it here. Those puppies ought to be here any day now, too."

Richard and Gloria James showed up at my home the following afternoon as we were unloading cleaning supplies from our final trip out to her old house. Everything was ready to go on the market.

"I'm going inside," Leigh murmured to me. As she stepped toward the door, I grabbed her by the wrist and anchored her in place.

"You don't have to run from anyone, Leigh."

The elderly couple picked their way down the drive. Gloria walked with a cane these days, following a recent knee replacement surgery. Her husband was a brittle diabetic and just as poor in health. Their son, prior to his arrest for drug crimes, had been their sole caretaker.

I had to wonder how either of them thought they could take care of a child. If not for a crooked judge, they wouldn't have had a chance.

"Hello, Mr. MacArthur. This isn't a bad time, is it?"

"No. We're just finishing up. What can I do for you?"

"We wanted to apologize to Leigh for what's happened. Your visit gave us a chance to talk and come to our senses. Thank you, young man."

I was hardly as young as I appeared. The magic flowing through my veins slowed aging. We didn't live more than a decade or two longer than most humans, but we looked better during our lifetimes. So did our bonded mates.

"We don't want to take it to court, now that we know you'll be here to help Leigh. I… we can't use Sophia to replace Dennis. He's gone now. There's no bringing him back, and he made his decisions," Gloria said.

"Where's Leigh so we can tell her in person?" Richard asked.

Leigh stepped out from behind my vehicle. "I'm right here."

"Leigh, we're sorry. We were so carried away with our pain. And after Dennis died, we just lost sight of what was best for Sophia. He wouldn't have wanted this. He wouldn't have wanted all of us fighting this way."

I glanced at the open backseat and saw a rear-facing child seat. Sophia was with them of course, her wide-eyed features alert and aware of her surroundings.

"Do you mean I can see her now? Right now?"

The older man nodded. Without another word, Leigh dashed for the car and slid in beside Sophia. I watched with a smile on my face.

"You did the right thing," I told them both as Leigh reconnected with her daughter. Those sporadic, monitored visits to their home hadn't been enough.

"We made contact with the social worker. We can't leave her here with Leigh just yet, not legally, but you're both welcome in our home at any time until we hear back from Mrs. Johnson."

"Thank you, Mrs. James. Have you set a date and time for Dennis' funeral?"

The older woman nodded. They only had about a decade on me, but the vast differences in our appearance came as a benefit of my shifter traits and healthier lifestyle. "We plan to put him to rest Saturday afternoon. We'd like it if both of you came."

"Of course." I hoped Leigh didn't disapprove of my agreement.

I invited the couple inside my home for coffee while Leigh bonded with her child in the living room. We gave her complete freedom from our prying eyes and stayed clear. She didn't need a monitor. She wouldn't harm Sophia.

"Cream, sugar?" I asked. A little friendly interaction went a long way, and despite the minor difference in our ages, I treated them with the same respect I'd give my gram.

"Yes, please," Gloria answered.

"If you don't mind my asking, Mr. MacArthur, how old are you?"

"Ian, please. And no, I don't mind. I actually get this a lot. I'll be fifty-four next month."

Their eyes bugged. I've heard every kind of joke, from having great genes to having the same physical fitness trainer as Brad Pitt. I didn't look my age and I never would.

"Well, you sure don't show it," Gloria commented.

A sweet soprano drifted from the living room into the kitchen. The lullaby was a familiar tune, but I'd never found it particularly pretty until now.

"Is that Leigh?"

"It is. You didn't know she could sing?"

"She never talks about singing. She only told me she likes to hear the choir at church." We had talked about volleyball, her sports injuries, and her failure to complete college, but singing never made the conversation. She had a beautiful voice.

"Leigh used to be the best in the choir before…" Richard's voice trailed.

It became crystal for me then, and I was able to understand everything about the sorrow on her face during the service. I finally knew her reasons for attending despite their unwelcoming behavior.

"Would they let her in the choir again now? Look, I know you don't much like her the way you used to, but even you have to admit she's paid her dues. What do we have to do to get this town to accept it?"

They looked at each other. "I think everything has to start with us, Ian."

Chapter Seven

~LEIGH~

My husband-to-be arrived in jeans. He wore them well, but I couldn't help but mourn the loss of the classic fairy tale wedding from my childhood fantasies.

In my dreams, I'd wear an exquisite white gown with trailing lace while a half dozen bridesmaids beamed proudly from beside the altar. They wore blue, my favorite color, with wine-colored sashes around their waists. I had flowers in my hair and a piano player skillfully announcing my arrival with the wedding march. His hands would glide over the ivories and I'd emerge to find a captive audience who melted before my beauty on my special day. My father would lead me down the aisle to a handsome man in a flawless tuxedo, join our hands, and give me away with tears in his eyes.

The crushing reality was a Wal-Mart dress from the clearance aisle and two of Ian's friends in their Sunday best. My dad died two years ago from throat cancer and my friends scattered like cockroaches when the shit hit the fan after Sophia's birth.

One glance at the man beside me sped my pulse rate to a jackhammer pace. Ian was a good-looking man, a kind man, and there were worse guys to marry. I'd hoped his kindness would soothe the butterflies in my belly, but it didn't. I nervously smoothed my fingers over the edge of my yellow and white sundress.

"It's not too late to change your mind," Ian whispered in my ear.

"I should be telling you that." It was his crazy idea, after all.

"Nah, I'm good."

The simple ceremony lacked fanfare. An old tape player running in the background provided our Wedding March and the magistrate stood by a long table where our wedding license waited. He spoke a few solemn words regarding the sanctity of marriage before asking if we each accepted the other. Then he had us sign the papers. Envying Ian's steady handwriting, I tried to script my own name without my pen shaking all over the line. He was unwavering, steel nerves and perfect composure.

"I now pronounce you husband and wife. You may kiss your bride."

Instinctively, my eyes shifted from the judge to my new husband and found Ian closely watching me in return. Before I could concoct a phony excuse or claim modesty, Ian's mouth lowered against mine.

Ian swept me away with his intensity. My fingers threaded through his silvering hair and anchored him in place as surely as the arms around my waist held me to his military-honed physique. Years after his retirement, he was still built like a soldier at the peak of his career.

His tongue darted between my lips, prompting me to open my mouth in acceptance. My nipples tightened beneath my strapless bra and our audience vanished from my memory. Only the tangle of our tongues mattered, along with how much I wanted to guide Ian's hand from my waist to my breasts, or better yet, to place it between my thighs where my panties dampened.

I came away from the kiss breathless and red-cheeked, the heat spreading all the way to the neckline of my dress like a badge of embarrassment for everyone to see. From the corner of my vision, I caught sight of Ian's strange champagne-colored eyes with a smirk on his face, watching me.

Seconds after we exited the courtroom, I twisted to whisper in his ear, "Did you really have to kiss me that way in front of everyone?" To keep from meeting his gaze, I smoothed the skirt of my dress and picked at a minute speck of lint.

"We certainly won't have to worry about anyone questioning the validity of our marriage now, will we?" he countered.

"Point."

"Photo time," Dani called out.

I liked Russ and Dani. They were the perfect couple, polar opposites in appearance and completely adorable. I envied her confidence as much as I was jealous of her big breasts. She'd lucked out in the curvaceous figure department with striking, proportionate measurements all around.

"You both look so cute together," Betty said.

"I—we do?" I asked, startled.

"My dear, you are always beautiful, but even my failing eyes can see you and my grandson look marvelous together."

Betty remained clueless. I had to wonder if his plan was for her benefit as much as it was to help me. At her age, she didn't have much longer to see her grandson happily married, and in a way, this made Sophia her great-granddaughter.

Prior to the wedding, I'd signed something drawn up by Ian's lawyer and faxed to us, forfeiting any and all rights to his pension, properties, and holdings. I didn't want those, and even if I did, how much of a bitch would I look for trying to steal a veteran's hard-earned savings?

At the end of the evening, after a restaurant dinner with Russ, Dani, and Betty, we all went our separate ways. I hugged Dani and Russ in the parking lot outside the restaurant then Ian and I drove Betty home.

By the time Ian had pulled into his driveway, I could barely breathe. My vision swam a little as I crossed the threshold into my new home.

"What's wrong?" Ian asked.

"Nothing. It's still hard for me to believe your living room is as big as my whole house," I confessed. The whole floor plan of my former home could be shoved into the room he dedicated to his big screen television and social furnishings. The bedrooms were as generous, providing more space than I even needed.

Ian's personal bathroom had a shower worthy of my dreams. I'd nearly chosen the downstairs bedroom by the kitchen for its personal bathroom, until Ian coaxed me to check out the entire house. I didn't regret it. It was worth sharing a restroom with the man for the umbrella shaped shower fixture. I soaked beneath it for a half hour, enjoying the luxurious spray, unrushed and without fear of the water heater crapping out.

I found Ian on the couch with his laptop and a beer in front of a movie. According to Betty, he liked to watch action flicks for background noise while working on government projects.

"Hey, finally settled?"

"I think so," I replied. Taking the seat beside him, I nestled into the couch corner and brushed out my damp hair while he fetched me a beer and snacks, too.

Some wedding night. Bride and groom retire to their honeymoon to chastely watch Liam Neeson films all night with bowls of popcorn and a goodie bag from their friends.

A wicked part of me wanted to test the boundaries of our new marriage by offering my body. I had trouble reconciling that he came into this deal without expectations of benefitting from our arrangement.

I mulled it over until the credits rolled an hour later.

"Well, I'm going to bed. G'night, Leigh."

"Night, Ian."

And then my chance was gone. The whole town probably thought we were wrapped naked around each other by now.

I stole a peek at his retreating shape when he left the room. Ian was an excellent example of a man for his age. I still couldn't believe he was fifty-three. Hell, I hadn't wanted to believe he was out of his thirties yet. He must have belonged to the same vampire club as Brad Pitt, Johnny Depp, and Keanu Reeves. In each of his pictures — there were many framed photographs of him receiving some medal or another — he looked exactly the same except touches of silver in his dark hair grew more prominent over the years.

My own personal Dorian Grey, unaging and beautiful.

"If you need anything, you know where to find me," he called back from the stairs.

"Okay."

I remained on the sofa long after Ian left, feeling cold and numb all the way to the tips of my toes. The day's events instilled a surreal sense of disbelief, and I found myself waiting to awaken from the dream.

To prepare myself for the difficult day ahead of me, I set my alarm for an ungodly hour and lay down in my bed to sleep. It wasn't like the neighborhood where I'd lived, where the gangbangers drove their cars at all hours of the night, bass thumping from their trunks. The silence unnerved me and made it difficult to sleep.

When I awakened in the unfamiliar bedroom, my eyes blinked open to gradually adjust to the shaded interior. There weren't any water stains or cracks in the ceiling, and no fear of the roaches crawling over me in my sleep. This was home, and I had every reason to be grateful to my savior.

Once I made the bed and parted the blackout curtains, I washed my face and shuffled into the kitchen to find Ian had beat me to the punch. I'd thought I would surprise him with bacon and eggs, but I found the man in his flannel pants with a mixing bowl of pancake batter.

"Well shit," I muttered. "How are you awake already?"

He twisted around to look at me and grinned. "The early bird gets the worm."

"Uh huh."

"How'd you sleep?"

"Lousy," I answered honestly. I plucked a banana from the fruit bowl and busied myself with peeling it to avoid prolonged eye contact with the sexy soldier at the stove. His navy blue tee clung to him so snugly he may as well have gone without it. I could see every muscle through the tightly stretched cotton. I wanted to *touch* every muscle, too.

"Do you mind if I make coffee," I asked.

"Coffee sounds great. There should be some ground beans left in the fridge, and the maker is at the end of the counter in the bottom cabinet."

Leftovers made up the bulk of his food stock, as well as a near empty gallon of milk, bottled beer, and a sack of apples. I found the coffee beans behind an unopened ketchup bottle in the door compartment.

"What is going on with this kitchen?" I finally demanded.

"Huh?"

I don't know what came over me, but I began removing things from cabinets and setting them on the counter. The man's kitchen was a disorganized mess of misplaced goods I began tidying on a whim.

"Needs a spice rack."

My confused new roomie turned to look at me. His brows raised.

"I mean, nothing in here makes sense. There's no flow," I said.

All of his pots and pans were at the opposite end of the kitchen away from the stove, and cooking utensils were scattered across several drawers, as if he tossed them in whichever was closest to hand at the time. I discovered pantry items in cabinets with the bowls or tucked away wherever there was room.

"Peanut butter with the plates," I muttered in disbelief.

"That bad, huh?"

My hand froze on the offensive sandwich spread jar. "I'm sorry," I blurted out right away. "I didn't mean to be bitchy or seem like I don't appreciate what you're doing for me, 'cause I do. I just thought—"

"Nah, it's okay. It's your kitchen too, now." Grinning the whole while, Ian gave me this boyish, heart-melting shrug like I'd embarrassed him. It was the one time when his crow's feet showed, and even then, they were only a few faint lines at the corners of his eyes.

He served me a breakfast of chocolate chip pancakes and maple syrup, but the irregular size of the chocolate pieces led me to think he'd broken up a candy bar. A glance at the wrapper in the trash confirmed my theory.

"You went out of your way for me," I said in a conversational tone once my plate was clean. He moved to rise, so I leapt from the chair to beat him to the punch, collecting the empty plates from the table. He chuckled and offered me the last sausage link from his plate. I was too ravenous to turn it down.

"I want you to feel comfortable here," he pointed out as he helped load the dishwasher, or at least tried to. My competitive spirit forced me to hip bump him out of my way. "Feel free to change anything else you'd like if it'll make you feel comfortable. There's going to be social workers in and out of this place for a while, I guess, so." He leaned against the counter, fixing his pale eyes on me. "It needs to feel like a home and not a bachelor pigsty."

"It's not a pigsty," I blurted, quickly jumping to his defense.

"It's not exactly a place for a baby either. We can remedy that after the weekend when you're up for it. I'll withdraw some cash for now, but Monday I'll call my banker up and get a monthly allowance deposited into an extra account for you."

With the dishwasher filled, I returned to rearranging the clean plates and plastic cups. I'd expected a rich bachelor like him to live like a movie star inside his home not a frat boy in his first apartment. "Allowance?"

"I'll start you off with a couple grand to spend on this place. After that we need… you need to get some more clothes. Appropriate clothes," he muttered, seeming to speak to himself more than he was talking to me.

"What's wrong with my clothes?"

"You wear them till they're worn thin, sweetie," he pointed out, gentle as ever and aware of my embarrassment. "Look, your sleeve has a hole at the elbow."

Heat crept up my neck and into my cheeks, but I wasn't sure if it was caused by his words or because he'd moved in close. His hands smoothed up my arms, over the threadbare sleeves of my shirt.

I wanted to kiss him. I wanted him to grab me like he did in front of the judge and prove our marriage wasn't a mere convenience or act of benevolence. Most of all, I wanted to forget my ex-boyfriend and the father of my child would be put to rest in the town cemetery, closing the worst chapter of my life for good.

"You should pick Sophia out some pretty new clothes, too. Monday, we'll stop by Social Security to get your name changed then the DMV for your driver's license update."

"Ian?"

"Hm?"

One step forward placed me in his personal space, allowing me to loop one arm around his shoulders. I didn't need to stand on tiptoe since we were almost the same height.

"Thank you."

Before my nerves failed me, I leaned in and slanted my mouth over his. Ian's firm lips parted at the questing sweep from my tongue, and the next moments were dedicated to shared exploration rather than a forceful invasion. Our kiss was unbridled passion and longing, a hunger nurtured by weeks of mutual attraction rather than a sudden flash of lust. Orange juice flavored his tongue, the perfect accompaniment to the sweetness of feeling his mouth against mine.

I learned more about Ian MacArthur in the thirty seconds of our embrace than I did since our meeting on my doorstep. He became more frenzied, desperate, dragging me in by a hand molded to my ass. The close quarters exposed me to his erection, stiff and unyielding where we trapped it between our bodies, prompting me to wiggle just enough to stir a moan out of him. It was an empowering change of pace from the way I usually felt about myself.

Ian did find me attractive. He did want me, and maybe I wasn't fooling myself if I dreamed of a future with him beyond our agreement.

His sigh clenched my belly as he squeezed my ass one last time. "We better get ready for the funeral. I told the Jameses we'd be there early to help out at the wake."

Are we not going to talk about sucking face in your kitchen? His cavalier attitude sort of peeved me until I looked down and saw a hard-on tenting his pants.

"Right. I'll just go get ready then." And take care of the ache between my thighs while I was at it. Living with a sexy man was going to be its own sort of trial until we figured out where to take our marriage.

Chapter Eight

~IAN~

I don't know what came over Leigh, but I liked it and wished I'd handled the aftermath with more dignity. We dressed in our funeral attire and made the drive to the James residence before noon, where the bustling household had filled with mourners. Cars filled the street, parked up and down the block on both sides of the road. We had to park at the corner and walk back.

"What if everyone looks at me crazy?" Leigh asked.

"We'll do it back to them. I'll have you know my experience as a military officer grants me the ability to pull off insane very well."

Her giggle warmed my spirit, and in return, I tried to give her the strength to make it through her day. We ascended the walking path to the front door hand in hand, putting on a front as a happy, newlywed couple. Leigh squeezed my fingers until my hand tingled from the loss of circulation.

The entire house silenced, save for Sophia's fussy squalling. I felt like a character in an awkward romantic comedy, waiting for the punch line to the joke or for the audience to laugh. All eyes turned to us and while a pervading sense of tension made me regret the offer to arrive early to provide support.

"Leigh! Ian, thank you for coming." Gloria limped to us with Sophia cradled on her right side, only to pass the infant to me and throw her arms around Leigh. She was the very model of acceptance and love, startling me as much as my wife.

My wife. The strange reality of it hadn't yet sunk in until I held her child against me. Sophia had ceased fussing almost immediately. Held securely in my arms, she looked up at me with curiosity and waved her chubby little fists.

I offered to drive to the cemetery and the Jameses accepted with grace and gratitude. To my surprise, the small and tasteful service was well attended as if Dennis James hadn't been a petty thug and drug dealer. Maybe he had been more at one point in his life, but I had trouble seeing beyond the mess he left behind.

Thank you, I thought. *Thank you for leaving me this wonderful woman and beautiful child.*

With Sophia in her lap, Leigh sat beside Gloria and held the woman's hand while I stood behind them resting my hands on Leigh's shoulders. When the coffin was lowered and the service was over, we returned to the James residence for a repast with the close friends and family.

"Hold Sophia for me, Ian?" Leigh asked me.

"Sure. Pass her over."

While Leigh helped in the kitchen, I walked Sophia around and tried to socialize with mourners.

"Hello, Mr. MacArthur. I guess the new marriage means you'll be in town for a time, eh?"

I turned around to face a graying man ten years my senior. I smiled at the old war veteran. "I told you last time we talked, Ian's fine. And yeah, I suppose I'll be around for a good while now. I usually only take a few government contracts a year, if I can help it."

I knew Henry Banks from taking my grandmother to bingo at the VFW Hall a few times a month. When I wasn't around, he often did it.

"How's Betty?"

"She's doing well. Why don't you stop by and see her?" I encouraged him.

As we lapsed into talk about my grandmother, a crowd of ladies surrounded me to see the deceased's daughter. She was passed from arm to arm and loved by many.

"She's going to have his eyes," one woman said with admiration as she passed the baby back to me. I had no idea where she drew that conclusion. Sophia had Leigh's eyes without a chance of them being brown.

"I suppose we'll see soon enough," I replied, neutral and cordial all at once.

We blew off church the next day since Gram was feeling under the weather. Leigh and I checked in on her for a time, and then on Monday, I coerced my wife to take my Escalade to town for a shopping trip and to fetch groceries for Gram. While she was gone, I walked the half mile to Russ' house at the end of the dirt road. A long time ago, when I was barely an adult, I'd built the cabin to be close to

Gram when she denied my request to move in with her after boot camp.

A young man needed his space, she'd said. Years later, when loneliness drove her to move closer to town to be in the community, she gave my childhood home to me and told me to do as I pleased.

So I rented it out to Daniela Reyes, and in doing so, introduced her to the love of her life and my best friend.

Russ passed me off another bottle of Shiner while Dani tended the grill for a reversal of roles. Watching my pal's mate flounder as he called out suggestions was better than most television shows.

"So, what's the latest news? I've missed a lot between the wedding and the funeral."

"Well, Dani was down at the feed store fetching some oats for Daisy when she overheard a couple of the guys gossiping on the sidewalk over a game of checkers. They're saying drug problems out in town are worse than ever."

"It's true. I had a flight over town a month ago and saw all kinds of crap. Mostly weed and small time dealing. What did she hear?" I brought the cool beer to my lips for a swig and listened. As a consistent resident for the past three years, Russ knew more about the local community than I did.

"Crack. Methamphetamine. Apparently drug dealers are cooking meth out in the boondocks. I'm pretty sure I caught a whiff of something the other day, too."

"Out here?" I jerked up straight in my seat and stared at him. "Aw shit. Here I thought it was limited to a bunch of kids dealing weed or prescription pharm they stole from their grandparents."

"Well, they've graduated to making meth labs in shacks," Russ said bluntly.

I grimaced. His news robbed me of the taste for my beer.

"Are the police doing anything about it?"

"They're a five-man police force, Ian. What do you think?"

"Six if you include Chief Montgomery. Not enough to take down a drug ring on their own." Ideas manifested in my head.

"Oh no. No, no, no, man. I know that look on your face. I know when you're up to no good. We're not a two-man SWAT team. We're not police investigators or whatever you'd call the drug folk—"

"The DEA," I chipped in to be helpful. Russell growled and shot a dirty look at me.

"Either way, we're not them. We're military operatives currently enjoying some relaxation from our last job fighting insurgents."

"You live here too, Russ. You think Dani wants to pick up and leave?"

"I really don't," Dani called from the grill.

Russ' consternation failed to wipe the smug look off my face. I knew I had him from the moment his girlfriend stepped over to join us and turned her brown eyes his way.

"Russ, I love living out here. Remember the murder in town we heard about a month ago? It was drug related. Safety and security is the whole reason people move to small towns like this. We leave the cities like Houston behind to be *safe*." Dani shivered. She kept a couple guns of her own in their house, and boy did she know how to use them, but it didn't change that our peaceful community had transformed.

"Fine. I'll do some sniffing around when I'm in town too," the disgruntled bear shifter agreed.

"Why don't you do something about it, Ian? You're skilled. You have decades of leadership under your belt," Dani suggested.

"I'm skilled at military command, sweetheart. What are you suggesting for me to do with it?"

"Well, I heard that Sheriff Vasco doesn't plan to run again. He's going to retire."

I stared at her. "Why didn't I think of that?" Russ had invited me to join the volunteer fire department weeks ago, and I'd told him I would consider it. Becoming Sheriff MacArthur would allow me to help even more people.

Dani grinned and lingered near Russ to tousle his hair. "Give it some serious thought at least. So how's Leigh? I thought she could use a friend and maybe I'd stop over to talk to her some."

I shook my head. "She's handling it all okay, but you'll have to wait. I sent her out to go shopping since the social worker plans to officially return Sophia to us today."

"You're letting her drive *your* vehicle?" Russ stared as if the shocking news was on par with letting her run free with my bank account.

"Yes. She's a grown woman. If I don't show she can be trusted, why should anyone else believe it?"

"Hey, darlin'? Would you go see where Trigger got off to?"

Dani arched one of her dark brows at Russ. She didn't fall for his excuse to get rid of her, but she humored him by walking away from the deck and into the grass, whistling a few times.

I knew the question was coming before it even left my pal's lips.

"Did you bond fully with her yet?"

"Not yet. Ever since my eagle recognized her I can't get her off my mind. The more I do for her, the deeper it pulls me in. I wanna tear the clothes off her most days, but she's in no shape to be feeling that kind of way."

Russ nodded. "It's like when she's hurtin', you're drowning in her pain, and her happiness is the only thing that can help you to breathe again."

"*Yes.*" I sagged into the seat and let out a frustrated groan.

"It's about time, old man. Revel in it and be happy you found her."

"Yeah. You're right. Maybe it's about time I told her what I am, too. I gotta let her know it isn't about wanting to get her on her feet anymore."

I needed to let her know we were soul mates.

~LEIGH~

Dad and I used to joke about Target being a middle-class Wal-Mart. Growing up the only child of a widower made me close to him, and in the final weeks of his life, I'd never felt more lonely. I should have realized it was time to cut Dennis loose from my life when he didn't try to help me through my grief, but if I had, I wouldn't have Sophia. She was my bright star and the one accident in my life I didn't regret.

I stared at the condoms on the shelf. We weren't using protection when we conceived Sophia, and I was sure we were both high when it happened anyway. Sex with Ian was inevitable in our near future. I knew we both wanted it, and it had to be safe between us.

I blindly grabbed a box and stuffed them beneath a box of diapers. After a few steps down the aisle, I considered my memory of Saturday morning. I scurried back to the display and swapped them for the larger size.

A stop at Redbox on the way home yielded a newly released horror movie from some big Hollywood studio with a monstrous special effects budget. After a few days of Ian's spy thrillers, I needed a break.

I wasn't the type to conduct frivolous shopping sprees. Ian had another plan and forbid me to return until I spent at least a grand. He claimed it would distract me until my 4 p.m. appointment with the social worker. With a trunk load of groceries and new clothes, I pulled into the drive an hour prior to the lady's expected arrival.

"Do you need help?" Ian called from the door.

"Yes, please."

We unpacked it all in record time. I'd run every kind of errand imaginable from visiting government offices to following up at the bank to finish paperwork for my new account.

The doorbell rang after I put the fresh crib sheet on Sophia's mattress. I beat Ian to the door and came face to face with the social worker charged with my case.

"Good afternoon, Mrs. MacArthur. Someone here is very thrilled to see you."

Eager to hold her again, I reached out and took my daughter from the caseworker. The woman entered after I stepped back to make room. I struggled to maintain my emotions and failed, tears sliding freely down my face no matter how I tried to keep them in.

"Thank you."

"You don't need to thank me, Mrs. MacArthur. You fulfilled the court's obligations."

At some point, I'd ceased to exist as merely 'Leigh' and had become the responsible and respectable Mrs. MacArthur.

"Is there something for me to sign?" I asked.

"No," she assured me. "You'll find everything has been handled regarding this matter. Enjoy your life with Sophia. I'm proud of you for coming so far."

"Thank you," I whispered again. I touched my cheek to the top of Sophia's curls and closed my eyes before sinking to the couch. We lay on the sofa and snuggled until Sophia's belly made her kick and squirm with hunger. The rest of my evening with her passed like a dream. She ate and received a bath before I dressed her in a pink onesie I'd washed the previous day. After a few soft coos and a cherubic smile, my baby fell asleep without a fuss.

I could have stood beside her crib watching her sleep for hours, but I rewarded myself for a job well done by unwinding with a cup of yogurt and a movie. Ian settled beside me as I pressed play. My dog lifted her head to look at Ian then collapsed into her bed again, too tired to approach for ear scratches. She had settled by my feet between the couch and Daddy's old coffee table. Ian leaned down to rub her.

"Where have you been all evening?" I asked.

"I thought I'd give you some space to be with Sophia. How's she liking it here so far?"

"She's a baby, silly. She'll like anywhere as long as she's dry, warm, and has a full tummy."

Ian chuckled. "Then maybe I should ask how her mama likes it here."

"Her mama loves it here," I replied. I pressed a few buttons and skipped to the main feature. Ian didn't budge from beside me. "I thought you hated horror movies."

"I like them from time to time." In other words, he didn't want to make me sit downstairs alone.

"You don't *have* to babysit me every night, Ian. I'm fine. I can watch a movie on my own."

Hurt flashed in his eyes. *Crap.* I swore internally at myself a few times for my poorly worded dismissal. "Ian, I'm sorry. I mean you don't have to feel responsible for entertaining me every night on top of everything else you've done."

"It's fine," he assured me. "I'm not your chaperone." The man rose from his seat despite my clumsy protests and apologies. He took his unfinished beer with him.

"Honestly, Ian, you're welcome to stay. You don't have to leave on my account."

His crooked, half-hearted smile didn't assuage my guilt. If anything, I was even more of a jerk for chasing him out of his own living room. "I have to leave early in the morning for work related stuff anyway. I really should get to sleep."

Long after he left, I still felt like an ungrateful bitch for chasing him off. Ian was a good man who deserved a lot better than what I gave him in return. I watched the rest of the movie without receiving any actual satisfaction then took a hot shower to ease my nerves. I soaked beneath the steady spray for longer than necessary then retired to my bedroom. Restless, I spent the next hours tossing and turning in bed.

No matter how long I tried, my conscience wouldn't allow me to sleep. I didn't want him to go away on one of his trips before I had the chance to apologize again.

There was no telling if he'd come back at all. With his dangerous career, anything could happen and I'd receive a knock on our door one day to see a uniformed soldier on the porch. He'd share his bad news, telling me my new husband wouldn't be coming home. Then

I'd be a widow who regretted the last thing I said to my best friend was that he didn't need to babysit me.

Without another thought, I slipped from my bed and hurried across the hall into his room. He slept with his door open, the lights off, and the parted curtains allowed pale silver moonlight to shine over the large bed. His chest rose and fell with the even breathing rhythm of a deep sleep, so peaceful in his expression I hated to wake him at all.

"Ian?" I whispered in the dark as I laid my fingers over his bare arm. He was a slim man, but his build and preferred style of clothing painted a deceptive picture, concealing the muscles beneath.

The ground flew out from beneath me as I tumbled through the air. I hit the mattress beside him with the wind knocked from my lungs, his thick bicep across my neck. I couldn't even squeak, let alone scream. My hair fanned across his second pillow as the cool, untouched side of the bed cradled me. Somewhere in the back of my mind, beneath the absolute terror of course, I realized he had the softest mattress I'd ever felt.

"Leigh?" The pressure eased from my throat then rose completely away. "What the hell, woman? Are you all right? Did I hurt you?"

"No. You gave my heart a workout, but I'll survive it. I think." I hoped. I knew for damn sure the stiff object against my hip wasn't a gun.

"What's wrong? Why are you here at—" he glanced at the digital readout from the alarm on his bedside table "—almost midnight."

"I couldn't sleep, and I knew if I didn't come talk to you now, I might not have the chance until your business is settled and you come home and… that could be days from now." He'd warned me sometimes his contracts could take him away for a couple weeks at a time.

"I'll be back by Thursday. It's not a long trip. Mostly, I need to ask a favor from Argus, and if I don't spend the evening in San Antonio, he takes it as an insult."

He hadn't moved. Neither had the unyielding presence beneath the blanket. Only his sheets and a light comforter separated our bodies, my nightshirt shifted to an embarrassing level above my waist. He could see everything, from my chunky thighs to my plain white and blue striped cotton hipsters. At least they were brand new.

"Ian?"

Despite the darkness, I saw the way his eyes roved over me, slowly digesting my current state of undress. One of his hands gently tugged my nightshirt back into place.

"Didn't mean to scare you so bad, Leigh."

"It's okay," I whispered back. I waited for him to say something, but he never did.

His mouth crashed against mine in a sudden kiss, the lack of warning offering me no time to prepare. It took several pulse-pounding seconds until my brain caught up with my body and realized my sexy as sin phony husband was kissing *me*.

I moaned beneath his mouth and twisted to face his body completely. With a couple kicks, I managed to dislodge the blankets from beneath me until they were at the foot of the bed, confirming my suspicions. Every hard, muscled inch was exposed to my questing fingertips.

Our mouths broke apart, each of us dragging in a gulping lungful of air, but Ian didn't stop there. The scoop neckline of my shirt gave him free access to my throat. He nipped my collarbone and ran his hand over my thigh, raising goose bumps on my skin. "Are you on the pill, Leigh, because I don't have any—"

"I bought some. There's a package in my top dresser drawer."

"You bought condoms?"

"For us." His cock twitched against my hip. Apparently I'd given him the right answer, but as far as I was concerned, it was the only one.

He kissed the pounding pulse point at my throat before descending lower, reaching my left breast. His lips sealed around my nipple for a teasing suckle through the soft jersey cotton while I moaned and writhed beneath him.

"Wait for me," he whispered against my tit.

Bare as the day he was born, Ian left me behind and slipped from the room. I had the tantalizing view of his deliciously muscled naked ass, at least before he was out of sight.

While he was gone, I laid there fretting in bed, wondering what he thought of me. Each precious second played against my insecurities until he reappeared in the doorway less than a minute later. To say his absence had dulled the mood would be a lie — it worsened my anticipation. His hard cock bounced with his movements, swaying as he came to a stop beside me on the bed. Foil tore then I watched him glide the latex ring over his dick and wished I'd done it for him.

"Ian?" I murmured shyly as he lowered one knee to the bed and leaned over me. Our lips touched in another electrifying kiss.

"Shh."

My nightshirt rose a little higher until I had no choice but to raise my arms and allow him to remove it. I wore no bra beneath the cute pink and white shirt, but I trusted in the darkness to hide my imperfections and round belly from his eyes. Silver stretch marks became the most prominent across my wide hips, something I wanted to conceal from him.

Ian eased back to kneel between my legs. He clicked the light on.

"Ian?"

"I want to see you."

A euphoric tingle of pure pleasure spread across my body from head to toe until fire seemed to consume every fiber of my being. I'd never felt particularly unattractive, but motherhood had added inches to my frame. Aside from my doctor, no man had seen me unclothed since the beginning of my third trimester, before the worst of the changes transformed my body. Ian was the first to see me this way. I wanted him to be the last.

His attentive eyes infused a sense of unfamiliar vulnerability, urging a hot flush to warm my cheeks. When I blushed, my entire upper body seemed to glow with color. He peeled my panties off last, and then there was nothing else to hide.

"You're breathtaking."

"Don't lie."

"I've never told an unnecessary lie in all my life, and I wouldn't now. You're beautiful, Leigh, and I love everything about the way you look. Every inch."

He bent above my body like a worshipper attending prayer at an altar. His lips skimmed my right hip and then my left while his thumb parted my folds. A little nibble to my thigh caught me off guard as much as the pressure circling my clit. He was an expert with his hands, merciless as he teased, using his fingers and mouth. Both of my nipples had hardened to unbearably tender peaks by the time his ascending path rose from my hip to my breast.

Moaning out his name was the proper encouragement. He filled me with one finger and then a second, pumping both digits in and out of my pussy. Eight long months had passed since the last time I had sex with Sophia's father, making me starved for the intimacy promised by Ian's touch.

"Ian. Ian, please."

"I don't think you're ready for me yet." A teasing tone filled his voice, accompanied by a husky hint of laughter. I twisted beneath him and raised my hips to the rhythm he set while plunging both digits in and out of me. If I wasn't ready now, I never would be. His fingers glistened on each stroke backward.

"Ian, if you don't fuck me right now, you're going to need those special operative skills to fight me off."

"You're adorable when you threaten me." Whether intimidated or not, he acquiesced to my demands, trading his fingers for his latex sheathed dick.

I'd always been afraid sex would never be the same again, but Ian proved me wrong from the moment he began sliding into my pussy. Even soaking wet and ready for him, he was a tight fit my body struggled to accommodate. I stretched around his unyielding width and pleaded for more.

"God, you feel so sweet, Leigh," Ian breathed out. He wore an expression of immense concentration on his face.

His rhythm was slow and sensual, testing the way our bodies fit together. My nipples rubbed against his sculpted chest, tickled by the few black hairs scattered over his pecs. Over and over again, he brought our bodies together, taking me as his wife in body as well as in name. Within moments, he lost the careful composure and snapped his hips forward to bury into me full tilt. Bliss consumed me, curling my toes and making me cry out his name in a jubilant shout.

"Oh, baby. We haven't even started yet. You'll have a lot more to scream about in a minute," he promised.

I shivered beneath him in delight. My pussy clenched around his girth, a reflex brought by the sexy whisper. Ian chuckled and kissed my ear.

Ian shifted to stretch his body over mine, finding the perfect angle. With his hard muscles pillowed against my softness, I ran my fingers up and down his back and felt the way his back flexed beneath my fingers each time his body rolled forward.

With my legs around his waist, I yanked Ian in closer and rolled him beneath me. The struggle slid him from my body, but a thrust of my hips reseated Ian's cock and reintroduced us to ecstasy. Before he could try to get the upper hand again, I leaned forward to brace my weight against his shoulders and undulated my hips until he swore and his eyes rolled back in his head. I wanted to lay my own claim.

"Don't stop, baby. Fuck, Leigh, don't stop." My breasts weren't more than a handful to fill his palms, but he squeezed and kneaded them eagerly, pinching the sensitive tips between his fingers. I clenched around his girth when he sat forward to capture one between his lips.

The partial loss of his dick introduced him to my g-spot. My muscles tensed and trembled on the verge of orgasm then I slammed him home again.

"I'm close, so close, Ian."

The base of his pelvis pressed flush against my clit in an intentional grind that pushed me over the edge. My climax was a series of starburst explosions, white bliss consuming every inch of my body. I spasmed atop him and threw my head back in a soundless cry.

He pulled me down by a handful of my hair. Something about the urgency in his kiss turned me on even more. For the first time in my life, I came a second time during sex, making my legs tremble and my body lay limp against his chest.

Post-orgasm contractions rippled along his cock like aftershocks. My husband moaned against my cheek and stiffened in release.

Overwhelmed with pleasure, I barely registered he was moving me or turning off the light. He tossed the condom into the wastebasket then tugged me close. Sleep claimed Ian before I finished pulling the blanket over our bodies.

Chapter Nine

~IAN~

Leigh smelled the way I imagined an angel would smell; light and sweet with lavender undertones teasing across my senses when I awakened with her tucked beside me. After a moment of admiring her peaceful features while she slept, I disentangled from her body and crawled from the bed.

Fuck, I hated leaving her after our first night in bed. Disgruntled with my own plans, I showered and returned to my bedroom to dress. Indecision had me torn between making enough noise to awaken her on accident or intentionally rousing her for a goodbye kiss. I did neither. I clothed myself as silently as a ghost and jotted down a message on the notepad beside the bed.

Leigh,

My cell phone is the ideal way to reach me when I am away, but if technology lets us down, you're welcome to call my associate in San Antonio. It's the best way to get me if you require my immediate response for any emergency matters.

I taped a business card to the corner of the note. The matte rectangle announced the name and contact information of Argus Prescott, the alpha of San Antonio's wolf pack. He led an extravagant lifestyle afforded by old money and inherited wealth. Thanks to traffic, I arrived a little before noon.

The pack lived in the middle of nowhere far beyond the city limits in a massive, southern plantation style home. I pulled off the highway and punched a code into the security panel by the gate. Automated, heavy wrought iron gates swung open to allow me access onto a half-mile long drive. A dozen wolves — all omegas and low in the pack hierarchy — roamed freely on the grounds. Two of their gray faces watched my arrival from the bushes as I parked.

"Ian?" a feminine voice called.

My attention snapped to the opening door. It framed the youngest Prescott, Ceres, a sweet girl I'd once held on my lap as a child. She popped out onto the porch barefoot, clothed in only cutoff jeans and a sleeveless pink tank.

"Hey, sweetheart!" I greeted her.

With an excited squeal, she raced toward me across the drive. I caught my goddaughter mid-leap and swung her around in a circle while she giggled. Too much time had passed between my visits, and thanks to the obligations of my job, I'd missed out on her graduation from veterinary school.

"Uncle Ian! Why didn't you tell us you were coming?"

"Last minute plans," I told her. "I also came to the profound conclusion that I don't visit you guys enough these days now I'm back in the states for a while."

"You really don't. Come on. There's someone I want you to meet," she announced with a big smile on her face.

Her longtime friend and admirer, Thomas, met us at the door. Even though they were both just a couple years shy of thirty, I still referred to them as kids. I'd known him since he was a chunky nerd tagging along with her for ice cream during my visits. Shit, he was more ripped than me these days. Evidently, life as a werewolf agreed with him.

"Uh, Ceres, sweetheart. I know Thomas."

"But," she said while clinging to young man's brawny arm, "you don't know him as…" She raised one hand and flashed me the tattooed green and purple band around her left ring finger. Interlaced vines and tiny flowers decorated her skin. Thomas wore one in black without the flowers.

"When did that happen?"

"The tattoo or the proposal?" Thomas grinned at me.

"Both. Hell, last I knew, you were still playing hard to get while he ran in circles." A little more than a year ago, I'd chided her about making a decision. It wasn't right to lead a man on or to play games until he changed.

"I took her a week ago for the tattoo, but I asked over the summer. Now they're driving me crazy with wedding plans," Thomas explained.

"Don't envy you, man." I dodged a bullet by marrying Leigh in front of a magistrate in a courthouse.

"The wedding is this spring, and I want you to be there," Ceres said.

"Of course I'll be there."

"Tommy, would you let Dad know Uncle Ian is here?"

"Sure."

As he loped out of sight to inform the head of the house about my arrival, Ceres turned to me and punched me sharply in the shoulder.

"Fuck! What'd you do that for?"

She took my left hand and gestured to the plain titanium band. "Why wasn't I invited? Was it a private ceremony? Who is she… or he?" Her green eyes grew a little wider, as if all of the pieces had finally fallen together. "Oh, my God, who is he, Uncle Ian? When do I get to meet him? Did you finally get married since it's legal now?"

"I'm not gay."

"Oh… awkward." She pressed her bare toes against the marble floor and cleared her throat. "Well, you never dated anyone that we've seen. Sorry," she babbled out.

"So you thought I was gay?" Torn between horror and laughter, I settled on a grin. "There's nothing wrong with being gay, but I'm sorry to disappoint you, sweetie. I'm straight."

"So who is she? What's her name?"

"Her name is Leigh."

Ceres perked up a little. She leaned in close again, all in my space, and sniffed my shirt in a way reminiscent of a dog. I used to think it was cute when she'd do it as a child, and it hadn't changed. "Human? I smell her on your clothes. She smells like cookies. Oh, come on, Uncle Ian. This isn't one of your cases in Saudi Arabia or whatever, can't you tell me something?"

I sighed. "I knew you'd give me the fifth degree, and I'm absolutely prepared to answer a thousand questions once I've talked to your dad."

"And rehearsed your story," she said. Argus stepped into view with Thomas alongside him. "Hi, Daddy."

His arrival saved me from a full-blown interrogation.

"Ian," Argus greeted me with warmth. "You don't normally visit in person unless you need something important, old friend. What's the problem this time?"

"Argus, you wound me. Didn't we help you when those hunters were calling for open season on wolves?"

"You did, and we're grateful for it, which is why I'm not plucking your feathers and throwing you out my door. You came in the middle of a busy time for us."

I grinned. Every time was a busy time for the wolves who had their fingers in more environmental protection ventures than I could count. Argus was a banker by career — my personal banker *and* lawyer. Whenever I needed something, I usually phoned in requests or sent them by fax. For the big stuff beyond his profession, I visited him in person.

"I need some of your wolves to do a sweep in the woods. Just some tracking work, nothing too big. If you think they'll spare someone, I'll need a raven or two for aerial surveillance. I'll need them for about a week, and I'll pay all of them well for their time."

Ravens and wolves worked closely together. Their symbiotic alliance meant one was never far from the other. Where a wolf pack existed, ravens usually made their roost in a nearby town.

"Whoa, whoa, whoa. Hold it. Ravens too? What the hell's happening?"

We went into Argus' personal office and discussed everything. I held no details back from my friend and painted a perfect picture of the drug problem creeping into Quickdraw. He listened and took notes, occasionally interrupting me to ask another question.

"Do you believe the town police are involved?"

"Not all of them. At least a few are on the up and up, but I'm concerned about the police chief's tendency to sweep things under the rug. I don't trust him."

"We'd better get Thomas in here then since he leads the second pack. We'll need a couple of his wolves."

"Thomas?"

"Yes. We've grown enough recently to require dividing our numbers." Argus dropped his gaze to the titanium ring on my finger. "Why didn't you bring your new wife with you?"

I imagined a dozen wolves greeting her with doggy kisses and wagging tails. Smirking, I suppressed the urge to laugh out loud at the ridiculous imagery filling my head. "She doesn't exactly know about all of this yet."

"Good luck. We recently brought a human into the fold, so I understand the challenge."

Once he called Thomas into the room, the three of us drew out our battle plans for Quickdraw. The younger alpha made arrangements with two of his friends from the raven clan to keep their schedules open in the coming weeks then promised his own help when needed.

Later, a chat over drinks allowed all of us to catch up on each other's lives.

Argus was newly single after thirty years of marriage, but he looked forward to the upcoming wedding of his only child. Eager as ever to share with me, Ceres revealed more about the upcoming wedding.

"You're really going to love our fiancée, Emma. She's a sweetheart. You guys can tell each other stories from your tribes!"

"Huh? What do you mean there's a second bride?" My eyes bugged out despite my effort to keep a straight face.

"Because Tommy was born human, we have a third fated mate," Ceres explained. "And maybe if you would bring your ass here to see us more often, you'll get to meet her."

Unlike other shifters, werewolves had the unusual ability to transform normal people during the full moon. As a former human, Thomas had what we called a split soul. His human half and feral half would always be at constant war. "So which one of you goes on the books?"

Ceres raised her hand and grinned. "I'll be the legal wife. We plan to visit the courthouse a couple days prior then do the big ceremony here at Dad's place with the three of us."

"I don't know whether to call you a lucky bastard or to feel pity for you," I said to Thomas. Multiple life mates could be a typical part of life for some shifters, especially those who participated in pack or herd life. Lioness shifters like my friend Sasha were often four or five women to a single exhausted, overworked man.

"I value my life, so I'll say lucky," Thomas replied. "They like to talk a lot, and I wouldn't survive the night if I said otherwise."

Ceres shot him a dirty look. "Okay, enough about us, Uncle Ian. What about you? How'd you meet her? What's she like? Do you have a photo of her? Is she on Facebook? Oh, my God, can I go friend her?" Ceres fired one question after the next.

"Here. She doesn't do social media, but I have this photo of her and the kid." I passed my cell phone to her. I'd snapped the photo of Leigh and Sophia's reunion when the social worker brought her by.

"She's so cute!" Ceres squealed over Sophia's picture. "And I love Leigh's hair. Oh, please, you have to bring her out for a visit. She, Emma, and I would have so much fun."

"Soon, sweetie, I promise. I have to take care of some things first." I caught them up on the recent business with Leigh only recently regaining full custody of her child.

"You married her because she kicked her drug problem and needed help?" Thomas clarified, raising his brows.

"I think it's sweet," Ceres said before elbowing him. "Don't listen to Tommy. Bring her back next time so all of us can meet her, Uncle Ian. Please? I promise we'll tell the omegas to keep out of sight, and we'll all do our best to pretend to be human. I mean, unless you do choose to tell her."

"I've given it some serious consideration. She's smart, and she'll begin noticing things eventually. I can't risk her finding out some other way, like the incident with Russ and Dani."

Argus winced. "Yeah. Sounds like you're making the right choice."

After dinner, the kids split and went back to their own home. I hung around with Argus for a while longer then eventually retired to the guest room where I dropped onto the edge of the bed. My silent cell phone taunted me. Not a single call from Leigh. I bit the bullet and phoned her instead.

What am I doing? She's not a child. She can fend for herself now, and she's more than proven she isn't the same drug-dependent woman. She doesn't need me checking in on her.

But I wanted to hear her voice. The call wasn't to check up on her — it was purely for me. I dialed my house line and waited with my breath held until she picked up the phone on the third ring.

"MacArthur residence." She sounded out of breath, winded like she'd sprinted for the line.

"Hi, Leigh. Are you okay?"

"Was exercising. One sec."

"Why are you exercising?"

There was a pause on her end of the line, then a quiet, nervous laugh. "I just felt like exercising."

Is she doing it for me? A cocky little voice whispered in my mind, bringing a smug smile to my face. "I think you're perfect just the way you are."

Leigh didn't answer right away. I pictured her with a rosy flush on her face. "Anyway, I hope you didn't call earlier and I missed it. Daniela invited me over for dinner."

"Why don't you go and buy a cell phone," I encouraged her.

"I didn't want to waste money. You were so generous and the amount you gave me was enough to cover the household needs. It just seemed stupid to get a cell phone, too."

"It's not a waste. You have Sophia with you and you'll be driving places for Gram and yourself. We'll have a line added to my plan."

"I don't know, Ian—"

"I insist. It's a smart purchase. How's Sophia by the way?"

"She's great. Your grandmother complained about you leaving again. She thinks since you've retired you shouldn't be doing these jobs anymore."

"Don't listen to her, especially since this job has nothing to do with the government or our military. I'm visiting a friend to discuss some important business negotiations, and they sort of sweet-talked me into bringing you along next time," I said.

"Really?"

"Really. My goddaughter, Ceres, is planning to be married in the spring, so we're both invited. Fair warning: she's incredibly excited about meeting you and thought I was gay until now."

A moment of stunned silence was followed by the cutest peal of giggles I'd ever heard.

"You definitely aren't gay," Leigh said. I pictured her blushing red and heard it in her voice. When I got home, we'd have to talk about the night we shared together and which direction it would take our blossoming relationship. It was imperative for her to understand it wasn't a one-night thing, unless of course, she wanted it to be.

I hoped she didn't want that to be the end of it.

"Anyway, I'm leaving sometime in the morning and should be home by lunch time unless I hit some serious traffic on I-45."

"I'll have lunch waiting for you."

I wished her a good night and ended the call after she bid me to have the same. As I settled down for bed, my confession to Leigh remained on my mind. It couldn't wait another day.

Chapter Ten

~LEIGH~

Ian returned around noon from his trip to San Antonio as I was completing a few household chores. Petunia barked loudly to announce his SUV pulling into the driveway.

"Wow. It looks great in here. You were busy while I was gone."

"I wanted it to be spotless when you came home. I even cleaned the fan blades. You're just on time, too. The pizza delivery man left right before you pulled in."

He opened the box and whistled. "Sausage and mushroom. You ordered my favorite. Wanna eat on the deck?"

"Yes!" I shouted it a little too enthusiastically. His curious glance and raised brows brought heat to my cheeks.

"You look great when you blush."

Emboldened by the affection in Ian's sunlight-colored eyes, I stepped forward to touch his face, tracing my index finger down his jaw and over the soft scruff he never seemed to shave. He had traces of silver in his beard I hadn't noticed before. It suited him, adding a hint of contrasting maturity to his striking features.

Turning his head, he brushed his lips against my fingers. My belly clenched as if he'd kissed me between my thighs. "We should eat before the food gets cold."

"Or before Sophia wakes up," I added.

Ian moved the pizza and breadsticks while I carried the lemonade pitcher and our glasses. We settled on the deck with the baby monitor close at hand and enjoyed the cool autumn breeze snaking in between the trees to dishevel my bangs. The sweet scent of earth and woods surrounded us, blended with fragrant pizza sauce and garlic bread sticks.

We chowed down and shared friendly conversation about his day with his old friend and my evening out with the neighbors. I didn't do long distance drives well and always fell asleep, so I admired his ability to make the five hour trek in high spirits. I couldn't wait to return with him.

"Leigh?"

"Hmm?" I had so much food in me, the only thing able to improve my day would be a nap stretched out in Ian's massive feather-soft bed.

Ian's expression changed, taking on a worried appearance. His brows creased, alerting me to something heavy on his mind. Our short friendship and even shorter marriage didn't hamper my ability to read him like an open book.

"What is it?"

"I decided to run for sheriff in the next election." The apprehensive expression remained.

"Won't you have to be here a lot if you run for sheriff, Ian? I thought you liked going away with your squad and taking up your government contracts."

"I do," he said. "And I can still do that, it just won't be as often as it used to be." I wanted to leave my seat to rub his tense shoulders. "But I want to do something for this area besides throwing my money around at people. Sophia deserves to grow up somewhere safe. To be honest, when I married you, I knew then I'd be cutting back on the work I do."

"This is great news!" I leaned out of my seat to throw my arms around his neck and kiss his cheek. "People around here respect you. You'd make a great sheriff."

"That's not everything. We need to discuss one more thing first. There's something I want to show you… and I know it's going to seem crazy, but I need you to have an open mind." He returned my embrace then ran his fingers through my hair, smoothing strands back from my face.

I raised my brows. His pale, champagne colored eyes watched me closely. "Okay? Ian, you're driving me crazy with this somber mood. Just tell me everything."

"The thing I need to show you has an incredible amount of importance for me, Leigh. I need to know I can trust you to keep this to yourself, because it affects more than me."

Was he going to let me in on something related to one of his top-secret government jobs? My pulse sped and my mouth went dry, prompting me to pour another glass of lavender lemonade from the pitcher. I sipped it nervously and cleared my throat before answering him. "Ian, I'll keep any secret you want me to keep. What's wrong?"

"I think it'll be easier if I show you first. Then we can talk about it."

Ian rose from his seat and pulled off his shirt, in the sexy way where guys grabbed a t-shirt by the back of the collar.

"Are you giving me a strip tease? You didn't get a tramp stamp of my name or something while away, did you?" I tried to ease the tension with some humor, sensing he needed it as much as I did.

Ian chuckled nervously and unfastened his jeans. I sat up straighter in the chair and stared at him. My child napped indoors, tucked safe and sound in her crib with a monitor on the table beside it, so if Ian was fishing for sex, he'd picked an excellent time for a second intimate encounter.

"Ian?"

His pants dropped and his boxers followed. He was perfect from head to toe, the very idea of masculinity. Because hard muscle and a lean build made his age indeterminable, I wouldn't have guessed my husband to be a day over thirty-five, despite the generous amount of silver in his dark hair. Ian's youthful features contradicted the loss of his chestnut brown coloring.

I lost the battle against my willpower and let my eyes drop below his waist. Even in its unaroused state, his cock was nearly as large as some of the guys I'd dated in the past when erect.

"Just remember it's me. Don't freak."

"Ian, I'm not going to freak because a hot naked man is standing in front of me. I'm freaking because you're being mysterious. What are you—?"

Ian's slim body contorted and a loud, cracking sound filled the air. A tiny shriek ripped from my throat. Before my eyes, he jerked one direction and shrank as a rush of ivory and brown plumage materialized into being. It may have all happened in a split second, but for me, it lasted an eternity. Ian wasn't there anymore; in his place, a proud American bald eagle stood on the wood patio deck. The eagle I touched in my very own yard less than six weeks ago.

When the raptor came closer to me, I slammed against the bricks beside the patio door. At some point, I must have leapt from my seat and stumbled against the back of the house.

It's Ian. I tried to tell myself it was Ian. The bird hadn't spirited him away, and he hadn't pulled a disappearing act worthy of Houdini. The bird *was* him. I leaned against the house until the threat of fainting was long over. My bird was him.

My heart leapt into my throat. Speaking became difficult, like a fist clenched my neck.

"Ian?" I whispered.

The bird tilted his head. They had the same gorgeous eyes, a too pale shade reminiscent of rose gold. How had I never drawn the comparison until now?

My racing pulse demanded for me to run, but the sensible part of me saw the man beneath the feathers and knew he'd never hurt me. Fighting against instinct, I crouched low and raised one trembling hand to the top of the eagle's head. I stroked him then let my fingers travel lower until I petted the silky feathers covering his breast.

"You're so… so gorgeous. I don't understand." I felt dizzy again. "I need to sit down. I need to sit down."

Ian was Ian again, a man crouching with me, his strong hands on my shoulders steadying me. Speechless, I couldn't even make lame come-ons or joke about his nudity.

"I'm a shapeshifter, Leigh.

"Not possible. *This* isn't possible." It became a struggle to control my breathing, and I was in danger of hyperventilating. Quick intakes of air whistled in and out of my lungs. "I am dreaming. Any minute I am going to wake up because you're walking through the front door and I've been asleep on the couch taking a nap."

"I knew from the moment I first saw you, that you were the woman I wanted. Because I'm a shifter and because I've been drawn to you. You met me once like this Leigh, because I wanted to see you again after I took you home."

The light-headed feeling didn't abate. When I wobbled again, Ian coaxed me to sit on the deck. I'd recently swept it clean of leaves and debris at least. "Like love at first sight?" It was hard having a conversation with a naked person, harder when the naked person had transformed from the shape of a bird.

"Sort of. You could call it such, I guess. I could have resisted if I wanted to, but the thing is, Leigh, I didn't. When I saw the way the people at church treated you, I couldn't let it pass."

"So you helped me because of what?"

"Because no one deserves to be treated that way, Leigh. Hell, I'd have stepped in for anyone, but finding you at the same time…" He sighed. "Come on. Let's get you off the ground."

Ian helped me up to my feet, but I stumbled against him and into his hard body. His strong arms surrounded me without hesitation.

"What's this mean, Ian? For me and Sophia. For… us."

"It means I don't only want you for a year, or until you're out of school and on your feet, Leigh. I want you for the rest of my life, for as long as you'll have me. I never intended to let you go without a fight. When I married you, I hoped you'd eventually come to want me, too."

And then I had visited his room in the middle of the night. I trembled, distracted by the memory of his lips against mine. I wanted to be afraid. I wanted to be terrified of a man who could turn into a wild animal in the span of a second, but in my heart, I knew he was the same Ian who rescued me from my shitty life decisions. Cold from the shock, I pressed closer against him to reap the benefits of his body heat.

"Are you okay, Leigh?"

"I'm fine," I whispered.

"If you want out, I'll understand."

"I didn't say that." The idea of ending it all and walking way away seemed scarier than the secret he'd revealed. I'd have to be a fool to go.

Sophia's sudden, piercing shriek interrupted our conversation. "I have to check her… um..."

"We'll finish this when you're done," Ian assured me.

I returned inside, glancing once over my shoulder to see him gathering his clothes off the deck. By the time I'd finished comforting my infant by changing a wet diaper, Ian had brought in our leftover goodies and clothed himself in his jeans. That was regrettable. We crossed paths as he exited the kitchen and moved our conversation to the living room where we settled on opposite ends of the same couch.

When Ian didn't speak first, I bit the bullet and started us off. "So… You turn into an eagle. Bet that was useful in the Air Force."

Ian's faint smile held a trace of amusement. "It was, actually. I'm the leader of a special group of individuals, each of us with a unique skill set related to our shifter traits."

"Wait a minute. Wasn't Russell in your squad? Are Dani and Russ eagles too?"

His rich, deep laughter filled the room. "No. Not eagles, sweetie. Dani is as human as you are, Leigh. My kind are incredibly rare."

Ian gave me a lot to think about and too many questions to ask at once. If Russ wasn't a human or an eagle, what was he? And had Ian settled for me due to the lack of women among his own species?

"I can see the question in your eyes. Russ is a bear."

Shit. A bear of a man and an actual bear.

"Does Dani know?" I whispered.

"Yeah, she does. Took Russ a while to tell her, though, and I didn't want to make the same mistake with you, Leigh. I wanted to tell you as soon as I knew I could trust you."

"I want to be pissed at you. I want to be so mad that you kept it from me. But another part of me wants to kiss you, because I missed you so much."

"I'll take the kisses," he offered helpfully.

So would I. We closed the distance between us at the same time, practically leaping at one another across the couch. His fingers tangled in my hair and our lips came together in a hard, bruising press. We were frenzied, as if a day apart had starved us of each other.

Ian tore away my camisole without a word. Warm sunlight spilled through the window over my bared breasts and upper body. He didn't need a bedside lamp to see me, and I didn't give a damn that he could. His mouth lowered to one nipple and then the other, delivering playful nips to the tip of each breast until they were stiffly budded peaks.

Without thinking, I snuck one hand in the waist of my pajama bottoms. I was soaked, and having Ian so close brought out the shameless side of me I never knew existed before. I circled my clit until his fingers closed around my wrist.

"You're not allowed to touch yourself," Ian whispered. His lips were at my ear, delivering a teasing nibble against my unpierced lobe.

"No? Why not?"

"Because it's *my* duty to give you pleasure, Leigh. I'm your husband."

A shiver coursed through me as Ian knelt and pulled down my capris. He tugged aside my bikini style panties before tonguing my slit. He lapped at my folds, making my body tense and my heart race with every parting lick and the discovery of my clit. Within seconds, he proved he was as skilled with his tongue as he was with his hands, introducing me to ecstasy I'd never experienced before. His lips closed around my clit, trapping the tiny nerve bundle for a series of torturous strokes. Just when I was on the verge of climax, he stopped and kissed the crease of my thigh instead.

The tiniest twitch of my hands toward my body resulted in his longer fingers encircling my wrists. He pinned me down with the lightest touch. It was all he needed.

"I couldn't wait to get back to you to do this, Leigh."

"Ian, don't stop… I need… I need…" I needed him inside me. To feel our bodies connected together as one.

"I know what you need." The sexy confidence in his voice convinced me it was true.

"Ian," I pleaded softly, squirming on my back until his mouth descended again. He lavished fleeting licks and split my folds with his tongue. At the end, he sealed his mouth around my clit and suckled.

Molten heat crashed over my body and swept me on the tide of passion. I arched my back and gripped his salt and pepper hair in one hand until the last contraction ended and I became a boneless heap on the couch. Afterward, Ian, traced lazy circles over my thigh. I moaned something unintelligible. My orgasm had made my limbs feel heavy as lead weights.

"Do you think I'm finished with you already, sweetheart?" His index finger teased between my thighs until my legs parted again and yielded access. One brush of his fingertip made me shudder again.

"Ian…" He bent his head and kissed me, brushing our lips tenderly at first. I could taste myself on his tongue, a discovery that turned me on more than anything. An overwhelming urge came over me to have Ian in my mouth, to feel the hot pulse of his cum. Somehow, it reinvigorated me.

"Bedroom. We need the bedroom," I gasped, pulling away from him.

"It's just us, Leigh. In our house."

Ian fished a foil square from his discarded jeans and tore it open. Licking my lips in anticipation, I watched him roll it over his hard length. He was definitely well-endowed for a bird-man, and I wouldn't have him any other way.

"My eagle wants to bond with you and claim you, Leigh. There's no undoing it for me after this, baby. I need to know if you want this. If you truly want *this*."

"I want you exactly as you are."

Ian flipped me onto my belly and dragged my lower half off the couch onto my knees. Before I could speak another word, he nudged his dick between my folds and gradually penetrated me, drawing out our merging one tedious second after the next. A pitiful moan parted my lips.

"Leigh?" I heard the question in his tone: had he hurt me this time?

"Don't fucking stop," I growled at him.

My encouragement inspired a series of ruthless thrusts. He took me hard and fast from behind, slapping our bodies together, and his pelvis against my softer ass cheeks. Each slam jerked me forward into the couch. His arm was like a steel band around my waist, securing me against him while one hand palmed my breast.

It didn't matter that it was only our second lovemaking. We both knew how we liked it and what we wanted from each other. Once we found the rhythm, we kept an urgent and desperate pace. My every nerve was alive and humming with power. Without me having to ask or guide him, Ian's other hand dipped below my belly and traveled south until his fingers curved between my thighs. He touched my clit with confident fingers and introduced me to ecstasy.

"Close, so close," I panted out.

His lips skimmed my ear. "You're going to be more than close, baby."

I clenched around his dick. Fuck, I loved it when he called me baby.

In a torturous move, Ian slowed his pace until the imminent threat of my release dimmed. Then, just as swiftly, he pounded into me with renewed vigor. The back and forth pace drove me toward my finish.

The first orgasm was comparable to detonating a stick of dynamite, exploding and igniting the next charge in the set. Arching my back, I screamed as the next rolling series of endless contractions lit through my soul, calling his name over and over more times than I could count. Through it all, his motions never ceased.

Just when I thought it was over, Ian's backstroke set off another chain reaction as he stiffened behind me in climax. His breathless reaffirmation told me exactly what I needed to hear.

"*Mine.*"

When I came to, Ian's concerned face was gazing down at me. He sat cross-legged on the floor with me over his lap, a sweaty sheen still glistening over his shoulders.

"What happened?" The sound of my hoarse voice startled me. One moment I was experiencing the best climax of my life, and in the next, I was staring up at my lover from the floor.

"You passed out," he answered with a sheepish look on his face.

"I passed out during sex?"

"I think you were still kind of hanging on at the end there, so, technically, it was after sex, but yeah."

I tried to lift one hand to weakly swat at him, but it only fell back to my side again. "Is that a shifter thing?"

"It's actually rare, hon. Or so I've been told."

"Nngh… maybe it's a credit to your sexual prowess that it made *me* faint then."

Once I assured Ian I was fine, he helped me from the floor and stole a tender kiss. We spent most of the afternoon sprawled on the couch together while I listened to the sound of his strong heartbeat. He was right. It was our home and no one could see us enjoying it in the way we wanted. It wouldn't last once Sophia was older, but for now, I planned to enjoy every minute, especially until she awakened from her nap.

"I never meant to mislead you, Leigh," Ian broke the silence.

"I know." I raised my head to look into his eyes, and for once, I saw the vulnerability beneath his masculine bravado. Ian was tough, but he needed me as much as I needed him. "Your secret is safe with me. I promise."

Chapter Eleven

~IAN~

Leigh forbade me to from telling Dani and Russ she was in the know, but I warned her Russ would be able to smell the change in her scent and know we had bonded.

"So? Bonding doesn't mean you told me the truth about his furry side," she pointed out. "Or your feathered one for that matter. Let me have a little fun with him."

"True."

Our friends visited us for lunch a couple days later. While they were around, we made Thanksgiving plans for a big dinner at my house to save my grandmother the obligation of attempting to cook. The women shuffled around the kitchen while Russ and I drank beers in front of the television and discussed plans for an upcoming trip to Israel.

"Food is ready. Here, give Sophia to me," Leigh said.

"Nah, I got her, babe," I said.

"How are you going to eat with her flailing her fists into your plate?" my wife demanded.

"I'll manage," I insisted. "It can't be worse than trying to eat with Russ nearby while on a surveillance mission in the east."

Leigh and Dani promptly burst into giggles. My squad mate's betrayed look only added to our amusement.

"You think he's a grump now when he's hungry? You haven't seen how scary he gets when he hasn't had a full meal in a couple days," I continued.

"Russ is such a teddy bear; I can't imagine him being scary at all," Leigh said.

Amidst her own giggles, Dani shot an affectionate look at Russ. She eased behind the couch and leaned over his shoulder to kiss his cheek. I didn't realize Leigh's pun was intentional until they continued during our lunchtime chatter.

"You ought to send Leigh over for firearms lessons, Ian."

"Bear with me a second, Russ. Shooting lessons? Like me firing a real gun?"

"Hell yeah, why not? Dani shoots as well as some of the men I've seen in the military. I'd suggest for this guy to teach you, but he's shit with a handgun anyway."

"I am not," I protested. "I just prefer a rifle."

"What do you think, Ian?" Leigh turned to face me.

"I think it's a good idea. Crime is sort of on the rise lately anyway, so it won't do any harm for you to learn."

"Hopefully, you can put a change to that once you get in office as sheriff," Dani said.

"I haven't won yet. The election isn't for months."

Both girls laughed as if my chance of losing the election was an impossibility. "Yeah, sure. You'll win by a landslide, Ian. This town loves you and what your family's done for it. Betty's already got a sign in her yard," Leigh said.

"Where the hell did she get a sign?" I asked.

"I kind of put it there yesterday when Sophia and I went to sit with her." Leigh grinned. "It was her idea. We went out to the sign maker in town and had a couple dozen made up. We could *barely* contain our excitement."

"Hey, Leigh, where did you get this?" Dani called from the kitchen.

Russ pulled me aside the moment Leigh left the room. They remained in the kitchen to ogle some of Leigh's recent shopping discoveries.

"What's with all the bear puns from her today, man? Am I paranoid and imagining it or does she know?"

"She knows," I confessed. "She wouldn't let me warn both of you."

"Asshole. That little brat had me sweating bullets." Russ playfully slugged me in the shoulder.

I grinned at him and took out my phone to check my messages. "They're here. Thomas and Ceres are going to park their truck at the community center. They brought two ravens."

"Aw shit. Are we going now?"

"Might as well get it done, don't you think?"

"I guess so. Dani's kind of grumpy with me anyway. Maybe an evening away will give her a chance to cool off."

"Really? She seemed fine to me."

"It comes and goes, man. Sometimes I wonder if all this shifter stuff is smothering her. Today she's fine, but last night was just damned awful. Everything I did upset her."

"Think a couple days away will help? Dani can have some space to relax if she's feeling overwhelmed. Maybe it's time to arrange for a weekend campout with Taylor and Juni soon," I suggested.

"You know how Sasha feels when we leave her out," Russ mentioned.

"Yeah, but…" I whistled. "Shit, I hate leaving her out, too, but she's still sore over splitting with Taylor. I didn't want to rub salt into a raw wound for either of them."

"They'll get over it. We'll only make it worse if we keep trying to handle them separately."

"You're right. I'm a little weirded out that you're being the sensible one, but you're right."

Russ slugged me in the arm. "Anyway, let's go get our lunch."

~Leigh~

The bite of a chilly afternoon wind whipped against my cheeks. As soon as the men had declared they were heading into the woods in their shifter forms, Dani and I spilled onto the patio deck with them. Maybe it should have been weird to see Russ stripping down in front of me, or even weirder for Ian to do it with another woman present, but nothing about their behavior seemed sexual.

"This isn't awkward like I expected it to be," Dani whispered.

"It's for science," I replied.

We nodded.

"We'll be back for dinner," Ian assured me. My husband handed off his clothes, which I folded after giving him a chaste kiss to his cheek.

"Why are you taking off naked into the woods?" I asked.

"Need to know info, hon," Ian said.

"And I don't need to know."

"You got it."

"Fine, fine. You two be careful then. Don't, you know, get waylaid by some flirty lady eagle wanting to hatch chicks."

"Never any fear of that."

The transformations happened in a blink of an eye. One minute there were two smoking hot naked men on the porch, and the next second there were wild animals. Ian flapped his powerful wings and took to the air, showing off by soaring high then plummeting toward the ground like a feathered bullet. Even Russ in bear form seemed to roll his eyes.

Ian landed on the wooden patio railing and leaned close until I understood his silent request. I dipped down to smooch his beak; then a satisfied eagle flew away into the distance. After Russ trundled into the woods, we sighed and headed back into the kitchen.

"Movies with Sophia then?" I suggested.

With two mega-sized bowls of ice cream and a bag of popcorn to share between us, we settled in the living room with a romantic comedy. Sophia enjoyed tummy time on the floor at our feet, babbling at a plush patriotic designed eagle toy. She gummed on the soft beak and squished the blue wings in her chubby fists.

"I love your dress. Where did you get it?"

"I picked it up from the new thrift store in town. What I like most is the skirt, because I can carry my revolver under it," Daniela explained. She hiked up the dress to mid-thigh level and revealed the holster. Her legs were a little slimmer than mine and I envied her.... her ample bust line.

"I don't think a thigh holster would fit me."

"Russ had this made for me after I passed the course for my concealed handgun license."

"I've never shot a gun in my li—"

Tires squealed in the dirt road in front of my house then the windows imploded, showering the carpet with glass shards. Projectiles sailed through the open space and thumped into the walls.

My terrified dog fled upstairs. As my instincts kicked in, I threw myself onto the floor and wriggled into place on top of Sophia to shield her. "Should we run?" I called up to Dani.

"No! Just stay down!" she urged me. On her hands and knees, she pushed with her body to shove the sofa on an angle between the windows and us. "Fuck, I can't text Russ. I have his phone!" She dialed 911 and put it on speakerphone.

"911. What is your emergency?" a relaxed voice spoke to us.

"Someone is shooting into our house!" I yelled back, fearing I couldn't be heard.

"Where is your location?"

I rattled off the address and hoped the operator understood my shaking voice. She calmly repeated it back and let us know a car was on its way and to stay on the line.

"Can you make it into a safe place?"

"N-no, and I have my baby with me. Please hurry."

I didn't dare grab Sophia and run for it while bullets flew through the destroyed windows into our living room. More glass shattered behind my head, indicating Ian's television was trashed. With my body curled over my squalling, kicking child, I was her first line of defense against any wayward bullets. We had nowhere to run and no place we could hide, but in the midst of all the shooting, the door slammed open and heavy steps thudded through the entrance way.

An African-American man burst into the foyer with a scrawny white guy beside him. Both needed a good meal, and only one had his teeth. They leveled handguns into the living room as they spun to face us. "Get the fuck down and—"

Dani didn't give them the chance to finish his command. Her revolver barked loudly and the black guy fell thrashing to the ground. The toothless white guy remained upright beside him and fired a round at my friend. A bullet missed her head by a narrow margin, carrying forward into some knickknacks on Ian's fireplace mantle instead.

"Bitch, drop the fucking gun!" When Dani didn't lower her weapon, he pulled the trigger and shot her.

Dani jerked and stumbled back as a bullet slammed into her body. She squeezed off rounds until the revolver clicked dry and the other shooter went down.

"Dani!" I cried.

She stumbled to the couch and slumped in the corner, profuse amounts of dark blood staining her new dress. A steady trickle seeped from a bullet wound on her left shoulder. My fledgling knowledge of human anatomy told me it was close to a large blood vessel, but probably hadn't punctured it.

One of the shooters wasn't out. He sat up with a groan and swung his gun arm up. Without thinking, I rushed toward him, snatching the lamp from the table and yanking its cord from the wall. I bashed him over the head before he could aim then secured his fallen firearm. They weren't dead, but I didn't trust leaving a weapon within reach.

"My friend's been shot!" I screamed at the phone when I returned.

"Fuck, fuck, fuck!" someone shouted outside. A growl preceded several gunshots then a noise resembling a dog's whimper.

"Do something, dude!" another voice shouted.

"You didn't say the motherfuckah got attack dogs 'round here!" With the windows blasted out, their voices carried across the lawn into the room.

From where I knelt beside Dani, I couldn't see much out the window but besides an ancient red Nissan parked by the road. A figure in a dark hoodie jumped into the bed of the truck then the driver peeled down the road.

"Are you and Sophia okay?" Dani asked.

"Forget us, we're fine!" I don't know what had come over me, but I went into action. Using a baby blanket for a makeshift cradle sling, I secured Sophia against me to provide her comfort. She continued to squall, but the angry red color faded from her cheeks. With her beginning to quiet, I doubled over and folded an afghan from the back of the couch and guided Dani onto the hard floor. "I'm going to apply pressure to this, okay, Dani? And to your back where it exited."

We remained that way until sirens heralded the arrival of EMS and the police. According to the paramedic who helped her onto the stretcher, my friend's injury wasn't a gusher, more of a slow trickle, which meant it hadn't hit a major artery. I'd probably saved her from going into shock.

"Let me grab my purse, and I'll come with—"

"No! Stay here to tell the boys what happened," Dani insisted. "They'll be home soon. You need to be here to tell them what happened."

"Are you sure you'll be okay?"

Dani smiled weakly at me as they wheeled her into the ambulance. "Positive. These vans carry morphine."

Once I had Sophia settled and in her crib, the cops asked me question after question, having me repeat the story long after they seemed satisfied. They took photographs and waited for my husband to arrive while I nervously shot glances at the kitchen. I'd left Russ and Ian's clothing on the patio table outside.

"I don't *know* where my husband went."

"Does Mr. MacArthur have a cell phone number where you can reach him, Leigh?"

It was on the kitchen table. I sighed. "Ian went for a walk. I think he and our neighbor were planning to set up a deer stand or something somewhere, and he owns a couple hundred acres or so. There's no telling where they went."

"I'm right here. What the hell's going on here?" A glance over my shoulder revealed Ian striding from the kitchen. Russ wasn't far behind him.

"We heard the sirens. What's happening?" Russ stared into the living room then at the blood stains on the couch. His face went white as a sheet. "Where's Dani?"

"She told me to stay behind and tell you guys what happened." I relayed the story to them in detail like I had for the cops, and once I was done, Russ took off for the hospital in Ian's SUV.

"Are you sure you're all right?" Ian demanded. His eyes darted toward Sophia's bedroom door then swept over my body. His hands followed, quickly assessing whether or not I had sustained an injury. He lingered at the blood on my jeans.

"I'm fine. I'm fine, Ian. We're both fine!" I tried to convince him when he moved as if to dart to Sophia's room next. "Sophia's okay, too. Not a scratch on either of us. It's just… I was so afraid, and I didn't know what to do, but somehow I did everything right." The rest of my attempt to speak broke off into a sobs. With the worst of it over and the excitement at its end, my dwindling adrenaline left stone cold exhaustion in its wake.

"Christ. I'm so sorry I was gone, Leigh. I'm sorry," he whispered against my hair. He hugged me tight in his arms and refused to let go until my shaking ended. Afterward, we both walked to Sophia's room together. Even though the paramedics and I had both checked her, Ian looked her over himself.

It seemed like hours had passed before the cops were gone. The damage left from the firefight and failed drive-by made Ian reluctant to remain overnight.

"We're going to Gram's for the night. I'm not making you guys stay here. Pack up."

He didn't have to suggest the idea twice. It took about twenty minutes to pack up a bag and everything Sophia would need for a night away from home.

"Have you heard from Russ and Dani yet?"

Ian glanced down at his phone and shared the recent text message from Russ with me. "She's good, see? Russ is with her now and he says it's nothing major."

"She was so brave, Ian. You should have seen her." I wiped my eyes and got ahold of myself before I broke down, determined to be a strong wife Ian could be proud of. "I still don't know what happened outside, but there were growls. I thought maybe Trigger got loose and came to our rescue."

"I can explain, but it'd be better if you see it. Come on."

Ian picked up Sophia in her car seat and shouldered the diaper bag. He led the way to the forested walking path between the two houses while I led Petunia on a leash.

"Are you sure it's safe out here? Those snarls were so close."

"Trust me." Ian brushed a kiss against my temple then led me deeper onto the path. The last rays of sunlight cast shadows all around, but we weren't in complete darkness and the trees shielded us from the wind.

"Okay, lovebirds, you can come out now."

"Lovebirds?"

Leaves rustled to my left. As my gaze snapped from Ian's placid features, I caught sight of two wolves emerging from the brush. I staggered back a step and nearly lost my balance.

"It's okay, sweetie. They're with me."

"With you?" I questioned. My voice raised on the last word.

Both marvelous creatures moved forward to greet me with their proud heads raised. A rust-colored smear of dried blood stood out against the larger, charcoal and white-furred male wolf. The female had more blood around her blonde muzzle than he did, but no visible injuries. I never knew wolves could have green eyes.

"Ian, he's hurt." Petunia peeked out from behind my thigh at the two wolves. She didn't fear them as much as I expected.

"He'll be fine," Ian assured me. "Go on, guys. You don't have anything Leigh hasn't seen before."

The two wolves simultaneously canted their heads at Ian then glanced at me. The male had a skeptical look in his blue eyes.

"Seriously. Go ahead," Ian urged them.

The two animals underwent transformation, losing their fur and lupine shapes to rise onto their two hind legs. In the blink of an eye, they were a man and a woman barely any older than me. The girl wiped her mouth with the back of a wrist and grinned.

"You okay, Thomas?" Ian asked him.

"It hurt like a bitch, but I'll survive," Thomas replied. He glanced down at his side where a puckered, pink scar remained. My attention wavered between his muscles and the nude woman standing beside him. She was classically beautiful by every definition of the word, with long, wavy golden hair. She had a fit, tanned body like a runner or tennis player.

"Thomas, there's a baby. Keep it clean," the blonde chastised with a slap against his arm.

Thomas chuckled and kissed her cheek. "Sure. Don't worry about being buck nekkid in front of her. Worry about my mouth."

"Meet my goddaughter, Ceres, and her mate, Thomas. They're going to help me with some problems in the area."

Ceres stepped forward instinctively to hug me then paused and dropped her arms at her sides. "Hi. Uh. I wish we met under better circumstances."

Don't look down, don't look down. My eyes involuntarily flicked down at Thomas' crotch. Were all shifters hung like horses? Hoping he hadn't noticed, I tore my gaze away to look at his face instead. He smirked at me, inspiring fears he could read my mind.

"You'll get used to it," Ceres assured me. "When Thomas first became a werewolf, it took us hours to coax him out of his clothes. He was so shy it was adorable. Anyway, how's your friend? Is she going to be okay? We watched EMS take her away, but we didn't want to risk anyone seeing us."

"She's definitely not coming home tomorrow," Ian said. "But her boyfriend says nothing critical was hit."

Ceres was right. As we talked, I found it easier to ignore their nudity and to focus on the conversation. They walked with us down the forest path to Russ and Dani's house where we planned to borrow his truck for the night. He and Ian kept keys to each other's rides.

"We were on our way back from…" The girl's eyes drifted to Ian then back to me. "Anyway, we heard gunshots and knew they came from this direction."

"There was a third shooter about to come inside after your friend shot the other two. I distracted him so Ceres could catch him from the side," Thomas explained.

"Are you going to be okay?"

"Oh, yeah. I'm good. I'd rather be the one to get shot than Ceres anyway. It's a small price to pay."

"That last guy won't be using what's left of his hand for much." The corner of Ceres' mouth rose.

"I'll tell the police to keep an eye on local hospitals then," Ian said. "I can't thank you enough for coming to their rescue."

"No problem, man. We're going to hang around in this area and camp out. My cell is nearby, so we'll ring you if anything happens."

"Feel free to use my house if you need anything."

Ian fed a super condensed version of the story to his grandmother. By morning, it would probably be all over the news that a robbery had been foiled on a veteran's home in the country.

Ian hadn't fooled his grandmother, and he hadn't fooled me either. The problem was trying to determine who he'd meant to convince with the story.

"Go have a soak in the tub, baby. I'll get Sophia her bottle and put her to bed."

Trusting him with my baby, I indulged in an hour-long soak until my skin became pruney, as if I could wash the terror of the day down the drain, too.

Ian wasn't in bed when I emerged from the bathroom, but Sophia was fast asleep with Petunia curled up beside her playpen. I found him on the porch, leaning against the rail with a pack of cigarettes in one hand and his phone in the other. I recognized the contemplative expression on his face.

"You smoke?"

Wearing a guilty expression on his face, he ceased swiping mid-text and glanced away. "I used to when I was a lot younger," he explained while tucking the device into his pocket. "While you were in the shower, I found Gram's stash. She tries to hide it, you know."

I nodded. "I smell it now and again mostly out here on the porch, so I sort of guessed she indulged."

Ian chuckled and set the pack on the porch railing. "Hell, she's over ninety years old. I figure she can do what she wants by now if it makes her happy, but she thinks it upsets me."

"Does it?"

"A little." He took a step closer to me and wrapped one arm around my shoulders. With one sweet kiss, my husband assuaged my worries and chased away the remnants of my fear. "Before you and Sophia came around, Gram and the team were all I had. I didn't retire from the Air Force because the career tired me, Leigh. I left because after Russel's wife died, I realized how fragile human life can be. I wanted to be around for her last years. She's… she *is* my mother. As close as I've ever had."

"I think Betty is too stubborn to leave you any time soon, Ian." I hugged him then leaned back to peer into his golden eyes. "Why are you out here alone?"

"Thinking."

"That much is apparent." I cupped his face in both of my hands and skimmed my thumb over the soft, silver-peppered scruff on his jaw. "If I'm going to be your wife and your mate, you need to trust me with the things troubling you. What's happening, Ian? I deserve to know as much and why someone tried to shoot me in my own home. Were you texting Russ? Is Dani okay?"

My husband dragged in a deep breath then guided me inside from the porch to the guest bedroom. Grateful to have him with me, I crawled beneath the sheets and tugged him in to join me. Sophia slept peacefully in the playpen beside us.

"Now spill it." Moving closer let me set my head on his shoulder, fanning my hair over his bicep and the pillow.

"Okay," he agreed. "Something is going wrong in this town, and I think the drug problem runs deeper than a few misguided kids dealing Xanax bars after school. It's worse than teens picking narcotics from the medicine cabinets of senior citizens. Someone put a hit out on me because I've been digging around in their business."

A hit. It was something straight out of one of his movies. The news should have terrified me, but instead, I felt a rare surge curiosity. "Are you going to clean up the town?"

"We're going to try. I made contact with a few people I work with. I don't trust the local police or the county boys."

"You don't think—"

"Maybe," he said. "Ceres bit someone hard enough to sever a blood vessel and some tendons. If they check into a hospital, I'll know about it. This problem in Quickdraw has gone on long enough."

"Is that why you decided to run for sheriff?"

"Partially. Everything I said about that before was true. If our own department is corrupt, then it needs to be cleaned out, top to bottom."

"I should be terrified right now, but…" A strange sense of levelheadedness pervaded my emotions, imploring me to remain calm. I'd first noticed it during the firefight between Daniela and the thugs. "I have nothing but absolute faith in you right now. Isn't that weird?"

"Of course you do."

"But why?" I raised my head from his shoulder.

"Along with turning into animals, we shifters have some, ahh… more passive abilities specific to our type of animal. As my bondmate you get to enjoy them whether I'm present or not for as long as I'm alive. You'll never suffer any kind of impairment — mental or physical — for long. And you'll be more rational than the average person."

"So," I began while twisting to roll onto his chest. It put our faces close, noses almost touching, eye to eye while I studied him in the dimmed bedroom lighting. Ian was an enigma, and nothing in the past prepared me for living life with a supernatural fantasy guy. "You're sexy, you turn into an eagle, filthy rich, good in bed, and you have some sort of magical healing aura?"

"Mmhmm. All eagles do. The Ojibwe believed we carried away sickness to the Creator. I wished I'd been there for Russ' wife, but we were both away so often together I never knew she was ill until she was beyond my help."

"Ian?"

"Hm?"

"Can Dani and I do the same thing now with the healing?"

"Yeah, you can, but not her. Why do you ask?"

"She was so brave," I repeated for what must have been the fifth time. "And she made me feel brave, too."

"Because she pulls it from Russ. He inspires bravery in others."

"One day, real soon, you're going to have to explain all of this to me because this is some need to know information."

Ian chuckled and opened his mouth to reply, only for the phone to buzz with an incoming message. Hiding nothing, he enabled the touch screen with a slide of his thumb and began reading the message.

We picked up your guy. You know where to meet us. We're on our way there.

~Ian~

As I stepped down from the porch and approached Russ' truck, I shot a glance over my shoulder to the raven perched on the edge of the roof. Harrison would remain as lookout over the night, and he had strict instructions to warn Leigh if any suspicious activity occurred on his watch.

I left my wife with my pistol and the key to my grandmother's gun safe. After a five minute primer lesson on how to operate the handgun, Leigh's confidence skyrocketed. I wished we weren't in my grandmother's house and short on the time for hanky-panky. Seeing her with my gun turned me on.

Not once in all of my entire career had I ever used my privileges with the government for personal gain, but I was more than willing to use them to protect someone I loved. Leigh didn't know it, but all of our vehicles were tagged in law enforcement systems as special class federal vehicles. All six of us could speed to our heart's content with or without a siren, but we kept concealed equipment to use in emergencies. One button would blast sirens and flash lights. My foot remained anchored to the accelerator the entire way.

A black Mercedes awaited me at the safe house in the middle of the country, almost smack dab between Houston and San Antonio. Juni and Nadir occupied seats inside, one nibbling a stale donut and the other drinking coffee.

"Glad to have your help on this, Nadir. I know you just got home for your R&R." Nadir's Middle Eastern descent gave him the edge we needed during missions in Afghanistan. He'd spent the past two years in deep cover making sacrifices the rest of us couldn't imagine. Now he was home spending his first days lending me a hand.

Nadir scoffed and shook his head. "Don't think anything about it. We're family."

"Did he talk any yet?"

Nadir and Juni shook their heads.

"No," she said. "We waited for you. We didn't tell Russ we found him either, because we knew the moment we did, he'd rush out here from the hospital and we'd be lucky to have anything of him left for you to interrogate."

"Good thinking."

Juni worked Comms and Nadir was our Intel agent. Together, there wasn't much the two of them couldn't accomplish for the squad. I relied on them when legitimate methods of acquiring information were a bust or when I needed someone tracked down.

"How are we gonna do this one?" Juni asked. "The usual?"

I nodded and strode into the room to find my helpless target secured in a chair. He hyperventilated beneath the black hood, aware of the approaching footsteps.

"Who's there? Look, man, I need a doctor. Y'all gotta let me out of here. I didn't do nothin', you can't just hold me up in here like this."

Without concern for concealing my identity, I removed the black bag and stepped back until I came into focus for our captive. The man in the chair was slim, scrawny like most backwoods drug users. The partial halo of dark skin from repeated burns on the lower lip was the telltale sign of a crack addict, along with a half dozen other visible symptoms of drug dependency. Under these circumstances, pity wasn't part of my emotional repertoire.

"Ian MacArthur?"

I answered him with a sharp right hook to the face, juggling his head back and nearly knocking him unconscious. Usually, I was the calm and calculated one. The cool squad leader who never lost control. I had Russ' role today, and I played the part with ease.

This fucker could have killed my wife and child.

"Didn't expect to see me again, did you? Thought I was dead in there? Who sent you?"

"Fuck you," he spit out. "I know I got rights. Where's my lawyer?"

"I don't think you get how this works. There's no police involvement. No one, and I do mean no one, knows where the hell you are right now. You're a ghost no one will ever find, and judging from the looks of you, no one will ever miss. Now someone sent a truck load of you to my house to kill me, and I want to know who. *Now.*" Taking him by the shirt collar, I tightened the material until it cut into his throat. After giving him a ragdoll's treatment, his rebellion gave way to fear and he was thirsty for air again.

"I d-d-don't know much."

I cuffed him again, hard enough to knock the chair onto its back and for his head to strike the padded floor. We'd added that installation after Russ nearly cracked someone's skull open during an interrogation. The guy had spit in Juni's face and the southern gentleman in Russ had exploded violently.

"Don't!" he shrieked, flinching away as I dropped to a knee beside his head with my fist raised.

"Ian!" Juni cried from the door. "What are you doing?"

"I'm fucking doing what needs to be done," I growled at her. My fist began its descent, but she ran forward and grabbed my arm at the elbow. Nadir hauled me back with one arm around my waist.

The scuffle ended with me in the control room after Juni shut the door in my face. I dropped into her chair at the computer console and watched them unfasten the bonds to release our prisoner. His limp, mangled hand had basic first aid to prevent bleeding out and little else, but I recognized Nadir's work. He and Sasha had worked closely during the final year of her active duty, making him our backup medic.

"Are you okay?" Juni asked gently. "I'm sorry, I really am." Our detainee had tears streaming down his face. I'd shaken him up good enough that he flinched back from her initially when she reached out. "I'm just going to have a look at your hand, okay? We want to get you some medical help, but I need you to cooperate first so I can help you."

"I'll get him something for the pain. He must feel awful right now," Nadir commented. He came out of the room and glanced at me after the door was shut. "Was all of it acting, or did you really lose it? That wasn't normal for you. You're always the cool-headed one."

So much for being calm and rational. "I really lost it for a second, but the end was acting," I admitted. We had a system here of good-cop, bad-cop, usually with Russ as the bad guy and one of the girls or Nadir as the good guy. The girls had the best luck thanks to their specific animal totems. Juni was our lucky rabbit and Sasha had the gift of timing. She always knew when to ask the right question.

"He's at ease with her already. Once she has him calmed down and comfortable, he'll spill whatever she wants." Nadir plucked a medical kit from the cabinet and dropped it on the table beside me.

"What are you giving him?" I watched him withdraw a small vial of clear liquid.

"Some morphine," Nadir replied. He withdrew a small amount of liquid, recapped the syringe, and returned to the room.

My operatives went through the usual song and dance. They got the guy comfortable and even got his name out of him. His name was Kevin Watson, and a quick look into our databases revealed he was the thirty-two-year-old, unemployed son of our town's bar owner with a history of possession charges.

"When do I get to leave?" I heard him ask. "I have rights. I know I have rights. You guys can't keep me here like this, can you?"

"Soon, my friend. I promise it will all come to an end soon," Nadir assured him. "You're very fortunate Ian has the pull to keep you out of prison for your crimes. You participated in an attempted murder. Did you know an infant was in the room?"

"No, no. Montgomery never said anything about kids. He just said to go in hard if we saw MacArthur's vehicle parked in the drive. Told us the wife would be with his grandmother."

Bingo.

"Ask him about Chief Montgomery," I told Juni over the communication link. She wore a small earpiece while in the room with our suspect.

"It sounds like Montgomery really screwed you guys over," Juni said. She flashed the guy a sympathetic smile and pulled up a seat. "Does he normally do shit like that?"

"Hell yeah. Thinks he can get away with doing whatever he wants 'cause he's police chief."

Nadir whistled. "Sounds like a real asshole. Maybe there's a way we can help you and keep you safe. I guess if he knew you were talking to us, he'd have you locked up."

"He would. He knows people, man. I'll be in TDCJ and down at Ferguson Unit like my homie, DJ."

"DJ?" Nadir leaned forward a little on his seat.

"Dennis James. He got pinched by one of the honest cops. Uhh… What's his face… fucking Hunt caught him. Montgomery told us we're on our own if we get busted doing shit, and Dee got sloppy."

"Why didn't he try to make a deal? They gave him a pretty stiff sentence for the drugs he had on him, didn't they?"

"Yeah. That's 'cause Montgomery knows people. This place is fucked up, man. I knew it was over for him when he got sent to Ferguson. You can't hide once you're in there."

"I take it that means they have a few men on the inside."

Kevin nodded. "Yo, man, can I have another shot of whatever you gave me? The pain is starting to come back."

I chuckled. "Dose him up with something light and lemme make a couple calls. Our problem is bigger than I anticipated."

Chapter Twelve

~LEIGH~

"I'd like to visit Daniela Reyes," I announced to the young woman at the nurses' station.

The cold, clinical environment of the county hospital surrounded me. Doors opened and closed, wafting the scent of chemical deodorizers.

Once I had directions to Dani's room, I made my way down the hall and knocked on the door.

"Come in!"

I stepped into a vacant room then shut the door behind me for privacy. The bathroom door was half ajar, but sour vomit assaulted my nose.

"Dani? You okay in there?" I hesitated outside the door, waiting to see if she wanted any help.

"Yeah. Just a sec, Leigh."

The toilet flushed, and then I heard her at the sink. After a few swishes and gargles, Daniela's pasty face appeared in the doorway. "Sorry about that. Mind helping me back to the bed?"

Holding her gown shut in back with one hand, I helped the wobbling woman back into her bed. "You don't look so good. Hospital food not agreeing with you?" I expected to see Russ asleep in a chair. Rumpled hospital blankets were strewn over the back of it, indicating he'd been there. Tentative about making myself at home, I sat on the edge of the seat.

"The food is godawful. Russ went to get me McDonald's while the breakfast menu is available." Dani did a double take and looked around the room in confusion. "Where's Sophia?"

"With her great-grandmother. Betty assured me she can still change a diaper and swaddle an infant. Plus, she has Ian's goddaughter helping."

"Good, I'm glad everyone is safe. I heard an animal growling outside during the shootout, so I just assumed another you-know-who was involved."

I crept to the door and peeked into the hall. Without a nurse in sight, I took a minute to catch her up on the news. I told her about the wolves outside and the young man who knocked on our door that morning. His name was Harrison and he had kept watch over the house all night for Ian.

"Ohhh. Russ mentioned wolves coming to visit, but didn't say much." Dani's distracted demeanor was at odds with her usual bubbly personality, setting off my maternal instincts. She looked like she needed a hug, so I leaned in and gave her one, careful of her bandaged shoulder.

"I'm so sorry you were hurt, hon."

"You aren't the one who hurt me, Leigh. I just feel awful right now."

"Is everything okay? Should I call the doctor in? Would you like me to go and let you rest some more?"

"No. No doctor. It's… I'm pregnant. The hospital labs confirmed it for me after I arrived," Dani admitted. She picked at the edge of her hospital gown sleeve. "Russ doesn't know yet. I don't really know *how* to tell him."

The news caught me by surprise and my gut instinct to congratulate her hung on the tip of my tongue. "I'm going to go out on a limb and guess you guys weren't trying."

Dani shook her head. "I had an IUD in, but you know how the doctors tell you there's always a tiny, insignificant chance they can fall out or become ineffective? Mine's gone. I never even noticed."

"Are you gonna tell him soon?"

"I think so. I don't — do you think he'll be happy?"

"Dani, he'll be ecstatic. The question is, are *you* happy? Are we celebrating this baby? Do we get to go hog-wild at the mall buying booties and blankies when you get out of here?"

A fragile smile surfaced on Dani's face. I relaxed immediately. "I think so. I lost a baby once, you know. When I was married to my ex-husband, the one I killed two years ago. The doctors gave me the whole song and dance about it being a natural occurrence sometimes. Said nothing could have prevented it." She shook her head. "Michael blamed me for losing his son."

My belly knotted in worry again. "Is this baby going to be okay?" I gestured to her bandaged shoulder.

"Thanks to you, I didn't lose as much blood as I could have. He or she seems fine." She nibbled her lower lip and glanced down at her tummy. "They're going to send an ultrasound tech in around noon to check. I have until then to tell Russ."

"He'll be thrilled, Dani, I just know it."

Maybe his ears were burning, because Russell chose that moment to push through the door. Two large takeout bags and a cup holder with coffee and orange juice filled his big hands.

"You didn't answer your phone, and I wasn't sure what you wanted... so I grabbed two of everything," he called out, setting the food and drinks on the table. "Oh, hey, Leigh."

"Morning, Russ. I came to check on Dani and we got to chatting."

"Sorry I took so long, darlin'. I ran home to feed Trigger and Daisy, too." He looked like hell with dark circles under his eyes. He fidgeted more than usual.

Dani fetched a hash brown out of the bag. "Go ahead and have some, Leigh. I can't eat all of this and neither can Russ."

"Sorry, I wasn't really thinking when I placed the order." Russ' boyish grin wiped the nervousness from his face.

Poor guy. He must be so worried about Dani.

Russ lowered Dani's hospital rail out of his way and sat beside her on the bed while she dug into her biscuit sandwich. I helped myself to the spare. We all ate together and made idle chat until Russ began talking all in a rush.

"Dani, I love you. I was planning to wait until Christmas to lay this on you, but there's no time like the present, right?" He rubbed his hand up and down her thigh over the blanket. She gave him an odd look.

"Russ, what are you talking about? No time to do what? To give me breakfast?"

The bearshifter shook his head and fetched a black box from his windbreaker pocket. My eyes — and Dani's too — darted to his open palm immediately. All of my concentration became devoted to not inhaling a piece of egg.

"You're more than my mate, darlin'. You're my soul and the air I breathe. Living with you isn't enough anymore for me. I want you to be my wife. Marry me." He opened the box to reveal a sparkling ruby surrounded by diamond-encrusted leaves. The gold setting glimmered in the diffuse hospital room light.

I had been granted the privilege of witnessing a beautiful moment. Tears burned my eyes and I held my breath, knowing Dani's answer before it came from her lips.

"Russ…" Tears streamed down her face. "Yes! Oh, my god, yes! But there's something you need to know first."

"What is it, darlin'? You can tell me anything."

"Remember how I haven't been feeling well lately? The ER doctor ordered some tests before you got here last night. I'm pregnant."

"I'm going to be a father?" The joy on Russ' face was almost painful to see. Sophia's father hadn't looked so happy when I told him I was pregnant.

I dreamed of a day when I could relay the same news to Ian. Sophia was my world, but fantasies raced through my thoughts of giving my husband a child with his shifter heritage — a little sister or brother to grow up alongside Sophia. As Russ doted over his wife-to-be, I eased from my seat and crept to the door. I pulled it shut behind me to grant them privacy.

Once I fished my phone out, I asked Ian via text if it was safe to call. My phone rang less than a minute later when I reached the hospital elevator.

"What's up, sweetie?" The sound of his tired voice thrilled me.

"I'm so glad you're okay. You've been quiet since you drove off last night, and I worried about you," I babbled out.

"I'm fine. We'll be on our way back to Quickdraw soon. How's Dani?"

"Engaged and pregnant," I chirped, unable to hold the news to myself.

"Hot damn. Tell 'em I said congrats."

"We'll have to do it later. I snuck on out before Russ had the chance to begin bawling over her."

Ian's rich laughter warmed my heart. I leaned against the side of the elevator and closed my eyes. "I miss you."

"I miss you too, baby. Thomas and Ceres are behaving, right?"

"Thomas didn't show up this morning, but Ceres and Harrison came in to eat breakfast when I left Betty's house. She said he found a peculiar smell by the river bottoms and wanted to loop back one more time."

"Sounds like Thomas. They're good kids—"

"Ian, they're older than I am. Stop calling them kids."

"Habit," he admitted. His sheepish laugh painted a picture in my mind of his broad smile and glinting eyes.

I stepped out of the elevator to the ground floor and moved for the parking lot. "Tell me the truth, Ian. I know you can't go into details, but I need to know if you're going into something dangerous."

First he was silent, then I heard him inhale a deep breath. "It'll be dangerous, but I promise, I'll be home to you."

"That's all I need to know. Let me know when it's over."

"I will. Do one favor for me. Tell Russ to check his cellphone. I'm calling the squad together."

~IAN~

"Why the fuck was I excluded?" Russ demanded.

"Because Dani needed you, and we knew you'd fly off the handle," I said.

Russ appeared less than impressed with my response, but as the squad leader, I called the shots and chose team members.

"Fine," he grumbled. "I just wish you'd trusted me enough to tell me what was going on."

"Ian trusts you, Russ. You know that, just as much as we all know how much you love Dani. Our informant would be a smear on the concrete floor if you were there during the interrogation." Sasha set her hand on Russ' shoulder. "Be reasonable."

"I said fine." The cross expression faded from his face. "I am fine. Sorry. I just get so angry where Dani is concerned. Can't help it, guys."

Once his cooler head prevailed, we returned to our debriefing.

"Our informant tells us there are a handful of small-time dealers, but the guys we really want are woven into the Quickdraw PD and our county sheriff's department. There's a couple in the higher echelon." I slid my finger over the touch display and opened an image. "Chief Montgomery ordered the hit. My snooping around in his town and asking questions scared him. They know if I run for sheriff in the next election, they don't have a chance in hell of bribing me to shut up."

"Yeah, because you're already making legitimate money hand over fist," Juni chirped. "You don't need their payoffs."

"Ian's incorruptible," Nadir added. "They have good reason to be scared."

"Do we have authorization?" Sasha asked. "We need to do this by the book if we're going to go in."

"We have everything we need. Unless your hands—" I gave a pause to look at Sasha "—or your paws are forced, we're not to engage in combat. We don't want a meth lab of dead junkies with claw marks in them. This isn't Baghdad and we're not at war."

"Look, I can't be held responsible for that," Sasha said. "I'm sorry I almost broke cover that day, but I don't regret killing them all."

"Nice kitty," Nadir murmured.

Sasha hissed at him.

"If you're in a bind, by all means, let your claws out. I want to go in hard, get the evidence we need, and get out. Subdue if possible before taking any lives."

"If the sheriff is in on all this, who are you planning on handing the evidence over to?" Taylor tucked a knife inside his boot.

"Texas Rangers. I called my friend, Charles, to give us a hand. He's on his way out from Dallas," I explained.

Juni's eyes grew round. "You have friends in the Rangers, too?"

"Ian has friends everywhere. You should know that by now, darlin'." Russ clapped Juni on the shoulder.

"Officially, it's their case, but we're gonna make it all easy for them and have this wrapped up nice and tight by the time they arrive." I rose from my seat and passed out earpieces. "Juni spent a lot of time making these to fit our unique shapes. They're for us to use in our animal forms."

Sasha stared at the circular device I handed her. "Ian, this is a cat collar."

"It's extendable, Sasha. It'll adjust whenever you shift." Juni opened her laptop and logged into her tracking program. "With this, I'll be able to follow all of you. We tagged the wolves and their ravens already. If you swap to your human form to communicate, I'll be here at Ian's place to direct you."

"Sounds good," Russ said. He turned his collar around in his hands a few times then tried to fasten it around his neck.

"That's for your wrist, Russ," Juni said.

"Oh."

"Taylor, since you, Ian, and Russ are the only animals native to this area, I'm counting on you to get as close as you can without provoking them to put a bullet in your ass," Nadir said. "I'm staying behind with Juni to operate the video systems."

"Sweet. I can do that. You just want some good surveillance feed as evidence, right?" Taylor asked.

"Right. We need clear visuals on faces and activities," Juni replied.

Once preparations were made, our team split. Juni and Nadir remained behind at my place to run the control center, but I had the most difficult job of them all: I refused to allow anyone to confront Montgomery before me.

***

"About time you got here," Kevin complained. His voice crackled through the wire we'd taped to his chest. I listened from my hiding spot outside of a leaning shack in the woods.

Confronting Sheriff Montgomery wasn't enough. We needed him to freely confess what he'd done. My contacts with the Texas Rangers had approved the ruse, lending legitimacy to evidence I planned on collecting.

"Where the hell have you been, Kevin?"

"Taking care of my damn hand, man. You didn't say MacArthur had fuckin' attack dogs. You gave us bad info, Sheriff."

"You assured me you and your boys could handle MacArthur," Sheriff Montgomery spat. "If you can kill him, you could have shot a couple mutts."

"Well, he wasn't there. Just pay up and I'll go."

"I'm not paying you for an unfinished job. You were sent to kill MacArthur and his junkie slut. That's what I hired you for. Last I checked they were alive and your boys were arrested. Such a shame they tried to escape and were shot."

"We told you we weren't gonna kill Leigh! You promised she wouldn't be there. I only went because you swore he'd be alone. I can't go back there again! He'll be expecting it. I can't even hold a gun right now. Look at my hand."

I smirked. Ceres didn't play around when it came to taking someone down. He was lucky to have escaped with his throat intact. Hell, he'd be lucky to make any sort of deal at all to keep from going away to prison for life.

"Then I guess you're no use to me anymore, Kev."

"Hey, man… what the fuck? Put the gun down!"

As much as Kevin deserved to get shot, this wasn't the way to do things. I needed him on a witness stand. Abandoning my post outside, I circled round to the front and kicked the door in.

I had a split second to make my decision. The gun swung around toward me, but my sharp reflexes gave me ample time to twist out of the bullet's path. It struck the wall behind me instead, shattering the glass in a picture frame. I usually saved the inhuman reflexes for the battlefield when there weren't any witnesses left to tell tales. For Montgomery, I made an exception. I was on him in a second, smashing my knuckles into his chin. He stumbled back and lost control of his gun when I twisted his arm and dislocated his shoulder to disarm him. Kevin, the junkie we'd used as our bait, high-tailed it out the door without a backward glance.

Unwilling to go without a fight, the sheriff swung his heavy fist around and clipped me in the temple. I blocked another punch and flipped him to the floor. The chunky, out of shape police chief didn't have a chance against me, but I lacked mercy.

"You sent men to kill my wife." My fist pounded into his face, cracking cartilage in his nose. My eagle craved vengeance *and* his blood, demanding his death for daring to put my mate in danger.

"Ian," Juni spoke up through the communication channel.

Montgomery groaned, his attempt to speak coming out as a hoarse croak.

"You're going to pay for what you've done here, Montgomery. All this time, you knew about the bullshit happening here." I punched him again, bruising my knuckles. He grunted and spit blood to the side.

"Ian, stop!" Juni cried. "You'll kill him if you keep up like this."

"Maybe I want to kill him," I growled out.

"You don't," she disagreed, adopting the placid tone reserved for our detainees.

"She's right, Ian," Nadir said. "Listen to us. You do not want this man's blood on your hands. You're better than that."

Montgomery's head lolled back. Blood trickled from his nose and split lip, and all I wanted was to finish what I began.

"Fine," I hissed between my teeth. I waited for the anger to recede, breathing in deep and measured breaths. Even my eagle had been ready to surrender to our shared anger, enraged by the man's decision to place Leigh and Sophia in danger. "Get to talking, Montgomery. Tell me everything."

"Ian. Ian, you don't understand. There are things going on in this town that you can't comprehend. Things you won't want to be involved in. You'll wish he killed you and Leigh both if you go through with this."

"Right now, my squad is leading a raid against three different meth labs and crack houses set up in the boonies. We're taking your supply line down."

"You'll never find the supply line. Those are only decoys. They don't mean anything."

"Then tell me where to find the real source. Tell me now and it'll look good on you later when the DA presses charges against you. Maybe they'll cut you a deal."

Montgomery's bitter chuckle unnerved me and shattered my righteous indignation. "You can't stop what's happening here. No one can."

"You won't be able to get any information from him, Ian. That guy's out of it. Give it up," Nadir said.

"Yeah, you're right," I replied. I stood and left Montgomery on the floor to look out the window. There wasn't any sign of Kevin. "Our witness is gone."

"I saw it," Juni reassured me. "Thomas has him cornered outside." The wolf growled low to confirm. "Your help is on the way, Ian, not that you need them."

"Sit your ass on the floor until the Rangers get in here to arrest you," I barked at him.

I patted Montgomery down and found a second firearm concealed in his boot. About five minutes later, tires screeched on the blacktop to herald my backup's timely arrival. Somehow, I hadn't given in to my bestial nature. Death was more than he deserved for everything he'd done.

Montgomery's wet cough held too much amusement for my taste. Crossing to the window, I glanced outside at the two trucks with their flashing lights. Once I verified my friend was one of the responding officers, I pulled open the door and stepped outside.

Shamed and stripped of his authority, Montgomery surrendered to his own cowardice in the early hours of the morning a week later. Officers found him hanging by a bed sheet in a cell. He'd taken his secrets with him.

Chapter Thirteen

Four Months Later

~Ian~

"Leigh? Baby? I'm back."

Three weeks away from my wife and daughter felt like a lifetime. I loved my job and hiring out my services to the government, but for the first time in my entire career, I couldn't wait to be home.

Following the dramatic end of Chief Montgomery's reign over Quickdraw, the drug trade calmed down and the remaining police officers quietly resumed cleaning up my hometown. Everyone knew about my upcoming campaign for County Sheriff, and thanks to the part I played in bringing the crooked chief to justice, my election was guaranteed.

Shortly after Leigh, Sophia, and I spent our first Christmas together, I resumed taking government contracts. Russ and I planned to build a comfortable savings account to allow us to remain home for the unforeseeable future. He wanted to spend the next year with Dani and their child. I wanted to be there for Leigh to provide the support she needed.

This is it. The last job until Leigh's out of school. Nothing to stand between her and me now. And even then maybe I am done for good. Maybe it's time to retire and pass the torch to Nadir. Maybe it's time to become a real family man and run things from behind the scenes.

It was time to end my career. For Leigh and Sophia, I'd give up anything.

I stepped through the door, eager to pull my two favorite girls into my arms. Once I found them. Leigh's scent led me to the backyard and I leaned against the door, watching. She had a large blanket spread out over the grass and Sophia playing beside her. Petunia napped in the sun nearby along with the single puppy we'd kept. Wedding magazines piled up within her reach, another sight that brought a smile to my face. Russ and I had been in full agreement with the girls' plan for a double wedding.

I wanted Leigh to have the fairy tale ceremony she deserved.

"Hey, beautiful," I called out loud enough to catch her attention.

"Ian!" Leigh jumped to her feet and met me halfway across the yard. Her kisses welcomed me home; the joy surpassed only by the toothless grin Sophia gave me from the blanket.

"I didn't expect you back so early."

"Well, we managed to wrap everything up sooner than expected. A couple of the guys hung around to play at being tourists, but Russ and I couldn't wait," I indulged her in another kiss, "to return where we belong." Now that Dani was in her approaching her third trimester, Russ didn't plan to take another job for a while.

"Da da da da." Sophia clapped and held her arms up toward me when we approached. I scooped her up and kissed her cheek.

"Yup, I'm home, princess." Tiny hands touched my face and unshaven jaw. Patting my cheeks, my soon-to-be adopted daughter gazed deep into my eyes.

"Da daaaaa."

"I hope you love me as much when I'm chasing boys off our porch with a shotgun sixteen years from now."

"Ian." Leigh swatted me.

"I'm joking." With both of us around to teach her good from bad, hopefully, I'd never need to do it.

"I was about to take her inside for naptime."

"I'll carry her up," I volunteered. Both dogs roused and followed on my heels, dancing behind me every step of the way.

Sophia settled in for her afternoon nap without fuss, as if she'd been waiting for me to tuck her in. Leigh met me at the bottom of the stairs, shaking her head.

"She always falls asleep so quickly when you do it," she complained.

"I have a way with women."

"Come back outside with me, the day is beautiful."

Leigh pulled me by the hand to the patio. I chuckled at the college textbooks piled on the table. "How's the schoolwork going?"

"Great, actually. Dani proofread my essay, and I have a project I have to give for some of the senior citizens at the assisted living center near school."

"Yeah? What's it on?" With encouragement from Sasha, Dani, and even me, Leigh had returned to school. I couldn't be prouder. She'd graduate with her degree in another semester.

"The healing properties of music therapy and its effect on individuals with Alzheimer's disease." She rattled out a mouthful of words that made me grin. Leigh had an amazing singing voice to begin with, but she was thrilled to discover her area of study benefitted from our bonding. She wanted to use the powers transferred through our link to help others as a music therapist.

I whistled. "Sounds like good stuff."

Leigh's cheeks colored. "It is, I think. Will you listen and be my guinea pig before I go perform?"

"Of course. You know how much I love to hear your voice."

She blushed again, a trait I never tired of. "There's something else, actually."

"Yeah? What is it, hon?"

"While you were gone, I got myself a new doctor and had a visit."

"Are you sick?" A concerned wrinkle creased my brow. I glanced my wife over as if any illness would be visible in her appearance, still haunted by the memory of Katie Hawkins sunken cheeks and thinning hair. She'd tried to endure chemotherapy without Russ, afraid informing her husband of her illness would recall him from active duty to be at her side. Maybe it was too early to make the determination that I couldn't live without Leigh at my side, but I could easily and honestly say I didn't *want* to be without her.

"No, silly." Leigh only laughed before giving me a reassuring pat to one thigh. "I visited the lady doctor. I, um… had something put in." She showed me the tiny scar on her arm and guided my fingers to touch the slim, hard presence beneath her skin. "I didn't know how you felt about kids, but I know Sophia is all I need right now."

"Leigh—"

She held up a hand to show she wasn't finished. "Right now, Ian. But one day after I'm out of school, if you'd like me to get it removed, I'd like that too," she whispered.

"A little sibling for Sophia."

Leigh nodded. "Yes. I want a baby with you, enough that I kept thinking about it." Heat suffused to her face, bringing a rush of pink color. "But even more, I want to feel you without anything between us. No more condoms."

Certain traits of a shifter's personality were ruled by our animal aspects, driving us to mate frequently to preserve our species. The arrival of spring brought mating season for eagles, a sensitive time for me. I was completely erect in the time it took to rise from my seat. Maybe she didn't want the child now, but the only thing concerning my eagle was her confession of desire. She'd said it. She wanted my baby.

"I need to be inside you right now." I fumbled with my belt, but then Leigh took over. She had my pants lowered and my cock out within seconds. I'd never been so hard in all of my life.

"Fuck," I swore out loud when she took me into her mouth. Her lips formed a perfect ring around my dick, teasing only the tip with her tongue. It was the worst and best kind of torture. I wanted to fuck her so deep and so hard she saw stars.

"Leigh, baby, how long? Do I need backup?"

Her mouth came off me with a wet pop. "No. It's been in long enough." Leigh's hand slid over my ass and squeezed. One forward movement slid my cock into her mouth again. I watched it disappear inch by inch until her nose nestled against the base of my dick and my balls touched her chin. My head tilted back in ecstasy.

I was already close to the edge before she began bobbing back and forth. Skilled fingers teased my balls, and then she pulled back. Her lips pressed against my hip while she left my dick exposed to the air.

"I love what you're doing to me, baby, but I need to be inside of you. Right now."

We didn't waste time; Leigh's clothes fell away between our united efforts. One swift yank pulled her against me, her back to my chest and her ass cradling my dick. She wriggled against me, sliding up and down until I couldn't take it anymore and bent her forward.

Without a condom to separate us, I snapped my hips forward and drove into her. The exquisite sensation of her pussy surrounded me all at once, and required me to linger in place, buried balls deep in her body. I couldn't move, overcome by how amazing she felt. Our fit was puzzle piece perfection, like two halves of the same whole merging together once more. When she adapted to my size, I set a fast rhythm like our usual lovemaking. I needed a hot and fast fucking, a primal mating to assert my claim of her. She could do whatever she wanted to me later, but right now, her pussy belonged to me.

"*Mine,*" I hissed out between my teeth, while Leigh moaned and clutched onto the edge of the patio table. I didn't care that we were outside, her bared ass exposed, her gorgeous tits jiggling for anyone to see. I throbbed inside her and experienced every tremble of her walls. "Tell me you're mine."

"Yours, baby. I'm yours. I'll always be yours," she panted out.

If I could have called in victory like an eagle, I would have. Instead, I groaned my pleasure against the shell of her ear.

"Touch me, Ian," she pleaded. "I want your hands on my breasts."

I teased her full tits, pulling and rolling each pink tip between my fingertips, visualizing them in my hands. Each one was a perfect palmful. Leigh moaned and rocked back against me, her hands clutching the patio table edge for support. Keeping one hand on her breasts, squeezing and kneading, I slid the other down her side to her hip. The lush curve received a light smack, and then I gripped her thigh and plunged within her body with renewed vigor.

Flesh slapped against flesh as we both gave in to our carnal desires. My wife's fast, breathy pants climbed higher and higher in pitch. Leigh's pussy tightened around my cock, a vice-like grip that pushed me over the edge.

"Sweet God, Leigh, I love you so much."

I gave her the words in my heart as I tightened in orgasm behind her, releasing burst after burst of my seed inside her body's tight embrace. Leigh reached back with one arm and hooked it around my neck. We held each other close and rode out the aftershocks together, until she was limp and pliant in my hold.

I carried her off the wooden deck into the sweet smelling clover. After I sank to my knees and lowered Leigh to lie beside me, I held her close and secure in my arms. We didn't move from where we lay in the grass, naked as the day we were born, our legs entwined and bodies close. We exchanged lazy, drugging kisses that made me linger on the border of sleep, and then I made love to her again face to face with one of her legs over my hip. Taking it slow gave me the chance to lavish her breasts with tender affection. I trapped one nipple between my teeth, stimulating the tender peak until her pussy clenched around my dick and she shuddered in orgasm.

"I'm so glad you're home again," she whispered against my cheek when both of our breaths had slowed.

"Me too, sweetheart." I didn't dare to part from her, leaving my half-hard dick surrounded by her warmth. "It feels so good to make love to you without a condom." So good I couldn't bear to leave.

"Mmhmm," she agreed. "Can't wait to see you in your uniform for the wedding." She ran her fingers down my chest.

Having Leigh in my arms, her body nestled in close, was everything I wanted.

"Tell me again, what you said before."

"I love you," I whispered, dropping a kiss on her lips.

"I love you, too, Ian. With all my heart."

Somehow, fate had brought two lost souls together. Sophia and Leigh completed me, the family I'd needed and looked for all my life. They were worth fighting for, and for them, I'd finish what the team and I began in November. The town may have become quieter in the wake of Chief Montgomery's suicide, but I wouldn't rest until the remaining dealers were off the streets.

I couldn't rest until our hometown was the place Sophia and our future children deserved.

BOOK 3: THE PURR-FECT SOLDIER

Chapter One

~TAYLOR~

When put to the vote, wrestling always won over any other television program.

I rolled my eyes and went with the flow, settling on the bench with a bowl of ramen, squeeze cheese, and diced summer sausage in my lap. It was Mack's secret recipe, a damned delicacy in this place. I only trusted it because I watched him make the shit.

One of the guys changed the channel just in time for the starting chatter about how some wrestler was going to beat some other guy's ass. The announcement was made in the classic series of threats and bravado. They screamed at each other at the top of their lungs, made aggressive gestures, and then the announcer took over.

"Sup, Taylor? I heard you gettin' out soon."

I glanced toward my right. A beefy guy with a chest like a gorilla sat beside me. He wore his hair trimmed low on top, bald at the sides and back. Upraised prison tats went up and down his arms in black ink like pigmented scar tissue — the sign of a shitty job done with a hypodermic needle and ink from a BIC pen.

"Sup, Slick. Yeah, I am. About fucking time, too."

"Parole?"

I nodded.

"Damn. You know we got that thing coming up. We could use you, bro."

"I don't wanna fuck up my chance at parole, dawg. Sorry." Getting mixed up in a riot was the last thing I wanted or needed.

"Yeah, you right. You right. Besides, the Deuce wanted me to let you know he needs to have a word with you. You gotta meet him tomorrow during rec."

I nodded again. "Sure thing. Morning or evening?"

"Evening."

At the end of the night, long after the wrestling program ended, the doors opened and a guard in a starched, gray suit entered the room. Lights out. We were all shuffled one row at a time to our cells like cattle. The doors rolled open, we stepped in, and they shut behind us.

I shared a cell with a big white guy called Mack, aptly named for his physical resemblance to a Mack truck. He and my werebear friend Russ had something in common, with muscles bulging off their muscles.

"Yo, Tay, I can still have all your stuff when you go, right?"

"Yeah. Do I look like I wanna take twenty bucks worth of noodles with me into the free world?"

I tossed my prison whites aside to be washed the next day then crawled into the top bunk. With my eyes closed, I imagined the feel of the grass beneath my paws. The fresh air against my fur, whistling over my ears. Anything beat the stench of the prison and a couple thousand men in a hot box.

One more week and I could punch Ian in his damned face for suggesting the stupid idea of sending me undercover into a nearby penitentiary. Ferguson Unit had been my home since late March, and if I didn't love him like a brother, I'd probably pluck all his feathers once I got out. All this time, six months, and I wasn't anywhere close to digging up the info he wanted. All I'd found out was that a con named 'the Deuce' had a street thug named Dennis killed. Dennis was the baby daddy of Ian's new wife. She had dated the guy before his criminal behavior got him put away for twenty-five years. But that was another story.

"Bitch, turn the fucking lights off!" someone screamed from his cell at the poor officer busting her behind to keep ahead. My months of incarceration fostered a new respect for working women. I used to think girls like my female squad mates, Sasha and Juni, were the only ones who had it hard. Then I met these women. The officer yelled something back, and fifteen minutes later, the overhead cell block lights dimmed.

Eventually, a voice on the loudspeaker announced count time. I watched her go by with her sheet of paper and flashlight, a curvy figure in stiff grays with abundant brown curls fastened into a bun.

I can't wait to get out of here and get laid. How the hell do these men manage this for years?

I watched her pass by a second time, sighed, and rolled over to go to sleep. The monotony of day-to-day life began at three a.m. when we were roused for breakfast. I choked down overcooked scrambled eggs and eventually reported in for my job as the warden's personal janitor.

I had Ian to thank for it as much as I had him to blame for being in prison in the first place. He pulled strings, got me put where he needed me to be, and, in return, I reported shit to the prison officials. I was playing both sides, leaking info to make friends with inmates and tipping off the prison administration.

By evening, I had nervous jitters.

What the hell did this guy want with me? I couldn't have offended him. As the unchallenged leader of the prison minorities, the Deuce had enough pull to get guys in my cell at night if he wanted. It only took one crooked officer to make it happen. And if they resorted to that, I'd have no choice but to shapeshift and take them out. I'd explain the claw and teeth marks later.

I shuffled down a corridor, nearly a half mile long, following a train of men with the same destination. Hard cement covered every inch of the floor, echoing loud voices surrounding us. A stressed guard watched us with his hand on his can of pepper spray, his face like a bulldog's, the smell of a hard day clinging to his sweat-drenched body.

The prison's main areas sweltered during the summers. Air conditioning was a gift granted only to the administrative offices and infirmary. Officers and felons alike suffered in misery.

I reached the end of the line where a trio of male officers waited with cheap exam gloves on their hands.

"All right. Come out of 'em," one demanded.

I bit my tongue and complied, removing my clothes and handing each article over one at a time.

It's not like I gave a damn about doing their naked dance in the hallway. It was the principle of it. Once prison guards finished strip-searching the group of us lined up for recreation, I was free to go. Pulling my shirt on again, I strode onto the grass, relieved by the caress of the evening breeze against my face. The fresh air rustled my sweat-dampened prison whites and carried the grassy scent of the pastures to me from the nearby field.

I sought the Deuce out and found the big man pumping iron at the weight machines. He had about fifty pounds on me, built like a freight train — hardly unusual since most guys had nothing better to do than work out excessively.

"Sup, man. Slick said you wanted to talk."

The Deuce passed the weight bar to his spotter and sat up, panting heavily. Sweat glistened on his dark skin, a mix of Hispanic and Black ancestry apparent in his features. "Yeah. I have an opportunity for you. Word around the prison is that you're gonna move local. Stay in the Huntsville area. That right?"

"Yeah. I came from Dallas originally, but I don't have any family left. A friend of a friend assured me I can pick up work easy in this area."

"Your friend's right, if you have the right skills. What you planning on doing?"

"Mechanic. I'm good with cars."

"Well then, I think I can hook you up. When you get out, man, you talk to my boy Tito up in Quickdraw. He runs the garage there."

"Yeah? Thanks, man, I appreciate it."

"You tell Tito I sent you, and maybe pass him a few messages for me."

"Sure thing. Whatever you need." This was it. My chance to get a foot in the door on their outside operations.

"Let him know his problems are—"

I smelled the guy coming from a mile away. The dwindling, evening sun glinted off the shiv swinging toward my back. I ducked and weaved out of the way, pivoting on a foot to face one of our attackers. My fist came up and blocked the assault as another rushed the Deuce from his left. We were outnumbered and the officer on the rec yard had taken that moment to chat with another inmate by the ball court. The boss in the guard tower was probably in the john.

Five of them against two of us. The Deuce was accustomed to prison brawling, but I was the one with the cat-like reflexes. I moved fast, my hands a blur used only to defend myself. I twisted the arm of my primary assailant, forcing him to drop the shiv. Then I kicked the back of his knee in and shoved him face first to the ground. He struck his face on the pavement and was out for the count. His prone sprawl allowed me a glimpse of the blue lightning bolts tatted to the back of his neck.

Gang fight. I'd seen more than a couple since going undercover. The power struggles never stopped.

"Fight!" the officer screamed. Her panicked voice began to rattle off details of the assault over the radio.

I snapped my foot toward another skinhead's face. He had all the markings of a guy in the Aryan Brotherhood, or maybe even the Circle. Hell if I could tell without analyzing his tattoos even closer.

"Holy shit! Look at Tay go!" someone cried. Nobody had seen me fight before, my skills a closely guarded secret until now. I'd only had to hand one dude his ass in the showers back in May, and Warden Johansen had him transferred off the prison unit after his recovery.

Two left standing. Where the hell is the guard? With one man between me and the Deuce, I couldn't defend him from the guy squaring off against him. He was shanked in the side, once, twice, a third time before the gas grenade exploded to my right.

Chapter Two

~JADA~

Tranquil music played through the storefront speakers as I sipped a frosty mocha Frappuccino. I waited for my afternoon client, a new mother with a spa day gift card from her doting fiancé.

I envied women like her with their shit together. A career, a good man, and a family—three of the four things my mom claimed every woman needed for success. Of course, Dani had an education, too. She had it all. She had the life I wanted for myself one day.

The clock ticked, only three minutes past four. The storefront of *Nirvana* had a shop counter beside a fifty-five-gallon aquarium of yellow labidochromis fish and cichlids. By the wall, a shelf held rows of shampoo, conditioner, and personal goodies for the clientele to purchase. Behind us, the salon floor held four chairs with mirrors on each side, as well as two shampoo basins and two hood dryers.

The shop was my baby.

With a tote bag on her arm, Daniela Reyes wandered past the storefront window. The door chime sang and announced her entrance, but I was right in front of the door to bounce to my feet and greet her.

"Afternoon, Dani," I chirped. "You ready for this day of pampering?" I aimed a smile at the woman as she stepped through the stained glass doorway. She'd been my first customer when I opened the doors to the spa last year, and she'd been a regular ever since.

"More than ready. I even left my cell phone behind in the car."

"Poor Russ. Forced to make do without calling you every five minutes to ask why the baby's squirming."

We had a good laugh at her husband and headed into the back. I settled Dani in a room for her wax and massage. At first, we worked in silence until the tough part was over. The backrub came last, a necessary treat.

"So, tell me, how is the baby doing?" I asked as I rubbed sweet almond oil into her knotted shoulder muscles. The aroma of eucalyptus and mint essential oils filled the small room from the nearby diffuser.

"Finally sleeping for at least five hours a night. Seven if we're lucky."

"It will get better, I promise. My cousin Padma said things began to settle out with her daughter around four months."

Serene music played as I treated Dani to an hour long massage, working her muscles loose from head to toe. At the end of her time, I settled the sheet over her relaxed body.

"Take as long as you need, Dani. No rush. Catch a nap if you'd like, and I'll see you in the front for your hair."

While my client dozed in privacy, I stepped to the front and smiled at the three women chatting together. Lisa and Naomi worked for me as hairstylists and had their own preferred customers. I had mine.

"Afternoon, Leigh," I greeted her, only to be embraced in an enthusiastic hug. "Back to freshen up your highlights, huh?" Like Daniela, Leigh MacArthur scheduled regular appointments with me, often visiting together.

"Naomi talked me into it," she said. "How's Dani? I saw her car outside."

"Relaxed and snoozing. It was sweet of Russ to buy her a package."

"Yeah, Russ is a teddy bear," Leigh said with a giggle.

A client for Lisa entered as I settled Leigh at my chair. With Daniela asleep, I had time to highlight and trim her friend.

"How's Mr. MacArthur enjoying his new job?"

"He loves it. He claims being sheriff is simpler than being an Air Force colonel."

We both shared a laugh. I'd voted for Ian, too, and my father had been relieved when the man won the election by a landslide.

By the time Daniela emerged from the back, I'd gotten Leigh under the dryer.

"Are you excited about the upcoming graduation?" I asked her.

"Definitely," Dani replied.

"I can't begin to tell you how happy my dad will be to have a bank in town. He hates driving into the city."

Daniela chuckled. "It's going to take a while to get established, but I hope it'll be worth it. Everyone says they'll open an account to support me, but you know how it is."

"Don't I," I groaned. "I'd be generous if I said even half the people who made promises came in. It was so disappointing."

"It'll happen, Jada. You've got a good place here and a smart business plan."

"Do you really think they'll give me the loan, Dani?"

"Keep this between you and me, but I'm absolutely certain," Daniela said while winking, "you won't have a problem with your approval."

I sagged in relief. "Thank you so much. I can't begin to tell you how grateful I am—"

"Then don't. You've given people a reason to come to Quickdraw over Huntsville. This town needs to grow."

"Quickdraw is home. I couldn't imagine moving anywhere else just to be closer to some big chain store. If we bring the businesses here, people won't have to move." I gestured toward my employees. Lisa, our barber, was busy with one of her male clients. "No one has to drive into the next city to get a job."

When complaints poured in from my customers about the local nail salon, I knew it was an opportunity to move ahead. I wanted to buy the recently vacated shop beside me and renovate it to include mani/pedi work stations.

"It'll all work out, Jada. Trust me."

"You should come out with us when your shift is over," Leigh invited. "We're going to have dinner over at the fondue place that just opened up on Main Street. Cheese, chocolate, and wine."

"I don't want to impose."

"Nonsense." Dani gave a dismissive wave. "The more company the merrier, or so the saying goes. Girls' night out, Jada. It'll be a fun way for you to unwind after a day on your feet. Please?"

Daniela's pleading face and attempt at puppy dog eyes won me over.

Two hours later, I was in the rear seat of Dani's badass car after the girls picked me up from my place. The Perfect Pot had a table waiting for us under a reservation, and soon we had two steaming cheese dips with various veggies and bread bites for dipping.

It was like an extension of our time in the salon, chatter consuming every subject from their school careers to their home lives.

"Did Russ say anything to you about a job?" Leigh suddenly blurted out to our friend.

"No. Is there supposed to be one?" Dani asked in return.

Leigh bit her lower lip. "I don't think so."

"So why are you asking me? You know about as much as I do," Dani assured her. "What happened?"

"Okay, so Ian says they're all done with this stuff, but yesterday some big guy in D.C. called and begged him to go to Palestine to handle some big problem."

I nearly choked on my wine. "Wait, what? Palestine as in the Middle East, not Palestine, Texas, you mean?"

"You know that security company he owns?"

"Yeah, he installed the system at my place. I love it," I replied.

"Well, he also manages private contract work for the military, too," Leigh explained. "Sort of like a mercenary. He stepped back from the business and promoted a close friend to take it over because he wanted to become sheriff."

"And be here for you and Sophia," Dani reminded her.

"Oh, wow. I mean, I had no idea he was Special Forces."

"You know Ian. He hates tooting his own horn." Leigh poured wine in all our glasses. "Of course, I love that about him, and a huge part of me is glad he's not going out as much anymore."

"Russ promises he's done with it all, too, but sometimes I think he's tired of the home life every day. I mean, they're going from nonstop excitement to posing as old men sitting on porches with games of Checkers."

"He's in the volunteer fire department," I pointed out. "He does get some excitement."

"When do they *ever* have anything to do?" Dani asked. She shrugged and dipped a breadstick into the fondue pot.

"Maybe we should go adopt a bunch of kittens from the shelter and put them up in trees." I giggled at my own absurd suggestion. "You know when he came in to get his haircut from Naomi, I overheard him telling her he *likes* being a stay-at-home dad."

Leigh sighed. "Ian says the same thing, but I feel awful leaving him with Sophia all the time when I'm in class."

"You ladies have good men. The last jerk I went out with hated kids." I sighed and pulled over the dessert menu. "How do you even choose one when these all look amazing?"

Leigh leaned over for a peek. "Oooh, turtle fudge."

"You can't go wrong with chocolate peanut butter," Dani said.

We indulged and ordered both of the sweet treats. I dipped marshmallow after marshmallow into a pot of rich chocolate laced with gooey peanut butter. The pieces melted in my mouth, the perfect end to a fabulous evening. I thought they'd have to roll me out of my chair and to Dani's car, but somehow I made it to the backseat.

"I had a great time, ladies. Thanks for inviting me."

Leigh and Dani exchanged mischievous grins. "We're heading down to The Outlets this weekend. Come with us," Dani invited.

"That's almost a three hour drive!" I protested.

"We'll take Ian's SUV and ride in style," Leigh promised as they parked in front of my house.

"I don't know…"

"What else do you have to do?" Dani asked.

After I agreed to accompany them on their wild shopping spree, I stepped up to my porch and unlocked the door.

My humble home was a single-level house with a shoebox-sized front yard, only a five-minute walk up the street from the spa. Before I had the day spa, I took clients off the street and styled hair in the second bedroom, tolerating the cramped quarters as a necessity.

Maybe the floors needed a good sanding and the windows could use new screens, but I couldn't complain when it was all mine. I paid it off before taking on a pile of loans to open my business.

Leaving my shoes on the porch, I stepped inside and clicked on the living room light. A love seat, modest television, and an aquarium shelf filled the space, leaving no room for anything else. "Did you miss me, girls?" I peeked down into a fish tank at my sorority of female bettas then pinched in a bit of their food. I had a second tank on the shelf above them, home to a single enormous male with a pearlescent body and lavender fins. I'd paid far too much money for him from a breeder two years ago, but I loved him.

My phone rang as I was wiggling out of my bra. I tossed it onto the corner of the couch and flopped into the seat. God, I loved that moment of setting the tatas free after a tiring day. "Hey, Mom," I answered. I put my feet up after tucking the phone between my ear and shoulder, the remote and PlayStation controller on my lap. I signed into Netflix and planned to let the next episode of *Orange is the New Black* drown out my mother.

"So, I have pleasing news for you, Jada."

"Uh huh."

"Hazim's son agreed to meet with you this weekend. Aren't you happy?"

"Yeah."

"You will have to do something with your hair, of course, and visit the store tomorrow to buy something nice to wear. No more of those frumpy clothes you're so fond of buying. That dress you wore to your father's family reunion resembled a potato sack, baby. You must pick something else. Now, he isn't Indian, but what does race matter? Love is love, as your father proves." My mom was Indian, but she'd married a white guy after she immigrated to the U.S. She was pregnant with me at the time, and Dad had raised me like his own child.

"Uh huh."

"Well, what do you think?" Mom asked. "Jada? Is this weekend good for you?"

"No," I replied automatically, absolutely clueless. I hadn't heard a word she said until then, but her tone implied that 'no' was the only correct answer. Last time she had set me up, I'd wanted to claw my egotistical date's eyes out. He'd spent most of the evening checking out every woman we passed.

"You did not even consider my request," she argued.

I didn't need to. My mom lived for one thing, and that was getting grandchildren out of me.

I'm not even thirty. It's not like the expiration stamp on my ovaries was dated for tomorrow, but she behaved like my eggs were already spoiled.

"He is a nice boy. What else are you doing this weekend that's more important than meeting a sweet young man? He will be coming home for good from the military soon, his mother says."

With my finger on the mute button, I groaned out loud. I had nothing against military guys, but if I was going to give up my freedom to date, I'd rather it be with someone in the same state. My mother's definition of soon could be as much as four years.

My show resumed where I left off, on a hot and heavy lesbian sex scene. "I'm going out on a date with a woman," I replied. "Two of them actually. Sorry, Mom, gotta go. Long day at the spa and all."

"*What?*"

"Love is love, right? Talk to you soon, bye!" I hung up, silenced the ringer, and tossed the phone aside.

I will not look. Not gonna break, I told myself, refusing to give my cell a second glance. Mom meant well, but I wanted to find a man on my terms. My budding business was everything to me, and I wasn't going to let some guy disrupt my focus.

So what if I was the aquatics version of a crazy cat lady?

Chapter Three

~TAYLOR~

"Are you ready to do this?" Nadir asked.

I glanced at my squad mate and longtime pal. He wore his hair long and loose against his shoulders like an Arab Fabio. He'd infiltrated so many terrorist cells the marines had granted him a permanent pass to break grooming standards.

"I don't have much of a choice," I replied. "Ian is counting on this."

"That's true," he agreed.

"What I don't understand is why the local police department can't handle the matter now that their crooked chief is gone."

"Because," Nadir said, "there are only five or six men on staff. It takes months of dedicated investigation following, observing, and stalking targets to put together a good case. Because the local police department doesn't have the authority we've been granted. We can play hard with the rules."

"But why not tell the new chief?"

"Plausible deniability. Ian believes the new man is as honest as they come, but we don't want to put him in an awkward situation."

"You don't trust his acting to be up to par, eh?"

"That too," Nadir said, grinning. "With the governor coming up for re-election soon, we have his power behind us. He wants this sewn up before elections next year so he can take credit for the decline in drug-related violence."

"Which means we better not fuck this up by leaking information to the wrong people. I don't know what he's scared about. He only has one true opponent and the guy gives me the creeps whenever I see him on the news."

"Yeah, but he's rich, and wealth is power in this state," Nadir said. "So have you rehearsed your story?"

"Hell yeah. I figured I'd go meet this guy tomorrow, come clean about my phony record, and say the Deuce sent me."

In the month since the attempted murder on the rec yard, I'd learned the man knew a hit was coming for him. He'd counted on my arrival, and his right-hand man at the prison let me know I'd performed to expectations. I was the kind of guy they were looking for.

"Well, I'm prepared to help you as much as needed since Ian and Russ aren't able."

"Yeah, law-abiding citizens can't be seen in the company of an ex-con. I get it, but don't have to like being isolated in this little shithole."

We passed through the unfamiliar residential area of Quickdraw. The place was new to me despite two of our friends living outside of the city limits. Here, I was a stranger, and the two of us were studied by curious, but friendly, faces peering through the half-lowered windows.

"What kind of place did you rent me?"

"It's not horrible."

I groaned. "If you gotta start it off by saying 'it's not horrible,' man…"

We pulled off the street and into a pebble drive in front of a small house without a garage. The neighbors waved to us, a family of two adults and four kids. I waved back as I stepped from the car and stared at the shack in front of me.

Peeling paint, torn screens, and rotting wood window shutters were part of my new home. I sighed. "It could be worse," I muttered under my breath.

"Here's the keys. You're paid up for six months," Nadir said when we reached the stoop.

We stepped inside and saw the interior matched the outside down to the yellowing water stains on the white ceiling. He must have rented the oldest place on the block. The floors were laminate and clean, but scratched and peeling. I had a master bedroom of less than average size, a smaller bedroom as big as my closet back home, and one bathroom.

There was an old, musty smell in the air, and the lingering scent of cigarette smoke, which had darkened the curtains and stained the walls.

"The guy who owned this place died of lung cancer a couple months back, I guess. His daughter rented it to me for cheap when I said an ex-con friend of mine would need a place to stay."

I grimaced. "Not surprising." I glanced at the forty-two-inch television and PlayStation 3 on a small, modest entertainment stand. "You brought my stuff?"

"Yeah. Your brother and I brought some things from your place a couple days ago."

My first stop was the bathroom for a shower while Nadir amused himself with my PlayStation 3. Once I finished washing away the prison funk, we made plans to fetch my Cadillac from Houston the next day then went to choke down some burgers from the fast food spot down the road.

"Come on. Admit it. This place isn't so bad," Nadir said.

"Yeah, for being out in the middle of nowhere," I replied. "I'll try to view it as a vacation. Hell, at least I can roam and hunt wild game."

Nadir scrutinized his burger. "This tastes like despair and greasy sadness. We should have hunted instead of buying fast food."

"Agreed, bro."

"Anyway, I'll be in town Saturday night," Nadir said. "Mom and Dad colluded with a friend to set me up and I've been invited to dinner."

I smirked, amused by Nadir's disgruntled frown. "Family on the first date, huh? Poor bastard."

"Yeah, laugh it up. Anyway, afterward, I can meet you up in the woods near Ian's for a hunt. That late, maybe we can drag Russ out with us, too."

"Maybe. Don't be so sure on it," I replied. Russell became such a homebody after the birth of his son that the rest of us rarely saw him anymore. Ever since Dani had questioned his desire to be the stay-at-home parent, he'd taken his job above and beyond the call of duty. Shit. Even a kid needed to experience the great outdoors sometime, right? Juni even offered to make a bear-sized baby sling if it would get him outside with all of us again.

"Yeah, I know."

We tossed our trash, drank a couple of beers, and then Nadir was on his way. True to his word, we drove down into Houston the next day, giving me the chance to check out my auto body shop. I'd trusted my baby to my little brother and right-hand man, Oscar. He thought my undercover jail time was karma for all the years I'd picked on him.

Later, after driving back in my newly detailed Caddie, I secured a job at Tito's Scrapyard & Auto. In my first hour on shift, I learned the place was crooked as a barrel of snakes and one of the other mechanics dealt pot on the side.

This is going to be easy. They don't even try to hide the shit they're doing.

I was on my way back into town from a visit with my brother two days later when I saw her alongside the road. A young woman stood in front of a raised car hood while smoke billowed into the wind. In only a few seconds, I drew conclusions and determined she'd be stuck out in the sun until someone arrived to help.

Not my business. It's not my business.

Through the driver's side window, I caught a glimpse of her brown sugar skin, neatly pinned black hair, and the sharp, curve-hugging business suit accenting her body's best features. The sleek pencil skirt made her look like some kind of fertility goddess, drawing my attention right to her hips.

She was on her way somewhere important. Had to be.

Fuck. Why can't I ever mind my own business? I wondered. A second later, I'd pulled into a gas station half a mile down the interstate then rounded back to park behind her. As I left my car and shut the door behind me, she moved back a step to remain on guard.

"Can I do something to…?" The offer died on my lips as the wind kicked up, kissing my acute sense of smell with cinnamon, cardamom, and some other unique scent. Spicy and sweet, like the foxy woman in front of me. I stared.

"Can you what?" she asked, defensive and wary.

"I… help? With your car?" I finally asked. The world around me—open interstate, speeding cars, and rumbling Mack trucks—became insignificant, and the only thing I could see was her gorgeous face. All that mattered was her big brown eyes and glossy, pouting lips.

Mine. She was meant to be mine. And I'd do anything I had to for her to realize we were fated for each other. Swallowing down the nervous tension clenching my throat, I put on an easygoing smile.

"All of a sudden, my car got really hot, and I have no idea what the hell happened."

"Mind if I take a look?" She waved me toward the engine, but kept her eyes on me like I was some stalker preparing to shove her into my car.

Smart girl. Fuck. Why now of all times? Stumbling across the woman I was meant to love while I was pretending to be a drug-dealing loser was the last thing I expected or wanted.

I waved off the steam pouring from the radiator and engine.

"Your radiator is busted, ma'am."

She cussed under her breath and looked at the time on her cell phone. "Figures, on the day I need it the most…"

"You headed somewhere important?"

"Yeah. I'm signing for a business loan today, and I need to get all the way to Houston to my bank. If I don't do it today, it'll have to wait until after the weekend..."

"And you were all excited about doing it now, am I right?"

She nodded.

"I'll give you a ride," I offered. "Are you from around here?"

"Yeah, I live in Quickdraw. I know I can get a ride home from my friend who works there, but I can't just leave my car alongside the road like this all day. Ugh. Maybe if…" Her finger slid down the phone screen, probably scrolling through contacts in her list. "I can ask my dad if one of his friends can tow it to Tito's."

"So after I drop you off, I'll come back for your ride and drop it off at Tito's."

One of her perfectly shaped brows arched. "And I'm supposed to trust you with my car keys while I'm fifty miles away?"

"You're in big luck 'cause I happen to *work* at Tito's now." I grinned, amused by her wide-eyed expression. "I'm normally under hoods, but I have experience with a tow truck. Go ahead. Verify it."

After she scrutinized my driver's license and phoned the boss, she returned it to me with a faint smile.

"Okay, Taylor. I'll accept your offer. I'm Jada."

"Nice to meet you, ma'am. I—" She raised her phone to snap a picture of me.

"What the hell?"

Jada maneuvered around in to the back of my Cadillac and snapped another photo of the license plate.

"What are you doing?"

"In case I go missing," she replied.

I stared at her.

"You can never be too safe," Jada insisted. "Besides, my dad wouldn't ever let me hear the end of it if he knew I was hitchhiking with a stranger."

"Yeah? Who's your dad?" After she slipped into the passenger seat, I shut the door and crossed to my side.

"Chief Hunt."

I cut my eyes over to the sexy girl in my passenger seat. Jada's exotic features and ochre skin tone clashed with my memories of a sandy-haired white guy at the Quickdraw police station. "Huh?"

"He's my stepdad," Jada explained. "He adopted me when he married my mom, but… well, he's just Dad to me. I love him. He's the only father I've ever known." Her eyes twinkled as if she had more to say on the subject, but she bit her tongue.

"That's cool." I took my eyes off her curves and focused on the road. "So which bank we heading to?"

"Prime Advantage Bank of Texas. It's at… ugh, wait. I'll just add it to my GPS."

"No, it's cool. I know the way there. I use that bank. Great coincidence, huh?"

I should have figured as much, and I was happy I'd only be dropping her off. As much as I'd love to see Daniela, we had to pretend to be strangers.

"So, you said a business loan," I prompted. A steady current from the air conditioner stirred her scent, subjecting me to the worst torture I'd ever experienced. It took all of my willpower to focus on the road instead of my increasing desire to get my head between her thighs.

"I'm expanding my business," she replied without giving any detail.

Wary girl. Guess that's a good thing. I'd dated a few girls who gave me their whole life story on the first meeting, which left no mystery to unravel later. Boring. "Oh yeah? What do you do?"

"I own the salon and day spa in town."

"Oh, I've passed by there. It's just across the street from the garage. Can't say I have any need to visit a spa, though."

"You'd be surprised," Jada said, opening up a bit more. "We cut men's hair and I have a couple clients who get regular massages." She glanced at me, and for the first time, a smile spread over her face. "One of my friends, her husband comes in for manscaping regularly. He's like a bear."

Fucking Russ. It's gotta be. Choking back my laughter was an exercise in futility, so I let it loose. "I don't even wanna know what all's involved with manscaping. Sounds painful."

"It's not that bad," she insisted. "When I wax guys, I get it done and over with quickly."

I winced. "I don't think you could pay me to lie down for a wax." I wasn't all that hairy anyway, unlike Russ who looked like he was settling down for a winter's hibernation. My body hair was fine and soft, the same tawny brown as my pelt when I took my cougar form. It blended with my skin.

"It's really not as bad as Hollywood makes it out to be." Jada's husky chuckle raised goose bumps on my skin. I imagined the sultry sound huffed against my ear, a bad decision I came to regret when my stiffening dick pressed against my jeans.

I shivered.

"You okay?" she asked, concerned.

"Yeah, I'm fine," I lied. "Anyway, I'll pop in for a trim one day."

Once she succeeded in gaining my agreement to enter her shop, Jada changed topics and told me about some of Quickdraw's popular spots. All two of them.

"So on Thursday and Friday nights, a lot of people go to the VFW Hall for bingo nights. Any other time, there's a little sports bar at the edge of town with cheap beer and overpriced alcohol. I think they water the beer down."

"Damn. What the hell does anybody do for fun?"

"Go to Huntsville," she chirped. "There's a country western club and some university bars people like to visit. Aside from that, we don't have much in the actual town."

"At least there's a liquor store," I grumbled. Drinking a beer after work would probably be the highlight of my day.

"Watch your wallet around there after dark, though. The hookers are pickpockets and a couple folk have been roughed up."

"Y'all's town has hookers? Like actual hos and prostitutes?" Snickering, I merged with the main highway and caught a glimpse of the sign. We had nearly an hour to go.

"Doesn't every place?"

"True enough. So their pimps get physical with folk?"

Jada shrugged. "Rumor says drug exchanges go bad, but the cops never turn up anything."

"Well, thanks for the heads-up."

We chatted the rest of the way, some of it small talk, some of it deeper, meaningful, and hard-earned information she appeared reluctant to give. By the time I dropped her off, I knew all about her struggle to bring better local businesses to her little town, and her dreams for expanding the salon's services. Before she left my car, I got her to accept my phone number and input hers into my phone.

The timing was crap, but hell if I was going to let her slip through my fingers.

"Thanks, Taylor."

I idled until she was safely through the bank doors before I pulled out from the parking lot. I activated the Bluetooth and impatiently waited until Russ greeted me with a sleep-deprived voice.

"Russ, you won't believe what just happened, man."

"Damnit, Taylor, Mateo is napping and it's my only chance to get some shut-eye myself."

"Screw sleep, this is more important."

"I'm gonna beat your a—"

"I found her."

"You found who, you flea-ridden fuzzball?" Russell grouched.

"*Her,*" I breathed, still shocked by the discovery. "You and Ian are starting a damn trend."

The gruffness in Russell's voice faded in an instant. "Holy crap, for real? Who is she, man?"

"Your manscaper." I had to get a small dig in while I could.

"Who? My man—no way! You mean Jada?"

"She's the one, Russ. And ha! You admit to getting waxed."

"Look, y'all know my back is awful. I look like I'm trapped between a shift or something. So one day, Dani sort of offhandedly mentioned... we're not about to have this damned conversation right now. What happened with Jada?"

I relayed the day's events, starting with spotting her broken down car all the way up to dropping her off.

"How did you stand it?" I asked him.

"Resisting?" Russ guessed, too insightful for his own good.

"I wanted to pull over to rip her clothes off." Our animal halves could be exceptionally focused, single-minded creatures. Ian had admitted his eagle had two modes, consisting of sating his hunger for food or his new wife. I'd envied him until now.

"It didn't kick in for me right off, remember? I was still mourning Katie." Russ quieted for a moment. He never really did stop grieving, and that was fine, the mating bond was a powerful thing to deny even in death. "When I finally realized Dani was the one for me, hell, I was already about to bond with her. So I guess I never did resist it."

"I better call Ian next, huh?"

"You better. With you being undercover, it's going to be hard pulling off a love affair."

"The timing is shit. What do I do, though? Ignore her and make a move later? What if she moves on?"

"Hey, don't forget, man, if she's really *the* one, she'll be drawn to you, too."

His words should have reassured me, but I had a feeling this whole thing was going to be a tricky balancing act. Good things cats always landed on their feet.

Chapter Four

~JADA~

Daniela and I stopped at IHOP to celebrate the approval of my business loan. I was floating on cloud nine, so happy I could barely sit still while we perused the menus.

"Thanks for giving me the ride. Let me cover the bill, okay?"

"It's no big deal, sheesh. You don't even charge me a fraction of what you should for my hair."

"I know what they charge in Houston, but that's not why I opened a business. Most of the people in Quickdraw are older with retirement pensions and limited income, you know? Why would I want to charge Granny a hundred bucks for a deep condition, trim, and roller set?"

"True. So, what about that guy who dropped you off? I had to look at his photo twice after you sent it. He's sexy as hell."

"I know! His eyes are unreal." I slid my phone from the table for another glance at Taylor's handsome face. He had chiseled good looks, like a male fashion model caught off the runway. I imagined the body beneath his tee and oil-stained jeans, picturing a flawless physique of lean muscle and tight abs. "And he's sweet, too. I know that shouldn't be an afterthought, but most guys like him act like I should feel lucky they want to be with me."

"And this one?"

"We just laughed and talked most of the way once he broke the ice. I kept trying to shut him down, but he didn't give up. He's amazing."

"Well?" Daniela gave me a look.

"Well what?"

"You're single, and he's new to town…"

"How do you know he's new to town?"

Daniela pursed her lips and shot me a mischievous look. "Well, I kinda saw him yesterday when I took my car in for an oil change. I don't let Russ touch my baby. He's great when it comes to guns and all of that stuff, but he doesn't know the first thing about upkeep for a vehicle."

"Ahh, gotcha. So he worked on your car."

She nodded. "Friendly guy. New to town," she repeated.

"Probably not single," I interjected.

"Didn't he give you his number?"

I rolled my eyes and turned to face the approaching waitress. We placed our orders before continuing the conversation. "Yeah, but I'm pretty sure it wasn't for personal calls. He has my car keys, remember?"

"Oh." Dani looked disappointed.

My friend brought Taylor up again on the way home, asking if I planned to give him a call about more than the car.

"Oh goodness, no. I told you, I'm probably not his type. Those kinds of guys always want a girl like the chick in the workout videos I loaned you. Look at me. He'd get lost in my fat." I groaned into one hand. I carried a lot of weight in my breasts and ass, but especially in the hips where golden stretch marks streaked my skin. Guys loved my hourglass figure until the clothes came off and they saw my voluptuous silhouette included tiger stripes, too.

"What rolls?" Dani asked irritably. "You're smaller than I am."

"You just had a baby."

"I'm only five pounds heavier than I was before I had Mateo. I've been this size for years, and I'm okay with it now. Wouldn't you say Russ is one of *those kinds of guys*?"

I shot her a skeptical look. "Just because some fairy godmother blessed you and Leigh with sexy-as-fuck men, doesn't mean she's got a third one hidden for me."

"And how will you know without checking it out?" Dani demanded.

"I don't know. Maybe. I'm just trying to focus on work, you know?"

Daniela reached across the center console and took my hand. "Live a little, huh? The loan is secured, meaning the shop space next door will officially be yours and your spa is going to be a hit. I think you deserve a good guy in that mix, too."

"Dani—"

"Or at least a good lay. When was the last time you got some, chica?"

My cheeks never showed a blush well, but I always felt the heat creeping into my face. "A couple years," I muttered. "It's definitely, ah, been a while."

A vision flitted through my mind of returning to Tito's and finding Taylor under the hood, his coveralls tied around his waist to reveal a sculpted upper body. He'd be all muscles and lean angles, like a statue carved from sandstone. A golden brown Adonis with beautiful topaz-blue eyes. I must have stared into them at least a dozen times on the way.

"Okay. You win, you win. I'll call him tonight."

***

"How did everything go?"

"From crappy to good," I answered my mother while I washed my hands in the sink.

"What happened?"

"My car broke down on the way to the bank."

"If your car's in the shop, how'd get you get to Houston?" Danny asked. He noisily chewed a handful of Oreos while loitering in front of the pantry. I shot my little brother a dirty look. In a few months, he and his buddies would be heading off to boot camp, so he was enjoying one last summer with us at home.

"You'll ruin your dinner, Daniel. Put them away." My mom shook a finger at him. "Now, what was it you were saying, Jada?"

I bit my lip and turned to start dicing the vegetables for the night's salad. "Daniela Reyes gave me a ride home."

"Nice girl. Speaking of which, the wedding invitations arrived today. Not for another three months, but I guess with so much family out of the state and country they wanted to get them out early. Did you know Russell's mother lives in Russia?"

I shook my head. Insignificant facts easily amused my mother, but the news didn't surprise me; the guy was built like a Russian wrestler. "I wonder if that's why he's named Russ," I mused.

"You said ride home, though. How'd you *get* there," Danny asked. Ignoring Mom, he popped another Oreo into his mouth. I figured some of it stemmed from a desire to binge on things while he could. There wouldn't be cookies in basic training.

The front door opened and shut. After a thrilling day of keeping the peace in Quickdraw, my dad usually thundered into the house, showered, then collapsed somewhere to play a boring tactical warfare game on his laptop. He poked his head into the kitchen first and brightened when he saw me.

"Hi, guys. Joining us for dinner tonight, too, baby?"

"Hi, Daddy. I—"

"Jada hitched a ride into the city," Danny snitched promptly.

"You little asshole," I shot at my grinning brother, hurling a pot holder at him.

"You took a ride from who?" Dad asked. He twisted to stare at me.

Kid brothers. Ugh. "His name's Taylor Jackson. He's really sweet and gave me a ride to Houston, and then he wouldn't even accept gas money from me for the trouble."

"Taylor Jackson," he repeated in a low voice. I recognized the look on my father's face, his expression darkening like storm clouds. He was trying to place the name with known troublemakers in the area. "Doesn't ring a bell."

I sighed in relief. "He works at the garage and is fairly new to town, so lay off a little, okay?"

Dad grunted and let it slide. Once he left the kitchen, I approached Danny to recover the pot holder. I stole a few of his cookies, too.

"Shouldn't you watch what you eat, Jada?"

Mom's words cut through me, a cold knife trimming the elation from my chipper mood. I sighed and started to put them back, but Danny pushed my hand away and shook his head.

"Eat them," he mouthed at me.

I tried, but the taste and desire for sweets was ruined by my mother's perpetual need to point out my weight at every opportunity.

During dinner, Mom didn't miss a chance to quiz me about Taylor.

Probably worried I won't show any interest in her military playboy from Houston if I find someone on my own, I thought bitterly. She'd probably promised my cooperation to the guy's dad like we were back to the days of dowries and courting. Doctor Hazim Zaman was a nice guy, or so I thought the single time I met him, but too old fashioned for my tastes.

I escaped the house as soon as I could, but the phone rang as soon as I stepped through my front door. My parents must have some kind of x-ray sense, a vision allowing them to see clear across town into my living room. That or they called my neighbors and asked if my car was in the drive yet. Both options rated high on the Creep-o-Meter.

A glance at the caller ID revealing Dad's number. I sighed. "Hi, Daddy."

"Did he tell you he's fresh out of lockup?" Dad asked.

"Huh?"

"Your new friend. Did he tell you he's been in prison? He has a list of—"

"You looked him up?" My voice raised, sharpening more on each word. My dad had always been tough on any guy I dated, but he'd never run one of my boyfriends through the system before. Worse, I hadn't even been asked on a date with Taylor yet.

"I sure did," he growled. "The name sounded familiar, so I asked Marty about him. The kid has a criminal record rivaling an east coast rapper. It's a wonder he isn't still behind bars."

"Daddy, did you seriously have Marty run a background check on Taylor the moment I left the house?"

"I did, and I don't regret it either." He sighed. "Jada, you deserve better than a thug. Why don't you take a lesson from your friend Leigh Denton and stay clear of troublemakers, okay?"

Before Leigh married Ian MacArthur, she'd gotten knocked up by one of the local pot dealers. My dad locked him up for selling stolen narcotics before she even had their baby.

I'd felt so bad for her then. Now she had a happy marriage and a bright future for her daughter.

"Okay, Daddy. He did a nice thing for me, but I didn't plan to hang around him, if that's what you're worried about. I'm gonna go to bed now though, okay?"

"I didn't mean to upset you, punkin."

"I'm not upset," I assured him. Miffed, exhausted, wishing sometimes I could make my own life's choices, but not upset. "I'm really tired, and I have a lot of stuff to do tomorrow with the spa."

"Okay. I love you."

"Love you, too."

I tossed the phone onto my bed on my way to the restroom where I drew a hot bath. I poured a generous amount of orange blossom bath salts into the steaming water then soaked while an audiobook played from my Kindle.

With business on the rise and an expansion in the works for my day spa, I didn't need to invite trouble into my life. I lay down in bed an hour later, forcing the memory of Taylor's smile from my thoughts.

I knew it was too good to be true.
At least I had a planned shopping trip with the girls.

Chapter Five

~TAYLOR~

Jada didn't call. I'd expected as much to happen once gossip spread about my so-called past. Daniela and Leigh both called to chat about her, but Jada's number never showed up on my call list, despite their efforts to convince her to give me a chance.

Nadir had the same shitty luck. His blind date for the weekend bailed. Her parents apologized profusely, fed him well, and then he showed up at my place for a few rounds of video games on my PlayStation over beers. Neither of us wanted to hunt in our crappy moods. We'd slaughter half the forest.

"Were you actually looking forward to meeting your mystery chick?"

"Yeah, maybe," he grumbled. "Would be nice to have what you three found, you know?" My pal hesitated for a moment then asked, "Have you seen Sasha recently?"

I shook my head.

"She's pretty depressed."

I sighed. "I know. I really wanted to be that man for them, too. Honest, dude. Her sisters are amazing women, but there just wasn't anything there beyond the sex and our friendship. You know what happened. If I stayed with them, we would have gone through that again."

"I know," Nadir said sadly. "I'm sorry for that. I only meant to say that you should call her. She blames herself even after all this time."

My ex-girlfriend Sasha was in a soul-mated partnership with two other lionesses. They'd wanted me to be their alpha, their pride's male, and I'd given it my all until the inevitable happened.

I still emailed Nandi, the youngest lioness of their pride. As much as I adored them, I couldn't give them what they truly needed.

At least I'd found my mate, even if she didn't know it. Nadir had no one.

Screw it. If she's not going to come to me, I'll go to her. If she's not interested, then I need to hear it from her mouth.

I made a visit to her salon on my first day off, hopeful Ian's plan hadn't blown my chance with my one and only. If I was lucky, there was a logical reason behind the extended silence… like dropping her phone in the sink or letting the days slip away from her with work.

Probably not. I had a feeling Ian's top secret plan had fucked me good.

A sign above the doors read *Nirvana* in cursive, golden font. Smaller, plain white letters beneath the store name indicated, 'salon and spa services'. The place was tucked between a vacant building and a thrift store.

I opened the door and stepped inside, finding myself treated to gentle music suited for meditation and the spicy scent of sandalwood, vanilla, and jasmine. A sexy brunette approached from behind the counter, clothed in a tiny strapless dress. Her blue eyes dragged over me from head to toe. "Can I help you, sir?" she drawled.

Glancing over the main room revealed no sign of Jada until I noticed her unattended purse at a nearby station. "Actually… yeah. Y'all got a barber here?" I asked.

"That's me. I'm Lisa. Whatcha need done?"

"Fade me up." I'd pay for a haircut if it could stall until Jada appeared to see me.

I settled in the chair and offered my name to the spiky haired girl as she fastened the black drape around me.

"Hope you don't mind me saying this, but your eyes are gorgeous, Taylor."

I chuckled. "Thanks. I get that a lot."

"So, are you new in town?"

"Yeah. Rented a place over on Davenport Street. I work for Big Tito."

Lisa's trimmers began their work as she engaged me in casual chitchat. I watched her in the mirror.

Too skinny, I thought. I'd always liked plump girls with hips. Something I could squeeze and hold onto during sex. A girl I could fuck hard without fearing I'd break her. A girl who could carry her weight with confidence without giving a damn about what anyone thought but me and her. Lisa was pretty, but the attraction was nonexistent.

Jada had me firmly under her spell, fantasizing about how soft she'd feel in my arms, the sweet scent of her skin, and how much I wanted to taste her lips on mine.

"How's that look?" Lisa asked, interrupting my fantasies about Jada.

Taking some time to admire my reflection in the mirror first, I couldn't find a thing to complain about.

"Looks great. Thanks. What do I owe you?"

"Fifteen."

I gave her a twenty instead and told her to keep the change.

"Here's my card and my number, you know… in case you wanna be a repeat customer sometime. You can gimme a call whenever or—" her brown eyes drifted down to my pocket and the cell phone inside it "—you can text me at that number. Any time."

"Hey, Lisa, I'm gonna go—"

I twisted toward the source of the voice to find Jada framed in the doorway at the salon's rear, staring at me.

"Hi, Jada."

"Hi," she replied, guarded.

"You two know each other?" The disappointment blossomed on Lisa's face, her expression falling like toast, jelly side down.

"I gave her a ride to Houston the other day," I offered, remaining vague. I stepped from beside Lisa and approached Jada at the back of the room.

"Got some time to talk?"

"What do you want to talk about?" she asked.

"Why you didn't call. Did I do something? Did I upset you?"

"You didn't upset me." She fidgeted.

"Then what's wrong? We were all cool when you got out of the car, now you can barely look at me."

"You didn't tell me you were fresh out of prison."

I sighed. A quick glance to Lisa's direction revealed her sweeping the mess by her station while pretending not to eavesdrop. Her eyes had grown wide.

"So I did some time."

"You didn't tell me that."

"It's not exactly the first thing I cough up when I meet someone. How'd you find out?" I asked, trying to play it safe.

"My dad told me. Word gets around in a small town, so I guess one of your homies down at Tito's must have spread the word."

Damnit. I knew this was going to happen. "Please, hear me out."

She hesitated, brown eyes fixed to my face. "Why were you in jail?"

"I didn't kill anyone, Jada. I'm not a rapist, child molester, or a murderer. I made some mistakes that put me in a bad situation. That's all. I served my time." I hadn't lied to her yet; I made the mistake of letting Ian talk me into this mess, and I'd never laid an aggressive hand on a woman in all of my life. Kids were great, and I'd sooner fuck someone up for harming a child.

"What. Did. You. Do?" Jada repeated, enunciating the words.

With a heavy heart, I told her the crimes in my file. She'd probably look me up by name later to see the phony record in the system, if she didn't have her dad do it.

"My conviction is for assault and battery. I have a couple small possession charges, too."

"Are you a dopehead?"

"I don't do drugs."

"So you deal them." Disgust laced her voice. "Get out."

So much for Russell's claim about fated mates feeling mutual attraction. I didn't have a chance, and I wouldn't hang around to beg like the damned dog shifter at Big Tito's.

I held on to my dignity and walked out.

~JADA~

Lisa stared at me when the door shut. "I can't believe you let that sexy-ass man walk out of here because he *used* to deal drugs."

"It's a pretty damning background."

She shrugged. "Everybody makes mistakes."

"You know as well as I do that shady business happens across the street. It's like he got out of prison and went right back to it."

Lisa shrugged a second time. "Ain't got anything to do with me. Or you. So he got a job — a good paying job, I might add — at a shop that's got a reputation. Doesn't mean he's dealing. It's better than no job, right?"

"I guess."

"He gave you a ride to Houston, girl, without wanting anything in return. Didn't he have Tito cut you a deal on that new radiator, too? Shit, when mine had that leak, he charged me about eight hundred dollars."

"So? Giving me a ride and a discount on some work doesn't mean he's a law-abiding citizen now."

"I'm just saying give him a chance and find out instead of assuming." Lisa glanced toward the door. "If you don't want him, can I have him?"

"What kind of question is that?" I demanded.

"Well, if I walk over there and chat him up again, are you going to flip tables later over it?"

"I kinda sent him packing, so why should I care?"

"Because I know you. You'll regret it later and wonder if you made a bad mistake. You'll feel *awful*."

Sulking, I glanced at my phone. "I'll give him one date." *Daddy is gonna hate it. Good thing I'm a grown woman now. Lisa's right. I'd feel terrible. Hell, I already feel terrible for how I treated him just now.*

Taylor answered on the first ring, a little overenthusiastic for my tastes, but a pleasant change from the usual guys who played games. "Hello, Ms. Hunt." He sounded like a kicked puppy, contradicting my previous idea regarding his enthusiasm. The guilt washed over me anew.

"Dinner, Lottie's Italian Cafe, seven o'clock."

"Huh?"

"You want a chance, I'm giving you one. So don't be late."

Lisa flashed me a thumb's up. After I ended the call, she forced me into my own salon chair and plucked the curling irons out of the cradle.

"You can't go on a date looking like this."

"What? I'm not trying to impress him." *Not yet.*

"He just got out of prison. He probably hasn't been laid in *years*."

"I'm not planning to have sex with him on the first date!" I cried.

"I'm just sayin'. Take some protection with you anyway, girl."

I rolled my eyes. My hair was so sleek and straight it was impossible for me to get a curl into it. Lisa had a secret with the hair spray and a method for pinning them afterward. By the time they fell for my date, I'd have lovely, loose, mermaid waves.

"Don't you dare show up without dressing sexy," Lisa warned me as I headed out the door half an hour later.

"It's only a first date."

"With a man who looks like he belongs on GQ's cover," she shot back at me.

"His looks aren't why I like him."

"Ha! I knew you liked him!"

Once home from the salon, I pulled out a black dress with a fitted waist and sweetheart neckline. Ever since high school, I'd had trouble squeezing into dresses without stretchy busts and flowy skirts. The hem fluttered two inches above my knees, modest but sexy without danger of showing him my panties. Paired with strappy wedges, I looked and felt amazing.

Lottie's Italian Cafe was one of the nicer eateries in town. Nice as in there was an actual wine menu. I arrived on foot at a quarter to seven, expecting to wait for Taylor, but I entered to find him already at a table. He'd traded in his worn jeans and t-shirt for khaki slacks and a button-down shirt.

Damn, he cleans up nice.

Taylor stood and seated me like a gentleman. "I ordered some wine. I hope you don't mind. An old friend recommended one."

"A friend from prison or before that?"

"Before that." He had a warm, endearing laugh paired with a smile capable of melting ice. "My friend Nadir is practically a career wine snob. If it comes in a bottle, he's had it, no matter what part of the world it comes from."

"Nadir?" Both of my brows shot up. "My folks had a Nadir over for dinner this past weekend." *What are the odds?*

"A marine named Nadir?" Taylor asked.

"With a year left before discharge," I replied.

"Small world. I didn't realize your families were close," Taylor said. He took a long gulp from his ice water.

"His dad and my mom both work at the same hospital in The Woodlands. I was, uh, kinda supposed to be there. For a date." I cleared my throat and took a sip of wine to wash the sour taste from my mouth.

"So you're the one who stood him up?"

"I had good reason! My mom told me about it after I promised my friends Dani and Leigh I'd go south of Houston with them," I defended myself. My ears burned.

"Chill, it's cool. I mean, it's not like he cried or anything. He was kinda bummed he came all this way out to Quickdraw, but then we zoned in front of the PlayStation a few hours and all was good."

Desperate to ease the growing tension between us, without even understanding why it mattered, I gripped onto a possible change of topic. "Got a PS3 or PS4?"

"The three. I've bought way too much to upgrade systems now," he replied.

So he's a former drug dealer who likes to video game when he isn't peddling weed, I thought. With the menu spread open before me, I perused the entrees and made a quick selection before the waitress returned to take our orders.

"So… am I right if I assume you're a gamer, too? What's your favorite game?" he asked.

Leaning forward, I watched him from across the table. His bright blue eyes held mine, shameless and inquisitive. For the first time, there was a man interested in what *I* liked to do.

"I'm hopelessly addicted to Minecraft," I admitted. "I built a full out city with a mine down to the lava pits and everything."

"Nadir and I build sky cities in creative mode when we're not playing Borderlands," he confessed. "Creepers piss me off too much to deal with them."

"I have that game, but I kinda suck at it." I shrugged. "Maybe we can play sometime though."

It seemed a perfectly reasonable and innocent suggestion. We were both saved from an immediate reply by the arrival of our food. Afraid of looking like a pig in front of my hunky date, I ordered a light mushroom ravioli and soup instead of my preferred meal.

Taylor had a sixth sense. He saw through the bullshit and eyed my plate like it was an alien creature. "That's it? That's all you're gonna eat?"

"Ravioli is filling."

"For about five minutes maybe," he retorted. "That's a *snack*, not a dinner. Here, try the shrimp."

He passed over two large shellfish from his plate without making a dent. Wafts of lemon and garlic-scented steam made my mouth water with anticipation.

Damn him. I love shrimp.

By the time we cleared our plates, he'd snuck several more shrimp over for me to eat.

"No dessert?"

"I'm watching my weight," I replied uneasily.

Taylor's brows rose. "Okay…"

Ugh. Leave it to a guy to make me feel awkward about it. "I'm always nibbling on sweets, so I try not to overdo it."

"You know, you're sexy as hell the way you look now."

The compliment brought a rush of pleasure. "Yeah, well, you're not so bad looking yourself."

Who was I kidding?

He was absolutely fucking gorgeous, and as far as I could see, his personality matched.

***

"I saved you! Ha! Ha!" I threw up both of my arms and whooped in victory, rubbing it in until Taylor shot me a look from his side of the couch.

"I softened him up for you," he grumbled in his sexy baritone. He sulked the way my brother would when I beat him at a fighting game.

"You were hiding around the corner almost dead," I shot back.

Maybe first-person shooter games weren't so bad after all, or maybe it was the company and his easygoing smiles.

I don't know what happened. One moment, he was sharing his cannoli with me — since I refused to order dessert — in the next, I was accepting a last-minute invitation to game with him for a couple hours after dinner.

"I won fair and square. Now pay up." I grinned and shifted on the couch, stretching out my legs toward him.

I'd never received a foot rub from a man before, especially not on the first date. His electrifying touch sent sparks up my calves and warmed my skin. Thank God I'd recently waxed. His fingers were magic, introducing me to a slice of the heaven I gift to my clients at the shop.

"You've done this before," I accused.

"Not as many times as you're probably thinking," he replied.

I didn't have anything to say on it because I didn't want to begin to imagine his hands on some other woman's feet. Or anywhere on her, really. So I closed my eyes and enjoyed the relaxing massage.

"Hey," I asked, "what time is it anyway?"

"Going on ten."

Ten o'clock already? Crap. I opened my eyes and reluctantly slid my feet from his lap. His hands were like magic.

"I should probably head home. Time ran away."

"Always does when you're having fun. I'm glad we did this, Jada."

"Me too."

He walked me to the door and opened it for me. I stepped out, but paused in the doorway to turn around and look back at him.

"Thanks for um… a fun time," I said. The man in front of me contradicted everything about the record my dad shared with me over the phone. He was sweet, respectful, and I didn't catch even a whiff of drugs in his place. His bathroom was clean and tidy, and the rest of the home was small, but undecorated.

New. A fresh start.

Taylor had served his time, and I wouldn't be the asshole to deny him a second chance. Surrendering to my impulses, I stepped in and grabbed him by the shirt collar for a kiss, my heels bringing me to the perfect height for our lips to meet.

If his massages were bliss, his kisses were sin incarnate. Carnal desire jolted straight through me, dampening my panties and making my pussy clench. His tongue didn't meekly explore my mouth, it laid claim, and I mirrored his hungry enthusiasm.

"Wow," he murmured against my lips.

Wow indeed. He kissed me again, equally unwilling to part. His strong arms enfolded me, tugging me in close to his hard body.

No. I am not gonna fuck him on our first date, I chided myself. I wanted to, though. I had the craziest urge to push back through the doorway and rip all his clothes off. I felt him hardening against me and imagined the thick cock waiting beneath a layer of khaki. My fingers burned to slip between our bodies for a touch.

Stepping backward, I distanced myself until I moved down from the steps. "I'll see you this weekend?"

"Yeah… this weekend's great."

"Or earlier if you want." I bit my lower lip and watched for his reaction. His blue eyes lit up.

"I'm free after work tomorrow, too."

"Good. I'll see you then."

"Sure you don't want a ride?" he asked, dubious. "It's dark out. Why don't you let me drive you instead?"

I chuckled and shook my head. "No, a little walk won't hurt me." I smiled one last time and hurried out onto the road. Most neighborhoods in Quickdraw lacked sidewalks, forcing residents to follow the side of the road. I lived two streets over from Taylor, farther away from the business quarter.

Long stretches of darkness spanned between Main Street's occasional streetlamp. Outside of the downtown business strip, the residential communities sat in relative darkness, lit by only their own garden lamps and porch lights.

The cool night breeze ruffled through my hair, carrying the faint stench from a pair of nearby dumpsters. After raising my purse higher up my shoulder, I hurried across the narrow street. Taylor lived on my side of town, thankfully, half a mile from the police station and down the road from my shop.

I traveled a road lined by quiet homes, my placid neighborhood tucked behind the town's only veterinary clinic. A dog barked to my right, my neighbor's black and white border collie greeting me. Across the road, two teens smoked on the curb, oblivious to my passage.

Certain someone was following me, I clutched my house keys in one hand and my cell phone in the other, prepared to speed dial my dad. Twice, I looked back over my shoulder, but I saw nothing and hurried forward across my driveway.

The headlights of a passing truck illuminated the road, sending shadows over my lawn. They also reflected off a pair of unnaturally bright blue eyes. They shone back at me from the bushes, set in a tawny, feline face.

"Holy shit."

As my heart slammed against my ribs, I fumbled the keys and stepped back onto the porch. The creature didn't move, a silent observer from the bushes. Somehow, I managed to turn the key in the lock and hurry inside, where I immediately went to the window overlooking the yard. A large mountain lion stepped out from between my two hydrangea bushes. It watched me through the window then fell back into the growth.

"What the hell is it doing in town?" I breathed out a relieved sigh and considered calling Animal Control. A wild cougar could cause all sorts of havoc.

I called my father instead.

"Hey, Daddy?"

"What's wrong, punkin?"

"If a big animal like a wolf… or a mountain lion came in town, what would happen?"

"Probably shoot it, darlin'. Why?"

I hesitated. "Is that necessary?"

"Wild animals like that only venture into town when they're hungry, punkin. *Real* hungry. Which makes 'em dangerous. Did you see something tonight?"

Lying to Dad made me feel awful, so I opted for the truth. "I think I saw a mountain lion in my yard. I mean, it's real dark, so maybe I was mistaken."

"I'll send an officer around just to be safe. I'll feel better if you stay in the house tonight."

I shivered and moved to the window again. My sandy-furred friend hadn't returned. "I don't think he wanted to eat me."

"Like I said, Jada, a wild animal like that doesn't come into town unless it's hungry."

"He could have caught me at any time, Daddy. I mean, he walked right past a couple teenagers across the street and they're still out there smoking."

"You sure you weren't seeing a cat? Mr. Kendall has one of them fancy special breeds and it wouldn't be the first time he's gotten out."

"If it was a house cat, it was on 'roids, 'cause he definitely didn't miss out on leg day. He must hit the gym more than Danny 'cause I've never seen a house cat that tall and buff in all my life."

"Well, I'm glad you called. Lock your door and make sure you turn your porch light on."

"Lock my door? Is the cougar going to pop in for a visit?" I teased.

"Ha ha," he quipped. "Humor me, okay? You should be locking your door anyway, a young woman living alone. You should have a dog over there with you. And a gun."

"What's a dog going to do? Maybe I'll walk outside and recruit my feline stalker," I teased him.

We said our goodbyes, and then I ended the call. By the time I laid my head on my pillow, I was exhausted. Stretching my body along the cool sheets, I snuggled into the silk and closed my eyes, letting the pillow top mattress embrace my curves.

Sleep came easily, my dreams visited by prowling mountain lions with piercing blue eyes. I couldn't get the animal out of my head.

When Dani and I met for lunch the next day, I told her about the mountain lion and my increasing certainty that I didn't have a close brush with death.

"I felt the same way when I found a black bear in my backyard," Dani said.

"A black bear? Did Russ shoot it?"

"No. This was before Russ and I moved in with each other. Before we were really dating. I came down one morning and this bear was laying in my new hammock."

"Seriously? What did you do about it?" I asked.

"I fed him," Dani answered, laughing. "My dad hated that I did it, but he was miles and miles away, so what was he going to do? Ground me?"

We shared a laugh. The idea of a bear snoozing in her outdoor furniture made me think of Tumblr and America's Funniest Home Videos. "God, I hope you took photos, 'cause I'd love to see that. What happened to him?"

Her eyes twinkled. "Oh, I still see him sometimes. I did take a few photos on my phone of him. I like to imagine he lives on our property because he knows it's safe and I'll always give him food."

I plucked a cheesy, beef-covered nacho from the pile of Tex-Mex on my plate. "Too bad I can't do the same for a mountain lion. Daddy said they're likely to kill him if he's found."

"Better to set food out for a hungry animal than risk it eating a neighbor's house cat or dog, right?"

I crumpled a napkin and tossed it at Dani. "You're such an enabler. Anyway, you live in the boonies. I doubt I'll see Mister Cat again."

"Never say never."

After work, I enjoyed dinner and a movie with Taylor. Despite everything I ever learned about wild animals, I went home and thawed some grilled chicken breast in a dish. My mom, hoping to encourage me to eat smart and lose weight, had brought me a couple pounds of it for salads. I scooped a couple of handfuls into a pie dish and left it outside by the back door.

Then I tried to pretend it wasn't there. By bedtime, I felt silly for wasting good leftovers and was on my way to retrieve it for the trash when I heard a startling noise.

I followed the strange caterwauling sound to my back door and opened it to peer out.

Blue eyes stared up at me from the porch. With a shriek, I slammed it shut again then scrambled to the window to look outside. The mountain lion lay on his belly beside the empty pan, watching me in return through the window.

Holy shit, Dani was right.

The creature rose to all fours and walked up to my door. He pawed it noisily, scratching the plain wood with his claws.

Did he want more food?

I hid behind the door out of his sight for a few minutes, but when I peeked out the window again, I saw his face right against it, waiting for me. I stumbled back, laughing at the hilarious situation.

"Okay, so you want more food, huh?"

I searched the freezer until I found some ribs I froze after the Labor Day barbecue. After thawing them in the microwave, I slid another dish out the door.

Eventually, after I'd taken a photo and a few videos of him, my majestic friend strolled down the steps and disappeared into the trees beyond my backyard.

I watched him leave and wondered if he'd return again.

Chapter Six

~Taylor~

"Her dad despises me," I grumbled.

Ian chuckled and passed me a beer. "I'm sure that's not true."

"He sent her an assload of texts during our second date before she even got home. Called the whole time we were chillin' at my place. She didn't notice because she'd muted her phone." Jada had called later, warning me her dad might pop around or stop at my job to see me. We nixed our plans for a third night out in favor of waiting a couple days. So I visited her as a cougar again, and found she'd taken Dani's advice to make me a pot roast.

Ian laughed at the story of my visit.

"I'm so glad to amuse you."

"I'm not laughing at you, man. I'm laughing 'cause you remind me of what I did to Leigh when I showed up at her place. And I'm laughing at Hunt. At this town, I guess. Word spreads fast when you're in a small town. People don't have much to do here besides tell other folks' business.

"Yeah, I know about everything except what we *need* to hear about." Who was dating who was a hot topic and spread like fire. Trying to find out who was dealing to who? Tight lips all around.

"Technically, you shouldn't even be here. You're supposed to use Nadir as your contact to keep us abreast of the situation with Tito and his gang," Ian pointed out.

"Don't be an asshole," I grumbled. "I'm isolated out there and Nadir can't babysit me whenever I get bored."

"You have Jada."

"Jada has a business," I reminded him, "and friends of her own. Besides, it would take another shifter to track down the way I came to get here. I stripped down in the woods at Kayak Pass and ran the rest of the way on foot. Uh, thanks for the clothes by the way, Leigh."

Leigh had tired of housing naked men at all hours of the day. The novelty had worn off after the first month. Now she kept an array of clothes from Goodwill in a basket by the back patio door.

"You're welcome." Leigh smiled, always cheerful. I had a feeling she was waiting for me to leave so she could get Jada on the phone and gossip.

"Well, since you're here. What's the word from the garage?" Ian asked.

I twisted around on my seat to glance at Leigh.

"What? Oh! Okay, fine. Fine. I'll leave you guys to have your chat in peace." She sighed and abandoned her seat beside Ian. Her fat and sassy mutt remained, too obsessed with us shifter guys to leave whenever we were around. Petunia set her chin on my knee and whined until I scratched around her ears.

"Aside from Lyle being a dog shifting mutt of some kind, I don't have much to tell you. I know he deals pot and codeine to some of the customers when nobody's looking, but there hasn't even been a veiled offer toward me yet."

"That's fine. You're new, they're feeling you out, and you need to prove yourself before they'll bring you in on it. That's usually how this works."

"I know. How far am I supposed to take this?"

"Anything and everything that won't put a civilian in harm's way."

I sighed. "Okay."

Ian read me like a book, raising both brows while leaning back to fix me with a skeptical look. "What's wrong? You having second thoughts now 'cause of Jada?"

"Kinda… I don't want to fuck things up with her."

"As soon as this job is done, you're free to tell her everything. We can come clean to the entire town, Hunt, and her family. He'll love you to death then."

"Yeah, I know. Nadir already coached his family on what not to say, so my cover should be fine."

"Take off this weekend with Jada. You need to look like an everyday Joe. Get out of town and get back to it Monday."

"Gotta love a drug-dealing asshole who doesn't open on Sundays," I quipped. "God forbid we all do some work on a Sunday, but selling some meth to that guy around the corner? Nothing wrong with it."

"We don't have solid proof Tito's involved yet."

"He's gotta be. I'm telling you, it's him."

"Get us the proof we need and we'll take him down."

***

What are you doing this weekend? I Swype'd on my phone to her.

Jada's answering text hit me an hour later.

Jada: *Sorry. I'm hanging out with my parents and Dad bitches if he thinks I'm talking to you now.*

Me: *It's no problem.*

Jada: *I don't have anything to do this weekend. I thought about working at the spa.*

Me: *What about letting me take you out somewhere?*

Jada: *What do you have in mind?*

Me: *It's summer, so how about a day at the beach?*

Jada: *I don't have a swimsuit.*

Me: *Buy one. I hear Amazon has free two-day shipping.*

My phone rang a second later, the lit screen revealing Jada's name and number. "Missed the sound of my voice?" I teased her.

"Seriously? Buy a swimsuit online?" Laughter and exasperation filled her voice in equal measures.

"Why not?"

"I have to try stuff on."

"We can hit up a store on the way out then." I pictured her prancing in and out of a changing room for my opinion on increasingly skimpy swimsuits.

Fuck. Yes.

"Fine. What time will we leave?"

"If we're on I-45 by eight, we'll have time to stop at the department store of your choice and get lunch somewhere on the island."

"Sounds like a deal."

I worked hard throughout the week, and by Saturday, I couldn't wait to spend time with Jada for more than a few passing minutes at the spa or a stolen hour during the evening.

On the day of our trip, I was up with the dawn, showered, and had my change of clothes crammed into a backpack. I stepped out of my house to find Jada's Camry waiting for me. She leaned against the driver's door, her ebony hair free against her shoulders. A dress in earth-toned colors complemented her skin in shades of gold, topaz, and brown, and the wedge sandals on her feet bumped her up close to my height.

"Did you seriously drive here to leave your car in my driveway?"

"Yeah." Her eyes crinkled at the corners. "Give the neighbors something to whisper about. Plus, I wanted to surprise you with these." She reached into the passenger seat and removed two white boxes. The sweet smell of fresh goods from the bakery hit my sensitive nose before she raised the lid.

"You're amazing."

"I know," she replied, grinning. "I brought coffee, too."

"Marry me," I teased.

If only there was a way for her to understand how much I meant it. From the moment we met alongside the highway, I had become hers and knew there'd never be another woman for me. It transcended a lust for her in the physical sense; I respected her wit, humor, and drive to transform her business into a booming success.

"I try not to get hitched on the third date," Jada quipped back.

A few minutes into the drive, she passed me a still-warm breakfast sandwich—melted cheese on egg with bacon, stuffed between a flaky croissant. We sipped coffee and chatted about everything but her dad's disdain for me.

"God, I love your car."

"Thanks."

"I can't believe you have a movie player."

"You can put something in if you want to. Otherwise, I'm gonna talk you to death." Or rather, ask her too many questions and possibly put her off. I couldn't help it, but I wanted to know everything about her I could learn. "The case is in the center console."

"Maybe after my hands aren't so sticky."

A glance at Jada revealed our box of snacks had emptied. She'd brought two donuts for each of us, and I'd polished mine off in the first fifteen minutes of our drive. "Where's the woman who ate with me at Lottie's?"

"Huh?" She peeked around at me, donut frosting clinging to her lower lip and corner of her mouth.

"You know, the girl who's watching her sugar." I reached over and wiped a bit of glaze from her chin.

"I guess I figured if you really like me, I can be myself."

"Good." That's all I wanted.

And she was all I needed.

***

We hit up a mall outside of Houston. Unfortunately, Jada didn't put on a fashion show and kept her purchase a mystery, hustling her goods to the counter before I could catch more than a hint of her chosen color. Damn. My patience was rewarded when she stepped out from the changing room at the waterpark.

Maybe I was accustomed to being around the wrong kind of girl, but I expected her to exit in a single piece, her curvy body hidden beneath an oversized cover-up.

Jada proved me wrong when she strolled out in a bikini. The black bottoms hugged her ass and full hips, drawing my attention to her thick thighs. She had muscle beneath the soft flesh associated with being a bigger girl. I fantasized about peeling it off of her with my teeth until my eyes locked on her cleavage.

"Holy shit."

Jada paused mid-stride, her confidence visibly wavering on the precipice, caught on a treacherous divide between fearless and uncertain. "Is it ugly?" The unspoken question in her eyes made me want to pound whoever came before me responsible for the doubt she displayed. *Am I too fat for this?* Someone always put those kinds of thoughts into a woman's head. Someone had made her insecure.

"No." I shook my head quickly. "Not at all." I covered the distance between us in two steps, and without giving her the chance to argue, I cupped Jada's cheeks with both hands and kissed her. "You're beautiful."

I didn't give a damn what anyone around us thought; I kissed her again, aware of the men checking out her round ass.

Then I kissed her one more time for the women watching me to leave no doubt in Jada's mind that she was the only one who mattered. I had eyes for her, and only her.

"C'mon," I said as we parted and twined our fingers.

She leaned into me as I took a step back, her eyes glassy, seeming not to realize the kiss was over and it was time to walk from the changing area.

"You okay?"

"Huh?" She snapped out of it. Her dark eyes darted left and right then fixed to me. "I'm fine."

If she felt even a fraction of the desire and unbearable need coursing through me, then I knew exactly how she felt.

"Wipe that smug grin off your face."

I flattened my expression, internally pulling on my Ian impersonation. Nobody could surpass that mean bastard's solemn stares once he was pissed off. Leigh didn't believe us, but she was fortunate to never see that side of him.

"You're such a smart-ass," Jada fussed. Despite her words, a grin raised the corners of her mouth.

We spent the day daring each other onto the highest slides. When the lines grew too long, we chose to lazily float along the tube river that wound through the entire park.

"I'm hungry. Are you hungry?"

"Well…"

"Baby, we've been out in the sun all day and ain't had a bite since those donuts."

So I talked her into abandoning her diet again for the weekend. We ate BBQ from the concession stand and shared an Oreo and ice cream funnel cake. Since she'd left her credit card in her locker, and mine was stashed in the zip-up pocket of my board shorts, she finally let me catch the entire bill.

If only she knew how much money I had. On top of bringing in a ton of cash from my detail shop, I earned money hand over fist anytime Ian set up work for us overseas. If we didn't come close to clearing half a mil each year, he wasn't doing his job.

The amount of money he'd paid me for going into prison was obscene, enough to make up for having to dance around with my dick out every time a guard thought I had some contraband tucked under my balls or something.

"This has been really fun. I'm glad you talked me into coming."

"It doesn't have to end, you know. We can grab a room and hit up the aquarium or something tomorrow. Laser tag, maybe."

"A room?" Jada leaned back on her seat and stared at me.

"Separate rooms. Kind of a waste of money though, don't you think?"

"Feeling that lucky, huh?"

I grinned. "Nah, nothing like that. Men and women can sleep in the same room without having sex." Contrary to my comment, I struggled to keep my eyes above her generous bust line. "*I* can anyway."

"It is a longish drive back…"

"C'mon. It'll be fun." My motivations were selfish. I wanted more time with her, away from gossips and prying eyes. Out here, I could be myself for the most part. Jada got to see the real me, a guy who loved the water and having fun.

~Jada~

After choosing an overpriced Motel 8 room for the night, we settled on sharing a meat lover's pizza with all the works and cans of lemonade from the vending machine. Taylor was the worst kind of influence.

Women like Dani didn't consider me to be too large, but when I sat down, my thighs spread and my tummy developed three distinct rolls. My breasts were too large for my frame — they may look amazing in a bikini or a corset, but the reality is shoulder pain, expensive bras, and tailored clothes.

Lacking anything to wear but my breezy summer dress, I'd convinced him to at least let me run into the Family Dollar to pick up cheap sweats and a t-shirt for the night. I had the first shower, emerging afterward in my unflattering navy blue sweats and oversized men's tee. Taylor wolf whistled then moved past me.

I listened for the sound of the shower and lay back on one of the two queen beds. An overactive imagination treated me to visuals of Taylor in the steaming stall, all bare skin and hard muscle without the interruption of his swim trunks.

Was he thinking about me, too? Hard cock in his hand, pumping and fantasizing about being inside me instead?

Fuck, I hoped so.

Then why can't I have sex with him tonight? So what if it's only the third date?

Because he was just in prison a month ago and probably has who-knows-what, the insidious voice of reason whispered into my thoughts.

But we could use a condom! My naughty shoulder angel attempted to convince me.

But you don't have one, said my devilish conscience.

Damn. And if he had one, I'd be freaked out and wondering why he came equipped to a beach date.

Everything about Taylor struck me as too good to be true, a thought confirmed when he stepped from the restroom with a white hotel room towel around his shoulders. Close-fitting, white boxer-briefs clinging against the chiseled muscle of his upper thighs, a black band low on his lean hips. His swim trunks hadn't been so tiny, so insignificant, or so fucking tight. I swallowed and raised my eyes away from his bulge.

"Wanna check out the sights and take a ferry ride before we hit the road tomorrow?"

My mind went to dirty, dirty places. *Oh yeah, I have some sights for you to see.*

"Jada?"

"Hmm? Oh!" I snapped out of my naughty little fantasy. "Yeah, sounds like a plan. We could drive around and check out all the tree sculptures."

"And eat at Joe's."

"You are so food focused," I said, laughing at the dreamy expression on his face.

"What can I say? I love seafood."

His heart-melting, crooked grin made me clench with desire, dampening my brand new cotton panties.

"Night, sweet cheeks."

The endearment made me roll my eyes, but I smiled. "Goodnight."

Long after Taylor was muffling his snores into the pillow, I remained awake in the adjacent bed, cursing my self-imposed chastity. Lisa would have slept with him after the first date for sure, regardless of the criminal record attached to him.

I wasn't her, and waiting would make the actual sex that much sweeter if we did come to it.

Confident in my choice, I rolled over and went to sleep.

Chapter Seven

~JADA~

I argued with my dad over the course of a week during occasional squabbles at dinnertime. He claimed I chose a hoodlum over him, and I accused him of butting into my life.

"Do you know how it looks when people see you at that place? Do you know how it makes me look?" he had asked.

"Daddy," I'd said in an exasperated voice. I didn't want conflict; I wanted to tell him about the feline protector who occasionally showed up at my place. "I go to take my boyfriend a freaking Aquafina and a brownie at lunch. Hell, half of the force goes there for their lube jobs!"

"I don't," he'd grumbled.

"I'm not saying they don't have some bad habits, or that Tito isn't up to no good, but the work is great."

My excuses hadn't soothed my ruffled father. If anything, he became more aggressive and finally talked a warrant out of the judge. The search was a bust, making him the laughingstock of Quickdraw for a solid week. Any time I went into the supermarket or stopped for gas, I heard whispers about it.

Mom blamed me, so I stopped showing up for family dinner until she phoned one Friday morning.

"Let's go away tonight, Jada."

"Go where?" I asked, guarded.

"Does it matter where? You never find the time to come out with me anymore. I'm the doctor, but I still find time to spend with you."

Mom's unintentional guilt trip resulted in me dropping all plans for the weekend. I left the shop in Lisa's capable hands, smooched Taylor, and left Friday afternoon for a drive into downtown Houston with my mother.

"What has happened to us, Jada? Why did I have to shame you into coming with me for the weekend, when you went away with your new boyfriend only a little while ago?"

I sighed. "I knew this was coming. This is what happened to us, Mom. Whether I come to hang out with you voluntarily or not, I know you're going to lecture me about my life choices. Because I'm not another doctor like you and Granddad. You guys don't do this to Danny."

My mother was a beautiful woman, a thinner, older version of me with her dark hair cut into an angled bob. All my life, she'd forced me onto one diet after another, wanting the perfect little girl.

"I only wanted the best for you," she said in a low voice.

"I know," I replied.

In under thirty minutes, our drive had become awkward, and I was trapped for at least another hour before we reached our destination. I sank against the door and stared out the window again at the strips of outlet stores bordering the highway.

"When I came to this country, I knew I wanted to help people. I had an amazing new chance given to me and wanted to use it to the fullest. So I became a doctor."

"I know, Mom…" I sighed when I-45's traffic slowed to a standstill, placing us in bumper-to-bumper conditions. Make that two hours before we arrived.

"This time I am telling it to you for a different reason."

"Not because I've shamed you by becoming an overpriced beautician?" I asked. The bitter question left my lips, regretted in an instant. "Sorry," I whispered, quieting.

My mother didn't answer. She focused her eyes on the rear of the truck ahead of us. Her brown eyes narrowed.

"I'm sorry," I repeated.

"No. I deserved that. Your life is yours to do with as you choose. I complain often about what you do wrong, but I never tell you what you've done that is right. I *am* proud, Jada. You turned that ugly little building into something beautiful where women will happily throw their money at you. Perhaps you are not healing bodies in the operating room, but you are healing spirits. That is just as important."

Tears pricked at my eyes, threatening to overflow and send me into a cryfest. A few blinks pushed them back.

"Thanks, Mom. That means everything to me."

"This boy of yours needs your help, too," she told me.

"Help him to what?"

"Help him to stay on a good, law-abiding path. Prove your father wrong."

I sighed and twisted the ends of my hair around my finger. "From everything I can tell, Mom, he's on the straight and narrow. Just because he works at Tito's doesn't make him a bad person."

"You know what your father thinks of that place."

"I do, but where else is a mechanic gonna work? Or is he just pissed because I'm not with someone he thinks is worthy of me?"

Mom drummed her fingers on the steering wheel and glanced over at me. "My father never approved of anything I did either, and if I'd listened to him, I wouldn't have you. I wouldn't have left India. You were never a mistake, Jada. You and Danny are the joy of my life and you've been worth every struggle I encountered since leaving home.

This time I couldn't hold back the tears. They leaked down my face, so I swiped at my cheeks and searched for a tissue in my purse.

"Makeup ruined," I muttered between sniffles.

"You're pretty without it," she replied. "I know you think I'm hard on you, but I just want you to be happy, sweetheart."

My mom had found an awesome place where aspiring artists could buy canvases, chat with their fellow customers, and create works of art while nibbling treats from the snack bar. We arrived just in time to join an instructor-led class.

We painted for most of the evening and drank too much, sharing a bottle of red velvet wine between us. Later, we walked arm in arm to the Cheesecake Factory where we sobered up over hot sandwiches and delicious, fattening desserts. For the first time in all of my life, Mom didn't chastise me about my dinner choices.

As we were both unwilling to undertake the long drive back to Quickdraw after an evening of wine-sipping and good food, we found a nearby hotel and checked in for a night.

Dad called just as I finished brushing out my hair from the shower.

"Hey, punkin. Is it World War III yet?" he asked.

"*Dad.*"

"What? I wanted to check in on my favorite girls and make sure everything was okay."

"We're having fun," I admitted. I sat on the edge of the bed in my nightshirt while Mom showered.

"That's good. I'm real glad to hear it." He fell quiet, as if he didn't know what to say next.

If I could make peace with Mom, I could definitely make amends with Daddy. I dragged in a deep breath and swallowed my pride.

"I love you, Daddy. I'm sorry we've been fighting. I wasn't trying to embarrass you."

My dad paused. "I'm sorry, too, Jada. I don't mean to butt into your life."

"I know you don't. Can we at least agree to disagree about Taylor?"

"All right," he answered, surprising me.

"Really?"

"Really. I can't say I trust him yet. I still plan to keep an eye on the kid, but I'll lay off of you. Anyway, I didn't call to take up all your time. Enjoy the weekend with your mama."

"I will. Love you," I repeated again, smiling.

"Love you, too."

I ended the call and found an unanswered text from Taylor, forgotten while out with my mother. We made plans to meet after Sunday dinner with my family, and then I set the phone down on the bedside table just as Mom emerged from the bathroom.

"Who were you talking to?"

"Dad called to check up on us. He sends his love and said to have fun."

"With Danny leaving for the Army soon, he worries, is all. Did you two have a nice chat?" Mom settled behind me with a brush and stroked the bristles through my thick hair. I watched her reflection in the mirror to see her admiring the golden brown ombre coloring the lower portion.

"Yeah, we did. Mostly. He said he'll lay off some."

"That's something, at least." She set the brush aside and began braiding my hair. "Speaking of which, I saw your former jailbird."

"*Mom.* He has a name."

She chuckled and nudged the ticklish spot above my hip with her fingers. "I know his name is Taylor," she supplied without waiting for me to offer. "He's very polite, and… incredibly handsome. You certainly have good taste where looks are concerned."

"You met him?" I twisted around to look at her.

"I may have needed an oil change. Anyway, what I wanted to say was I'm sorry for judging him before we met. He's a nice young man, and you have my support. Your father will come around in time."

She was right. As the next two weeks passed, my dad made a visible effort to cool his jets about Taylor dating me. If he still disapproved, he didn't show it, and the tension at home gradually eased.

As for Taylor, he wasn't what I expected. He was interested in the simplest forms of entertainment. Indoors, we enjoyed peaceful evenings in front of video games and watched movies, my cheek against his chest. Outside, he cheerfully suggested fun activities for couples like horseback riding, hiking in Sam Houston State Park, and rock wall climbing at the activity center.

"You don't want to go drinking or dancing?" I asked, dubious.

"I can drink at home, and I don't dance," he muttered. "What, you wanna go dancing?"

"No, I hate dancing."

"Then…" He gave me a puzzled look. "Why are we talking about dancing?"

"I'm trying to figure you out, is all." I stopped to lean against a tree by the path, winded from the uphill walk. We were in the final days of summer. Cotton clung against my sweat-dampened skin and the hair at my nape was wet. The smell of the trees and earth surrounded us. I inhaled the scent of clean grass and earth, the woodlands as soothing as an evening in *Nirvana*.

"Okay, instead of trying to figure me out, why don't you try asking?"

"Why don't you do any of the things the rest of your homeboys at Tito's enjoy doing?"

"You mean wander up and down the street like I don't have any damned sense?" He barked out a quiet laugh.

I chuckled, too, and ducked my head, cheeks warm. "I always see them smoking outside the bar or hogging the basketball court."

"I had enough of the basketball court while locked up," he said dryly. "I hang out with them sometimes, Jada, but if this is your roundabout way of asking if I'm into their other activities — I'm not."

"I wasn't implying…" I bit my lower lip and shyly peeked up to find Taylor's smile remained. "So, you really like the outdoors, huh?"

"Don't you?"

"Erm…" I tugged at the neck of my t-shirt and fanned air against my skin. "I'm sweating for you, so that must mean something," I quipped. "And I guess it is nice to escape the spa for a while to enjoy the fresh air."

Taylor's bright blue eyes and charismatic smiles *also* made the experience enjoyable. Gazing into them, I melted and my breath caught in my throat. One of his hands settled at my hip, sliding up and down over the loose-fitting brown sweats I'd worn to protect my legs from the mosquitoes.

The undeniable sexual appeal he exuded had become a pervasive presence, always simmering beneath the surface whenever he touched me. His touch was electric, sneaking upward to the band of my bottoms and beneath my shirt, fingertips gliding over the strip of bare skin.

"Of course, there's a bonus to being out here with you," he said, dipping down to place a line of kisses from my neck to my ear. His teeth closed around my earlobe for a playful nibble, weakening my knees.

"What's that?"

"I get you to myself, with no one else around."

"Well…" I lifted my arms to circle his neck. "You don't have to steal me away outdoors to be alone with me."

"Sure I do." His grin widened. "No signal out here. Well, a crappy one at least. No dads, brothers, moms, or friends butting in. Just you and me."

"You're awfully patient for a man who's been in prison," I murmured. Feeling playful, I teased with a movement of my hips. It placed pressure on his cock, molding my body to the obvious outline. It turned me on to know he was as hard for me as I was wet for him, my panties damp and uncomfortable beneath my outdoors attire.

"It's a gift," Taylor replied, his husky voice a low, sensual utterance in the quiet forest.

In a move that was pure evil, Taylor adjusted his position enough to wedge his hand between us. He cupped my pussy over the layers of clothing and returned my previous tease. Every knead and pet applied indirect contact to my clit. I gasped and rolled my hips against it, eager for more.

"Like that, don't you?"

I made a quiet sound in my throat and nodded. My head fell back and my eyes shut as I surrendered to his talented fingers, bold and unhurried. Pressure built in my core, and all I could imagine was having his cock in my hands, feeling the hot flesh beneath my touch and stroking him before he entered my body to become coated in my slickness.

"How long have you wanted me?" Taylor asked. His words, a seductive and warm breath, heated my cheek. "I can feel how wet you are through your sweats. You're fucking soaked."

"Since…" The breath hitched in my lungs. I moaned softly, eager for more, but his fingers retreated and left me wanting. "Taylor…"

"How long?" he repeated. He inhaled as if he could smell my arousal.

"Since the car ride. Since you gave me a ride to Houston. You were so sexy in your stained jeans and t-shirt." He gave a little of what I wanted, his hand over my mound without delving beneath my clothes. "I want your fingers inside me."

"I don't think I can stop myself at just my fingers, baby." His deep voice, smooth as silk, caressed my senses and made me putty in his hands. I trembled and turned my head to find his mouth and capture his lips in a kiss. As his tongue advanced into my mouth, I sucked the tip.

"You don't have to." I wanted him so bad. A dull ache throbbed between my thighs, unrelieved no matter how I rubbed against him. My heart raced with increasing desire while anticipation pooled in my core, a hot jolt of lust shooting right to my clit. "I don't want to wait anymore."

"Do you want a fuck now, or for me to make love to you later?" he asked.

"Damn you." I laughed in spite of myself and released a shaky exhalation. "Later. You're right. I'm not eager to roll around in fallen leaves and possible ant piles."

"Don't forget the mosquitos."

By the time we returned to Quickdraw, my thighs were killing me. I tried to imagine rolling onto Taylor in bed while my legs screamed with every flex.

"Raincheck, right?" he predicted with a grin as he slowed to a stop in front of my house.

"Yeah. When I can walk again without wanting to cry."

"Go take a bath, babe. I'll see you soon."

We parted with a kiss, and then I waved to him from the door. Taylor didn't pull away until I was inside with the door shut behind me.

Soon, I thought. In the meantime, I had my fantasies to keep me company until the perfect moment.

***

"Ugh. Bunch of thugs are hanging around outside again." Naomi peeked through the blinds on the storefront window. I was beside her with a big bucket of steaming, soapy water to scrub the window sills beneath them. I'd already mopped the floors. It was all I could do to burn the restless energy building ever since the weekend with Taylor.

"I wonder if that's why we have virtually no customers today."

"Call your dad and tell him to get out here."

I cracked open the blinds. One of the last days of Texas summer had reduced the world beyond my shop into a scorching wasteland. I'd gotten into the habit of taking cool drinks across the road to Taylor, much to Dad's displeasure.

"Are they dealing?" I asked Naomi.

"Nah, they're only standing ar—wait, wait, look. There's a car."

A beat up, ancient Caprice pulled up and idled by the curb. The passenger window rolled down and one of the kids stepped up to it. Money exchanged hands and the passenger took a small, semi-translucent plastic baggie from the peddler outside my spa.

I saw red. Before I knew what I was doing, I barged outside. The smell of exhaust assaulted me as the ugly blue sedan peeled away and around the corner. It burned my nose and made me choke.

"Hey, you guys get out of here." I crossed my arms and stared the three loiterers down.

"C'mon, baby, you don't gotta be like that." I recognized Jared, a punk teen who used to bully kids at my brother's school.

"I'm not your baby and you're scaring off my customers. So get lost or I'm calling the cops."

"Ah man, the bitch is gonna call her pops," the smoking man swore. He tossed his cigarette to the curb and ground it under his boot. Tyrese, the oldest and a college dropout, was the son of the local florist. His mother had poured her heart out to me during a massage once, lamenting how far he'd fallen from the tree. His father worked long hours at a local prison to help support the family.

"Get *out* of here," I ordered again, "and take your butts with you. I'm not having you littering or dealing on my sidewalk."

"Bitch, it's a free country. You don't own this shit," Jared said. He'd shaved half of his blond hair to reveal the marijuana leaf tattoos on his skull. Oh, so original.

My brows rose. "Yeah?"

Turning my back on them, I marched inside my shop. Their snickers followed me. *Stupid idiots think they've run me off. I'll show them.* "That mop bucket still back there, Naomi?"

"Yeah, but—"

"Thanks."

I grabbed it and stepped outside again with the bucket of filthy water. In one heaving thrust, I splashed its contents over them and drenched two of the boys at once. "Oops!" I cried. I splashed Tyrese and the third kid, his face unfamiliar to me. I dubbed him 'Saggy-Pants' instead.

Shouts and cries of profanity filled the air. They called out new and inventive insults I'd never heard regarding my weight and my face. If I was a weaker person, if I had less self-esteem, if I didn't have Taylor to convince me of how gorgeous I was — I'd let it bother me.

"What the fuck do you think you're doing, lady?" Saggy-Pants demanded.

"I didn't mean to splash you," I said sweetly when one of them stomped toward me with an aggressive posture. He was close enough for me to smell the sweet odor of marijuana on his skin. "I wanted to wash the butts off the sidewalk, but you stepped in my way. Oops."

Saggy-Pants raised his fist, expecting me to back down, but a wild kind of fury had taken hold and I was too far gone to turn tail. I'd brawl with him in the street if I had to; too experienced with my enormous little brother and an assload of male cousins who liked to play rough and dirty. He had another thing coming if he thought he could intimidate me in front of my own property.

"The hell is going on over here?" Taylor demanded as he jogged across the street to my rescue, a black knight in oil-stained armor. His fitted t-shirt stuck against his sweaty skin, clinging to every contour, dip, and valley of his chiseled torso. He wore his coveralls with the sleeves tied around his waist.

"Uh. Sup, man," Jared said.

"Hey, T.J.," Tyrese mumbled.

"They giving you trouble, Jada?" Taylor stepped in close beside me, slipping his arm around my waist. The smell of engine grease and sweat assaulted my nose, but I ignored it to kiss his cheek.

"Aw, shit man, is this your girl?" Jared eyed me up and down.

I was and everyone knew it. These bastards were playing dumb.

"Just cleaning out the trash, babe," I replied, gesturing toward the wet cement. Cigarette butts and gum wrappers floated in the gutter.

"We was just messin' around, T.J. No big deal, man. We're leaving," Saggy-Pants said.

I rolled my eyes. *Taylor walks up with his muscles showing and now they're all ready to hang it up and go. I can't believe this.*

"Lemme catch your asses around here bothering her again. See what happens," Taylor threatened.

"'Kay, dude, fine. Damn. Marco, c'mon, dude. We got a better place we can hang out," I overheard Tyrese saying to the one with the too-large jeans.

Their group ambled off like a pack of cubs with their tails between their legs. Once they were gone, I wriggled free and turned to face my boyfriend. "Were you keeping an eye on my shop?" I demanded.

A sheepish grin covered his face. He was unshaven, but the look suited him, dark stubble contrasting against his sandy brown skin. "Naomi used your phone to send me a text," he admitted. "I was on my way out of the shop for the day."

"I'm sorry."

"No, don't be."

"The least I can do is get you a cold drink. Come on inside for a few."

While Taylor scrubbed his hands and face in the restroom, I visited the cooler where I kept cold cans of iced tea and Cokes for my customers. I lingered in front of it, allowing the frosty air to cool my face.

"Okay, business is dead, so I'm heading out. See you tomorrow." Naomi glanced at the hallway leading to the rear of my shop then turned to me and mouthed, "Have fun."

I shoved her. She and Lisa couldn't believe I was still holding out on sex with Taylor. Maybe I was making excuses, but the time hadn't felt right again. He'd even brought me papers from the local clinic confirming he was STD-free when I made the difficult choice and asked one awkward evening when I was leaving his place.

Why hadn't he gotten bored and moved on yet?

Naomi flipped the 'open' sign to 'closed' on her way out.

"Where'd Naomi go?" Taylor asked. He stepped from the back, drying his hands on a paper towel.

"No clients booked, so she took off to get ready for a date or something."

"In that case, mind giving me a peek over at your new space?" He gestured toward the new archway in the wall connecting the two shops. I planned to hang a beaded curtain there when everything was finished.

"Yeah, c'mon, they installed the new counters yesterday and hooked up the plumbing for the pedicure stations. The skylights are all finished, too."

When everything was said and done, I'd have six manicure tables, four pedicure stations, a new massage room, and a larger reception desk.

"It's all looking good," Taylor said.

"Thanks." I beamed, proud as a new mother. My business *was* my baby, at least for now.

"You still going for stained glass on the front windows?"

My expression fell. "No, the cost was too much, but I did find an alternative. I can get a custom film put on them which will provide the same sort of effect I wanted. I just need to decide on a pattern."

Taylor moved in front of me near the curtained windows in question and slid his hands up and down my arms. His touch ignited goose bumps, sending sparks dancing across my skin.

"Your place is locked, right?"

"Yeah, but—"

Without so much as a grunt of exertion, Taylor plucked me up and set me on the counter. Squealing the whole time, I pushed at his shoulders.

"You could have hurt your back!"

Taylor's brows rose. "Huh? Doing what?"

"Picking me up," I fussed at him. "I weigh too much for—"

He silenced me with a kiss. Taylor took his time, his tongue making a slow sweep into my mouth. His hands slid down from my hips to my thighs and encouraged them to part so his body could wedge between them. My skin broke out in goose bumps as he nudged my skirt upward until the pink, bikini cut panties beneath were visible.

One hand skated over the top of my thigh and traveled low until he found the edge of my panties. He circled his index finger and teased me, filling my body with delicious anticipation for more.

Even when we broke away to breathe, he didn't stop. His kisses continued down my throat until I was putty in his hands, my core clenching hot and wet with need. He explored me top and bottom, teasing between my legs while fondling one breast. I moaned as he circled his thumb over a peak too prominent for my bra to conceal.

"You have the perfect pair of tits."

His mouth lowered to my breast and sealed around the nipple. He alternated between them, suckling through my shirt to leave two wet spots against the floral patterned fabric. Too bad I'd left my piercings forgotten beside my bathroom sink.

Taylor continued his downward path until his hot breath washed over the thin cotton covering my slit. They were already damp, a damning beacon of my desire for him. He licked me playfully through the fabric.

"Fuck," I swore on a moaned breath.

His fingers slipped beneath my panties and found me, my body so wet, so receptive for him, that two digits slid to the knuckle without resistance. I couldn't form words, only a weak groan.

Maybe it hadn't been about waiting for the right moment. Maybe I'd needed him to do this, to take charge. I shuddered and involuntarily clenched around his fingers, the edges of a potential orgasm teasing past my senses.

"Open your shirt."

I did it with a trembling hand, barely able to focus. He was doing things, *amazing things* to me, robbing me of concentration.

"You're stunning, Jada. I could kiss every inch of you and never grow tired of it."

"Why don't you?" I asked, breathless.

"Because I plan to occupy my mouth in other ways."

Taylor dragged my panties from beneath me with confident, firm tugs, and then they were hanging by one of my ankles, my pussy bared to him. With my thighs spread, he saw every inch from my perfect Brazilian wax to the piercing snuggled against my hood.

His breath caught in his throat. He hadn't expected that.

"Do you like it?"

His answer came without words, produced by the touch of his tongue against the small piece of metal. A jolt of electric pleasure sparked across my skin, clenching my core.

"I've been wanting a taste since the first moment I saw you," he murmured. His warm breath ghosted over my wet skin.

Trembling, I raised a hand to my breasts. They felt tight and tender inside the pushup bra. "Don't tease me."

A slow, upward lick parted my folds. From that moment, Taylor ignored my clit and kept me in suspense by focusing on every other inch of my slick nether lips. My thighs quivered and my toes curled in my sandals until one plopped to the floor.

"Taylor," I gasped out, taking him by the shoulders with both hands.

His tongue dipped within my slick passage, creating flutters in my stomach. Firm, strong fingers ran upward along my thighs, then cupped my ass and dragged me forward another inch.

"Better than any dessert." He blew a cool stream of air across my sensitive flesh.

With one hand remaining on my hip, the other moved between my legs, Taylor slid his fingers inside me again and I instinctively clamped down around him. He chuckled and flicked his tongue over my clit as fingers noisily slapped in and out of my wet body.

"Don't worry, sweetheart. I'm not going anywhere until I'm done with you."

Taylor alternated between slow licks, sharp nips, and hungry suckles while his fingers pumped within my tight channel. He built me up, brought me to the cusp of orgasm, and then he'd turn away and kiss my thighs. The infuriating man repeated the torturous cycle until I thought I would burst.

"Please," I sobbed. "Oh God, Taylor. Please, baby, please."

Squirming and thrashing, I came while holding him in a death grip at the shoulders. With my head thrown back, I screamed his name, thrusting my hips, pushing against him, driven wild until only nonsensical words fell from my mouth.

Taylor coaxed me to lie down on the empty counter, my skirt flipped above my waist and panties dangling from one ankle. One of my legs, limp and boneless like a noodle, fell from the side of the counter.

I thought he was done.

I was wrong.

His fingers slid free from my body, replaced by his tongue. He took my limp leg and hooked it over his shoulder while he feasted on my pussy. I writhed against the stone countertop and searched for something — anything — to hold on to.

He was a sadist, skilled in the fine art of sexual torture. And I'd become his very, *very* willing victim. When he glanced up from between my legs, I saw his pupils had blown so wide, barely any blue remained. He dipped down again and the world around me spun. Without warning, his lips sealed around my swollen clit. Just like that, I was his—exploding, lost, and convulsing on the table as another orgasm shot through me.

My second climax was merciless and more potent than its predecessor. My body was quivering, on fire, subjected to too much sensation at once. One of his hands palmed my breasts and alternated between pinching each nipple, while his tongue tip explored my pierced clit hood.

It was heaven and hell both, all at once. He left me gasping for air with my chest heaving and breasts bouncing wildly.

Soft kisses trailed their way up my trembling body. Taylor leaned over me and claimed my mouth with infinite tenderness. I tasted myself on his lips, salty and earthy, but the world around me remained hazy.

"Night, Jada."

"Ni—huh? You're going?" If I wasn't meek as a kitten, I would have tackled him to the floor. I wanted to spend time with him and had looked forward to a quiet movie on the couch. His place or mine, it didn't matter.

"Yeah. I got some stuff to do tonight. Trust me, I'd back out if I could. Sorry," he apologized again, contrite features genuine.

I tried to snap out of it, but my legs were uncooperative. My foggy mind didn't want to make sense of my surroundings yet or accept my boyfriend had eaten me out on my brand new reception counter.

"Besides, I saw how stiff you've been moving since the hike."

Damn him for being so observant. "What about dinner tomorrow?"

"I think dinner tomorrow is great." I wanted to be angry, but he won me over with his bashful smile. "If you're feeling up to it. Don't rush on my account."

"Oo-kaay?" I dragged the word out, still frazzled and out of sorts.

"I really am sorry." Taylor chuckled, that low and sexy sound I loved so much, and leaned down to kiss my forehead. "Don't fall asleep in here or your back will scream tomorrow… and that would be a shame."

"I'm not. I won't." I hated that we weren't at his place or mine, where I could have stripped and talked him out of his plans to leave, but I appreciated his decision not to hit it for a quickie and leave. "You don't want anything?" I dropped my eyes down to his apparent erection.

He paused and glanced at me. "You offering?"

"No. Yes. Maybe," I mumbled, indecisive. "Do you have to go?"

"Baby, I'm covered in crap from rebuilding a diesel engine. Trust me. If we were anywhere else and this was any other time… Damn." He inhaled slowly and gazed down at me, smoldering desire in his eyes. I could see his arousal, the silhouette of his hard cock visible beneath his coveralls. I dared to skate my fingers over the bulge and earned a sharp hiss of his breath in response.

"Girl, you have no idea how much I wanna stay."

"No, trust me. I know."

~TAYLOR~

The timing was shit. I should have been home, making love to Jada. Instead, I was standing around for a heist.

Tito never involved me in much of the criminal side of the business. Once or twice in the month since I began working for him, they'd asked me to pass a message to one of his dealers or hold on to some product. With each request, the stakes raised a little higher.

'Don't fuck up' became my motto, until I finally scored the big job. Without a doubt, I knew this was my chance to prove myself. This was the beginning of the end, my chance to earn a way into the inner circle and to see what his operation was really about.

He wanted us to break into the local pharmacy. It was a small, Mom and Pop kind of place owned by an elderly couple and their middle-aged daughter. Their only source of income and a business in their family for decades.

The daughter was in on it, an addiction to Vicodin driving her to help rob her own parents.

To impress Tito, I concocted a plan for her to claim she forgot to lock the back door while closing up for the evening and taking out the trash. We'd hide behind the dumpster, burst in, and take the store for everything it was worth.

We did.

I held her at gunpoint with an unloaded pistol for the camera, my identity concealed beneath a ski mask. My heart pounded inside my ribcage the entire time. I'd never pointed a gun at a civilian woman in all my life.

I hated the way it made me feel. My skin crawled and I broke out in a cold sweat. On my orders, she punched in the code to the narcotics safe, we emptied enough codeine to stone a rhino, and we bounced. After we were gone, she phoned the police to report the armed robbery.

She met up with us hours later for her share of the wealth.

"What'd the cops say, Vickie?" I lounged on an old couch we had set up in the garage.

Vickie shook out her auburn hair from her knit cap. "The usual bullshit. They took the surveillance tapes and dusted for prints. My folks are fretting and contacted their insurance."

"They don't suspect you helped?"

"Of course not. Now give me my take, man." She shifted restlessly from foot to foot.

"Keep your pants on," Lyle grunted. He worked at a table, counting out shares of the pills to divide between Tito's drug trade and the robbery participants.

"I need it, Lyle. My head is pounding and this is the only shit that works."

Lyle passed the antsy woman a black film canister. Vickie fumbled the lid off and popped two pills into her mouth. Without a further word, she gave us the bird then headed out.

"Is she always an ungrateful bitch?" I asked.

"Yeah. That's just Vee."

"You were awesome in there," a kid named Joey gushed at me. He had to be about eighteen or nineteen, and too young to be tangled up in this mess. "I can't believe Tito let you lead the entire thing."

I just laughed at him, unwilling to give any verbal encouragement.

"So, you ready for your share, T.J.?" Lyle tossed me a bottle of thirty. I threw it back.

"Nah, none for me, dawg. I never do the shit I deal with," I said with a head shake. "Bad business."

The dog shifter frowned at me. "What? You too good to get high with us, too? You don't wanna hang with us. You won't get high—"

"Sounds like a smart man," Tito commented from the doorway. He came in smoking one of his thin, black clove cigars. Flimsy tendrils of sweet scented smoke wafted from him.

"Besides, never know when my parole officer is gonna ask me to piss, you know?"

"Whatever, pussy." Lyle chuckled at his own joke. It didn't bother me in the least; my cougar would always be superior to his mangy mutt.

"Hey, Taylor, come on back into my office." Tito nodded toward the door.

I followed him, and once I was inside, the man shut the door then gestured with one beefy hand for me to take a seat. The inside of Tito's office was a pimp palace decorated with exotic fur, leather, and gold.

A legitimate pimp cup stood on display at the edge of his desk, a gold goblet with his name spelled out in bling.

Once I settled in the seat opposite his desk, Tito lowered his bulk into the one behind it. He gazed at me quietly with appraising brown eyes.

"Heard you got into it earlier with Tyrese, Marco, and Jared."

I snorted. I could play it two ways, apologetic or resolute in my behavior. True to my inner nature, I chose the latter. "They were giving Jada a hard time, making a mess outside her shop, so I told 'em I'd beat their asses if they show up again."

Tito blew smoke and nodded. "I'll tell the boys to keep their business clear of your girl's place. How's that sound?"

"Sounds good, man. Thanks."

"That wasn't the only thing I needed to have a private word with you about."

This is it, I hoped. *My chance to find out the real deal behind what's going on.*

"Yeah?" I asked.

"Beer?" he countered.

"Won't say no to a cold one." Tito removed one from the mini-fridge behind his desk and slid it to me.

Condensation from the frosty Corona moistened my fingers. I popped the cap off with my thumb and slouched back in the seat.

"So, let's skip past the bullshit and go straight to the truth. What sort of cat are you that's got Lyle's hackles all up in a shitty twist?"

I grunted and put on a show of being dismayed. "Fucker outed me like that?" It was against our unspoken shifter code of ethics to dox each other to humans. I frowned severely, suppressing the urge to leave and promptly bust Lyle in his face.

"Part of his job. He lets me know when your kind are sniffing about the place."

"Fair enough. I'm a cougar, which is partially why I came up this way. I was eager to find a place with lots of woods to run in."

Tito's eyes lit up with greed, but he quickly hid it beneath phony nonchalance.

"You the one Granny Matthews saw back there with her goats a week back?"

I rubbed the back of my neck. "I got hungry… it was late. I hunted and couldn't find shit out there." To be fair, I'd picked off an ancient member of her flock she'd mentioned wanting to put down soon anyway, and then I made sure the old lady wandered up on a few loose fifties in her yard later that day.

Tito chortled. "I guess the Micky D's after-midnight menu ain't good enough for one of y'all."

"Heh. Yeah, you got that right. Gotta let the animal roam free sometimes."

I couldn't fucking stand him. Tito was slimy, the kind of slimy that meant any self-respecting man wouldn't leave his daughter, wife, or girlfriend alone with him.

"I need somebody with your skills for this business. Lyle's loyal, but he's never gonna be anything more than a follower. I need a man with cajones. Some real smarts."

"I haven't really done anything—"

"I disagree. You chased those boys off and guarded what was yours, T.J. I need you to do the same for my operation. There's a lot of your kind — the furry and four-legged variety — moving into Quickdraw recently."

"Yeah?"

Tito took in a drag on his clove. "The sheriff who just got elected? He's one. Not sure what yet, just that he's got feathers that make Lyle sneeze."

I smirked. *Good. I should stuff feathers around the place just to set that little shit off.* The idea amused me and I was certain Ian would see the humor in it, too.

"Then there's that big redneck on the volunteer fire department."

Gotta be Russ, I thought. "Him, too? Haven't met him, but I know who you're referring to."

"Yeah." Tito rubbed his chin. "MacArthur's the troublemaker though. The other big fuck minds his business and keeps out of ours. People are more willing to cross us these days than they used to be before he came around."

"Sounds like a real Boy Scout."

"Yeah." Tito laughed then he got down to the real question. "How close are you to your girl's daddy?"

"Not at all, man. He hates me."

"Shit."

"So if you wanted me to try to get him on the payroll, you're out of luck there. I'm not even allowed in his house."

"We'll worry about Hunt later. For now, I got another job for you to do, direct from the big boss. Needs to be fast and discreet. Think you can do that?"

"Discreet is what I do, Tito."

***

Judge Fitz awakened to the press of cold steel against his balls. His wife was paying a visit to their pregnant daughter out of state, so I snuck into his home around midnight.

It took me about two minutes to disable the home security system and pick the locks on the rear door.

As for the big golden retriever he kept in the house? It piddled on the floor and ran to hide under the table when it smelled the cougar on my skin. One growl from me guaranteed he remained there.

I made my way to the upper levels and crept down the hall toward the master bedroom. Fitz never stirred until it was too late.

"I know there's a gun under your pillow. Touch it and your dog'll be the only one with balls in this house. You got me?"

The judge trembled in his bed. "What do you want?"

"I came to deliver a message. We both got some mutual friends and they ain't cool with what's going on lately."

"I can't let all of them off. I just can't. MacArthur will become suspicious sooner or later. You don't realize how much pull he—"

"I don't care how much pull he has, old man." I tapped the knife against the crease of his thigh above his femoral artery. I heard him gulp. Fear permeated the air, seeping from his pores to drench his t-shirt and thin cotton boxers. He was petrified.

And I hated myself for doing it, even if he was a crooked official.

"All right. Tell Tito I understand. I'll do better."

I grinned and tapped the steel blade against his body again. "Good. Real good. Next time, I won't wait until your wife isn't home. I'll go visit her personally. Her and that baby girl of yours."

"No, don't!"

"Then do the job we pay you for and keep our people on the streets."

With my free hand, I reached beneath the pillow and removed his handgun.

"What are you doing?" Fitz demanded. Pressure from the knife in my other hand halted his attempt to stop me from taking his pistol.

"Can't have you shooting me in my back, now can I?"

He couldn't tell it, but I was sweating bullets under my mask, afraid he'd have a coronary while I held his jewels at knifepoint.

Perspiration trickled freely down my neck until I was clear of the wilderness bordering his home.

Finally, I'd made a breakthrough.

I knew how they were getting off and back onto the street, and most importantly, I'd earned Tito's trust.

Chapter Eight

~JADA~

"Bye, Jada!" Anna called from the door. My happy customer stepped outside into the dwindling sunlight, its glow casting highlights of gold against her newly henna colored hair. I waved to her and resumed sweeping the clippings from the floor.

I beamed with pride and admired the vibrant shade.

"You did a good job there. Could Naomi do something like that to me?" Beth, another client, asked from Naomi's chair.

"Mm, well, we could, but it wouldn't be that color. Your hair is darker, so the most it'll do is add a bit of a red tint to your hair when you're in the sun."

"Oh," the woman said, disappointed.

"But if you want, we can color it today," Naomi said.

"Let's do that then. I want some real bounce to it, too, girl. Make my hair swing."

I chuckled and stooped over to sweep up the mess from the floor. I had a few more calls to make around to the rest of the local businesses in the area. I'd decided, soon after chasing the troublemaking boys from in front of my shop, that it was time for all of us to take back our neighborhood. As store owners, we couldn't wait by as passive observers to our neighborhood's deterioration.

Most of the business owners had agreed it was time to take a stand. Before, we'd been afraid to call the police for fear of making trouble. We didn't open our mouths to chase them off. I'd proven it was possible to stand up to the filth giving our town a bad name.

I saw Mrs. Keller, the young woman who owned the dog grooming salon down the road, open her door and threaten to call the police on teens making her customers uncomfortable.

I even bought No Loitering signs from the general store and passed them out as the shops were opening.

It was too early to determine if our actions would be enough, but it was a start and better than what we'd had before.

"It's a good thing you got that system from MacArthur Security," Beth said. "Stirring the hornet's nest in town is going to upset a lot of people, Jada."

"I know, but it's worth it. Besides, I'm insured. Let's hope it doesn't come to that," I said. "And if it does, I keep a gun in my purse now."

Bells chimed from the front of the shop, signaling Lisa's arrival to the salon. I waved to her, smiling.

"Oh good, Lisa, you're here. Mrs. Hatton called and wanted to know if you could fit her two boys in this week. She wants them cleaned up before their vacation."

"Oh, yeah. I'll give her a call back and set it up." She tucked her purse away behind the counter.

"Everything okay? You seem a little distracted."

Lisa ran her fingers through her short hair and peered around the quiet room. Naomi was chatting with Beth while she applied dye to the woman's hair.

"We need to talk, Jada."

The smile dropped from my face. "Okay. Let's go into the back."

With one hand between Lisa's shoulder blades, I led her to the rear room where I kept my desk, filing cabinet, computer, and physical business documents. African violets filled a pot on the desk beside a family portrait of my parents, Danny, and me.

"What's going on?"

"You know how I mentioned my parents are having problems with my little brother recently, right?"

"Yeah?" I sat on the edge of the desk.

"Well… I caught him buying drugs today. Down at the park. I was jogging and spotted him trading cash for a baggie of weed by the recreation center."

"Oh, Lisa, I'm so sorry."

She forced a faint, thin smile. "I caught up to his dumb ass and took it from him. Threatened to tell Mom and Dad. He said some not so nice things and took off. But, that's not what I wanted to talk to you about."

"What then?"

"It's about *who* was selling to him."

~TAYLOR~

Quickdraw's only recreation center was positioned beside a small park, the brand new playground equipment recently funded by Ian's generous donations. It was a favored position for illicit activities, so I hunkered down beside the center's doors with my hands in my pockets.

"Sup, T.J."

I glanced up at the approaching teen, a repeat customer I'd peddled to twice since Tito asked me to begin distributions. His freckled face made me feel like I was selling to a child.

"Fifty bucks, kid. Take it or leave it. You want quality shit then you pay quality price."

"What? That's twice the price from last week."

"Don't like it? Go buy that sorry shit from the Dixie Quarters and risk smoking Windex with it, too."

"Man, a buddy told me he heard they cut their weed with oregano and shit."

I snorted back a laugh. "You heard right. So pay up or get out of here."

"Whatever," the kid mumbled. He thumbed some bills out of his wallet and passed them over, taking an envelope in exchange.

"I don't fucking believe you," a quiet, female voice seethed behind me.

My heart leapt into a slamming rhythm, the noise of my pulse drowning out all other sound. *No,* I thought, panicked.

I glanced from my customer and into the wide brown eyes of my girlfriend, my future mate, and the woman I loved more than my own life. *No, not now.*

"Jada, wait."

Jada spun on her heel and stormed down the sidewalk. I'd be lucky to catch her before she reached her car. My customer smirked and tucked his score into his pocket.

"No. Screw you," she raged at me.

"It's not how it looks, baby, I swear."

"Oh really? Because it looks crystal clear to me." She jerked her arm from my loose grip.

"Woman, give me a fucking chance to explain."

"What kind of explanation is there for it? I didn't want to believe it, you know. I didn't want to believe Lisa when she told me she saw you selling to her *brother*. I wanted to give you the benefit of the doubt and think better of you."

I couldn't lose her. Not after everything we'd shared together, and not when I was so close to finally attaining the peace Russ and Ian received from their mates.

If I didn't come clean to Jada now, I risked losing her forever. Fuck the mission. None of it was worth anything if I lost her.

"Jada, please, give me ten minutes. After that, if you never want to see me again, I swear I'll walk away and never bother you."

"I'll give you five."

"Can we get in your car at least so nobody overhears all of this? It's serious."

Jada humored me and climbed into the driver's seat. I joined her in the other side and twisted to face her. "I don't really have a criminal record."

"Bullshit. I saw it and read a whole yard of crap you've done." She fired up the engine and tore out of the parking lane down from the rec center. I watched her troubled features as she focused on the road.

"It's phony. Made up stuff our digital expert created to make a paper trail. My real name is Taylor Morrison. I retired from the U.S. Army four years ago to open a mechanic shop in Houston. I've spent the past seven months of my life undercover to help out a close friend of mine with the shit going down in this town."

Jada gaped at me. "Seriously. *That's* the story you came up with?"

"It's true, every word. Ian asked me to do it because nobody around Quickdraw would know my face. Baby, I've never so much as smoked a joint in all my life. I was in the Army for over twenty years. If I tested hot on a piss test, I would have lost my career."

"Wait. Ian? You mean Sheriff Ian MacArthur?"

"Yeah. Leigh's husband and my commanding officer."

"So you're doing what, exactly?"

"There's a whole lot to it that I can't talk about, but what I can tell you is that I don't like peddling drugs to anybody, but it's a necessity right now if I want them to trust me and think I'm one of *them.* If you don't believe me, you can ask Ian *and* Leigh. Dani and Russ, too."

"I've talked to Dani about you. She never mentioned knowing you."

"Call and ask her again," I pleaded. "What do you have to lose, Jada? Just call."

"Fine." Without looking at me again, Jada suddenly hit the brakes and turned off the main street onto an old dirt road. The car jittered and bounced as she sped over railroad tracks, then we came to an abrupt stop. "And if they don't verify your story?" she asked while taking out her phone.

"They will," I insisted.

A moment later, Russell's distinct, southern drawl greeted her with a warm welcome.

"Hi, Russ. I need to talk to Dani—no, wait. You're just as good. I want to talk to *you*."

I listened to her end of the conversation, anxiety rolling through my gut.

"I busted your friend Taylor selling dope by the rec center. Anything you wanna tell me about this?" she demanded.

Come on, Russ. Don't let me down, man.

"Really? 'Cause he says he knows you and you'd vouch for him."

She was silent on the phone for a long while, making the occasional acknowledging grunt. Several times her gaze flickered toward me, but I couldn't read her. My stomach twisted and each breath squeezed my chest just a little tighter.

"Thanks, Russ. Please tell Dani I'll see her for lunch tomorrow as planned." She ended the call and set her phone in the center console between our seats. "First Sergeant Taylor Morrison," she murmured. Her throaty, humorless laugh twisted the knife in my heart and dashed my hopes of an easy reconciliation. "You fucking liar."

"Jada, I'm sorry from the bottom of my heart for lying to you. I never thought I'd meet someone like you while doing this."

"So was I just a part of your cover? Flirt with the shop owner across the street?"

"No, it's nothing like that. When I helped you out alongside the road, I didn't know who you were. I didn't know anyone in this town except for my friends. What I did know was I couldn't let you walk away until this was done. I had to get to know you."

"All of this has been a lie… I don't even know you. How can I separate the bullshit you've told me from what's true?"

"I'm still the same guy who took you out to the splash park. The guy who likes laser tag and rock wall climbing. Nothing's changed about me but the kind of work I do."

"You're still dealing drugs."

"Not because I want to do it, but because I have to do this. Look, baby, I can't tell you everything. It's for your protection more than anything else. Ian's asked me to do this with the full authority of the governor. No one else is allowed to know because of the danger involved."

"Trying to find the root of the problem in town," she murmured, gaze on her lap.

"Right. Do you remember Dennis James?"

"Who doesn't? He used to be a nice guy until he got involved in dealing. He and my little brother, Danny, used to play ball after school. He taught him to dunk."

"I found out someone murdered him over this shit, Jada. Whoever he was working for got to him all the way in prison, and it's not going to end there unless we do something to stop it."

"Does this really change things?" Her brown eyes watched me, filled with emotion.

"Give me another chance," I pleaded again. "I'm trusting you to keep this secret between us because I care about you and I don't want this to end."

"Okay," she whispered.

I leaned across the armrest to kiss her, only for Jada to meet me halfway. Her lips parted, yielding access to her mouth and the chance to stroke my tongue against hers.

"You forgive me?"

She drew back then nibbled my lower lip in response. "This time. God, that's so hot that you're undercover."

"Hot?"

"Yes." Her fingers walked over my bulge and teased, making the hard dick beneath the denim flex in response. "My father is going to hate you if he catches you dealing," she whispered between kisses. "So you better not disappoint either of us by getting caught again."

"I won't," I promised. "But you can't utter a word of this to him. I'm sorry I put you in this position."

Her fingers rubbed over my dick through my jeans. "I guess I'll have to be a rebellious daughter for now."

I tried to ignore the unbearable tension until her fingers snapped the button and my zipper descended. In the outdoors privacy provided by the abandoned rail station, we had no witnesses and were free to behave as we wanted. I groaned as she took me in her hand and lowered her lips to the tip.

"Fuck," I groaned as my head fell back. "This isn't how I imagined getting into your pants, Jada."

"Lucky you, then."

I tried to protest, but was promptly silenced when she drew the tip into her mouth. Her plump lips sealed around the head and I was lost to the sensation.

Jada knew what she was doing. Her tongue teased around my flared crown then wiggled over the turgid length, tracing the pulsing veins and leaving glistening trails in her wake. Before I could utter a word of encouragement, she thrust her head down and bobbed in place, making obscene, incredibly sexy slurping sounds while her tongue moistened every inch.

Fisting my fingers in her hair, I guided her down and up in time with slow pelvic thrusts. "Fuck, baby. Yes. Get all of it."

She came close. No woman had ever deep-throated me before or even tried. Jada took me in until I experienced the tight squeeze at the back of her throat, where the angle hindered her from traveling farther. She hummed, and the vibrations made me swear out loud.

~JADA~

It wasn't like he'd lied about having a kid, or lied about where he'd been with the boys. He'd lied because of a job for the government, because he'd been tasked with saving our little town. My home.

The sexy truth of it made me wet until all I wanted was to touch myself. Or have him buried between my thighs, plunging his hard cock into my pussy.

I hated liars, but Taylor had earned a well-deserved pass.

"I'm close, baby. I'm close," he groaned.

Taylor laced his fingers into my hair and guided me along, pumping faster each time my mouth came closer to meeting his balls. I had him at my mercy, writhing in the car seat and practically panting for breath.

When I slid back and let his cock fall from between my lips, his disapproving moan made me smile. I was so hungry for him I could barely stand it. My thighs pressed together, panties soaked from the anticipation.

"No, wait. What are you doing?" he asked.

Now the tables are turned, I thought, delighted by the reversed roles.

I giggled at his breathless words. "If I let you come now, I'll have to wait for you to be ready again to fuck me. And like I said, I want you *now*. I won't wait or take another raincheck." Kissing the mushroomed head, I flicked my tongue against the small slit for a taste of his pre-cum. His dick was as long and thick as I'd imagined, soon glistening at its tip with another clear drop.

"Here?" he asked.

"Here. Right now."

Taylor didn't question it again. Instead, he dragged me into his lap and onto his erection. With a little wriggle, I placed myself in the perfect position, my panties the only barrier between us.

He ruined them with one tear, ripping the seam at one hip then the other; then he tossed the useless rag aside. With my skirt gathered up around my waist, I was bared to him again for the second time, my jet curls neatly groomed, trimmed down and waxed to a perfect strip above the hard cock jutting from his pelvis. His cock twitched, proving how much he appreciated the sight and making me glow with pride.

"Do we need a…?"

"I'm on the pill," I whispered, answering an unspoken question I saw in his eyes. "Do *you* think we need a condom, Sergeant? Do you trust *me* to be clean this time?"

His hip movement answered, nudging his cock between my glistening folds. I took over by directing the tip to my entrance. Then I slid it through the moisture gathered between the silken, pink lips. Groaning, he watched me through half-shut eyes.

"You're so big," I breathed out loud, surprised by the tight fit.

Needing him too much to be daunted by the size, I lowered in slow increments, drawing it out as a tease. We both groaned in mutual enjoyment. Then Taylor bucked upward and speared me in two quick strokes. His thick girth pressed into my body, parting my swollen lips until the delicious stretch was over and he'd filled my greedy channel completely. His cock seemed to go on forever.

"Oh fuck," I whispered.

Somehow, we rocked to a perfect fit. With his hands on my hips, his fingers curved around to my cheeks and spread them apart. A bump of his pelvis introduced me to the last inch, pressing my clit against his pubic bone.

"God, you're so tight."

"And you feel amazing," I breathed while undulating my hips. The enclosed confines made things a little more difficult, but I'd meant what I said. I wanted him. *Needed* him. Going home to a bedroom wasn't an option.

Taylor shoved my blouse up and fumbled with my bra. He took one look at my pierced nipples and swore under his breath. The moment he claimed my breast in his mouth, I clenched around him, earning another pleased groan and a flex of the cock filling my body. I giggled as he reached down to adjust the seat back, reclining it to give us more room. It wasn't a bed, but it was our moment. A perfect moment of passion, intense longing, and mutual need given satisfaction.

"You're beautiful, Jada. I know I've said it before, but damn, girl."

"Say it as much as you like," I replied.

Taylor's hands squeezed my ass and jerked my body in close each time I drew away. With him beneath me, I maintained most of the control over the speed of our lovemaking, and I loved every second of having him under my spell. My hips rose and fell, unrushed despite his attempt to urge me faster. My tight sheath flexed around him, squeezing and constricting to my timed movements until his eyes rolled back and his breaths quickened.

"You like that, baby? I wanna hear you come."

Taylor groaned in response before leaning forward to reclaim my tits. He nipped my left breast then gave the other the same treatment. The tiny circles he traced with his tongue jostled the horizontal barbells through my nipples and sent riveting shocks dancing up and down my spine.

Groaning, his mouth fell away from my bosom, and one hand gripped my face. Taylor kissed me hard, our tongues twisting together in a sensual dance interrupted only by our erratic breaths. My pulse became a frenzy, every muscle tensed as my trembling core tightened around him.

My climax rushed over me, a crashing wave of pleasure enhanced by his exploring fingertips. One found my clit and teased, intensifying the moment into a white-hot explosion.

I couldn't move. I was paralyzed by the sensation, crying out and gasping for breath in quick pants. Taylor took over without missing a beat, hammering away at me, my pussy so slick with juices it dripped down to his heavy balls.

Penetrative sex never made me come. Usually, I had to help it along with a vibrator. Taylor had me there before he even touched me with his hands. I shuddered and clenched around him again as his creamy warmth flooded me. His guttural groan of relief sounded like a growl in the close quarters.

"That was the best," I murmured against his cheek as we both began to come down.

"I don't wanna move."

"Me either."

We didn't. The first hour or so after our lovemaking was spent touching each other, our fondling interspersed with occasional moments of conversation.

"We probably shouldn't fall asleep here," Taylor reminded me when I yawned. His fingers traveled up and down my back, lulling me closer to sweet dreams. He felt so warm beneath me, an inviting pillow and absolutely, 100 percent mine.

"Fasten me up then?" I asked.

"And hide those gorgeous breasts? All of these piercings are fucking sexy."

"Play your cards right and you'll see them again soon." It took a moment, but I managed to get back into the driver's seat and turned my back to him so he could fasten my bra. "Can you handle the hooks or does your knowledge only extend to undoing them?"

"Sure." Taylor secured my bra and smoothed my shirt down. He didn't let me go without kissing the back of my neck. "Thank you."

"Hm? What for."

"For trusting me again."

I twisted around to face him. If his excuse had been anything less, I would have walked out of his life. "I don't like lies, Taylor. You told me the truth at least, and your fibs had an actual purpose. I still don't like it, but I understand."

"If I keep anything else from you, it's because the job requires it, or I plan to tell you soon when it's safe for everyone involved, okay?"

I bit my lower lip. "Okay. I can handle that. Do you have to be at the shop tomorrow?" I asked.

"Nah. The day's all mine."

"Come home with me then," I offered.

"You're inviting me back to *your* place?"

"Of course. Now that I know I can trust you not to stash crack in my bathroom toilet or something."

I nipped his ear, and then the wind played tricks on my hearing, transforming his chuckle into a rumbling purr. The noise vibrated through the hand I'd placed over his chest.

I felt deliciously sore during the drive home, aching from our frantic union and still wet for more. I anticipated his return inside my body as I pulled into the driveway. The neighbors waved to us.

Moments later, we were inside the house with nothing but clothes between us. I bumped the door shut behind us with my hip, tossed my keys onto the hook, and threw myself into my man's arms. My weight didn't budge him. He caught me, making me feel weightless.

I spent the rest of the night learning the many ways I could get Taylor to plead for more and groan my name. The man had more energy than I'd anticipated and stamina that spoke well of his military days. He was in amazing shape.

In the pale blue, fluorescent glow of my bedside aquarium, I admired his lean physique. My fingers ran trails over his smooth chest, enjoying the muscular contours. "Are you really forty-five?"

"Yeah, why? Do I look it?" He'd sprawled on his back in my bed with one arm behind his head, the other behind my shoulders to hold me close as the sweat dried on our skin. My hair was also a mess, wild from our vigorous lovemaking and Taylor's habit of running his fingers through it while we fucked.

I walked my fingers over his flat abdomen and traced the dips between the muscles of his six pack. "Far from it."

"Good genes."

His words were an understatement. He had *amazing* genes. "I wouldn't have pegged you to be any older than thirty. Though I guess I could say the same about your two friends, too."

He chuckled. "Like I said, good genes and a lot of training." His blue eyes flicked to the tank on my nightstand. "So why do you have a dozen fish tanks in your place? The bedroom, too, woman? Really?"

"I like fish," I said defensively. "It's a relaxing hobby, albeit a little expensive sometimes."

"I would have taken you for a cat person."

"Maybe… they're kind of bitchy, but recently my opinion of them has changed. You know, even though they play with their food and walk in their own poop." I thought about the cougar who sometimes came to my back door and wondered where he lived when he didn't receive food from me. Were there other humans nearby feeding him, too?

Taylor chuckled and brushed his lips across my shoulder. "Bitchy, eh? I like to think of them as having better taste than most people do."

"I'll stick with my collection of placid fish." *Unless it's my mountain lion.*

"Ouch." In a dramatic gesture, he held his hand to his heart.

"I take it you're a cat person?" *Whoops.* Giggling, I wondered if he had a pet somewhere at his other home in Houston.

"You could say that. Besides, fish swim in their poop, so..." He stuck his tongue out at me in a childish gesture.

"You're horrible."

Although he was horrible, we chatted throughout the night. I drifted off to sleep feeling warm and secure in his arms. My sexy military man would clean up Quickdraw, and in the morning, I'd certainly have more questions for him.

Chapter Nine

~JADA~

"Did you break up with him?" Lisa demanded when she arrived at noon the next day to set up at her station.

I froze and glanced over my shoulder at her. "Not exactly…"

She stared at me. I could read her mind, knowing her so well I thought the words before they left her mouth. "You slept with that jackass after I told you what he's doing and where you could find him dealing?"

I needed to lie. Nothing could make me give Taylor up now that I knew the truth, but ignoring Lisa wasn't an option. "I didn't make it in time, so I didn't see him dealing anything," I fibbed.

"What? You actually need to see him selling meth to believe he's doing it?"

Weed, not meth. Not that the difference matters, I thought. "I like Taylor. Not even a month ago you were threatening to go chase him yourself."

"Yeah, before I knew he was a drug-dealing creep selling shit to my kid brother."

"Your kid brother is a grown man making his own decisions, *if* what you saw was an actual drug transaction."

"Jada, dammit, I told you I snagged the drugs he bought. I can't believe you."

At the time, making love to Taylor had been easy, but the consequences of staying with him became more difficult with each passing day. In the face of Lisa's indignation, it became difficult to maintain eye contact. Standing up to my dad had been easy, but losing my friend's support hurt, leaving a deep ache in my chest.

I was the world's biggest ass.

"I really care about him, Lisa. We'll talk. I'll talk to him," I said lamely.

"Whatever."

Lisa didn't talk to me for the rest of the day. After cleaning her booth, she plucked her purse from the table and left without a goodbye. She breezed past Leigh in a huff.

"Whoa. What's her problem?" Leigh asked me, startled by Lisa's abrupt departure.

"Flip that sign to 'closed' for me and lock the door, and I'll tell you about it," I called over as I secured the register for the evening.

Leigh took a seat on the couch in the waiting area until I joined her.

"I planned to ask if you wanted to have dinner with me at The Perfect Pot, but obviously something is up. What happened?"

"Everything is a mess, Leigh. Lisa saw Taylor selling to her brother, and now she's pissed because I haven't kicked his ass to the curb."

Leigh swore. "Crap."

"Yeah. Crap."

"So that's when you called Russ?" She bit her lip and smiled faintly at my startled look. "Sorry. They called to let us know you'd found out what was going on."

"So they're all in on it?"

"Pretty much. Ian is the one who arranged for Taylor to get in the prison, so he could try to work things from the inside. He's been wanting to root out the problem, especially since they broke into our home and shot things up."

"Yeah, I remember all that from the paper. Daddy told me you had the baby home and everything."

"Yup. Dani, too. So you can understand why the guys want to get the drug issue taken care of."

I sighed and nodded. "I understand what Taylor is doing, but I don't know what to do about Lisa. Or my dad for that matter."

"Hopefully this will all be over soon. But…"

"But what?" I looked to her for advice.

"What if you two 'broke up' for the time being? Your dad would get off your case, Lisa would be appeased, and when this is all over, you two can tell everyone the truth."

"Maybe…" *Maybe that's what's best for everyone,* I thought. Leigh rubbed my shoulder in unspoken support. "I'll talk to him tomorrow, after I sleep on it."

~TAYLOR~

A police siren screamed as I crossed the bridge leading to Quickdraw. I glanced into the rearview mirror to see police lights. I pulled over clear of any potential traffic and killed the engine.

The hell is this about? I wasn't even speeding, I thought while rolling down the window. I fetched my wallet from my pocket and placed it beside me after fishing out the phony driver's license. With both set in the passenger seat, I watched the side mirror until the cop's door opened.

A lanky blond stepped from the vehicle. I made eye contact with Chief Hunt as he strode toward me, a grim expression on his face.

Fuck.

"License and proof of insurance," Hunt said in a terse voice. His hand hovered near his holster, daring me to give him a reason to fire.

"Yes, sir," I replied. I breathed in calmly and slowly reached for the glove compartment. "I'm going to get my insurance card out of here, cool?"

"That's fine."

The last thing I needed was to make him twitchy. Hunt was a good man, a great cop, but he was nervous and my record of assault put him on guard. He was within his right to be wary thanks to the impressive list of charges in Taylor Jackson's fictional history.

After the glove box fell open, I pulled the insurance card from it and placed my driver's license on top. He perused both and held on to them.

"Step out of the vehicle."

"Is something the matter, sir?" I unhooked my seatbelt.

"Step out of the vehicle," he repeated.

I didn't question it. I knew better. Wordlessly, I stepped from the car and followed him to the side of the road with both hands down to my sides, clear of my pockets.

"I have it on good authority you were seen distributing an illegal substance," he said.

Shit. Had Jada's friend ratted me out? Using my poker face, I shook my head and feigned disbelief. "I don't touch the stuff. If you don't believe me, you can search me and my car. I'm clean, sir. I give you full permission to search my person and my vehicle."

Five minutes later, another officer arrived on the scene. Hunt patted me down with his witness present then stood me alongside the road under watch while he ransacked my vehicle. When that failed, Hunt called out their canine unit to verify it was truly drug-free.

"Chief," the officer whispered, "there's nothing here. The guy is clean. You keep him here like this, everybody's going to jump to conclusions. Think it's to do with your daughter."

Every word reached my keen hearing.

Hunt shook his head and returned to task, leading the dog around again. Finally, he gave me a sheepish look when their combined efforts failed to turn up a single bud of marijuana.

"Take the dog back," he muttered to the canine handler.

"Do you want us to stay?" the other officer asked.

"No. Go on back to the station, too. I can handle it from here."

I didn't move, and neither did Hunt. We remained at the roadside in a stare off, a sort of silent, bitter stalemate until both police vehicles pulled away.

The wind kicked up, blowing grit and road dust into my face. I didn't so much as move a muscle until Hunt returned my license and insurance card to me.

"There any reason why someone would want to lie about you, son?"

I shook my head. "I try to keep to myself. If I'm not spending time with your daughter, I'm at home. I don't go out much these days."

"I've seen you at the bar with Tito's boys."

"Just once or twice. I don't really enjoy the company, if you get my drift."

Hunt watched me, skepticism in his eyes. "There anything you want to talk to me about in private, Mr. Jackson? Anything you think would help us out?"

I shook my head again. "No, sir. Nothing comes to mind."

Hunt watched me closer. "For some reason, my daughter seems to think you're a great guy. She swears up and down you're a changed man."

"I am, sir."

"Prove it to me then. Find another job."

"There isn't another place in town for a mechanic like me to work," I pointed out.

"Go as far as Huntsville then or even Livingston. Get out of this town. Go to work in a place where you'll get some real money. A couple of the boys at the department say you worked on their vehicles and did a tip-top job. Tito's isn't the only place with openings."

"Maybe. Most people in the other towns ain't so friendly to a guy with a record," I told him. "It's not for lack of trying or being lazy. Am I free to go?"

"Yeah. You're free."

I tapped Jada's number into the speed dial as I drove away. She answered on the third ring, quicker than usual.

"Hey, baby. You busy right now?"

"Not really. What's up?" she asked.

"Your dad pulled me over as soon as I crossed the bridge. I think Lisa squealed and told him what happened."

Jada swore into the line. "Waiting for you? Seriously? *Ugh*. Yeah, she definitely told Dad. Come over to my place so we can talk, okay? No, wait. I'll meet you at yours."

I arrived to find Jada waiting for me on the porch, her car nowhere in sight. She'd walked and had taken a seat on the plastic porch chair with her hands in her lap. Jeans hugged her curves, worn with a low-cut, gold-toned blouse.

"Hey," she greeted me without getting up. "Dad didn't rough you up too bad, did he?"

"Nah, your dad is a good cop. Searched my car real good, but didn't find anything." I pulled my keys out of my pocket and unlocked the house. Jada remained in the seat after I opened the door. "You comin'?"

"About that…"

"Yeah?"

She bit her lower lip nervously and glanced away from me to the street. A car slowed down and its passenger waved to us through an open window. All of the shine was gone from her expression when she returned the friendly gesture. "I was gonna wait until tomorrow…"

"Baby, what's wrong?"

"I don't know if we should continue doing this while you have your business in town. Lisa's really upset, and I don't know if Dad really believed you."

"What are you getting at, Jada?" I lingered in the doorway while she stood and kept her distance. "Come inside," I coaxed gently.

Reluctantly, she joined me inside after a cautious glance over one shoulder, as if certain someone was watching. Of course, in small towns, someone was *always* watching.

Once the door shut behind us, she released her inhibition and flew into my arms, squeezing me into a possessive hug. "I'm saying we should break up publically, not for real. When all of this is over, we can be open about our relationship again."

While sensible, the news still slugged me like a sucker punch to the gut. All the air left my lungs, and I deflated at the thought of going days without contact. In the little time since my lion had met her, she'd become my personal sun.

Time with Jada was the one thing I looked forward to each day of separation from friends and family. Without her, I'd have nothing.

"I understand."

"I'm not doing this because I want to, Taylor. I'm only thinking it'll be easier for you to do your job if Dad's not snooping around you because of me."

"No, you're right," I assured her. My fingers traveled up and down her back, finally reaching her ass to squeeze and knead it in my hands. "If we're going to do this, then I have a secret I need to share with you. Something important to me."

"You mean you have more than being an undercover military spy?"

"Yeah. Something I'm trusting you with. Something only a small number of people know."

"Okay…" She eyed me up and down with caution after I released her.

I stepped back from her and pulled my shirt over my head. My belt followed.

"Uh, Taylor. I've seen all of this already." A smile touched her lips, and then her appreciative eyes roamed over my body until I kicked both jeans and boxers away. "But one more time for the road isn't a bad idea."

"I'm not stripping for sex." The cougar inside me growled, as eager to reveal itself as I was to share the secret with my chosen.

"Are you so sure about that?" she teased.

"I'm stripping because I've kept one last secret from you, and I hope after you see this, your feelings about me won't change."

Chapter Ten

~JADA~

I loved the sight of my boyfriend's military-trained body. As I walked my nails over his washboard abs, his stomach muscles flexed and his thick cock twitched.

"Remember, I'd never hurt you." He stepped back again until he stood beyond arm's reach.

My brows knit in confusion. "Taylor, you're freaking me out."

"I know. Just trust me, please."

Taylor's light brown skin transformed into a sandy pelt as his muscled body shrank and he fell onto all fours. Large paws replaced his strong hands, and then a long tail flicked behind him. He had a massive body for a mountain lion, with the same proud poise he carried as a man and a whiskered face with keen, familiar eyes.

Instinctively, I stumbled back against the door. My bottom hit the wood with a dull thump, but the gorgeous feline didn't move in on my personal space.

"Oh, my God," I whispered. It was the same cougar from my yard. *My* big cat. I was positive, unable to mistake the piercing blue depths gazing back at me.

A thousand questions gave way to the incredible, urgent need to touch him. I stepped forward and ran my fingers over the creature's face, touching the silky fur covering one cheek. He responded sweetly. Enormous yet docile, he was still my Taylor — the same affectionate man who held me as I fell to sleep. He purred noisily, a motor hum emanating from his chest.

"I can't believe… you've been visiting me all this time." I lowered to one knee in front of him, and a dry, pink nose touched my throat, stealing my breath away when whiskers tickled my neck.

He was human again moments later, but crouched on the floor in front of me, placing warm human flesh beneath my explorative touch. His lips skimmed from my jaw to my throat, breathing me in.

So much about him made sense.

"I mean, I knew shifters existed, but—"

"Wait, what?"

Did he expect me to go screaming out of the house? I wondered. "My cousin Suraj is a tiger shifter. They're rare in India and sort of a treasured national secret."

"I guess we both learned something new about each other." Taylor straightened and offered me both hands. One effortless tug pulled me up from the ground, but I drew free to keep my distance again.

"I need to think." Which couldn't be done while he sauntered in front of me without a stitch on his body. I gestured toward the clothing pile. Taylor caught the message and stooped to collect his duds. One glimpse at his cock was enough to make the inner muscles of my pussy flutter with need.

"Wait a minute. This means you've been following me!"

Taylor smiled sheepishly. "I meant what I said about hating you walking home at night alone. I honestly didn't realize you might think it was creepy until Russ warned me about how angry Dani was about him visiting her."

"What?"

"Dani told you about her bear, right?"

"The hammock bear, yeah."

"Well, that was Russ. All of my squad are shifters, but we have different animals," he explained.

"Dani and Leigh, too?"

"No, they're human women like you, but they accepted the guys." He inhaled a deep breath, expanding his strong ribs. "The way I hope you'll accept me."

"Is this everything? No more secrets?"

"No more secrets," he assured me. "This is me, Taylor Morrison, cougar shifter. And… I knew from the moment we met that I was meant to be yours."

"What do you mean?"

"Every shifter recognizes their true mate, Jada. We may not all find them, but we always know them when we do. You feel it, too, don't you?"

Four steps closed the distance between us and each one brought a jolt to my pounding heart. I lifted to my toes and touched my lips gently over his in a brief kiss.

"Since we've met, I can't get you off my mind. You're all I can think of. Lisa catches me daydreaming about you." I bit my lower lip, wondering how Lisa would feel once Taylor revealed his true identity to the town. "I can't stand the thought of this fake break-up, of not seeing and touching you, but it's the best thing. For both of us."

"I know," he agreed quietly, lacking the poker face I'd come to know so well. In front of me, his emotions were laid bare, exposed, and honest. "I know it's for the best, but it doesn't make me happy."

"Have…" I bit my lip. "Have you ever felt like this before?"

"No." Taylor shook his head and offered one hand. I set my palm in his and let him lead me to his small couch. "I wanted to. I tried. It was just never right. Not until you came into my life."

Our fingers twined together as we settled on the cushions. "Can I ask a question?"

"Shoot."

"Are all shifters male?"

"What gives you that idea?"

"Well, of the four shifters I know of, all are men. Is that a weird coincidence or is it a shifter thing?"

"No, we have females."

I studied Taylor's melancholy expression, surprised by the deep sadness in his eyes when I asked about female shifters.

"Did you lose someone? A mate?" I wondered out loud. The entire town knew Russ was a widower. It seemed plausible to believe Taylor could be one, too.

"Yes and no." Taylor released a heavy breath then took my other hand, holding them both between his larger palms. "Shifters can't interbreed, which means we either have to find a willing mate the same breed as us, or find love with a human. I… I was with a trio of lionesses for a while." He didn't look at me this time, focusing his attention on the double living room windows, but I caught a hint of blue peeking at me from the corner of his eye, as if judging my reaction.

"Three at once?" My voice squeaked.

"Yeah." He managed a faint smile. "Even in their human guises they prefer to live in prides. It's natural for some of us to fall into our animal habits."

The knowledge formed a lump in my stomach. "So, um, what happened? I mean, three women. Wouldn't most men kill for that?"

"As much as I cared for them, they weren't for me, Jada. Not the way you are. Fate stepped in and guaranteed we weren't compatible that way." At my confused look, he elaborated. "We couldn't have children. And for shifters, it's not something we just want. We need it. It's an innate, driven urge we all have, so we try to find mates who understand and want kids, too. When we can't procreate… or if we lose a child, it's devastating."

Taylor's voice hitched and my heart broke for him. "Is that who you lost? A child?"

He nodded in reply, jaw tense and gaze trained on the floor.

"I'm so sorry."

"We were five months along when we lost her. Not long enough to see her face, but long enough for me to know my irresponsibility caused it. It's my fault. I caused her the pain of losing a child. Most times when we meet for assignments or get-togethers, we can barely talk."

"Oh, baby, no. You can't blame yourself for something like that. I'm sure whoever she is—"

"Sasha," he said in a low, melancholy voice. "Her name is Sasha."

"I'm sure Sasha doesn't blame you either." I couldn't summon an ounce of jealousy for the woman who seemed to hold a small piece of his heart. Instead, I hurt with him, and wanted nothing more than to wash away his pain. "Do you… still miss her?"

"I miss her friendship," he said honestly. "I miss the way things were before we complicated it with a relationship. We were just friends with a physical attraction to each other, but we gambled and lost. And since she's part of the team, it makes things tense sometimes."

"So you miss hanging out with her the way we do?"

He chuckled weakly. "No. We never hung out like this. Not really. She hates video games. Couldn't drag her to a waterpark. Now one of her sisters? Isisa would come along with me for fun times, and I do miss *that*. It was like… how do I explain this? It took all three of them to come close to fulfilling me the way you do, Jada."

"Do you see them anymore? Her sisters, I mean. I feel like I have so many questions because I've never met someone in, uh, a polyamorous relationship before. It's the sort of thing you watch on a television show." I nibbled my lower lip and weakly made a joke, trying to lighten the mood. "So you had sister-wives? Is it okay to ask this stuff?"

Taylor laughed quietly, some of the warmth returning to his voice. "Yeah, it's fine. I still talk to Nandi sometimes, but… is that gonna be a problem for you?" he asked.

"There's nothing wrong with talking." I scooted into his lap and one of his arms automatically curled around my waist. "I trust you. You've hidden nothing from me that wasn't necessary."

"Thank you."

"You don't have to thank me for that, Taylor. It's the right thing to do. Do you mind answering a few more things?"

"Shoot."

"How does a relationship work with three women? Did you move from one to the next each night?"

"Nah. They had their thing before I even became involved. None of them are related, so sometimes they slept with each other. Sometimes I'd join in. It was…" He rubbed the back of his neck, a thoughtful expression on his face. "Different, I guess. I sort of felt like a fourth wheel at times. That answer your question?"

I pursed my lips thoughtfully. "Don't mountain lions usually mate and leave? How much like a mountain lion are you?"

Initially, he stared at me, then the light returned to his eyes and a crooked smile brightened his features. "I don't have any way to prove to you how much you mean to me, Jada. You'll have to take my word for it and trust me."

"Tell me more about true mates."

"All right," he agreed. "Every person in the world, human or shifter, has a soul mate. A fated mate they're meant to cross paths with at some point in their life. It may not happen when we intend for it to happen, but according to my parents, it happens when we *need* it most. Us shifters have a more acute sense of determining when it's happened. It hits us harder. We know right away, unlike humans."

His words made the decision to separate for the time being hurt even more. I peered up into his blue eyes, my brows furrowed. "And that's why you're always in my thoughts."

"Yeah. It gets a little creepy sometimes until you learn to ignore it. And of course, it's going to suck when we're apart now."

"We can still talk at night. And… now that I know you're the kitty who followed me home, maybe we can arrange something as long as you don't get yourself shot by a neighbor."

"Yeah?"

I nodded.

"I'll come tonight, if you mean it."

"Only make sure no one sees you, yeah? Most people would shoot a cougar on sight."

"I'll be careful, I promise. I was sloppy that night." The man sighed and sank back against the couch with his eyes shut, slow and rhythmic respirations moving his muscular chest. "I've been sloppy since the day I met you. My inner beast wants to claim you, and I can't fucking think when you're on my mind."

"Wait, wait, *claim* me? I'm not a mountain or a parcel of land for you to stick a flag in."

"Ha ha."

"Seriously though, what do you want to claim?"

"Shifters bond during sexual intercourse."

"We've had plenty of sex."

"Yeah, but I wasn't going to claim you without having this talk first, Jada. It's hard to explain, but it's sort of like our spirits join and become one. You have to accept it or it's worthless."

His serious tone and solemn expression gave weight to his words. As archaic as it sounded, claiming a mate obviously meant something important to him.

"So… it'll be like marrying you."

He nodded. "I know what I want, but I understand if you need time to decide. There's no rush."

"You tell me you can't get your mind off your dick when I'm around because of this, and now you tell me it's no rush?"

"Once I give myself to you, there's no taking it back, Jada. If I bond to you and for some reason you want out… you're free to leave, but you'll take part of me with you. I need to know this is what *you* want."

My eyes widened at the thought of leaving him after accepting his bond. I shook my head and opened my mouth, but my tongue had gone dry, my lips too chapped for comfort. I licked them uselessly and dropped my head. "I'll think on it," I finally uttered. "What about Leigh and Dani… have they?"

"Yeah. They did. They're your friends, so feel free to talk to them about it."

He held me for a while longer, enfolding me in his strong arms. I lost track of the time until my ringing phone jerked me back to the present.

One missed call from Daddy.

Taylor glanced at the lit screen before I put it away. "So, I guess you should storm out of here soon, huh?"

I kissed his neck instead and found the pulse point at his throat. My breath warmed his smooth jaw before I leaned in to nibble his earlobe. The act earned a small sound — one part encouragement, one part dismay. Taylor was so responsive to my touches, easy to arouse, thickening his cock from the moment my lips took their exploring path across his skin.

When I snapped open Taylor's jeans, his hard dick practically sprang up to greet me, untethered by the boxers left behind on the floor.

Mine, I thought. A sudden sense of possessiveness came over me, a desperate yearning to make him forever mine. It had to be the mating talk at work on my subconscious. Gliding my hand up and down, faster and faster, I watched his head fall back and enjoyed the rhythm of his hips, how his abs tensed and flexed, his pelvis rolled. A single, dewy drop beaded at the tip until I wiped it over the fat crown of his dick with my thumb, using the moisture to jerk him.

I felt the desire for him in my core, a longing and a soul-deep ache craving his fulfillment. I groaned out loud and released him, forcing myself to stop. A clock was unnecessary to tell the time since one glance at the darkening sky beyond the window told me night would arrive soon.

"Come once it's completely dark, and I'll finish what I started."

"Fuck," he breathed. He didn't budge from the couch.

I wanted him as much as he wanted me, wishing I could stay, strip him down, and make love to him until the sun set and our tiny town went to bed.

"I'll see you soon."

"Soon," he repeated, his breathless word a promise.

Then I stormed out of his home and onto the porch.

"And you can fucking lose my number while you're at it!" I screamed behind me, my fury displayed to an audience of three on the porch of the adjacent house.

"You okay, Jada?" his neighbor asked, a gossipy old man. Mr. Daniels liked to share other people's personal business while playing checkers at the general store. He'd share this.

"Fine," I snarled back before I stalked down the drive and out of Taylor Jackson's life.

Chapter Eleven

~TAYLOR~

With a few hours to spare before nightfall, I took the opportunity for a shower and some rest. Dozing on my couch allowed me to catch up on some much needed sleep, but it wasn't the same without Russ or Nadir around to roll me off of it for catnapping.

Between Tito's new jobs for me, the time with Jada, and my own investigation, sleep had become an elusive thing I hoped to catch up with once the mission was over.

Memories of Jada's touch haunted my lucid dreaming state, and for a moment, she was there with me again, the sweet smell of her skin surrounding me with lingering traces of sandalwood and vanilla.

I wondered if she called the girls and asked them about the bonding ceremony. If they'd told her how pleasurable it was for both participants, if she was curious about how it would feel if we claimed each other as mates.

"Dispatch, be advised we have an officer down."

The report from the police band radio caught my attention, rousing me completely.

"EMS is en route to transport Chief Hunt to East Texas Medical Center."

I flew off of the couch and to my phone, hitting Ian's home line on speed dial.

"MacArthur residence," Leigh answered cheerfully.

"Evening, Leigh. Ian available right now?"

"No, but I can make him available," she chirped. The noise of the television grew fainter in the background as she moved through the house. I expected her to ask about Jada, but she didn't.

Suddenly, the thundering rush of a shower filled the phone line with noise.

"Ian! Why don't you save me some hot water and do your job. Taylor's waiting to check in," she chided. I would have chuckled at her playful tone if the circumstances weren't dire.

The water squeaked off. “It’s only been fifteen minutes,” Ian grumbled.

“More like thirty,” she shot back. “Here you go, Taylor. Chased him out for you.”

“Thanks, Leigh, you’re a peach.”

“She’s my peach, so hands off,” Ian grumbled over the line. “What’s going on that you had to call me instead of Nadir?”

“Do you have the police scanner on?”

“No. Why?”

“They rushed Hunt to ETMC.”

“Shit.” In the background, I heard Ian scrambling around and his wife asking what was wrong. “I was in the shower, so didn’t have my phone nearby. I’ve got a slew of text updates. They found his car overturned in the ditch. It was on fire, Taylor.”

“Crap. Is he—”

“The station is calling. Hold tight and I’ll call you back.” Ian disconnected without further word.

For the next fifteen minutes, I paced my living room floor and tried to get ahold of Jada. She didn’t answer my calls or reply to my texts. The phone rang as I was grabbing my car keys.

“Ian, man, please tell me what’s going on. Jada’s not picking up—”

“Jada is fine, Taylor,” Ian cut in. “An officer is driving her and the rest of the family to the hospital as we speak.”

Sweet relief flooded through me, tempered by the tragedy of Chief Hunt’s accident. For a moment, I’d wondered if her failure to answer my calls meant she was hurt, too.

“What happened?”

“I’m on my way to the scene. Russ is out there now and says it looks like Hunt was rammed. There’s lots of glass up on the road.”

“Those fuckers!” I swore.

“Taylor, it gets worse.” Ian’s voice had gone hard and flat, a tone I recognized from our military days. “Russ can’t say for sure yet, but he’s fairly certain the fire wasn’t an accident. We need you to find the responsible party.”

“I’m on it, man.”

***

A celebratory atmosphere greeted me at the garage when I arrived around ten the next morning. Someone had splurged on name brand sodas and poured a couple dozen cans into an old cooler of ice. Lyle grilled outside by the back door. My sensitive nose picked up the juicy scent of beef burgers and beer soaked brats.

"Hell, I didn't know we were having a party. Yo, Joey, toss me a Big Red." The heavy door swung shut behind me.

"Hey, hey, T.J!" Joey greeted me with a wave and a grin. The sad fact was, he was a smart kid. Good with cars. He just made stupid decisions, and involving himself in Tito's drug operations was going to cost him.

"What's up?" I asked, accepting the frosty can of red soda he passed over.

"You hear the good news?"

"What news?" I asked, playing it safe.

"Chief Hunt is toast. Word on the street is that he was life-flighted by chopper to Houston last night, and died this morning. Ain't that fucking sweet?"

What little sympathy I had for the kid vanished in a puff of smoke. One hand tightened into a fist down at my side, the bite of nails in my palm grounding me to the moment and helping me to keep my self-control.

"Taylor. My office," Tito called me from the doorway. Drink in hand, I sauntered after the man and took the seat across from his desk.

"Something you need, Tito?"

"Only a friendly chat. Sorry about your girlfriend's Pops, but it's gotta be nice to have him out the way now, right?"

Fucking shitbag murderers. "Hell yeah, dawg. Fucker was constantly riding my ass and disrespecting me."

Am I overacting? Hell, maybe I took it too far.

Focusing on the internal script I devised in my head was the only way to diffuse my fury. The show. The performance. I had to sell my hatred of Hunt, otherwise I'd bust Tito's face open and leave his teeth on the floor.

"Besides, she dumped me yesterday afternoon after her daddy searched my car. Seems like karma got his ass, yeah?"

"Shame to hear it. That's a fine piece of woman. I'd stick my dick in that ass if I could. Anyway, that fucking pig Hunt wasn't the only distraction around here. MacArthur's poking his nose into the shit already."

The thought of Tito putting his slimy hands anywhere near Jada made my skin crawl. I dragged a deep breath into my lungs and tried to appear aloof. "I hear he's a legend around here."

"A legendary asshole," Tito spat. "If we didn't have him around, we'd be set, but getting that man is impossible."

"Sounds like you've tried." *Admit it, you piece of shit.*

"A few of the boys may have been party to an attempt on the man's life. That mess cost me the last police chief. The boss man wasn't pleased."

I whistled, feigning awe as part of the performance. "Shiiiit, too bad you don't have another chief in your pocket along with Judge Fitz. How's it working out with him now anyway?"

"Whatever you did worked."

"Heh. You need to know where to apply the pressure, is all."

Tito grunted. "If only MacArthur was so easy."

"Why isn't he easy? The man isn't bullet proof, right?"

"He isn't. Getting to him is the hard part. It's like he has a sixth sense for this thing. He's never around in an easy place."

"What about a hit at his place?" I asked. My stomach knotted with tension as I faced the internal dilemma of advising Tito on how to take out my best friend.

"Tried that," Tito replied. "Now he's on to us and it's impossible."

Almost a year ago, a bunch of thugs had driven up to Ian's house and kicked in the door. They'd failed to kill him because Russ and Ian were out conducting an investigation in their animal forms.

Since then, he'd had gates, a twelve foot fence, and cameras installed to surround his hundreds of acres.

"So, what's stopping you guys from doing it when he's in town?" I asked.

"Like I said, he seems to have a sense for this thing. I called you in here for a specific purpose. Lyle says your sort are attracted to the same area like bees to honey. Where one shifter goes, a dozen more will follow. I need someone capable of taking out MacArthur, and the boss is willing to pay fifty thousand dollars to see it happen."

It could be the opportunity to blow the case wide open. Who was the damned big boss pulling the strings around Quickdraw and why was Ian's death worth so much to him? "What if I kill him?" I offered slowly. "Nobody has a reason to suspect me. Hunt maybe, but one of your guys took care of him, right? Let me handle this one."

"This ain't the same as putting the fear of God into an old man. He's a shifter like you, remember?"

"I've killed before." I had. "It's no big deal." It was. Maybe I'd killed in the service of my country, but I'd never enjoyed it.

"Good. The boss wants it done sooner than later. Get this done, T.J., and maybe you'll be meeting him in person to receive your payment." Tito slid a gun across the desk to me.

I had no choice but to accept it.

***

"Nadir, get the team together. They want Ian dead next."

"What?" By his slurred voice, it sounded as if I'd woken Nadir out of a sound sleep. He rarely kept normal hours.

"Tito's giving me a chance to prove myself and get rid of an obstacle. I need you and Juni to prep Ian for a hit."

"Another attack at his place?" Alarm raised the volume of Nadir's voice. "What the hell did you agree to?"

"No. Nothing like that," I assured him, pulling a beer from the fridge. "Ian's got to die, and it's gotta be soon, man. I told Tito I'd give this my personal touch to get him out of the way. I don't want Leigh or Sophia involved at all."

"Fuck. Okay, yeah. Lemme get in touch with him and see what we can do." Drawers opened and closed in the background, followed by the sound of rustling clothes. "Did you have something in mind?"

"It needs to be public. Something fast, so Tito's thugs don't have time to go and check the body, but with no chance of hitting bystanders."

"Give us a day to get something together—"

I cut him off, voice sharp. "I don't have a day."

"Are you kidding me? Stall it out and tell Tito you're working on a plan. Tell him you're gonna case Ian some, get his daily routine down 'cause you don't want to land your ass back in prison."

"I don't know about that. They're expecting me to produce results."

"Taylor, look, man, I know you're upset, but if we rush this, there's a good chance Ian will *actually* die. None of us want that. As for Tito, he wants you to get this done. Not botch it up in hate."

"Fine," I relented. "Three days, no more. Soon as you guys concoct something, I want to know."

"Of course. Have you talked with Jada? We got the news today about her father," Nadir said.

"No. Her shop is dark, and her car isn't in her drive."

"She's staying with her mom and brother. My folks took some casseroles over yesterday evening."

The knowledge only partially relieved my anxiety. "I've tried calling."

"Get over there and see her, man. She could really use you right now."

"I'm pretty sure if I knock on her mom's door, I'll be getting arrested."

Nadir sighed and I easily pictured him shaking his head at whatever dumb thing I'd said. "Go do what cats do best, Taylor. Paw at a window or something."

I took his advice.

Ninety minutes later, under the cover of darkness, I prowled through the bushes surrounding the Hunt household. They lived in a ranch style house on a large lot with several oak trees in the yard. Avoiding the lights, I peeked through the windows one at a time until I found Jada. She lay sprawled on her stomach across a twin-sized bed covered with tropical fish themed blankets. After turning a page in the book in front of her, she wiped her tear-streaked face with a tissue.

Certain she was alone in the dimly lit room, I batted at the window with my paw. Jada startled at the sound and glanced to the window. Surprise widened her red-rimmed eyes, but she hurried over without fear and opened the window and sliding screen.

"Taylor?" she whispered.

I answered by nuzzling her face then leapt inside after she moved aside. My transformation back into my human skin was instant and effortless, and then Jada was in my arms.

"I'm here, baby," I crooned against her hair. "I'm here."

"He's dead," she blubbered. Hot tears leaked against my naked skin. "Daddy's dead."

Guiding her to the bed, I snagged a blanket to drape over my lap then pulled her down against me. The book she'd tossed aside turned out to be an old photo album. Chief Hunt beamed up at me from a picture on the opened page. A younger Jada was pictured with him in front of a sandy beach on the shoreline.

I held her for as long as she needed, letting the minutes pass while my hand smoothed up and down Jada's back. She didn't speak until her sobs subsided.

"Thank you, Taylor… for coming," she added in a thick voice. Another shudder ran through her. Then she muffled the next sob against my chest. "I can't believe Dad's gone."

"He was a great man, and the world's a poorer place without him in it. I only wish I'd gotten the chance to know him as the real me."

"He'd have loved you," Jada whispered, sniffling.

"Is this your old room?"

"Yeah. Mom's kept it as is, though she keeps threatening to turn it into a sewing room."

Looking around was like peeking into Jada's past. Old pom-poms hung on the wall beside a framed school certificate and blue ribbon for the science fair. A colorful fish poster hung over the twin-sized bed.

"Taylor?"

"Yeah?"

"Can you stay tonight?"

"What if your mom peeks in?" The last thing I wanted was to upset her mom after she lost her husband.

"She won't. One thing Mom and Dad were always good about was respecting our privacy. As much as she may try to meddle sometimes, my room is like… sacred ground."

"Okay." I kissed her brow, decision made. "But I'll have to sneak out before dawn. Easier to slink through town when it's dark."

"Deal."

We crawled under the blanket and cuddled close on the narrow bed. The somber circumstances kept potentially lustful thoughts at bay. My cougar's perpetual need for Jada diminished in favor of providing her comfort.

"I promise, Jada, I'm going to get whoever killed your dad," I vowed.

"How?" she asked in a tiny voice.

"Best you not know the details. Just know that I'm not going to let them get away with this. Until then, you stay away from Tito's, okay?"

"Did he do it?"

"Nah, he doesn't have the guts. This came from above him, and that's who I'm after. I take down their boss and I get them all."

The beast inside of me demanded a chance to soothe her. I relinquished my control and shifted in the bed, exchanging human flesh for fur, hands for paws. Without a word, Jada snuggled into me and closed her eyes. Our embrace became as natural as breathing, no different in my feline form as it had been as a man.

"Your whiskers tickle," she whispered.

I responded with a purr, rumbling the noise and tucking my head beneath her chin. Jada stroked her fingers down my back. She made the tiniest sound, as consoled by my presence as any woman could be on the night after losing her father.

Exhaustion gradually claimed her, but before it took hold, she kissed my nose in unspoken appreciation. I remained beside my future mate until her breaths evened out and slumber relaxed her body. Then I stayed a little longer, breathing in her scent and loathing the necessity of my eventual departure. Before the sun rose, I snuck from the bed and let myself out through the unlocked window.

I wouldn't let Jada down. Someone had to be held accountable for her dad's death, and I was determined to find the person behind it.

Chapter Twelve

~Taylor~

"You ready for this?"

The driver, a husky Hispanic guy called Paco, twisted around in his seat to look at me. I sat in the rear of a white Volkswagen van, clothed in my dark sweats. My black and white bandanna was loosely tied around my neck, ready to be raised around my face.

"Yeah. Coast is clear, right?"

"Ain't a cop around here," Joey said. "Don't forget your shades, dude. You the only black dude around here with eyes like that."

"Sorta circumstantial," Paco muttered. "They can't pinch him over eye color and race."

"Nah, he's right. They can try and make shit hard for me."

Going into a hot zone never gave me the nervous jitters. I felt at home when on a mission, but this was different. This was my friend. My comrade. I had to pretend to shoot Ian down in cold blood, and I wasn't using blanks. One wrong shot would be enough to turn our charade into reality.

I took in a few deep breaths and hopped out of the van. A dark alley stretched between the post office and pharmacy, a place often traveled by pedestrians traveling on foot to pick up mail from their post office boxes.

The Quickdraw Post Office didn't deliver to in-town residents, so Ian picked up his grandmother's newspaper, bills, and correspondence each day if Leigh didn't fetch it herself.

I hung beside the trimmed hedge and watched Ian emerge from the quiet building. The sound of my own pulse thundered in my ears, deafening against the tranquil evening.

Ian walked down the post office steps, a handful of envelopes in his hand. *Now or never.* I leapt out with the gun raised, lined up my shot down the sights, and squeezed the trigger. Ian jerked back and stumbled from the impact. Blood splattered over the front page of the

Quickdraw Chronicle. Then the handgun barked and jumped in my hand, releasing another bullet.

A woman across the road locked up the doors to her gift shop. Shrieking, she leapt into her car for cover. She had to be calling 9-1-1 by now, if the shots fired weren't enough to bring the police.

The final shots were a blur. I ran my ass off down the alley and leapt into the van waiting for me at the other end. Paco peeled off down the road and hauled ass around the corner into the Dixie Quarters where cops rarely traveled. Back there, it was lawless squalor and one-bedroom shacks housing meth labs. Back there, social workers made frequent visits to remove children from neglectful homes.

Fuck, fuck, fuck. I pulled the bandana off and tossed it onto the floor.

"He dead?"

"He wasn't moving when I left."

Please don't be dead. Please.

"Whoo boy! MacArthur riddled with holes." Joey pumped his fist in the air.

"Pull in there, Paco. The shit-green house with the open garage. We'll spray paint this ride up in no time," Joey said.

Lyle met us in the house after we pulled the van in and shut the rust-spotted door. Empty beer cans littered his kitchen counters and the whole place reeked of wet dog. The disgusting odor turned my stomach.

"How many shots did he take, T.J?" Lyle asked.

"I damn near emptied the mag in his sorry ass. He never saw me comin'."

"Tito wants you to come by the old station first thing in the morning. By that time, we should know if you killed the bastard or not. Until then, we paint the van and lay low."

I pulled off my black sweatshirt and tossed it onto the grill to be burned. The bandanna followed, then Joey squirted a liberal amount of lighter fluid over it before tossing in a match.

"You guys can lay low, but I'm heading back into town this evening. It'll be suspicious if I disappear."

"I don't know about that," Lyle interrupted, ever the loyal dog to his master.

"Yeah, well, let's see you stop me. I did the job, and now I'm gonna head home to chill." I still hadn't figured out his breed, but I imagined it was something small and spineless. A beagle maybe.

To my surprise, Lyle stepped up to me and blocked the way. "I know you think you're hot shit, but Tito put me in charge—"

I rose up to my full height and hissed at him. Lyle shrank back a step, quickly put off by the hint of my cougar I allowed him to see.

"What was that about?" I heard Joey asking as I moved outside into the sunlight.

I took a dusty, dirt path as a shortcut, avoiding the main streets. No one gave me a second glance in passing. The moment I stepped inside, I flipped on the television to the local news. A reporter stood outside the Post Office, yellow tape stretched across the narrow street behind her.

"Sheriff Ian MacArthur was pronounced dead on scene. Police are on the lookout for an adult male suspect. Witnesses at the scene described an African American male, approximately six feet tall."

The reporter rattled off a vague description fitting at least a quarter of Quickdraw's residents. I shook my head.

Hours passed before Nadir's call came through on one of our untraceable, private lines.

"Everything's okay. We've got Ian with us at the bunker. He's going to lay low here for a while until it's time for him to resurface."

We kept a place for special circumstances. The bunker, located deep in the middle of nowhere, housed our goods, weapons, and computer equipment. It was a control center for our missions and a place where Juni, our communications expert, created new gadgets for us to use in security jobs local to Texas.

"Thank God."

"He's impressed by your shooting, you should know. He says the shot to the thigh hurt like a son of a bitch, but he's already up and walking around. Sasha had it stitched in minutes. It looked real. Better than we could have hoped for."

"Yeah, well, he was a good teacher."

He and Russ both. Sagging back against the couch, I closed my eyes and wondered what Jada was doing. I'd promised to bring her father's murderers to justice, and I had to see this through to the end.

"Now what's going on with our shitheads?" my squad mate asked.

I told Nadir everything, and by the end, I could laugh with him since the stone-cold weight in my chest had dissipated.

"You think this will get you to the boss?"

"They want me down at the old train station in the morning."

"Get some rest then."

"What about Leigh and Betty?"

"They know what's up. Ian explained it all to his grandmother yesterday and sent her to visit an old friend out of state. She's gambling on some riverboat casino as we speak."

"Lucky."

"Agreed. Leigh and Sophia are with Dani and Russ, playing the part of the grieving widow. He told her last night to prepare her for it."

"So what's the plan?"

"Hang on a sec. Ian wants to talk to you. He has an idea."

"Hey, Taylor. I have some thoughts about your meeting tomorrow. We don't know where they plan to take you, so I'd like you to wear one of Juni's GPS gadgets," Ian said.

"I'll sew that little button mic on my shirt since she's so proud of creating it."

"Good. What I also propose is that I come in my eagle form now, perch near your place, and follow you in the morning."

"Sounds good," I agreed.

We made plans for Ian to follow by air with one of Juni's tiny transmitters around his leg. The rest of the team would monitor my location and follow at a discreet distance, ready to act once Ian gave the signal.

Sleep was hard to come by, but somehow I managed a few restless hours. I woke up early and headed out, comforted by the sight of Ian circling overhead. An old beat up truck that may have been red at some point was parked by the abandoned building when I arrived. Tito waved me over through the window and told me to climb in.

"Where we going, boss?"

"You'll see."

A thirty-minute drive into the boonies brought us to our destination. The building resembled an old barn from the outside. Rotted wood planks and rusted barbed wire disguised the true operation.

Tito led me inside. The exterior was busted, but the barn had been gutted and given an appropriate makeover to house what may have been one of the largest drug manufacturing centers in East Texas. Workers in their underwear — stripped to remove any doubt of stealing the precious product — packaged drugs for distribution onto the streets. Their mules had to be carrying coke and meth as far as Houston. No. Maybe even Dallas.

His employees appeared to be all ages, genders, and ethnicities without discrimination. Anybody could cut cocaine and dry hash for Tito's small-time dealers to sell.

We passed a hydroponic growing room with rows of marijuana plants beneath hanging UV lamps along with some thugs with guns and cocky expressions who didn't bother to ask if I was strapped, too.

As we passed, a whisper reached me from one of the boys. "Yo, I heard he's the one who iced MacArthur."

We stopped in front of a closed door. Tito shot me a look. "Mind your manners with the boss, T.J. Don't embarrass me. You play your cards right in here and you'll be going places in this business."

"No worries, Tito. It's cool."

Tito pushed open the heavy metal door and gestured me in ahead of him. Much like his space at the garage, the office was decked out in an opulence that contrasted with the sparse squalor outside. Buck heads were mounted on the walls, but I gave them little more than a passing glance. Instead, my gaze focused on the man dominating the room.

The guy was bigger than Russ with trapezius muscles so huge he barely had a neck above his shoulders. His pale, bald head gleamed beneath the sunlight pouring through the old barn window. Deep down, part of me was glad the brains behind the entire operation wasn't a member of the Mexican drug cartels.

That would have complicated matters greatly.

"So, you're Taylor. I heard we got reason to celebrate because of you, kid."

"Yes, sir."

"Polite." The boss smirked then looked me up and down, sizing me up. "Call me Beau. Sir is so... formal. You and I are gonna be working too close for that."

"Good to meet you, Beau. I didn't do much, though."

"Ha! You hear that, Tito? 'Not much' he says." Beau chortled and crossed over to his desk. "No more of MacArthur poking his big fucking nose into my business. He's a difficult man to get to, but you caught him at a particularly vulnerable time. I respect that."

"I believe in getting the job done. I've made more money working for Tito than I ever earned on my own selling pot."

"That so?" Beau looked me over again.

"I got no reason to lie. You guys have a nice operation going."

"I started over in New Orleans, built my business up from the ground. I've got runs from Mexico into the bayou as well as this backwater dump," Beau boasted. "Once, I was like you, Taylor. Just a low man on the totem pole."

"And now you're the big boss."

The man chuckled and pointed his finger at me. "Exactly so, Taylor. I did what needed to be done, exactly as you're doing now. Which leads me to a question for you."

"Shoot."

"You ready to take over a part of this business?"

"Hell yeah. Why me though?"

"You did what nobody else around here had the balls to do. Thought I'd have to come personally to take out MacArthur myself after my boys botched the last attempt. But I didn't. You took some real initiative, offered to get rid of a problem Tito couldn't squash. He says you ain't a half-bad thief either, that y'all successfully knocked over McMillan Pharmacy with a plan you created."

"Don't wanna toot my own horn or anything, but yeah, I'm good at setting shit up."

A draft from one of the air vents blew a peculiar scent to me. Something about Beau was familiar, tickling my senses.

It's… I've smelled this before. The dry, almost spicy scent taunted me with its familiarity. The earthen muskiness brought to mind some of the reptiles I'd hunted while in the wilderness with Nadir.

He's a fucking shifter like us. Suddenly, Tito's unusual knowledge of our world made sense. He knew more beyond Lyle, because the big, all-powerful boss overseeing their criminal career was one, too.

"What kind of cat are you?" Beau asked, cutting to the chase.

"I'm a cougar," I answered promptly without missing a beat.

"Walk with me."

Beau led the way back through the warehouse, Tito trailing behind us several feet. From the corner of my eye, I spotted Lyle among the guards watching the workers.

"I don't have any need for another human on payroll," Beau said in a low voice, chuckling. "They're a dime a dozen, but men like you are rare in this business."

"Tito seems to do all right."

We stepped into the clearing outside the barn. Beau turned to me with a gun in hand. I hadn't even seen him pull it out. For a heart stopping moment, I thought he knew the truth. My pulse roared in my ears and my muscles tensed.

Ian watched from nearby in the branches of a tree overlooking the barn. His trilling call carried through the air, a warning that help was near. I counted the number of warbles, five in all meant five minutes stood between me and assistance. I saw him lean forward and partially open his wings, prepared to take flight and come to my aid. Like me, he waited to see what happened.

Beau flipped the gun in his hand and offered it to me, butt first.

"What's this?" I asked, accepting the weapon.

"The task is simple. You want the promotion, shoot Tito and take his place."

Damnit, I need Tito. Death is too good for him. Beau left me with few choices. Without further hesitation, I turned on Tito with the gun raised.

"What the fu—?"

The sharp retort of the 9mm filled the air, followed by Tito's pained yell. Red blossomed against his obnoxious yellow pants then he collapsed to the ground, gripping his bleeding thigh.

Lyle moved quickly to his master's side and growled, protective and loyal to the end. Too bad I couldn't shoot him, too.

"Like to have some fun with your kills, eh? Guess that's typical of cats. Don't worry, Lyle, you'll have a new master."

"You said shoot him. Not kill," I said when I came under the scrutiny of Beau's beady eyes.

"Rather keep him on as help. I get it." Beau nodded his head, impressed. "Pragmatic. Besides, I suppose he'll have some use. Tito's been in contact with some flesh dealers down in Houston. Working on some mergers."

The news turned my stomach. Swallowing down the bile rising in my throat, I maintained a neutral expression and answered with a terse nod. "I didn't know you guys were into selling hos, too. Is that moving to Quickdraw by any chance?"

"Yeah. You ain't soft about keeping a few girls in line are you?"

I shook my head. "Not really. Where are they coming from? Europe?"

"Some. We get a few from Latin America, too. Guatemala and Venezuela. You promise girls a better life in America and they're eager to come."

Girls. In my head I imagined scared and terrified teenagers who didn't know any better, fleeing from poverty and starvation in hopes of a better life.

It became more difficult to keep my cool.

"So what does this have to do with me?"

"You, my friend, will be taking over the business in Quickdraw. I need a man with some presence and power behind him to keep these fools in line."

Lyle hadn't moved from above Tito. From the corner of my eye, I saw the man watching me, his posture low and protective, as if he'd leap onto Tito and take a bullet if I changed my mind.

Maybe he would. Dogs were loyal, even if their masters were shit.

I turned the weapon on Beau instead. "Keep your hands where I can see them."

The amusement faded from his face and his black eyes hardened. "You're funny, kid. Now hand over the gun."

"I'd rather drag your sorry ass to jail," I spat out.

Beau didn't appear surprised by the revelation. "So, Tito brought me a mole." The big boss nodded to the two men by the door. "Kill him. Kill them both."

They raised their guns, but my reflexes were faster. I shot both as Beau exploded out of his suit. A massive, thirteen-foot-long crocodile was left behind, and it advanced on me with a burst of speed. Pulling the trigger while stumbling back from him meant most of my shots flew wide. Three sank into the croc's meaty, powerful body, but the rest hit the dirt at his sides.

Fuck me! I'd been guessing at a snake, not a muscled monster full of sharp teeth.

I managed to get enough space between us to rip out of my shirt and shift, but my pants hindered my escape, tangling around my hind legs. While I struggled to get out of my clothes, the enemy advanced.

Lyle leapt forward, transitioning from man to dog in midair. He kicked out of his jeans and wriggled from his shirt. I twisted and leapt to the side to avoid allowing him to come up on my rear. Batting with one claw kept him at bay, or so I thought, until the big, red-colored coonhound landed on Beau to attack him instead.

Tito may have treated him like shit, but Lyle loves him, I realized. *Loves him enough to be loyal and fight for both of their lives.*

Lyle growled and snapped his teeth in a failed attempt to get ahold of the crocodile. Beau knocked him off and slammed the dog aside with his strong tail. Then he turned on me.

If the crocodile got ahold of any part of me, the fight would end. He'd roll me, rip me to pieces, and I'd be dead before help arrived.

Light on my feet, I ducked and moved to the side, prancing out of his way. He snapped and twisted his body with his jaws open, seeking my foreleg. I landed safely to his left and tried to close my teeth around the back of his head. He jerked too quickly for me and I missed.

Damnit!

Our fight attracted attention from the guards inside. Three men rushed out with the guns raised and tried to make out the situation. As far as they were concerned, there was only one enemy. Me.

"Shoot 'em, man!" one of the guards cried out. Lucky for me, they were crap shots. Bullets struck the ground and spit up dirt. One grazed my left shoulder and drew a stinging line of blood.

Several vehicles rumbled into view down the dirt road, kicking up clouds of dust. They stomped their brakes then doors flew open as law enforcement officers flooded out. Texas Rangers. They'd arrived at last.

Among them, I saw our squad mates.

Sasha was leaned out a window with a rifle against her shoulder. One well-aimed shot took down a guard and drove the other two toward cover. It became a full on shoot-out between my back-up and the complex guards. Two more men ran out from the building and opened fire on the Rangers.

Ian dove down from the skies and raked his sharp talons at Beau's beady face, aiming at the eyes. The crocodile snapped at him. A single brown feather drifted to the ground as Ian soared upward out of range. Outnumbered, but not defeated, Beau turned toward the weakest of us within his reach.

Tito.

The wounded man pushed up onto his hands and made a frantic effort to escape. Beau charged after him. Before he reached his target, the coonhound raced in and placed himself between Tito and our common enemy.

Beau's massive jaws closed around the dog's leg. Then the croc performed the devastating attack I'd feared. Lyle yelped and screamed in pain as Beau rolled across the dusty ground. Blood splattered the dirt, and then the dog was free — bleeding, missing his left foreleg, but free. The coppery, metallic scent filled my nostrils.

Lyle and Tito were dirtbags, but I couldn't stand by as Beau devoured them. I darted in. My speed allowed me to keep out of Beau's biting range, but his strong attacks kept me from moving in close enough for a lethal blow.

Nadir charged in and squeezed off a round. He missed the brain, but the shock of a bullet wound drew Beau's attention off me. That split second was all I needed.

My jaws closed around the back of his neck, and he thrashed, putting up a futile struggle that ended when my teeth severed his spine. The gator went limp.

Ian's friends in the Texas Rangers knew about our special gifts. The Ranger in the lead, a balding man in his early forties, rushed forward with his gun drawn. I heard him shouting, "The puma is one of us!"

I shifted to my human form, and with the back of my wrist, wiped Beau's blood from my mouth. The Rangers stared. Two of the guys — I recognized their faces from another bust — had seen us make transitions before. For some humans, it probably never got old.

Juni tossed me a bag with clothes. I dressed while the authorities handled the workers inside. Sasha applied a tourniquet to Lyle's spurting stump while Nadir handcuffed Tito. If not for her quick intervention, the hound shifter would have died on the dusty pavement and bled out.

"Call for medical. This one needs emergency care," Sasha called to Nadir. She'd crouched beside Lyle to hold his remaining hand. Always kind and compassionate, she wouldn't abandon him to lie afraid and hurting. "I'm going to give you a dose of morphine, okay?" she said to him.

"Please, anything. It hurts so bad," Lyle moaned.

I loved her still, but it was a different kind of love. The love for a close friend and comrade had eclipsed any former physical attraction. Jada was the one who had captivated my heart.

Ian emerged from the trees dressed in jeans and a t-shirt. He joined up with the lead Ranger and shook his hand.

"It's going to take days to process the mountain of evidence here, on top of what your man has retrieved." The Ranger nudged his cowboy hat up his forehead.

"I told you he'd get the job done. You all right, Taylor?" Ian called over.

"You owe me a shit ton of paid leave after this."

"Deal."

***

Ian made a dramatic return from the dead, stunning most of the town.

Thankfully, neither Lyle nor Tito died from their injuries. The dog survived, barely, and in appreciation of his help at the end, I managed to convince them to cut him a plea bargain so he'd stand trial and testify in our favor.

He and Tito told everything about the operation and even ratted out a trio of Texas politicians in on the entire thing.

The next day, arrests swept over East Texas as warrants were issued naming powerful men and women. A half dozen judges, several politicians, and even corrupt law enforcement officers lost their good reputation when the hammer came down. A few corrupt prison bosses were swept into the scandal. Tito named two captains, a major, and a couple wardens across the state.

The family of Dennis James would finally receive justice for his murder.

When asked about Chief Hunt's death, Lyle clammed up and Tito claimed he hadn't ordered the hit.

"He says he won't talk to anyone but you about it. We need you in the room if they're going to get his confession," Ian told me.

"Okay. That's cool," I agreed.

While Tito's flesh wound had already received treatment, requiring his release to the jail, the same wasn't true for his dog. I arrived to the hospital and rode the elevator to the second floor where law enforcement officers waited outside the man's room. He lay in the bed, pathetic and pale, his carrot-colored hair bright against his pale, waxy cheeks. Ankle cuffs secured his feet and a restraint belt restricted movement of his remaining arm.

It wasn't like the cop shows made it out to be. No two-way mirror, no lawyers in suits. I nodded to the Ranger and officer standing watch over the confession; then I pulled up a seat beside the bed.

"Hey, Lyle. You look like hell."

"Whatever, pussy."

I let the halfhearted insult roll off me. "I hear you won't talk to them about Hunt. Why me?"

"Why'd you tell 'em to cut me a plea bargain?" he asked in return. "You hate me."

"Hate's a strong word. Besides, you saved my life."

"Wasn't trying to save you," he said, brown eyes boring into me.

"I know. End result is still the same though, ain't it? They told me you won't talk unless I'm here."

"Why'd you stop Beau from killing me and Tito? You coulda got enough shit to make your case without us."

"It was the right thing to do. A wise man once said, 'The only thing necessary for the triumph of evil, is that good men do nothing.' Maybe that makes me a pussy in your eyes, but my conscience is clear."

"All right. Tell that nurse to bring my shot of morphine, and I'll talk."

"Talk first. I won't have you drugged up and high. I wanna know about Chief Hunt. Was it you? Is that why you won't fess up?"

Lyle shook his head. "Wasn't me."

"Then who? Cooperating will go a long way in helping your case."

"Joey killed Hunt. He took one of our trucks and ran him down in his police cruiser. Said he wanted to impress Tito the way you always did whenever you was around. Said he wanted more responsibility."

"And the fire?" I asked.

"The kid started it when the gas tank began to leak. He told me he didn't wait around to see if Hunt was already dead, so he torched the shit to be on the safe side before he drove off."

"How do we know you aren't making this up?"

"Tell Tito I talked. Ain't like we got a way to communicate in here."

With some pressure, Tito confirmed Lyle's report of the events. The police arrested Joey an hour later for murder, fulfilling my promise to Jada to find her father's killer.

My work in Quickdraw was finished, but my life there had only begun.

Chapter Thirteen

DECEMBER

~JADA~

I stole a glance at Taylor from where I stood on the brides' side of the aisle. No man had ever looked finer in a military uniform than mine, but the two grooms were a definite close second. The love shining from Russ and Ian's faces was enough to make anyone smile.

The four men standing at the front were undeniably sexy, Nadir and Taylor both serving as groomsmen, while I, Dani's little sister Marta, and a few of her cousins stood in as bridesmaids.

The two brides, stunning visions in similar dresses, put the rest of us to shame, their beauty beyond comparison to the rest of us.

Daniela and Leigh walked down the aisle together, arm in arm. They wore strapless gowns, but the similarity ended there. Dani wore her waist length tresses in an exquisite updo, while Leigh's hung around her shoulders in loose spirals. As the taller of the two women, Leigh chose flats, but Dani wore heels. The fair-skinned blonde resembled a princess in her pale pink, ruffled, taffeta dress. Our Latina friend was equally beautiful in her airy, chiffon layers of pale ivory.

Lisa, Naomi, and I did a damned good job putting the two women together. I beamed with pride, sniffled, and dabbed my cheeks again with a handkerchief, moved by the brides' radiant expressions. Most of the town had shown up for the double ceremony and packed every pew in the church.

The same church where Leigh and Ian first met.

My mother had loaned both brides her own bridal jewelry. Something blue to honor the wedding traditions. Dani wore a thick gold necklace with large sapphires. The dangling gold segments fell in chandelier style, tapering to a V pointed toward Dani's corset-enhanced cleavage. Leigh had the matching tiara tucked against her blonde curls. Participating in the wedding preparations had given Mom something to do and occupied her mind from Dad's death.

I thought it would be too rough on her at first, but I was wrong, and for the first time in nearly two months, she was smiling again. Her eyes were bright.

I loved my mother. No matter how much we argued during my childhood, she'd always been Mom, looking out for me and trying to do what was best. The tears I'd struggled so hard to keep at bay spilled over my cheeks. I'd probably look a hot mess by the time the photographer came around to snap pictures of the bridal party again.

The joint ceremony was simple with each couple exchanging personal vows. We blew bubbles and tossed rose petals on them as they left the church. Some of the younger guests had tied a row of tin cans to the rear bumper of Russ and Ian's vehicles.

Taylor and I rode in his Cadillac to the wedding reception. Ian had rented Lottie's for all of their close friends and family to enjoy a private dinner. Soft music played over the speakers and two stunning tiered cakes were displayed in the center of the room. A single chocolate and strawberry groom's cake sat between them, the one flavor Russ and Ian could agree to share.

I ended up chatting with the two brides while Taylor moved away to mingle with his squad and their mutual friends. A tap to the shoulder pulled me from conversation about their honeymoon travel plans. I'd offered to watch Sophia for Leigh and Ian, thrilled to have a toddler to spoil. Taylor promised to help.

"Jada?"

"Hm?" I answered as I turned. I came face to face with Taylor and an angelic blonde. "This is Sasha. She wanted to meet you."

Sasha was my complete opposite; tall, lithe, and golden with white-blonde hair tamed into a chic updo. Picturing her as a proud lioness was easy. Without further introduction, the woman leaned in and embraced me, squeezing me with warm affection.

"You've got a good man here," she said. "I'm really happy for both of you." She had a peculiar accent I couldn't place.

"Thanks, Sasha," I replied as she ended the hug. I bit my lip and searched the restaurant for two equally hot blondes. "Are the other two with you?"

Sasha blinked her blue eyes in surprise, glancing from me to Taylor then back again. "They are, but we didn't all want to swarm and smother you."

"I'd love to meet them. Taylor has nothing but good things to say." I understood his relationship with the trio and felt no reservations.

He was mine, and nothing would change that.

Nandi and Isisa weren't what I expected. They had skin like dark mahogany, smooth and flawless. Their contrasting figures, one plump and curvy like me, the other muscular and toned, appeared beautiful in gold dresses. The shade was a perfect match to their almond-shaped eyes. Both greeted me with smiles, although only Isisa leaned in for a hug as Sasha had.

"I am happy for you. For both of you," Isisa said.

African. They're definitely from Africa, I thought. It made sense in a strange sort of way, considering their animal form.

"Thank you. It's great to finally meet."

Maybe another woman would feel awkward or even intimidated by the meeting, but I didn't, not when their open and genuine expressions held so much happiness for us.

So I told them about my new shop and learned Isisa was a lawyer with a practice in Houston. Their pride sister, Nandi, dabbled in self-publishing, a quiet introvert who often kept to herself.

"Any time you girls want to come down to Quickdraw for a day to relax, let me know." I took a card out of my small clutch purse and scribbled my cell phone number on the back. Sasha accepted it as if I'd handed her a precious gem instead. Her wide blue eyes filled with surprise.

We hugged again — Nandi, the shyest lioness, even squeezed me briefly — then the three breathtaking women moved on.

Taylor and I slipped out shortly after the brides and their grooms. Only a couple months ago, he'd begun construction on a new home in the Quickdraw outskirts where Ian and Russ lived. While I had given plenty of advice during the building stages, I hadn't yet had a look at the finished product.

And I couldn't wait to see.

~TAYLOR~

"So, what do you think?" I asked when we reached the empty living room. We had rounded back through another set of doors from the kitchen into a vast space with a row of big windows displaying the monstrous front yard.

"My opinion is the same, hon. You definitely have a lot to grow into," Jada commented, referring to the tour of my new, but empty, two story brick house. I'd built it between Russ and Ian's homes. "That's a big-ass yard. Who's gonna take care of all of that?"

A fifty-yard driveway snaked through the trees and a sprawling pasture to reach my place. Ian had given me my pick of the lots he owned, so I chose a place with room to roam.

"Russ will. They have a tractor over at their place."

In a week, I planned to bring most of my belongings from Houston. The four-car garage provided the space for both of my vehicles and room for Jada's car, if I could convince her to take the next step in our relationship. The rest of the place was a modest, brick exterior with wood floors and a woman's dream kitchen.

Jada never claimed a love for cooking, but she'd bitched about my tiny kitchen in the old place I'd rented. Prepared to house her immense wardrobe, I'd also given the architect specific instructions for an enormous walk-in closet with a built-in shoe rack.

Nobody owned more footwear than my girl.

"I haven't exactly had the time to shop for furniture," I muttered.

"You did this to yourself when you decided to buy and takeover Tito's business." She leaned up to kiss me, barely touching our lips.

Jada undid the buttons on my dress uniform jacket, but not before she skimmed her fingers over the rows of ribbons and medals one last time. I shrugged it off and draped it over my arm.

"You want me to go back to Houston instead?"

Jada's chin dropped. She bit her lower lip and delayed answering.

"Well?"

"I thought you'd go home after this was all said and done," she confessed. "Not because I want you to go home, but because you had your life back. I didn't think you'd pick up everything. Relocate your entire life."

"Jada, my life is with you, and your life is here. Your business. I'd never make you give that up.

"So what are you going to do about your shop in Houston?"

"Have my baby brother manage it." I grinned. "He's a bit of an idiot, but I think he can do it."

I took her by the hand and led the way upstairs. A brand new bedroom set had been the only new furniture purchase I'd made. Dark wood stood out against the cream walls and carpeted floor. My jacket found a new home atop the dresser, freeing my hands to slide up and down Jada's sides.

"You look beautiful tonight, Jada, but I think I wanna see you out of that dress."

She twisted around and bared the zipper to me. "Help me out?"

"Gladly." I tugged the zipper down, parting the royal-blue fabric until it slipped down and pooled at her ankles. My heart leapt at the sight of her, my soon-to-be-mate, clothed in a tightly laced corset and matching thong. I squeezed double handfuls of her plump ass and kneaded pliable flesh.

"I love when you wear these," I muttered.

Jada wore lace-top, black thigh-highs attached by garters to the corset. I imagined sliding her panties aside and fucking her in the skimpy lingerie.

"Unlace me?" With one coy glance over her shoulder, she filled me with feral lust and a raw desire to take charge. I plucked the knot loose then tucked my girl's body against me. Her ass perfectly framed my cock, both soft swells cradling it.

I growled and unfastened the front of her corset by memory, moving both hands over her curves to release the catches top to bottom. Both breasts spilled out as I dropped the restrictive device; then I cupped them and plucked the erect tips between my thumb and index finger.

"Tell me you want me, Jada. All of me."

"Taylor, you know I want you."

"No. All of me, Jada. I want… I want to claim you as my mate."

I released one tit and slid my hand down her subtle, soft tummy until I reached her panty line. Two fingers delved within after caressing smooth, completely waxed skin. Her pussy was so wet that one curving finger slid through her silky folds and into her body with ease.

"Did you think about it?" I asked when she only groaned a response.

"Y-yes," she stammered out, moving her hips, grinding. The tortuous movement placed pressure on my dick. "I talked with Dani and Leigh, too."

"What did they say?"

"That it'll be the best sex I've had in all of my life."

I chuckled against her ear then nipped the sensitive curve. "You think you can handle that?"

"Can you?" she countered, wriggling her ass against my hard cock.

I added a second digit, plunging in and out of her slickness, her body molding to me and clenching when I tweaked her nipple with the other hand. Jada's sassy teases faded into pleasured moans.

"It means we'll have a kid one day. Can you do that? Do you even *want* kids?"

Children were the one subject to never come up between us. Ever since I'd told her about my past with Sasha, she walked on eggshells regarding it.

"Taylor," she gasped out, moving and rolling her hips. "If you want a… yes, fuck, yes."

"It's not only about what I want, Jada. Do you want it?" I asked again, breathing against her ear, lips following her neck.

"Yes!"

It wasn't fair to tease her while discussing important subject matters, so I stopped. Both of my hands withdrew from her luscious curves, and then I stepped back to unfasten my pants. My hard dick strained for freedom until my boxers were around my ankles, balls so heavy and tight with the need for release that pre-cum glistened at the tip.

"Taylor?"

"Is this what you truly want, Jada?"

"I… do want kids. I've just never had a man I *wanted* to make a baby with. I'm not saying this to placate you." Jada's breaths remained quick but steady, her heaving chest causing both breasts to quiver enticingly. "I get it, Taylor. I didn't forget what you told me… this is like marriage."

I took her hand and kissed each of her knuckles while holding eye contact with her. "It is," I agreed. "I'll never love anyone the way I love you for the rest of my life."

"So… how do we do it?" Jada asked. "Do you bite me now or something like a werewolf movie?"

I stared at her.

"What? It's a legitimate question."

"You'll see." I chuckled despite the wave of goose bumps rising over my skin. "If I bite you, will you be upset with me?"

She shivered. "Is it necessary?"

"It may be." I stepped closer, bodies close enough to press my firm, rigid heat against her lower belly. "Once the mating bond starts, I won't be able to stop." I moved forward again, urging her back onto the bed without lowering myself to join her. I slipped her arms from around me and knelt, spreading her legs afterward to bare her sweet pussy.

Licking Jada was as much for my pleasure as it was for hers. I loved her taste, her smell, everything about the responsive way her body reacted to me. I was drunk on her, the worst kind of addict, and I lived for the way her brown eyes glazed over after orgasm. How she sighed my name while lying beside me in bed, drained of all energy and absolutely useless.

I started from the top, leaving no part of her neglected. Her mouth was a delicious treat, parting to accept the dart of my tongue between her lips while my busy hands traveled her curves. She sucked the tip of my tongue into her mouth playfully.

By the time I continued down, the tips of her breasts had pebbled tight. I nibbled one nipple then the next, their color as dark as cocoa and just as delectable. My tongue swirled over them in a time-consuming back and forth pattern, interrupted by the occasional scrape of my teeth, soothed only by another lick.

Once I kissed my way below her navel, I knew she'd never been wetter or more ready for my dick. I slipped two fingers into her to the knuckle.

"Fuck," I swore out loud, surprised by the moisture gathered by my exploring touch. She rocked her hips into the penetration, eager for more.

I responded by leaning down to lick her once, a tease before the main event. My tongue jostled the barbell through her delicate hood, prompting her to jerk and moan. Her toes curled as I traced her puffy folds with one finger. Then my lips closed around her clit, trapping the swollen nerve bundle for my tongue tip to flutter against it.

Two fingers plunged inside her, thrusting in and curving until I found her g-spot. She gasped out loud, raised her hips, and tried to rock against me in a desperate bid for orgasm. Adrenaline rushed through me, overwhelming my senses until it became a fight to remain selfless by bringing her to the first climax.

"Fuck, you're gorgeous," I breathed out, captivated by the sounds she made as I devoured her. I slid my finger down her pink slit again, parting her folds and denying her another penetration.

"Please!"

"Please what?" My words issued warm breath against her wet skin. She shuddered and writhed on the bed.

"I want you to… to…"

I wanted to hear her say the words, the seductive whisper of her requests always filling me with undeniable need.

"Taylor… I can't wait… I need it," she wailed out. "I need you inside me."

"Not until you come for me."

This time, when my lips closed around her tender button, I didn't stop until she squealed wildly and kicked with her legs. Her hips pumped, and then her mouth fell open in a soundless cry as her back arched against the sheets and her toes curled.

Without warning, I flipped Jada onto her belly and lowered atop her. One hand fisted my cock and directed the sensitive tip to her entrance, gliding my swollen crown through hot, wet folds. As I slipped between her glistening pussy lips, she inhaled a sharp breath.

A single stroke claimed her, and in doing so, I treated myself to a series of post-orgasm contractions. She clenched around me, hungry for my dick, spurring me to initiate a hard and reckless rhythm.

Sliding into her was like stealing my own little piece of heaven. Her pussy's tight embrace rippled in tiny post-climax aftershocks, inviting me to slam to the hilt and ride out her body's blissful reaction.

"Fuck," I groaned, gripping handfuls of her rounded ass. Her flesh was soft and pliant, jiggling beneath my hold. Without the presence of mind to speak anything else, I lapsed into silence. My feral instincts took over, my cougar demanding I finish what I started.

"Mine," I growled.

She liked it when I pulled her hair and fuck, so did I. I held a tight handful of her black waves in my left fist, and with my right, I brought my palm down against her cheek until it turned rosy and hot beneath my touch.

"Taylor!"

"Be mine, Jada."

Surrendering to the wild beast inside me, I thrust harder. Faster. Losing myself to the moment until nothing but her receptive grip mattered, hugging every inch of my thickness. The repetitious joining of our bodies created lewd slapping noises, wet skin to wet skin, my tight balls making methodic claps against her clit.

I bent down toward her neck. My lips were gentle at first, but the subsequent bite was not.

Startled, Jada cried out. I couldn't differentiate pain from surprise, no more than I could stop and reign in my cougar.

"Say it, Jada. *Mine.*"

"Yours! I'm yours, Taylor!"

The tension burst at once, a blessed sensation of the ultimate relief. I released stream after stream of hot cum into her greedy sheath, only to grind against her at the end. The delicious trembles of our mutual climax milked me for the last spurt. Then I sagged against her.

~JADA~

"Be mine, Jada."

Something wild overcame my man. With the sheets clutched between my fingers, I held on to the bed for dear life while he pounded into me from behind. Instinctively, I grabbed at him, squeezing with my inner muscles while he plunged forward. In. Out. In. Clapping our bodies roughly together until the wet slurping noises competed with my fast and erratic breaths. Out. Making me feel painfully empty, stretched, and craving him again.

The tender press of his lips against my nape sent a chain of tingles running down my spine, followed by a sharp flash of pain when his teeth clamped down on my sweat-glistened flesh. I cried out, pleasure and pain uniting as one indescribable sensation. I couldn't move, paralyzed by ecstasy as he plundered me.

"Say it, Jada. *Mine.*"

"Yours! I'm yours, Taylor!" I choked out, voice hoarse from my frantic gasps for air.

It was an explosion of sensation. A dizzying spiral that threatened to pull me under into oblivion. All I knew was Taylor's touch, his warmth as he filled me with his cum.

Everything I was, was his.

My legs gave out beneath me, and only Taylor's weight sagged down on my back kept me from sliding into a limp puddle on the floor. After a few moments, he dragged me further up the bed.

"Does this mean we're animal married?" I asked hazily.

Taylor chuckled at my question and tugged me closer, his skin hot against my sweaty body. My eyes drifted shut again as his fingers combed through my hair. "Like I said, it's the same thing as marriage to us. But…" He paused.

"But what?"

Taylor's weight left the bed. Curious, I rolled to my side and propped up on one elbow, watching him. How he managed to walk straight without wobbling after sex was a mystery. He fetched something from his pants then climbed back into bed with me. A small, black velvet box was set down on my pillow.

All I could hear was the blood rushing through my head as my breath caught and my heart thudded hard in my chest. *Is it…? No, it couldn't be. But what if it is?*

Taylor opened the hinged lid and all the breath whooshed from my lungs.

It was a modest ring with a trio of small pink sapphires. Gorgeous, gold, and of the style I'd have picked for myself, proving he'd paid attention to my tastes in jewelry. I prized colorful and unique over expensive.

"Marry me, Jada. I know it hasn't been long, but being with you for the rest of my life is what I want to do. I'd know it even if my cougar hadn't chosen you, because I love you."

"Marry you?" My eyes burned with unshed tears. For the second time that day, I wept tears of joy. Before the wedding, I hadn't cried since putting Daddy to rest, but it felt damned good to cry again over something good. Over something he'd be proud of if he were still around.

"I know it's mostly a sheet of paper, but if it makes this more real for you—"

"You jackass, I don't need a sheet of paper for this to be real to me," I sobbed. Tears rolled freely down my cheeks, and I tried to wipe them away with the backs of my hands. "I love you. Yes."

I held out my left hand for Taylor to slide the ring onto my finger. It fit snugly, not too tight, but perfect, as if it had been measured.

Meant for me.

SERIES EPILOGUE: A BEARY MERRY CHRISTMAS

Teotihuacan, resort owner and centuries-old dragon, paced the floor of the administrative office with a phone cradled between his shoulder and ear. "This is a ridiculous plan," he bit out in a terse voice.

"You had absolute faith in this plan two days ago. Why has your mind changed?" Saul asked.

Teo paused to glance at the security feed, his computer monitor displaying rows of tables beneath fancy cloth. He'd personally prepared each centerpiece as gifts for his guests to take home if they chose.

It was his gift, after all, a natural born talent of earth dragons to imbue vitality in the plant life around them. He could coax the tiniest seed into a vibrant flower within minutes.

"She loathes me."

"She has not spoken with you in years," Saul said.

"She will remember the times we have crossed paths in your home."

"Marceline is an incredible woman of intellect and integrity. She will forgive your past transgressions," Saul insisted. "Hang up and go speak to her or else."

"Or else what?"

"I will come and raze the entire island to the ground with such intensity that no amount of dragon's magic will resurrect your flowers," he growled into the phone, his best imitation of an angry, ancient wyrm.

The silence between them lasted for five seconds until Teo burst out laughing over the line. "It will be no more impressive than the tantrums you once threw as a child."

"I thought you could use the laugh, old friend. Chloe and I have done the most difficult work, although I do not believe my wife realizes our plan. You need do nothing more than appear and sweep your woman off her feet."

Teo laughed until his sides hurt then sank into the desk chair to watch the women in the monitor. *Sweep her off her feet?*

Marceline appeared as radiant as she had the first day he'd met her. The camera revealed her in deep discussion with some rich prick he couldn't recall inviting. The man's eyes watched her bosom closely, as if the words came from her tits instead of her mouth.

Teo growled, a low rumble vibrating in his chest. "I will call you soon with news of my success," he declared. He hung up without waiting for Saul to acknowledge him and marched from the office to greet his guests. Fashionably late, he swept into the room with a charismatic smile in place.

People waved him down at once. They all wanted the same thing — to garner his favor — but Teo had time for none of them. He weaved through the room, focused on his goal. Marceline was the only human in the room who mattered.

Luck seemed to be with him. Within moments of greeting Chloe and Marcy, another guest stole Chloe away.

And then he stole Marcy, too, coaxing her into the special garden and attached butterfly habitat. Her eyes widened as she took in the surroundings, and for one brief moment, she warmed up to him.

Then he ruined it in a single breath. With one ill-thought statement.

Fuck, Teo thought. As she strode away without looking back at him, the disgruntled dragon realized his error.

Hours after his failure, Teo retired to his personal island and stood at the shoreline, wondering how to take the next step. He paced along the sandy bank, absolutely nude from top to bottom, his fine tuxedo shredded in the water just beyond the resort's sea shelf. The refreshing swim in his dragon form hadn't helped to ease his mind, and if he phoned Saul, he suspected his friend would tell him to try again.

Of the hundreds on my island, she is the only one who expects nothing from me, and yet I want nothing more than to gift her with the finest jewels.

A dragoness would be content to accept precious gemstones and gold coins from him in exchange for her favor, allowing him the chance to later get to know her, and possibly earn her affection.

But many human women — Marcy included — led lives that seemed backwards to him, disinterested in a man's wealth until they had bonded.

Then they had the audacity to want to give equal financial support!

Such an absurd notion. Nothing should matter but the size of my hoard and that I am willing to provide for her.

And yet, it pleased him greatly to know she could find interest in him for more than his vast wealth — that she wouldn't be yet another gold-digging mortal searching for a favor.

Soon, I will try again. I will give her the time to forgive tonight's blunder, and then I shall make her mine.

***

Teo did not drown Marcy with priceless jewels, but he did discover every second of her time to be as valuable as the relics in his cave. He lived for the moments when a smile touched her lips, and he eagerly searched for reasons to bring them together. He escorted her to his private aviary where his delicate, feathered friends took an instant liking to her.

Later, it seemed only natural to entrust his wealth to her as well. He left her in his office with access to his account records.

He waited for her to call, but it never happened.

"Why do you remain here when there is a beautiful woman awaiting you?" Kekoa asked. "Does your heart no longer call to her?"

"It does," Teo admitted. "But she does not appear to be interested." He clawed the damp sand and muttered under his breath. For the first time in as long as he could remember, the crashing waves against the rocks and sandy shoreline failed to soothe his spirits. Wandering his personal island always brought him joy after a swim.

Kekoa laughed at him.

"What?"

"You truly know nothing of human women."

"And you do?" Teo shot back.

"I know they favor attention and play hard to get. I know women of quality value time over petty gifts. Give your *words* to her. Seek her and show her your attention hasn't waned."

Teo grumbled. "Two days have passed. How could my attention diminish in a mere two days' time?"

Kekoa rolled his eyes and sat beside him on the beach. "Trust me. Time passes more quickly for humans. She is not one of your dragoness bitches."

Teo growled and fixed Kekoa beneath a withering stare.

His friend raised his hands, pleading for peace. "The one you had here for a visit ten years ago, and the red I glimpsed in California, are all I have to go by. They didn't set a good example of your species."

"Fair enough. Very well then. What do I do?"

"Allow her to see more of you beyond the image you portray to the world. To your guests. Let her see the real you." Kekoa glanced at him. "And if that fails, human women appear to have an unnatural weakness for abdominal muscles. Flash your pecs at her once or twice and that should do the trick."

Teo stared at him.

Ultimately, he commissioned Marcy's artistic talents for a portrait, combining all aspects of Kekoa's advice into one endeavor.

It's been decades since I've had a portrait painted. Of course, I've always worn clothing of some sort as well, he mused. Moments after making plans to meet Marcy in his sterile, boring executive office, he cursed himself.

Teo went to the intercom and beeped his secretary. "I need this office furnished within the next half hour."

"Furnished?" Judy asked?

"Yes," he said impatiently. "Curtains, carpets, paintings. Things a woman would find attractive."

"Thirty minutes isn't enough—"

"Make it enough," he replied curtly before ending the call. Later, he'd apologize for his abrupt and rude behavior, but now, he had work to do. With help from Kekoa and a few of the other resort employees, they were somehow able to find furnishings and decorations in a miraculously short time, Teo himself even helping to arrange the room to his liking.

When Marcy entered a transformed room with personality, he couldn't wait to be rid of his clothing. Anticipation had made them stiff and uncomfortable against skin yearning to be free. His cock had already begun to tense, on the verge of achieving erection.

Marcy's eyes traveled downward to his dick. Her prolonged attention yielded a hot flush of masculine pride, then his cock twitched and swelled even further.

He ached, but most of all, he wanted her to find happiness in looking upon him, to feel equal pleasure to what he enjoyed whenever she entered the room.

"Am I to your expectations?" he asked.

Marcy abruptly swept her attention to his face. "Did you have a pose in mind?"

Teo's enthusiasm deflated. *Was Kekoa wrong?* he wondered. Marcy did not seem infatuated with his abs *or* the rest of him. He felt ridiculous and inexperienced with human women, and frustrated she did not reciprocate his interest by shedding her clothes as well. It was a foolish notion, expecting her to be as free with her body, but it hadn't changed how much he'd hoped to make progress.

"What would you suggest?" He held eye contact with her, refusing to show his disappointment.

At the end of their session, Teo reluctantly donned his clothes and searched for a way to prolong their time together. It came to him in a stroke of genius.

"I wish to see you again tomorrow."

And tomorrow couldn't come quickly enough, once she agreed. Teo floated through his day with dreams of confessing his feelings to Marceline.

Later, as he and Kekoa reviewed the construction progress of the island's new aquatics center, he absently muttered plans out loud.

"Tomorrow I will bond with her," he told Kekoa. "I believe you are correct. If money is the route to earning a dragoness' love, then certainly one's physical attributes are the way to impress a human woman."

"They like big cocks," Kekoa agreed. "You defend your female dragons quite readily but have poor experiences with them. Why?"

Teo sighed. "Loyalty, perhaps. Saul has no such qualms when it comes to speaking his mind about the fairer sex of our species, but I have always felt differently."

"Can you blame him?"

Thoughts of Brigid came to mind, making Teo laugh and shake his head when he recalled her air of superiority. "Ixchel was not as bad as Brigid. She did not mean to pay you insult, Kekoa, but you were a child then and it is unlike a female dragon to show affection to cubs not of her own flesh and blood,' he explained.

"You liked her." Kekoa leaned forward, curiosity on his brown face. "Enough to be her mate?"

"I did," Teo admitted. "Black dragons are a rarity among my kind, our females even fewer. I had hoped our year together would… inspire feelings between us beyond the contract to conceive young."

"She treated you badly," Kekoa said. "I loathed her for that more than I hated her for the things she said to me."

Teo snapped his head around to look at his friend. "What things did she speak to you?"

The wereshark hesitated, and spoke only when Teo gestured for him to continue with an impatient movement of his wrist. "She told me I was unwelcome and that if not for your pity, she would have eaten me. I was to leave once the cub was born, as you would no longer have an interest in guarding my life."

A bolt of fury streaked through Teo, knotting his stomach with anger. He clenched his jaw. "You didn't think to bring this to my attention?"

"Forgive me, Master. I thought you were aware."

Teo gritted his teeth and set one hand on the young man's shoulder. "No. At no point was I ever aware of her abusing you while beyond my hearing. You were a child, Kekoa. A child. You were my responsibility. I brought you here to this island to protect you, and had I known…"

I would have made her dwell on the mainland in one of my other homes. Visited her there for our matings. I would never have brought her home to upset you.

Kekoa nodded his head. "I apologize. I should have told you. Ah, I should go and conduct the interview scheduled for this evening. Already, there is a vast amount of interest in this new compound. Forgive me for becoming distracted."

"Ah, yes. That man." Teo crinkled his nose in distaste. A well-known doctor had applied for the position of director over the aquatics center, and while he was as sharp as a tack, Teo's feelings toward him remained undecided.

"I will prepare the cabana in the morning." The young man stepped away from the metal frame dedicated to the facility's future shark tank.

"Kekoa?"

The young man paused to glance back at him. "Yes, Master?"

"Teo. Call me Teo. Take the evening off to go spend time with Dante. I insist. He mentioned a desire to have company out on the reef and I mentioned you may have an interest in showing him the reef. Enjoy yourselves. *I* will handle Doctor Castlebury. If he is as eager as his cover letter implies, he will not mind waiting a half hour or so for my arrival."

"But your plans—"

Teo waved him off with a hand. "I will manage."

"Thank you… Teo." Kekoa tested the word out, as if it felt strange to his lips without the preceding title. "Tomorrow, we will meet at the private cabana. I have an idea." Smiling as he waved, he then turned and strode away to search out his new friend.

And Teo was left to his own thoughts, filled with hopes of earning Marceline's heart.

***

Teo was not prepared for the intensity associated with falling in love, and underestimating it nearly cost him everything he had fought to build between them. As days passed and they eventually bonded, it seemed only inevitable he would chase her away again.

He spent the first few days in disbelief, waiting for her to return. When the longing for Marcy surpassed his pride, he phoned Saul for advice.

"An angered woman requires time," Saul cautioned. "Did you apologize after upsetting her?"

"No, of course not. I did nothing wrong."

Saul made an exasperated sound and groaned into the phone. "You've broken one of the simplest rules of having a human woman," he grunted out. "You must apologize to her at once."

"Why? What wrongdoing have I committed, save for giving my expectation of having her for more than a passing moment of my life?" Teo inhaled a deep breath. Few things frightened him like the potential loss of his new mate to old age.

"If you require me to answer this for you, Teotihuacan, then you do not deserve her," Saul said simply. "Consider her feelings and place yourself in her shoes. How would you feel if she were to command you to give up your dragon shape and live a mortal life?"

"I would n—"

"Have you not asked her to do similar?"

Teo remained quiet.

"To accept your seed and bear your child is to forsake her *humanity*, Teo. Neither dragon nor human, she will watch all of her friends, family, and loved ones die."

"Saul…" Teo sagged in the seat and gazed across the sand into the crashing waves. "I have been a fool."

"A lovestruck fool," Saul said gently.

"What must I do?"

Saul chuckled into the phone. "Marceline is a fiery creature with strong opinions. Stubborn. Give her time to cool and consider how you might apologize."

"You have the talent for words," Teo grumbled. "What would you say in my place?"

"Marceline, I have behaved as an idiot. An absolute buffoon. I beg your forgiveness and promise I will never foolishly give commands regarding your body and well-being again."

"Asshole," Teo grumbled. "I wanted flowery words."

"Save the flowery words and voice your feelings. Speak to her from your heart."

Words from my heart. How do I tell her that with her beside me, my heart feels as large as this vast ocean, and without her, it is as empty as its surface?

"I will ask Chloe to speak with her," Saul offered.

"I… feel lost without her," Teo finally admitted. "She has taken part of my soul to Texas."

"Then tell her so. Give breath to your thoughts and let her know she is loved, once you are ready."

Teo disconnected the call and thought back on his friend's words. Saul made it sound so easy — *too* easy. He wasn't sure Marcy would forgive him.

Restlessness drove him to the beach. The sun had barely begun to set when Kekoa wandered down from the quiet house.

"Saul called back," Kekoa informed him. The dark-haired wereshark came to a stop beside the pensive dragon. "He asked me to let you know that Marcy is staying with them for a time."

"Good… That is… It is good." Teo paced back and forth across the sun-warmed sand, torn by indecision. *Of course she would go there. She and Chloe are close friends.*

"Is everything, well?" Kekoa asked, brows knitted together.

"Y—no," he answered truthfully. He wouldn't insult Kekoa's intelligence with a lie when his faithful servant had witnessed the final tense days of Marcy's stay with his own eyes. "Marceline left me."

"I am certain she only needs time to cool off," Kekoa assured him. Teo wished he shared the sentiment.

"Do I call her, Kekoa?"

"Some words are better said face to face."

"What if she has no wish to see me? She has been gone for many days without word."

Kekoa chuckled, earning the dragon's glare.

"I find nothing amusing about this," Teo muttered.

"Forgive me, my friend." Kekoa attempted to school his amused expression, but failed. Another chortle escaped. "It is a new side of you. A good one."

"You think I am a fool," Teo growled.

"No, I think you are a man in love. A dragon in love. It is new for you. Good, even."

"It doesn't feel good." Teo kicked at the sand and turned his face into the salt-scented breeze. The cool air brushed against his cheeks and stirred his dark hair.

Each passing day without Marcy beside him was pain more than he could bear.

"If you truly wish to know how she feels, go to her," Kekoa urged. "Look her in the eye and tell her what's in your heart."

"Saul said the same thing."

Kekoa's broad grin widened further. "Ha! I am wise as a dragon, then. Or he is as smart as a shark."

Teo snorted and clapped his friend on the shoulder. "Very well, I will go to her." *And hope it is not too late to undo my foolishness.*

About the Author

Vivienne Savage is a resident of a small town in rural Texas. While she isn't concocting sexy ways for shapeshifters and humans to find their match, she raises two children and works as a nurse in a rural nursing home.

To get on Vivienne's mailing list for news and upates, go online and visit http://eepurl.com/boj0p1

51036909R00201

Made in the USA
Charleston, SC
13 January 2016